THE **STORM BREWS** IN THE **NORTH**

BOOK TWO, PART ONE

RANCH BARLOW

MILTON & HUGO L.L.C.
4407 Park Ave., Suite 5
Union City, NJ 07087, USA

Website: *www. miltonandhugo.com*
Hotline: *1- 888-778-0033*
Email: *info@miltonandhugo.com*

Ordering Information:
Quantity sales. Special discounts are granted to corporations, associations, and other organizations. For more information on these discounts, please reach out to the publisher using the contact information provided above.

ISBN-13:   979-8-89285-627-0   [Paperback Edition]
              979-8-89285-628-7   [Hardback Edition]
              979-8-89285-626-3   [Digital Edition]

Rev. date: 12/29/2025

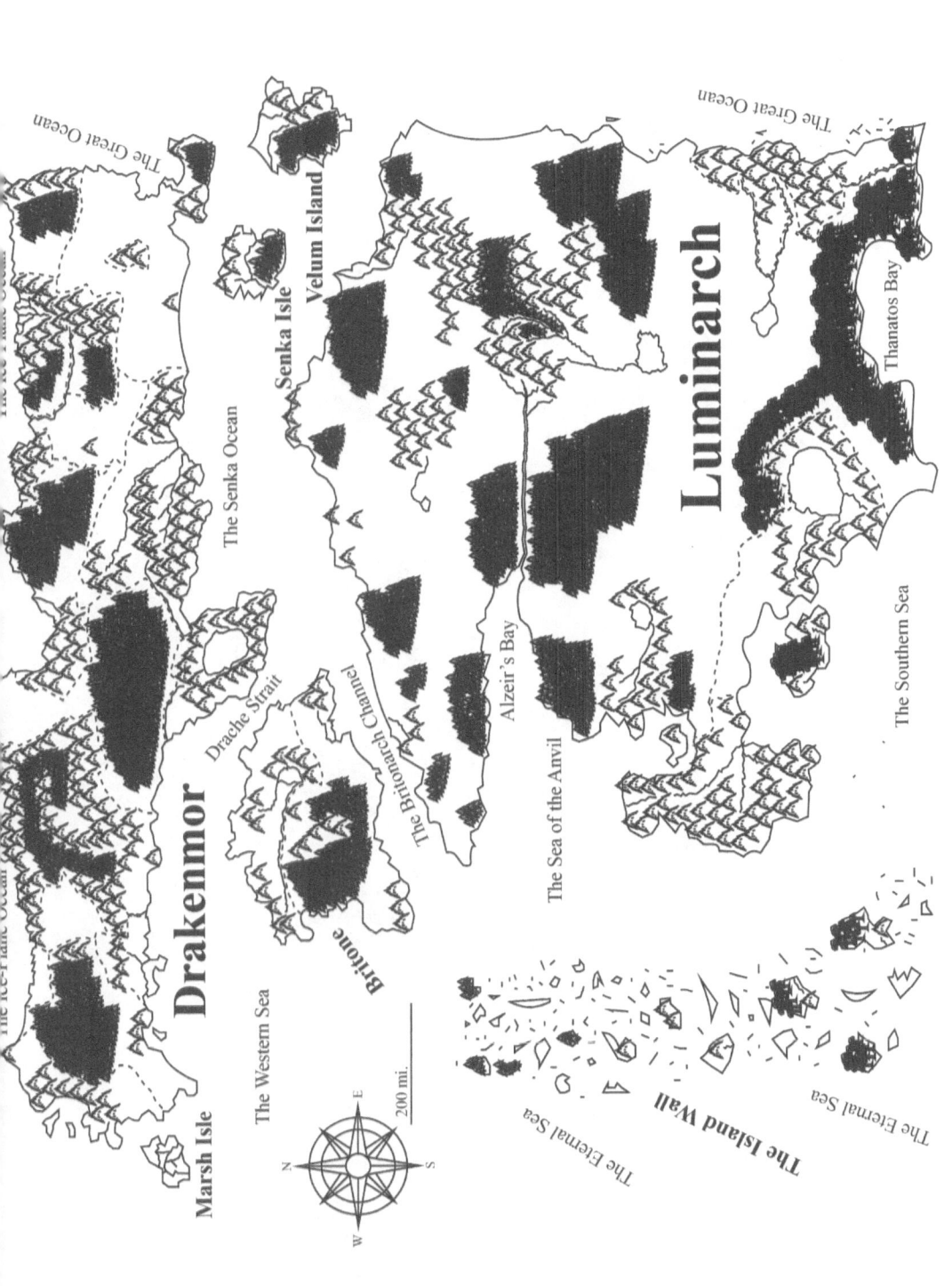

Drakenmor

Luminarch

The Great Ocean

The Great Ocean

The Great Ocean

Velum Island

Senka Isle

Thanatos Bay

The Senka Ocean

Marsh Isle

The Western Sea

Drache Strait

Britoune

The Britomarch Channel

Alzeir's Bay

The Sea of the Anvil

The Southern Sea

The Island Wall

The Eternal Sea

The Eternal Sea

The Eternal Sea

200 mi.

N E S W

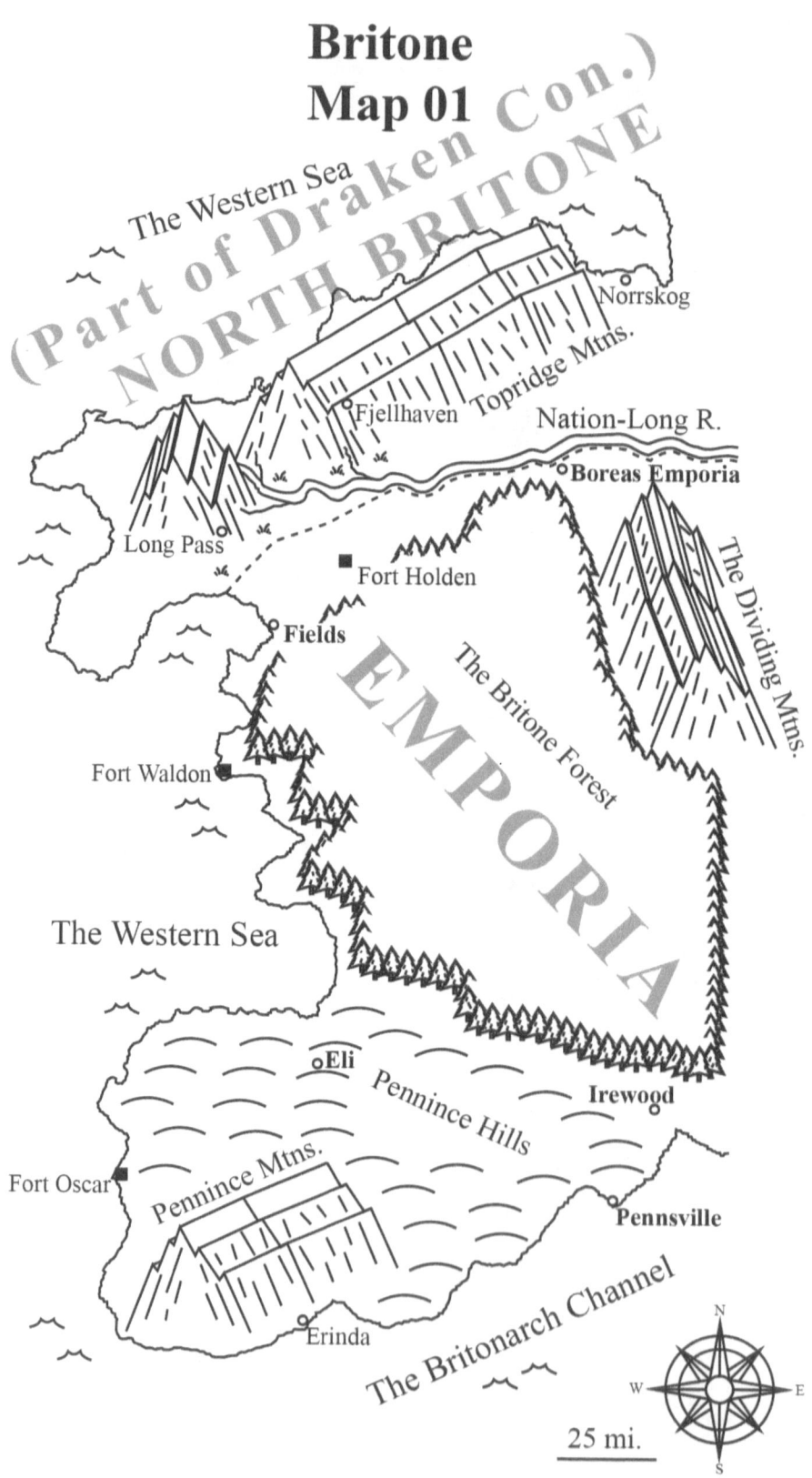

Britone
Map 02

(Part of Draken Con.)
NORTH BRITONE

North Spear Mtns.

Ljusby

The Salt-Flat Peaks

White Spear

Vinterdal

Nation-Long R.

Salt R.

Erobra Castle

Fort Arthon

Fort Gratham

Salt Lake

The Dividing Mtns.

Salt Spike

Salt Lake

The Britone Forest

Fort Alvin

Mutina

EMPORIA

Calm Sea

Delorin

The Britonarch Channel

25 mi.

N
W   E
S

Britone
Map 03

(Part of Draken Con.)

NORTH BRITONE

Fjordl uk

Drache Strait

Britonic Plains

Castle Lavvann

Fort Habstrast

Long-Grass

EMPORIA

Cane

Cane R.

Fort Mullen

Cane Mtns.

Halberen

Marendine

Halberen Bay

The Britonarch Channel

N
W   E
S

25 mi.

Drakenmor
Map 01

The Ice-Plane Ocean

Satt fjall Mtn.

Satt Fjall

The Western Sea

Skuggi Fjallsins

Sprunga

Voldugur Dalur

Sigur

Conartha Forest

Kolafjall

Glen Iar

Mirkwood Forest

Conartha Isle
Conartha Beag Isle

Skilagjald
Tindaborg

Two-Isle Bay

Jern hule

Conartha Beag Isle Forest

Torden Cave

Oddhvassa Vatn

MIRKWOOD

Beag R.

Beag

Ceann Baile

The Conartha Mtns.

Mirkwood Mtns.

Conartha Plains

Halsten

CLADAIGH AN IARTHAIR

Fiail Ard

Vermundr

Baile Corr

Linn Fola

Mirkwood Island

N

Baile

W — E

The Western Sea

S

25 mi.

Drakenmor
Map 02

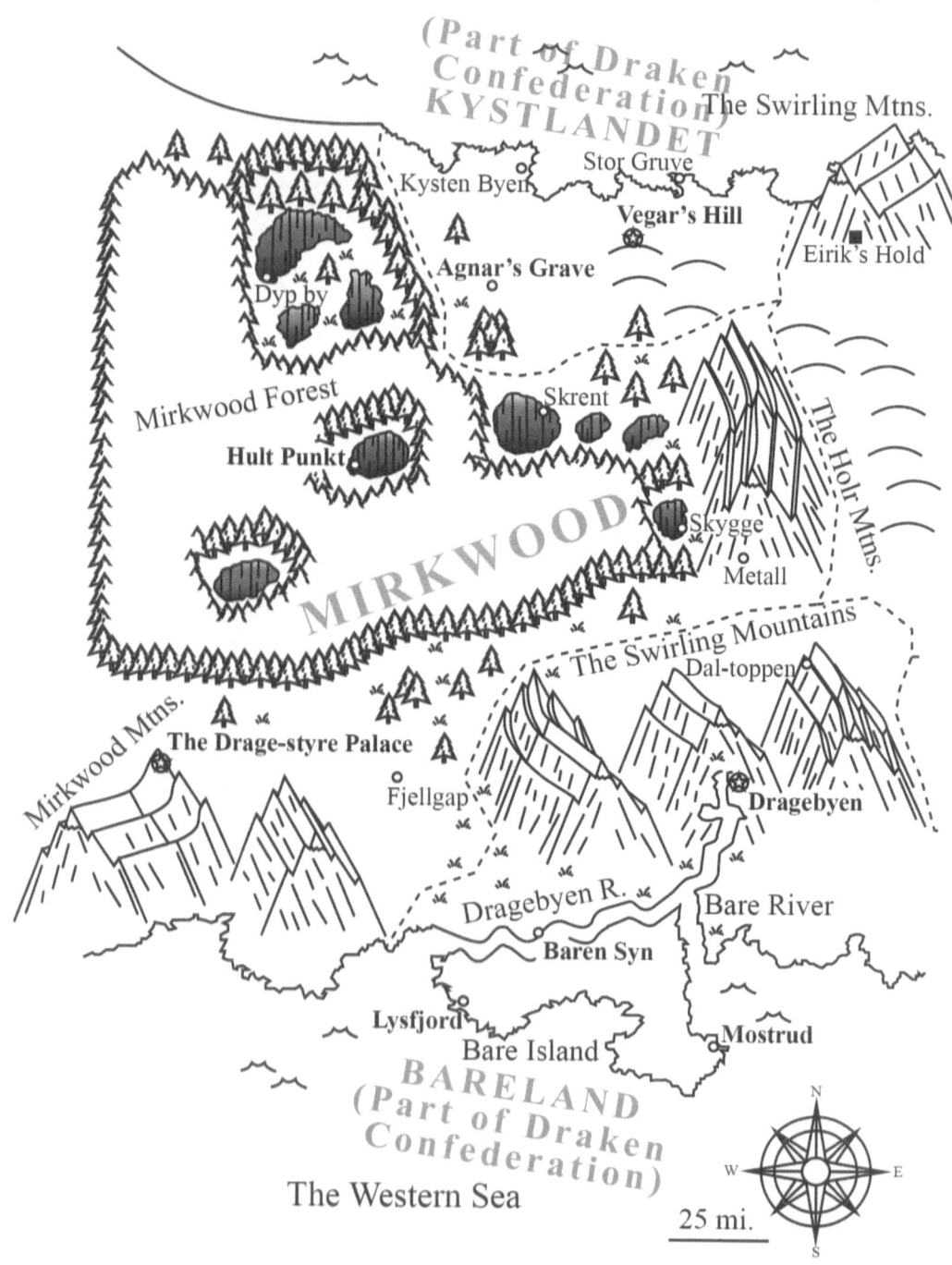

The Ice-Plane Ocean

(Part of Draken Confederation)
KYSTLANDET

The Swirling Mtns.

Stor Gruve

Kysten Byen

Vegar's Hill

Agnar's Grave

Eirik's Hold

Dyp by

Mirkwood Forest

Skrent

The Holr Mtns.

Hult Punkt

Skygge

Metall

MIRKWOOD

The Swirling Mountains

Dal-toppen

Mirkwood Mtns.

The Drage-styre Palace

Fjellgap

Dragebyen

Dragebyen R.

Bare River

Baren Syn

Lysfjord

Mostrud

Bare Island

BARELAND
(Part of Draken Confederation)

The Western Sea

N
W E
S

25 mi.

Drakenmor
Map 03

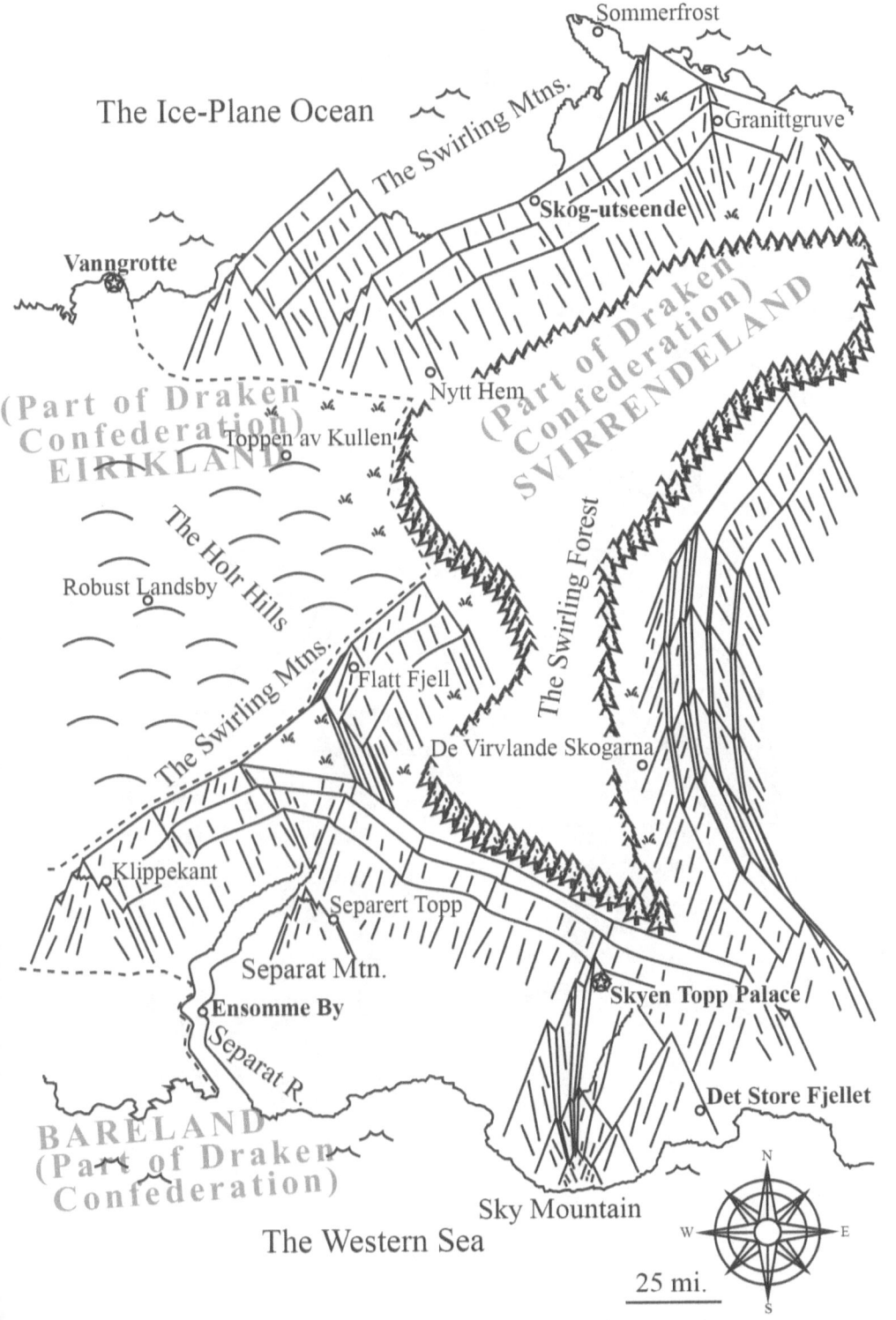

The Ice-Plane Ocean

Sommerfrost

The Swirling Mtns.

Granittgruve

Skog-utseende

Vanngrotte

(Part of Draken Confederation)
SVIRRENDELAND

Nytt Hem

(Part of Draken Confederation)
EIRIKLAND

Toppen av Kullen

The Holr Hills

The Swirling Forest

Robust Landsby

The Swirling Mtns.

Flatt Fjell

De Virvlande Skogarna

Klippekant

Separert Topp

Separat Mtn.

Ensomme By

Skyen Topp Palace

Separat R.

Det Store Fjellet

BARELAND
(Part of Draken Confederation)

Sky Mountain

The Western Sea

25 mi.

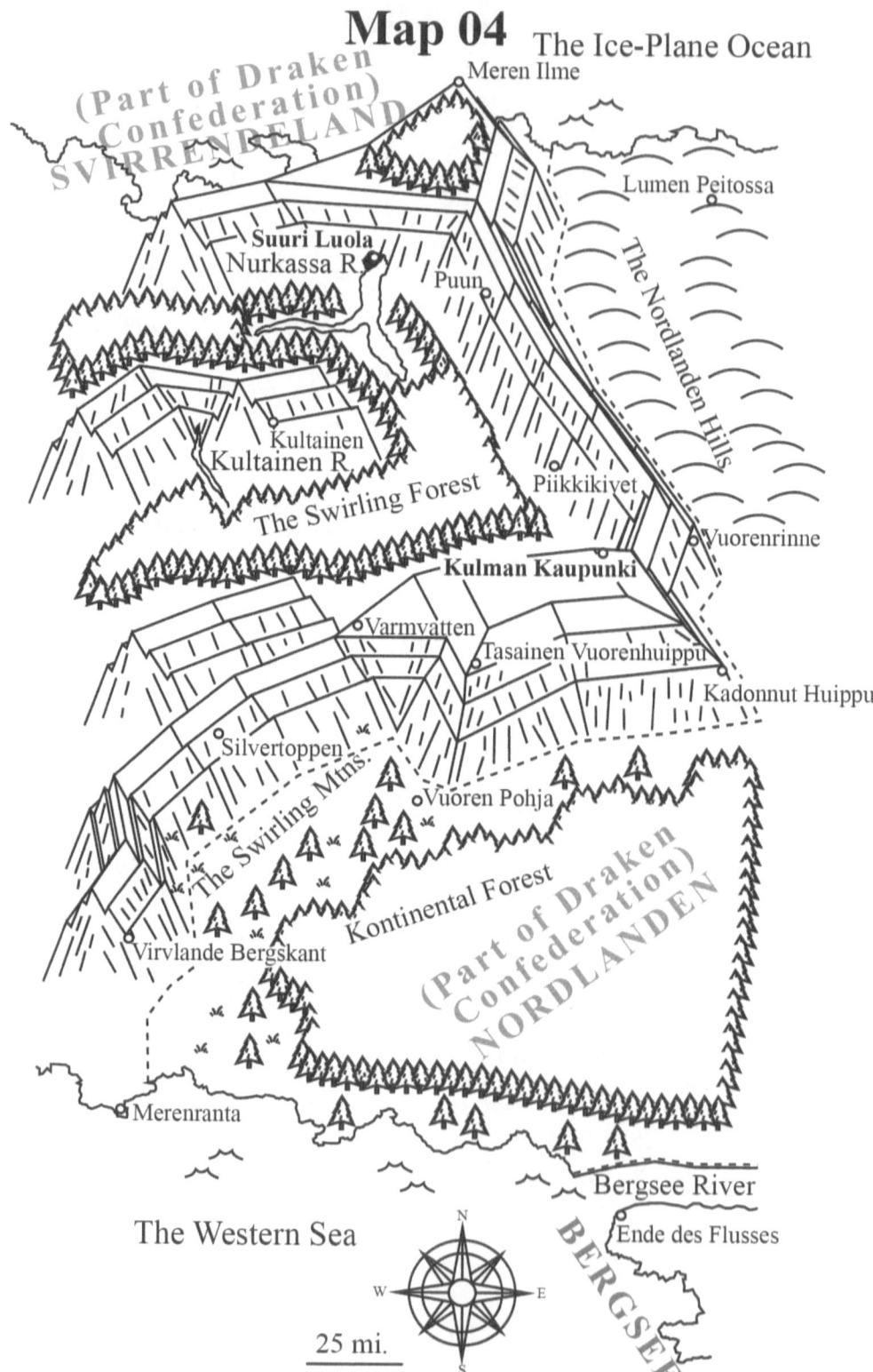

Drakenmor
Map 05

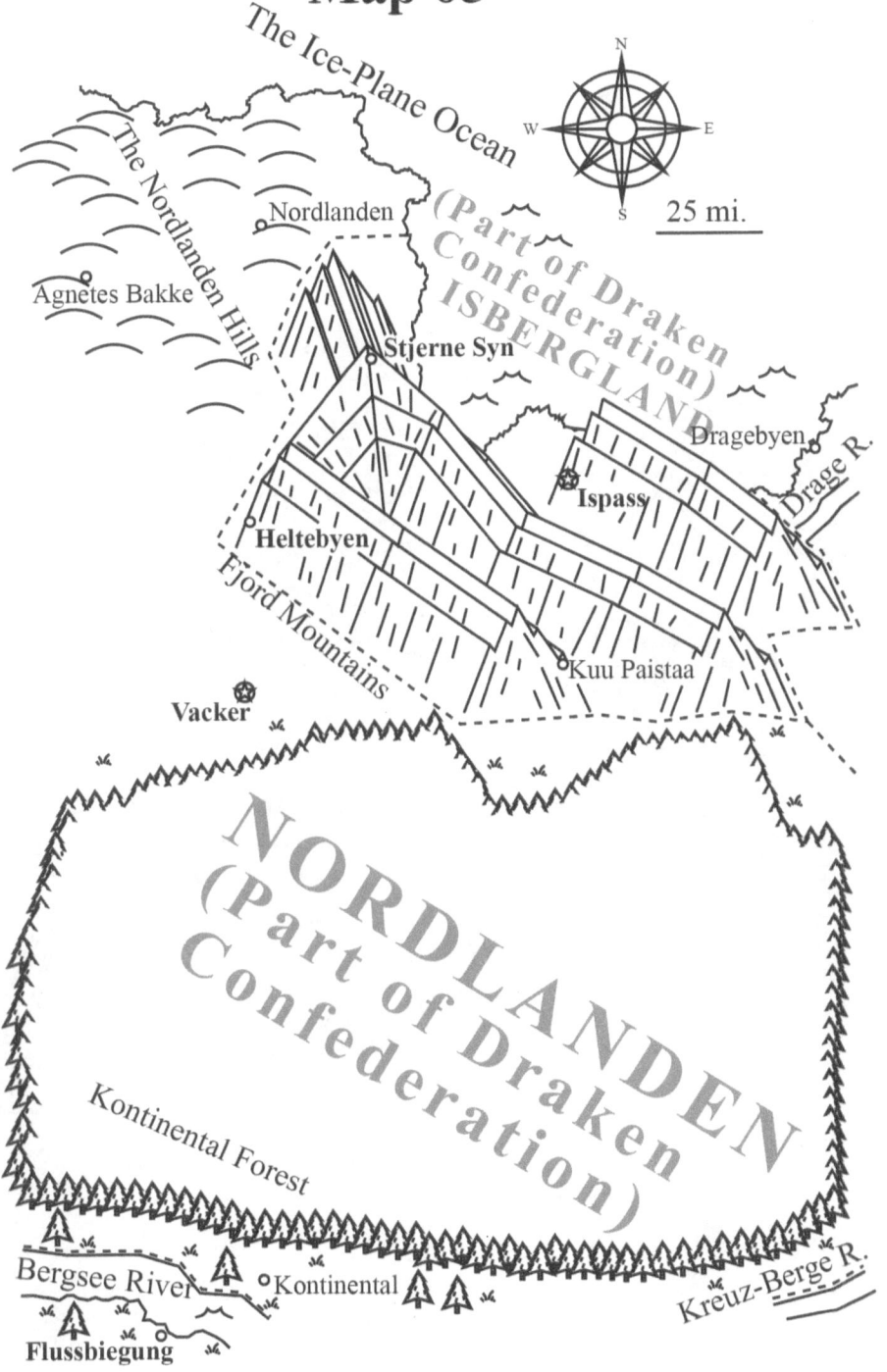

The Ice-Plane Ocean

N
W E
S

25 mi.

The Nordlanden Hills

Nordlanden

Agnetes Bakke

Stjerne Syn

(Part of Draken Confederation)
ISBERGLAND

Dragebyen

Drage R.

Ispass

Heltebyen

Fjord Mountains

Kuu Paistaa

Vacker

NORDLANDEN
(Part of Draken Confederation)

Kontinental Forest

Bergsee River

Kontinental

Kreuz-Berge R.

Flussbiegung

Drakenmor
Map 06

NORDLANDEN
(Part of Draken Confederation)

Blick auf die Berge

Bergsee R.

The Bergsee Mtns.

Kreuz-Berge R.

BRANDLAND

Grenzstadt

Metallfeld

Mondsee

The Feuer und
Wasser Gulf

BERGSEE

Uferfeld

Ufer des Sees

Unbedeckt

Bergsee Lake

Berggabel

Drache Strait

Felsiges Land

Spitze des Sees

Bergpass

Bergkante

The Senka Ocean

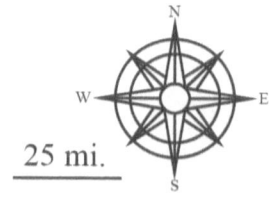

25 mi.

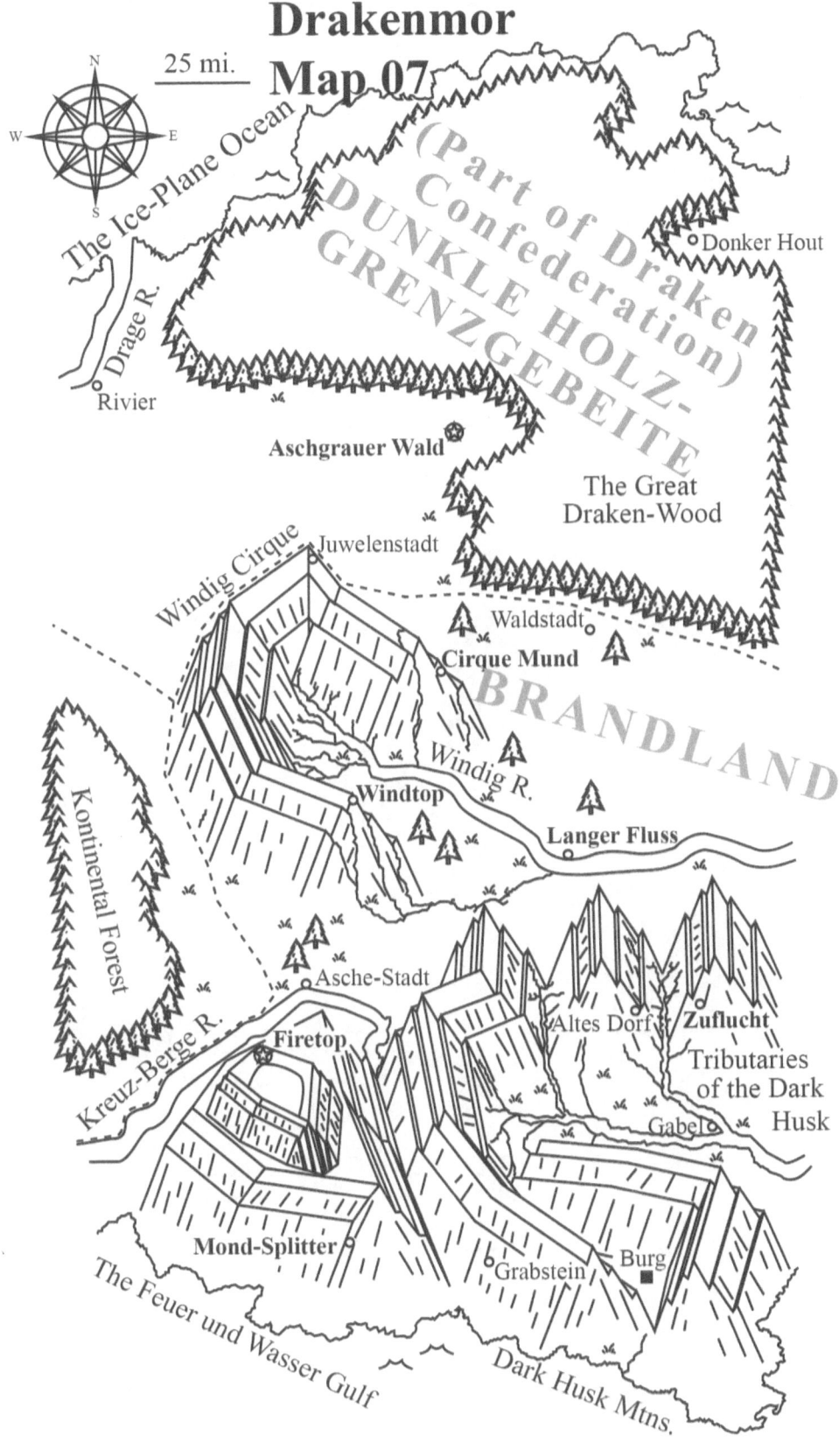

Drakenmor
Map 08

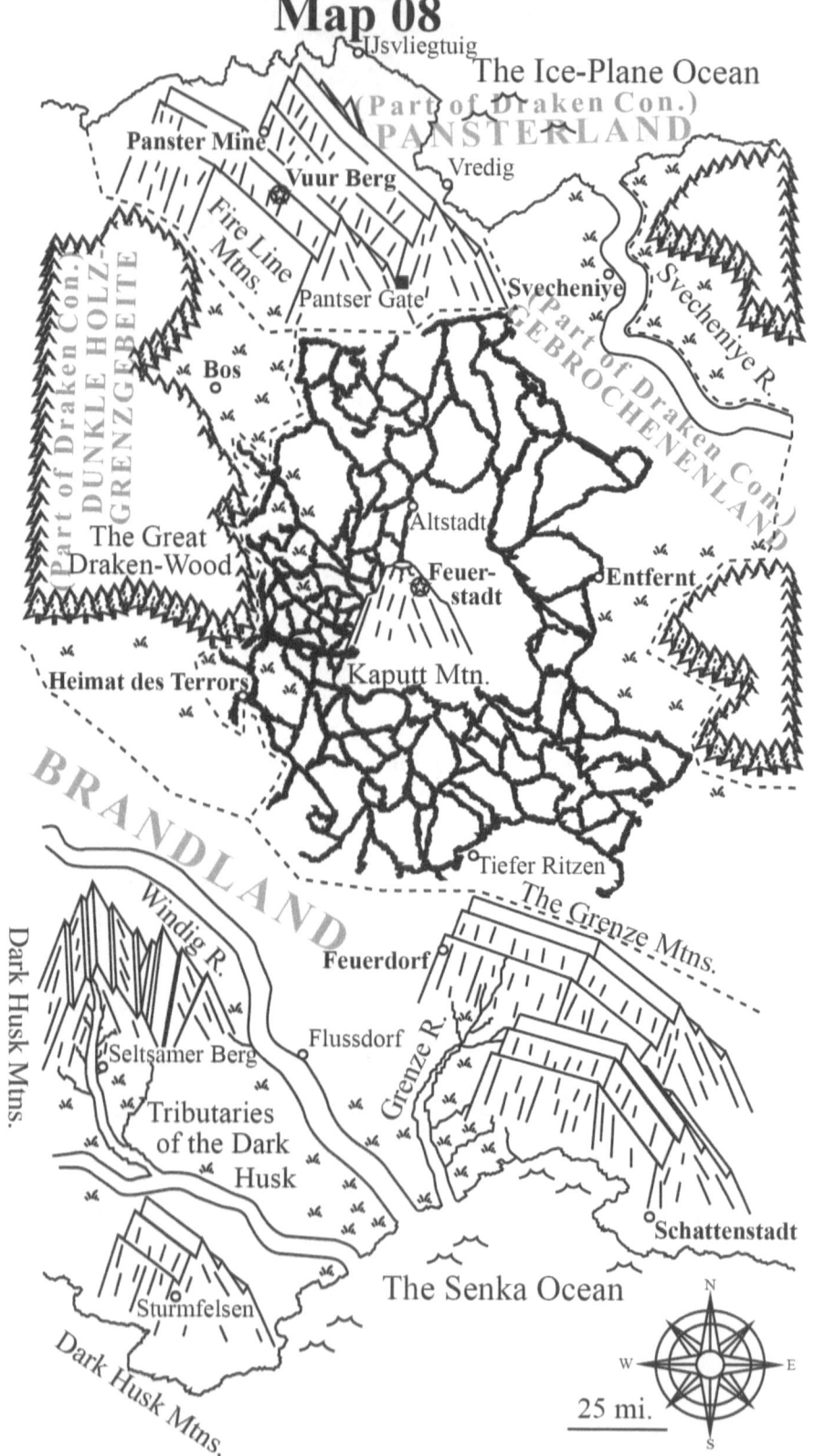

Usvliegtuig

The Ice-Plane Ocean
(Part of Draken Con.)
PANSTERLAND

Panster Mine

Vuur Berg

Vredig

Pantser Gate

Svecheniye

Svecheniye R.

Fire Line Mtns.

(Part of Draken Con.)
DUNKLE HOLZ-
GRENZGEBEITE

Bos

(Part of Draken Con.)
GEBROCHENENLAND

The Great
Draken-Wood

Altstadt

Feuer-
stadt

Entfernt

Heimat des Terrors

Kaputt Mtn.

BRANDLAND

Tiefer Ritzen

The Grenze Mtns.

Windig R.

Feuerdorf

Dark Husk Mtns.

Seltsamer Berg

Flussdorf

Grenze R.

Tributaries
of the Dark
Husk

Schattenstadt

Sturmfelsen

The Senka Ocean

Dark Husk Mtns.

N
W   E
S

25 mi.

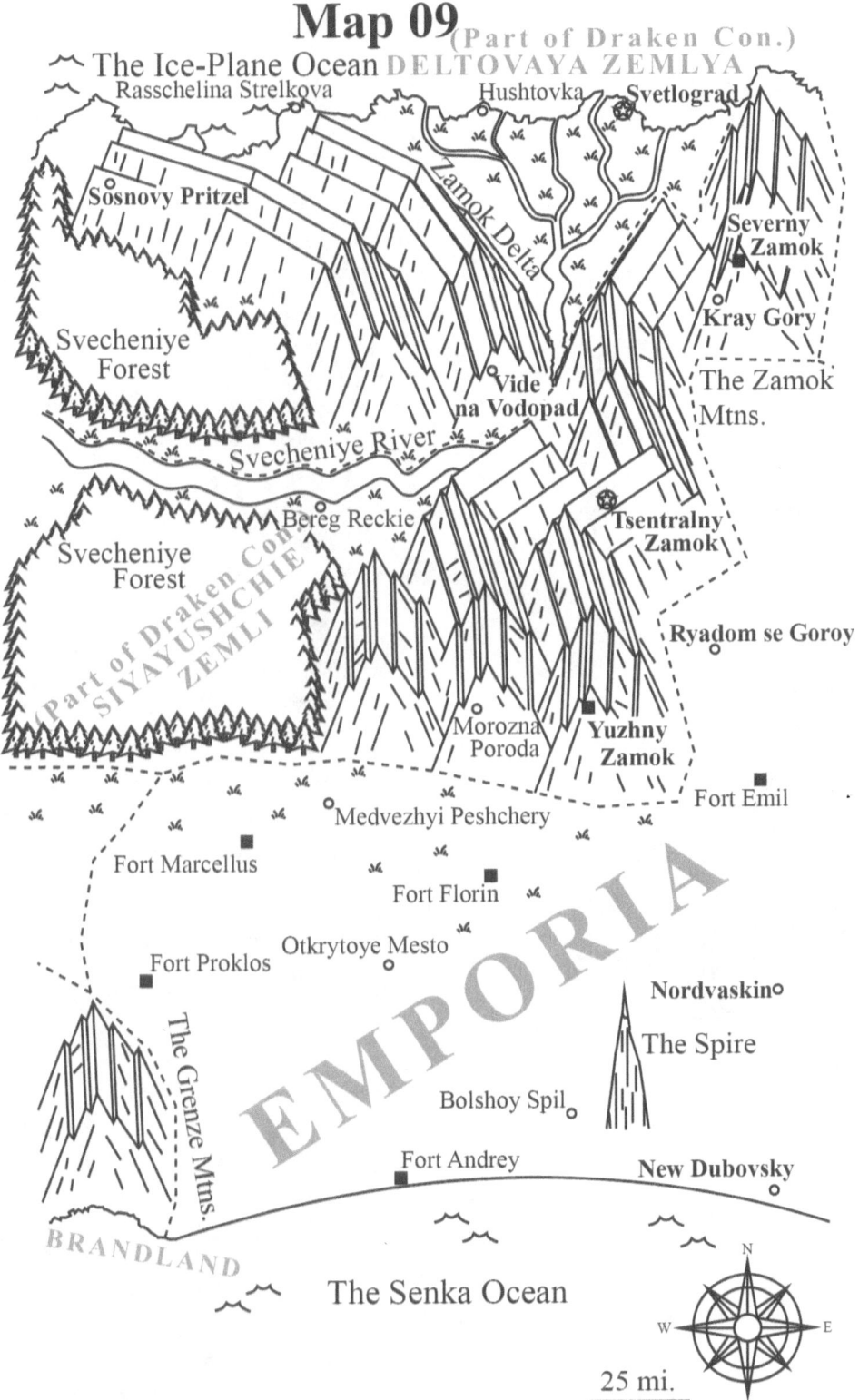

Drakenmor
Map 09 (Part of Draken Con.)

The Ice-Plane Ocean DELTOVAYA ZEMLYA

Rasschelina Strelkova

Hushtovka

Svetlograd

Sosnovy Pritzel

Zamok Delta

Severny Zamok

Kray Gory

Svecheniye Forest

Vide na Vodopad

The Zamok Mtns.

Svecheniye River

Bereg Reckie

Tsentralny Zamok

Part of Draken Con. SIYAYUSHCHIE ZEMLI

Svecheniye Forest

Ryadom se Goroy

Morozna Poroda

Yuzhny Zamok

Fort Emil

Medvezhyi Peshchery

Fort Marcellus

Fort Florin

Otkrytoye Mesto

Fort Proklos

EMPORIA

Nordvaskin

The Spire

Bolshoy Spil

The Grenze Mtns.

Fort Andrey

New Dubovsky

BRANDLAND

The Senka Ocean

N
W   E
S

25 mi.

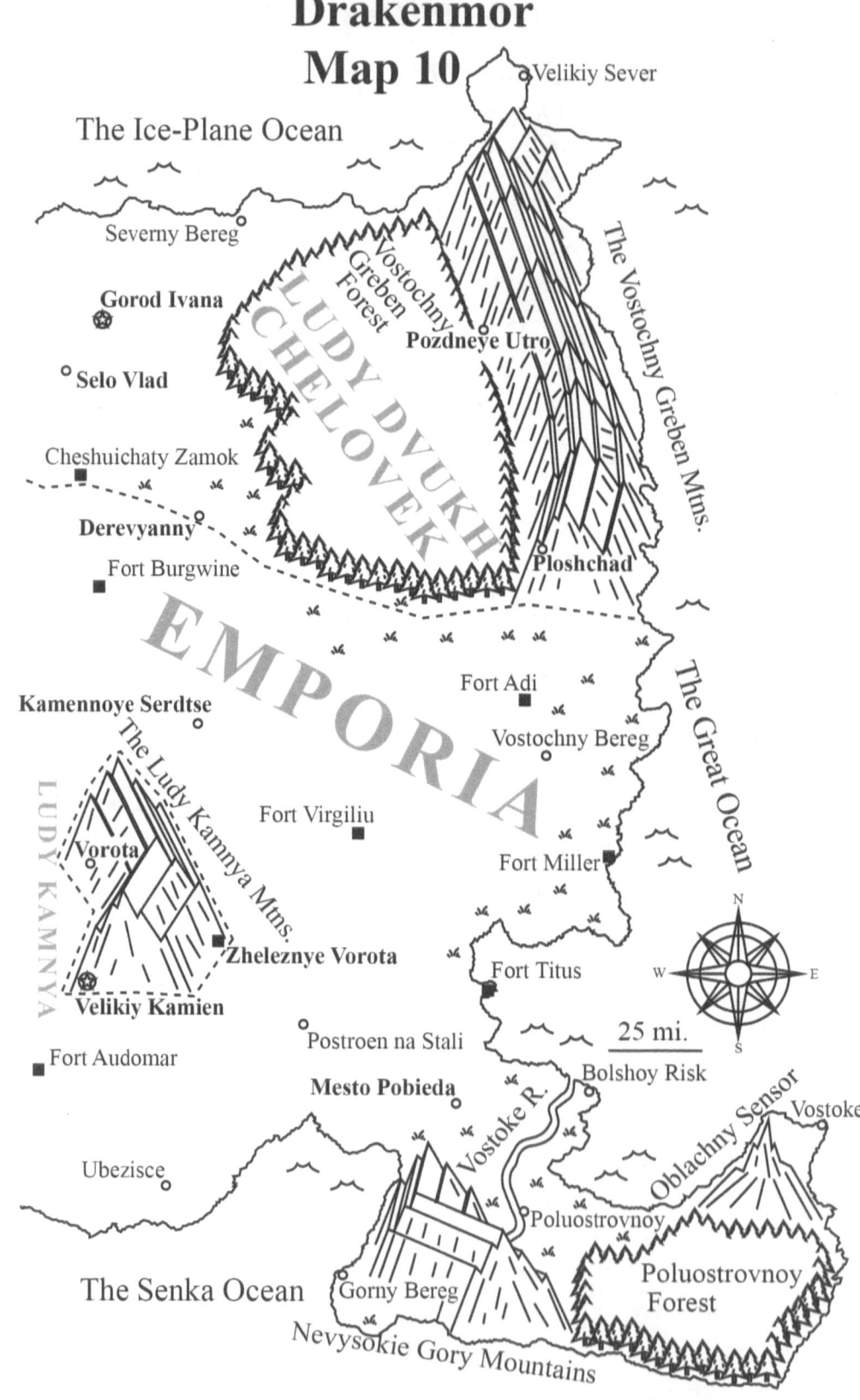

Island Wall
Map 01
City Names

LIBERTADIA

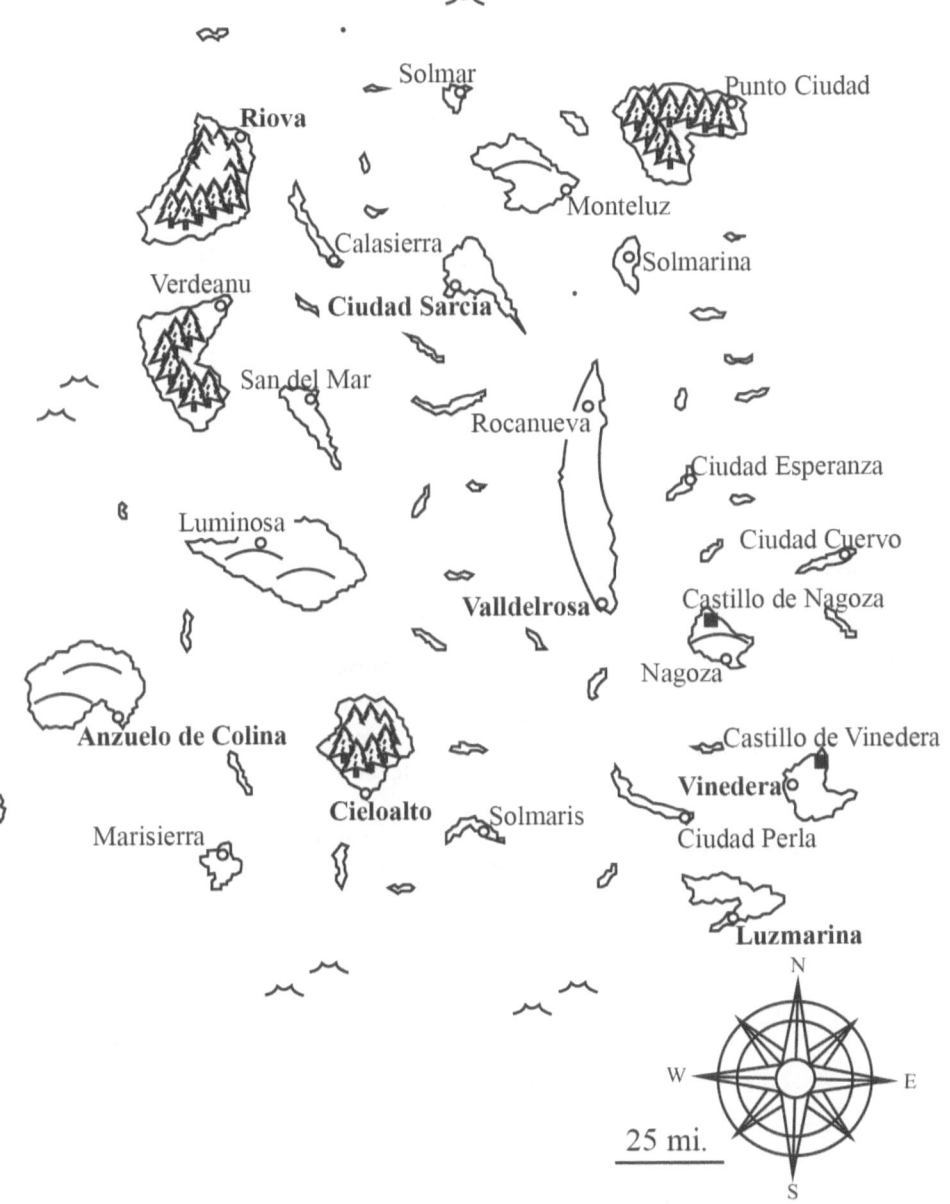

Solmar

Punto Ciudad

Riova

Monteluz

Calasierra

Solmarina

Verdeanu

Ciudad Sarcia

San del Mar

Rocanueva

Ciudad Esperanza

Luminosa

Ciudad Cuervo

Castillo de Nagoza

Valldelrosa

Nagoza

Anzuelo de Colina

Castillo de Vinedera

Vinedera

Marisierra

Cieloalto

Solmaris

Ciudad Perla

Luzmarina

N

W   E

S

25 mi.

Island Wall
Map 01
Island Names

LIBERTADIA

The Sea of the Anvil

Dorado Ensenada

Isla de los Perdidos

Punto Isla

Isla Riova

Isla Solmar   Cristal Orilla

Isla Elegida

Flecha Forest

Riova Forest

Eterno Oasis

Tierra Nieve

The Eternal Sea   Isla Astillada

Sarcia

Encantado Islote

Solmarina

Gemelo Norte

Isla Oscuro

Isla de Aislamiento

Gemelo Sur

Solmaria Isla

Zafiro Isla

Solmaria Forest

Isla Ancla

Hormiga de Fuego Isla

Larga Playa Isla

Isla Esperanza

Elysiano Puerto

Isla Enferma

Isla Port

Isla Adornada

Isla Vil

Dorado Puerto

Isla Espinosa

Isla Rest

Isla Cuervo

Isla de los Sin Nombre

Isla del Dedo Perdido

Isla Rana

Isla Castigada

Isla Nagoza

Cieloalto Forest

Isla Molusco

Isla Verde

Isla Plateada

Isla Ostra

Isla Torcida

Tierra Desnuda

Perla Isla

Cangrejo Isla

Isla Crow

Solmaris

Isla Vinedera

Isla Marisierra

Goldire Isla

Isla Granite

Luzmarina Isla

N

W   E

S

25 mi.

Island Wall
Map 02
City Names

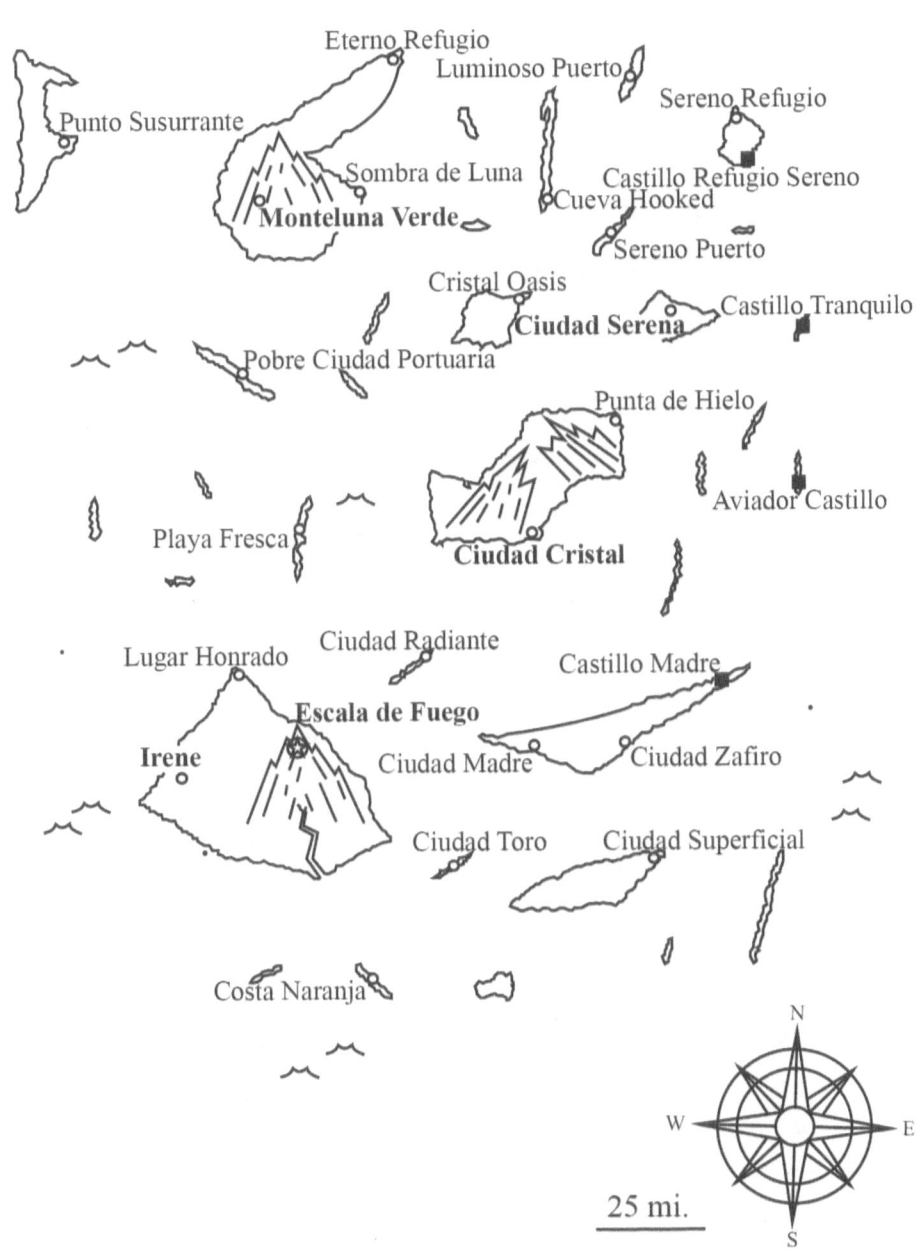

LIBERTADIA

Eterno Refugio

Luminoso Puerto

Sereno Refugio

Punto Susurrante

Sombra de Luna

Castillo Refugio Sereno

Cueva Hooked

Monteluna Verde

Sereno Puerto

Cristal Oasis

Ciudad Serena

Castillo Tranquilo

Pobre Ciudad Portuaria

Punta de Hielo

Aviador Castillo

Playa Fresca

Ciudad Cristal

Ciudad Radiante

Castillo Madre

Lugar Honrado

Escala de Fuego

Irene

Ciudad Madre

Ciudad Zafiro

Ciudad Toro

Ciudad Superficial

Costa Naranja

N
W   E
S

25 mi.

Island Wall
Map 02
Island Names
LIBERTADIA

Eterno Refugio

Luminoso Puerto

Susurrante Puerto

Sereno Refugio

Dorado Orilla

Isla en Forma de Gancho

Zafiro Orilla

Luna Mtn.

Sereno Isla

Sereno Puerto

Sereno Ensenada

Sombra de Luna

Cristal Oasis

Tranquilo Laguna

Pobre Puerto

Zafiro Laguna

Oriente Mtn.

Isla con Forma de Cuerno

Isla Coral

Occidental Mtn.

Isla Paralela Isla Airman

Tranquilo Santuario

Eterno Arrecife Encantado Ensenada

Cristal Refugio

Isla Viper

The Eternal Sea

The Sea of the Anvil

Escala de Fuego Mtn.

Radiante Puerto

Irene R.

Zafiro Santuario

Isla Mediana

Isla Larga Desnuda

Isla Escala de Fuego

Esmeralda Isla

Isla Costa Roja

Isla Deshonrada

Isla Costa Naranja Isla de Agua Caliente

N

W   E

S

25 mi.

Island Wall
Map 03
City Names

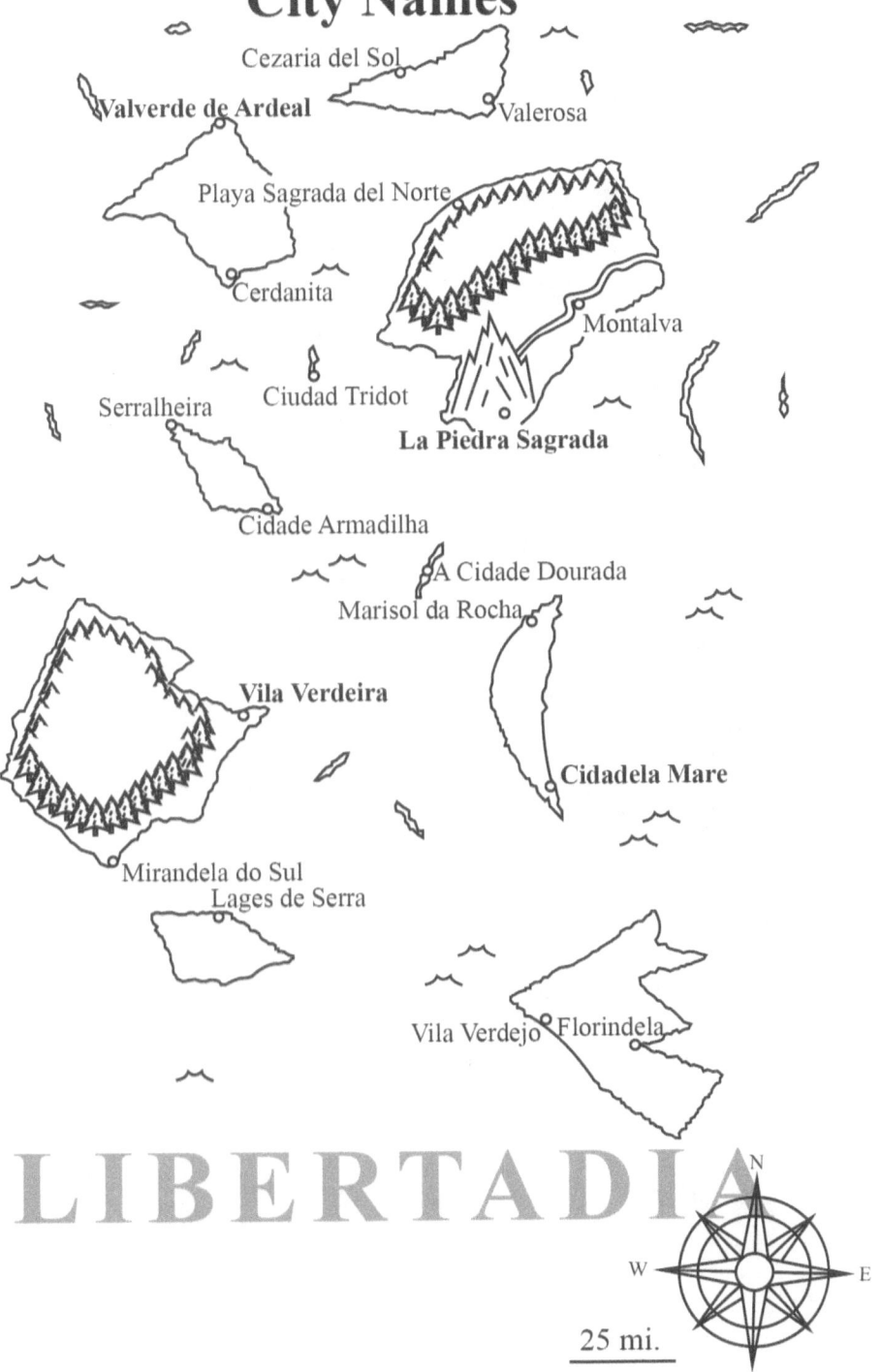

Cezaria del Sol

Valverde de Ardeal

Valerosa

Playa Sagrada del Norte

Cerdanita

Montalva

Serralheira

Ciudad Tridot

La Piedra Sagrada

Cidade Armadilha

A Cidade Dourada

Marisol da Rocha

Vila Verdeira

Cidadela Mare

Mirandela do Sul

Lages de Serra

Vila Verdejo

Florindela

LIBERTADIA

N

W   E

S

25 mi.

Island Wall
Map 03
Island Names

Isla Gem Shore

Isla Obsidiana

Isla Bloodvein
Maleficio de Roca

Isla Desperdiciada

Isla Maldita

Isla Piedra Sagrada

Piedra Sagrada Forest

La Isla de Ironmane

Juramento R.

Ilha Torturada

Isla Tridot

Ilha Malcriada

La Piedra Sagrada Mtn.

Pequeña Ilha

Ilha Torcida

Detenedor de Tormentas

Ilha Armored

Praias Douradas

Grande Floresta

Grande Ilha Floresta

Ilha Prateada

Ilha Anviled

Ilha das Baleias

The Sea of the Anvil

Ilha Batida

The Eternal Sea

Ilha Sangue Osso

LIBERTADIA

N

W — E

S

25 mi.

Island Wall
Map 04
City Names

LIBERTADIA

Praia do Solzinho

Pequena Cidade

Cidade da Espada

Vila Verdeira

Castelo do Sol

Vale Verde do Norte

Rio dos Sonhos

Castelo Serrilhado

Pescador do Litoral

Cidade de Jade

N

W   E

S

25 mi.

Island Wall
Map 04
Island Names

LIBERTADIA

Ilha do Solzinho

Espada Forest

Ilha da Espada

Ilha da Pequena Espada

Espada R.

Espada Mtn.

Ilha do Sol

Ilha Amarrada

Ilha Central

Ilha do Zeferino

Ilha Dinis

Ilha Devastada

Ilha do Recife

Ilha da Aldina

Praia do Sal

Ilha Serrilhada

Ilha da Luiza

Ilha de Jade em Desvanecimento

Ilha da Pedra de Frutos

The Eternal Sea

The Southern Sea

N

W   E

S

25 mi.

Luminarch
Map 01

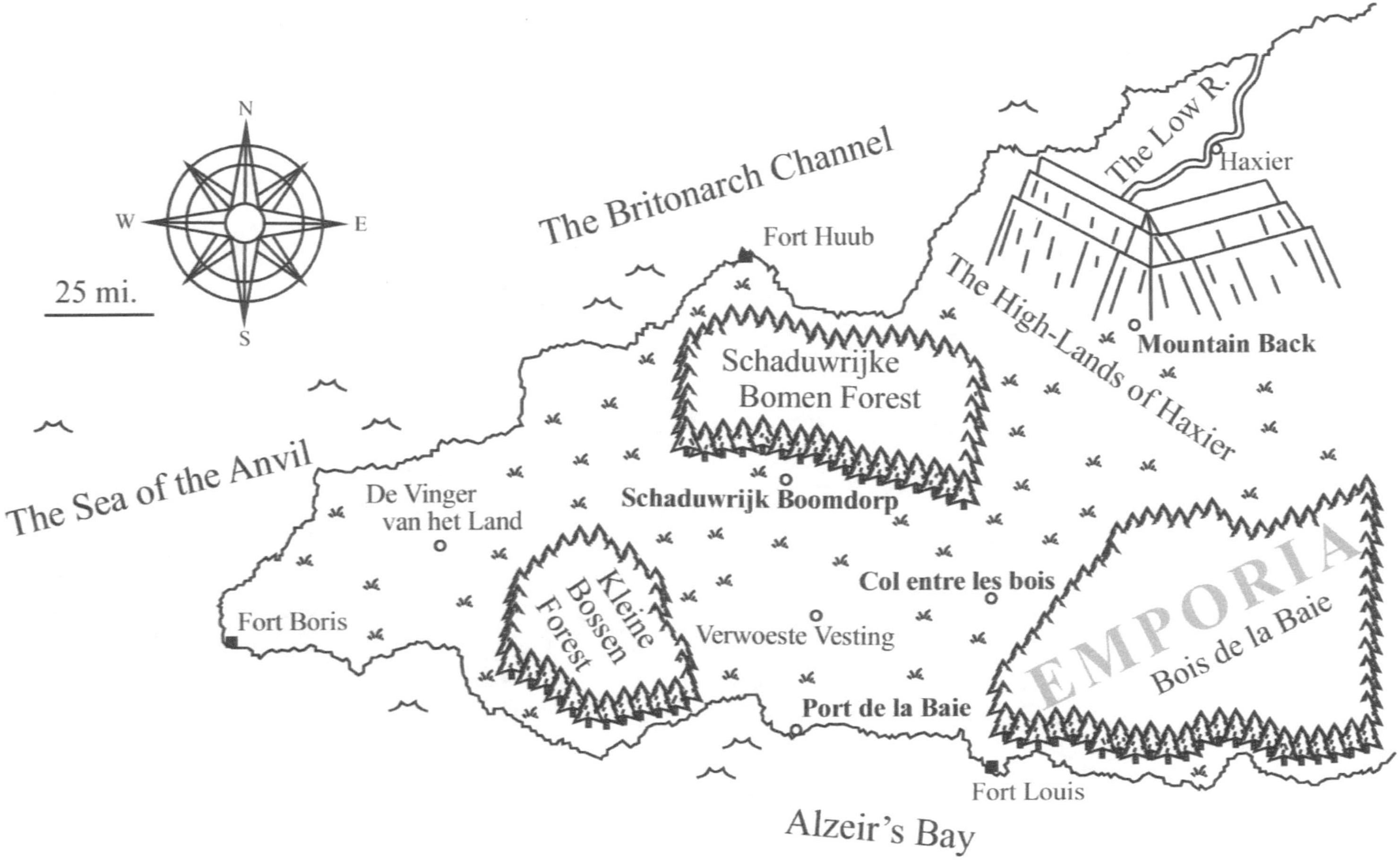

The Britonarch Channel

The Low R.

Haxier

Mountain Back

The High-Lands of Haxier

EMPORIA

Bois de la Baie

Fort Huub

Schaduwrijke Bomen Forest

Schaduwrijk Boomdorp

Col entre les bois

Verwoeste Vesting

Port de la Baie

Fort Louis

Alzeir's Bay

Kleine Bossen Forest

De Vinger van het Land

Fort Boris

The Sea of the Anvil

N E S W

25 mi.

Luminarch
Map 02

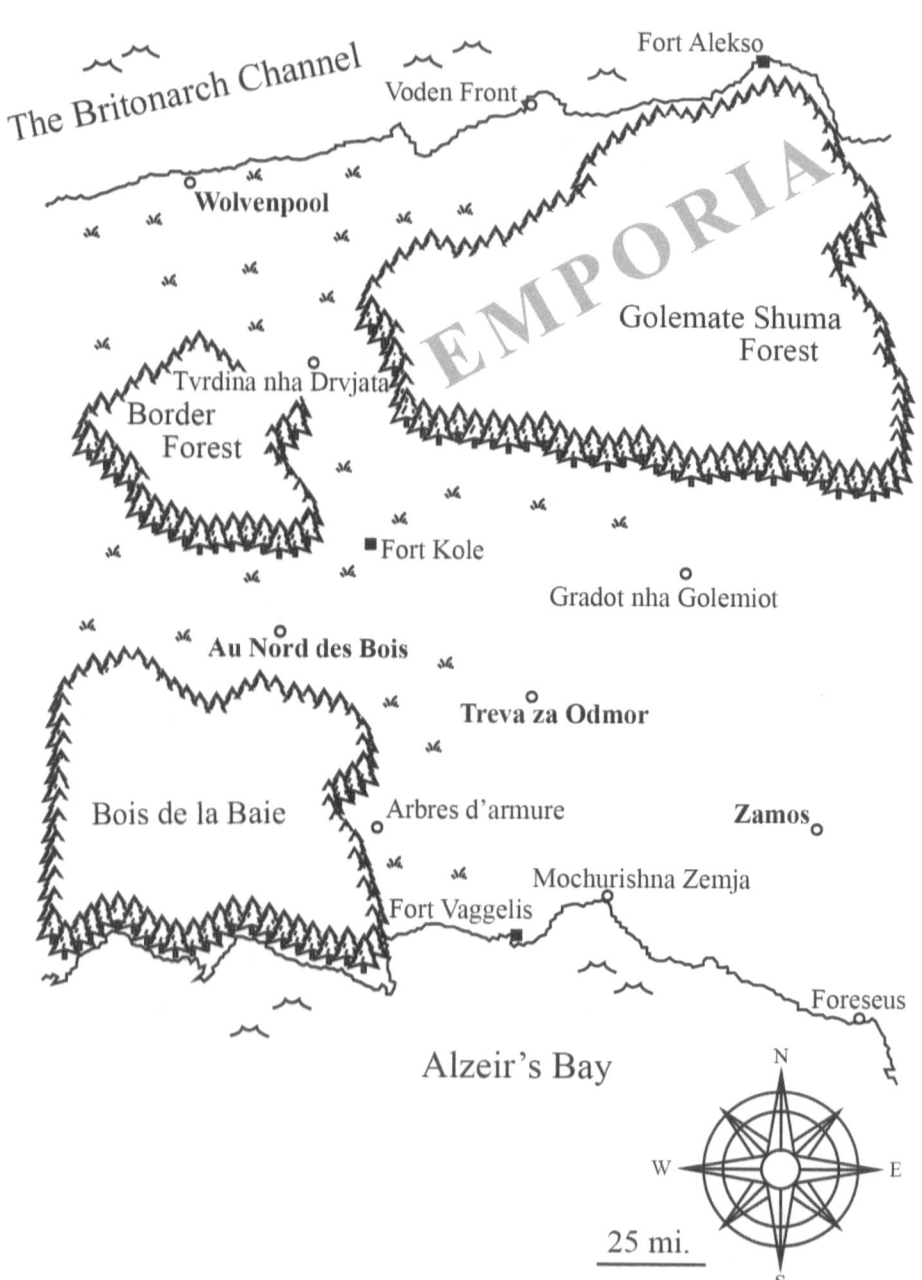

The Senka Ocean

Fort Alekso

The Britonarch Channel

Voden Front

EMPORIA

Wolvenpool

Golemate Shuma
Forest

Tvrdina nha Drvjata
Border
Forest

Fort Kole

Gradot nha Golemiot

Au Nord des Bois

Treva za Odmor

Bois de la Baie

Arbres d'armure

Zamos

Mochurishna Zemja

Fort Vaggelis

Foreseus

Alzeir's Bay

N
W   E
S

25 mi.

Luminarch
Map 03

The Senka Ocean

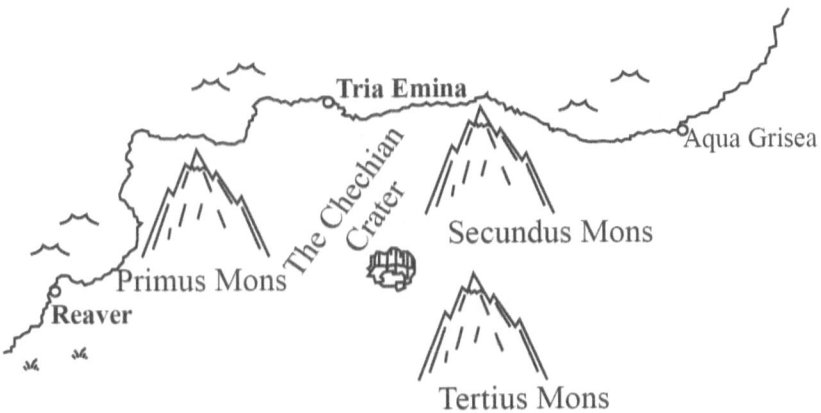

Tria Emina

Aqua Grisea

The Chechian Crater

Primus Mons

Secundus Mons

Reaver

Tertius Mons

Avena Flava

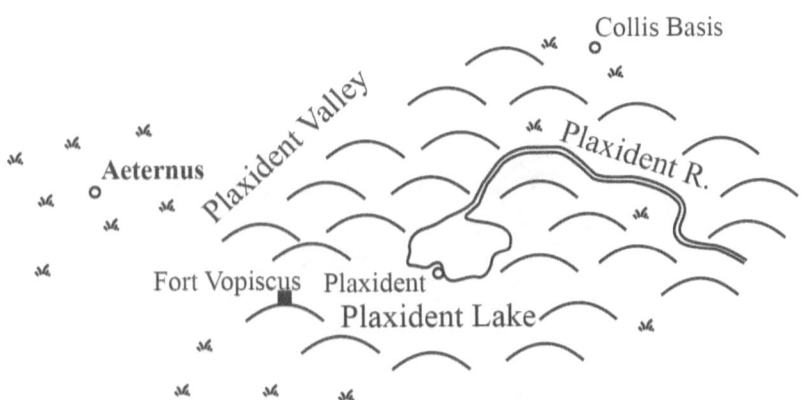

Collis Basis

Plaxident Valley

Plaxident R.

Aeternus

Fort Vopiscus   Plaxident

Plaxident Lake

EMPORIA

Emporenna

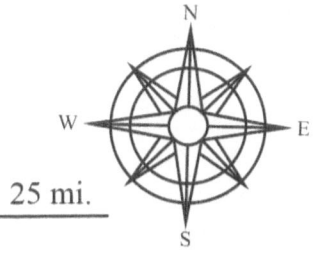

N

W   E

S

25 mi.

Luminarch
Map 04

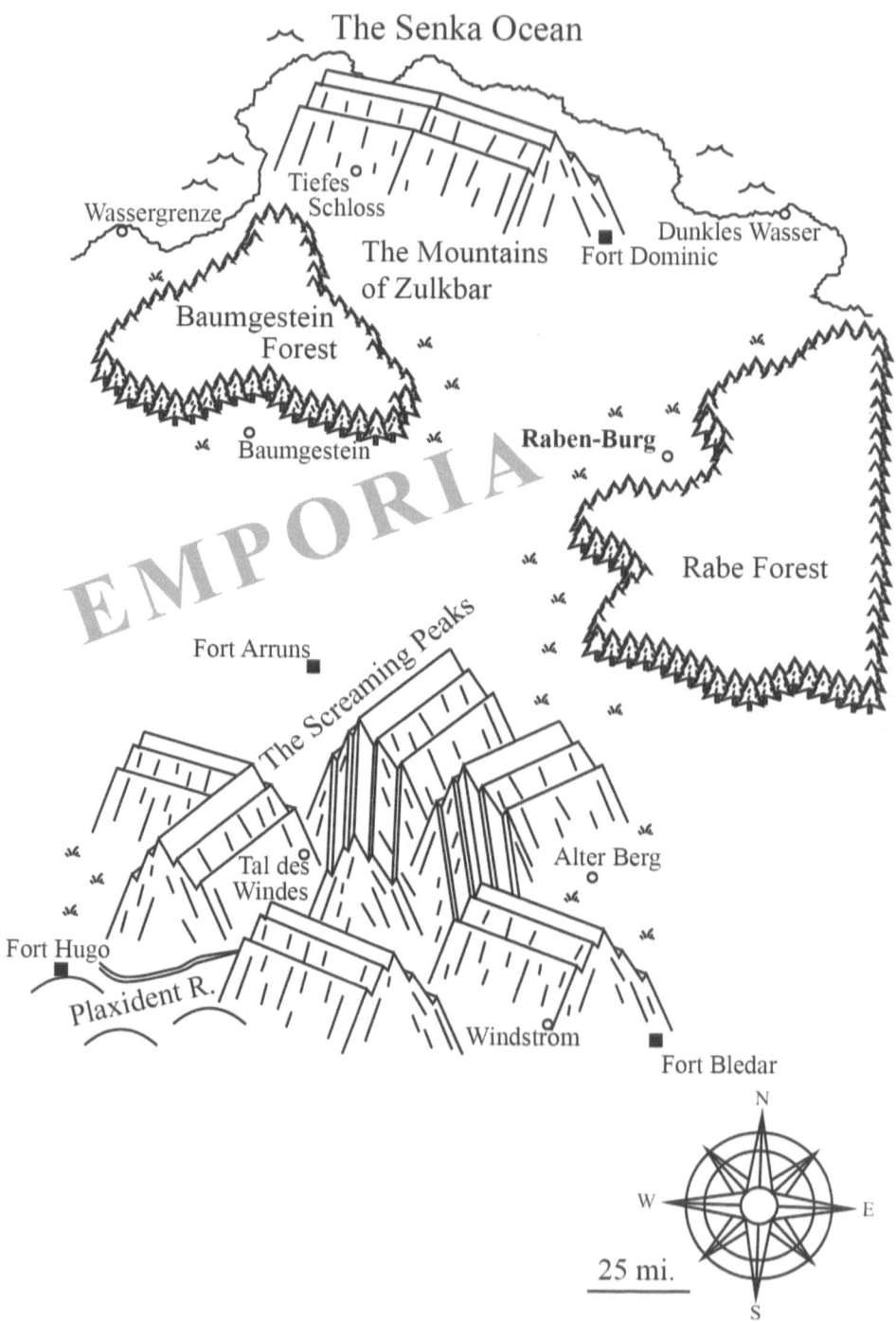

The Senka Ocean

Tiefes
Schloss

Wassergrenze

Dunkles Wasser

Fort Dominic

The Mountains
of Zulkbar

Baumgestein
Forest

Baumgestein

Raben-Burg

EMPORIA

Rabe Forest

Fort Arruns

The Screaming Peaks

Alter Berg

Tal des
Windes

Fort Hugo

Plaxident R.

Windstrom

Fort Bledar

N

W   E

S

25 mi.

Luminarch
Map 05

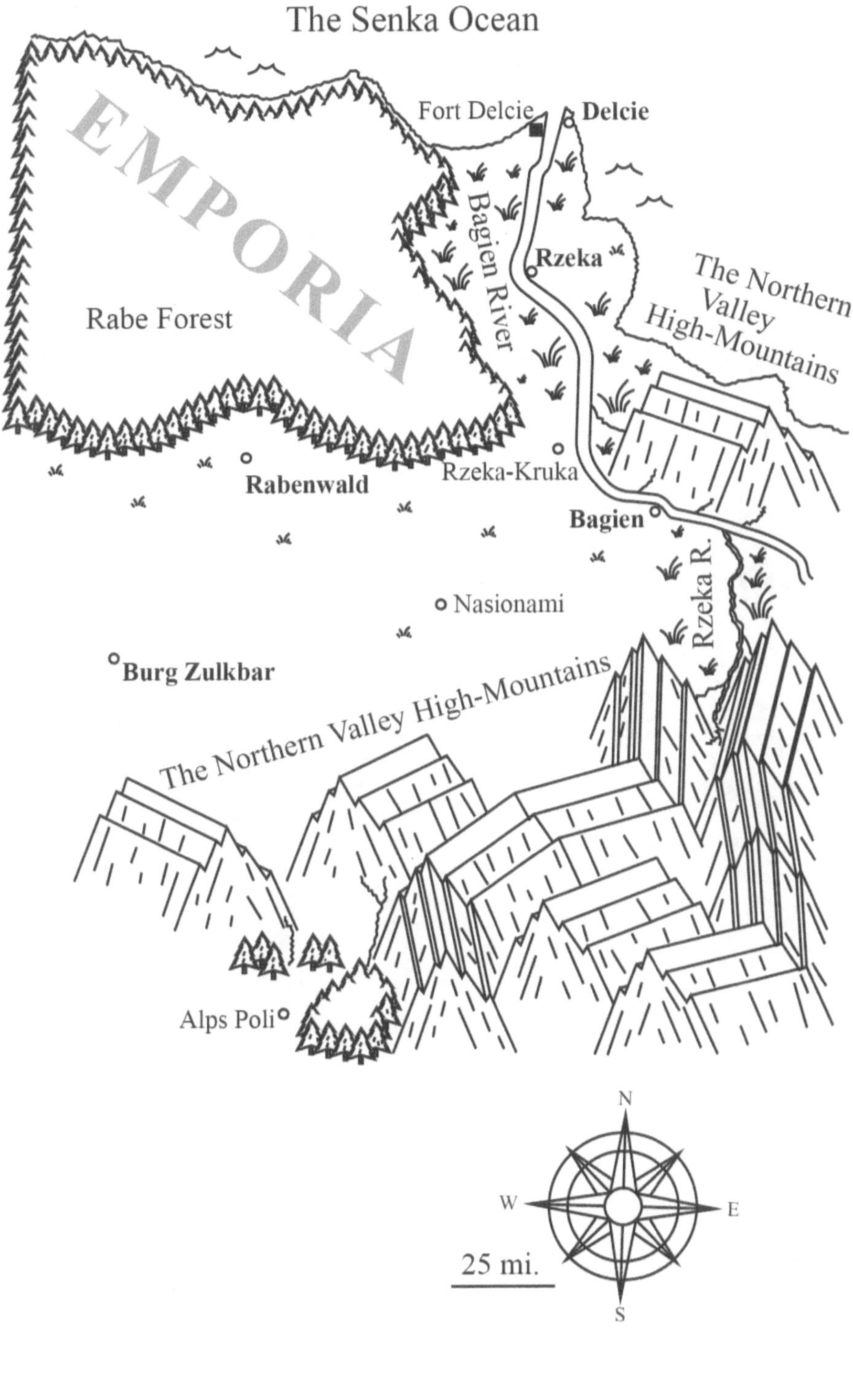

The Senka Ocean

EMPORIA

Fort Delcie ▪ Delcie ○

Bagien River

Rabe Forest

Rzeka ○

The Northern Valley High-Mountains

Rabenwald ○

Rzeka-Kruka

Bagien

Nasionami ○

Rzeka R.

Burg Zulkbar ○

The Northern Valley High-Mountains

Alps Poli ○

N
W · E
S

25 mi.

Luminarch
Map 06

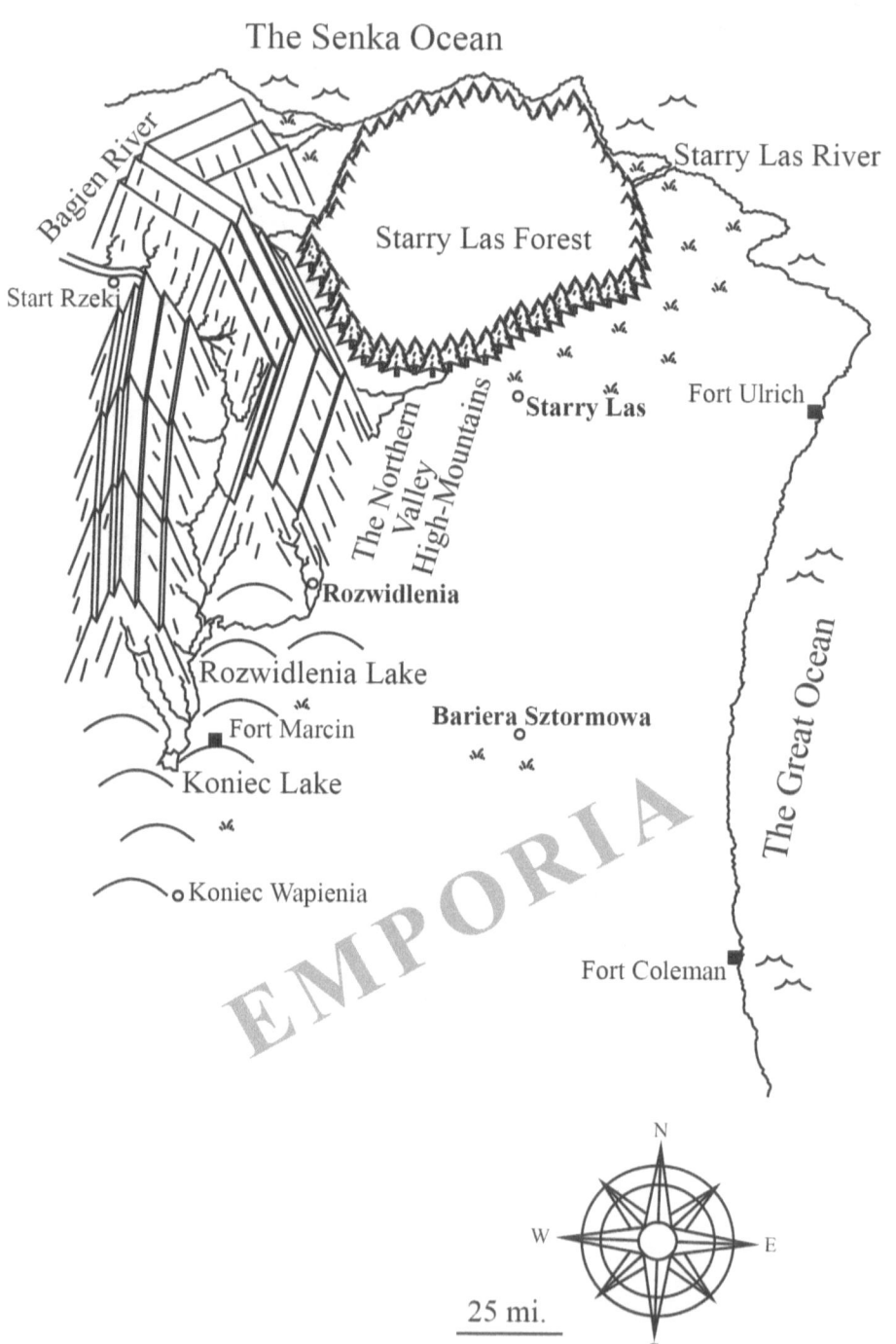

The Senka Ocean

Bagien River

Starry Las River

Starry Las Forest

Start Rzeki

Fort Ulrich

The Northern Valley High-Mountains

Starry Las

Rozwidlenia

Rozwidlenia Lake

Fort Marcin

Bariera Sztormowa

Koniec Lake

The Great Ocean

Koniec Wapienia

EMPORIA

Fort Coleman

N

W   E

S

25 mi.

Luminarch
Map 07

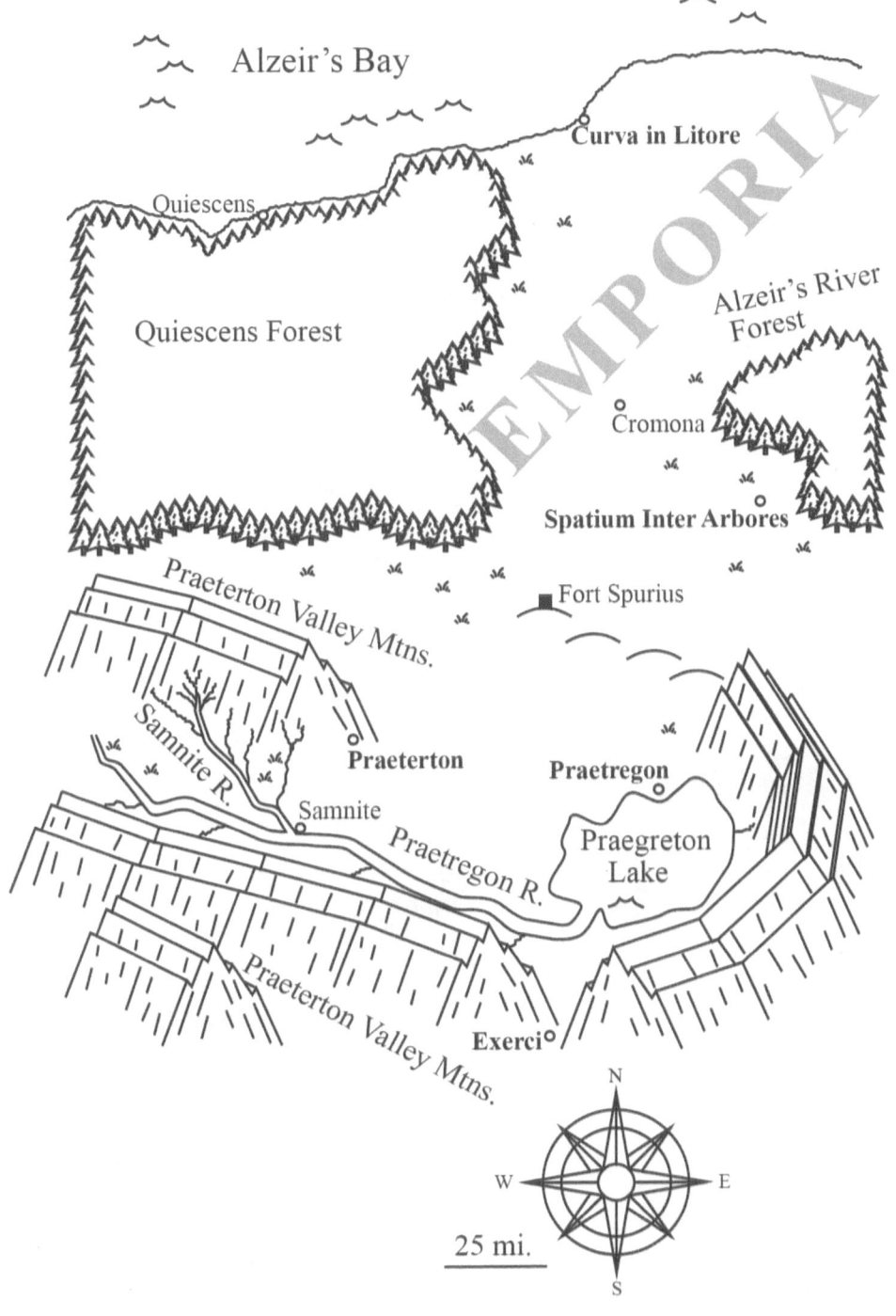

Alzeir's Bay

Curva in Litore

Quiescens

Quiescens Forest

EMPORIA

Alzeir's River Forest

Cromona

Spatium Inter Arbores

Fort Spurius

Praeterton Valley Mtns.

Samnite R.

Praeterton

Praetregon

Samnite

Praetregon R.

Praegreton Lake

Praeterton Valley Mtns.

Exerci

N

W   E

S

25 mi.

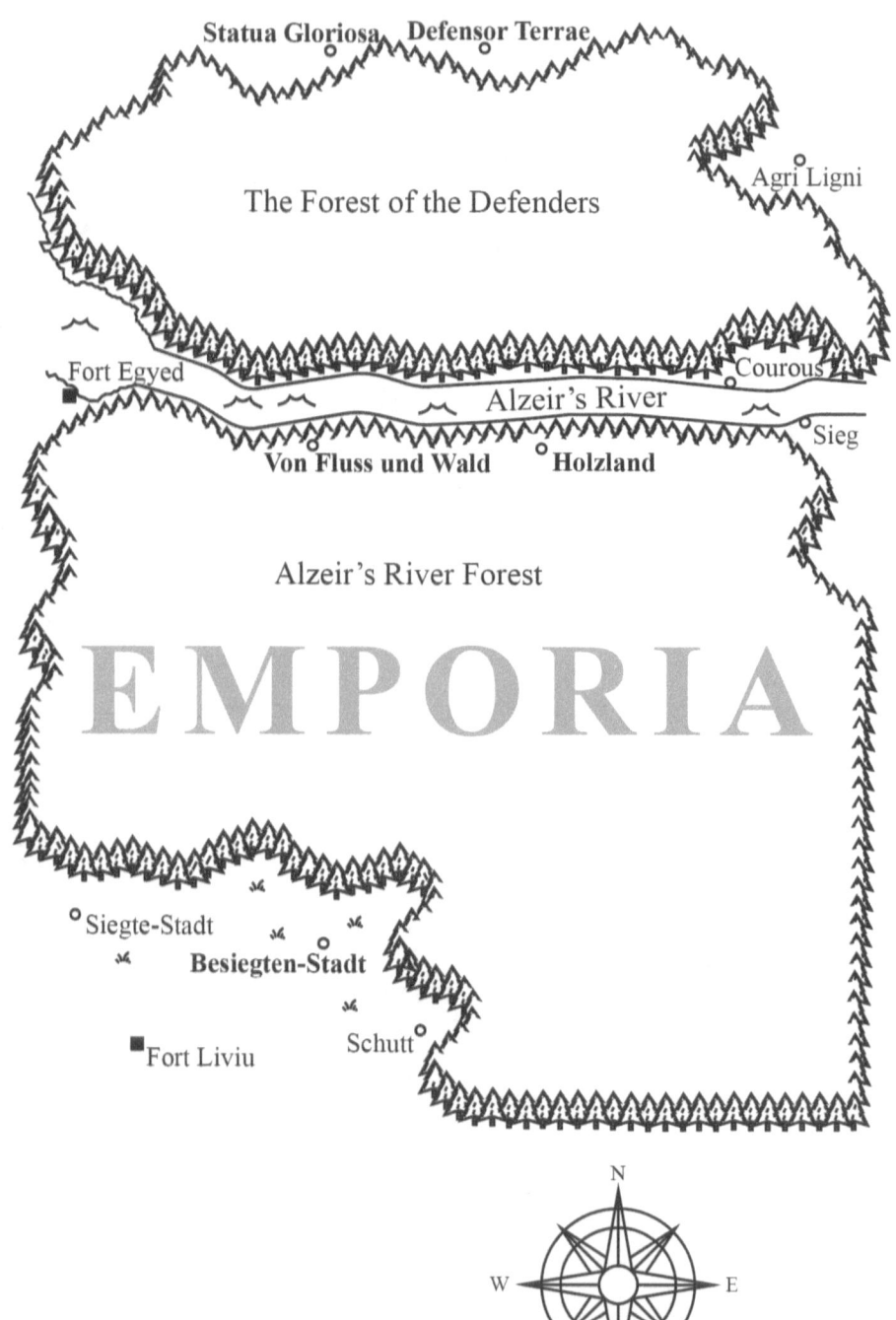

Luminarch
Map 08

Statua Gloriosa Defensor Terrae

Agri Ligni

The Forest of the Defenders

Fort Egyed

Courous

Alzeir's River

Sieg

Von Fluss und Wald Holzland

Alzeir's River Forest

EMPORIA

Siegte-Stadt

Besiegten-Stadt

Fort Liviu

Schutt

N

W

E

S

25 mi.

Luminarch
Map 09

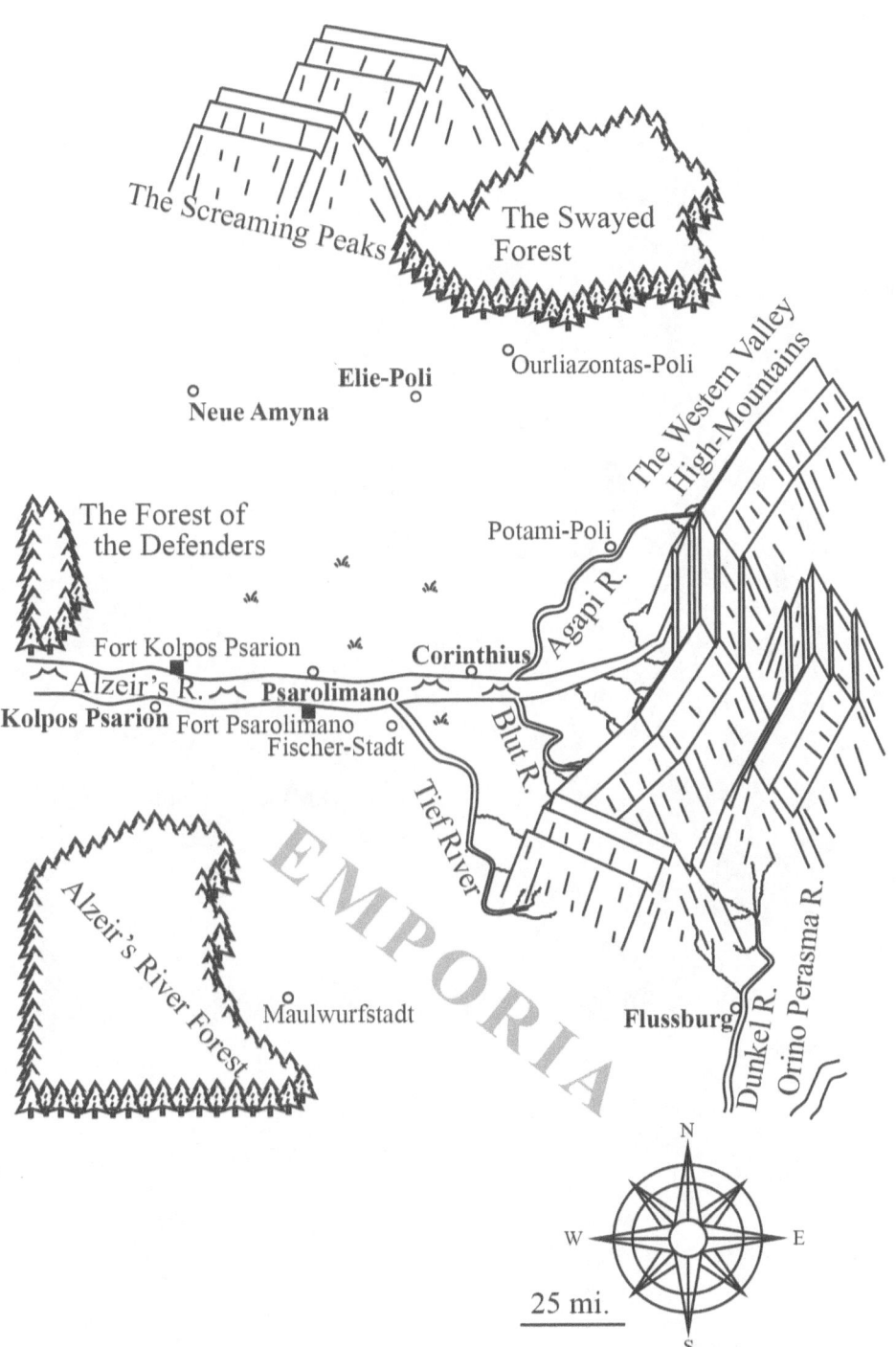

The Screaming Peaks

The Swayed Forest

Ourliazontas-Poli

Elie-Poli

Neue Amyna

The Western Valley High-Mountains

The Forest of the Defenders

Potami-Poli

Agapi R.

Fort Kolpos Psarion

Corinthius

Alzeir's R.

Psarolimano

Kolpos Psarion

Fort Psarolimano

Fischer-Stadt

Blut R.

Tief River

EMPORIA

Alzeir's River Forest

Maulwurfstadt

Flussburg

Dunkel R.

Orino Perasma R.

N

W   E

S

25 mi.

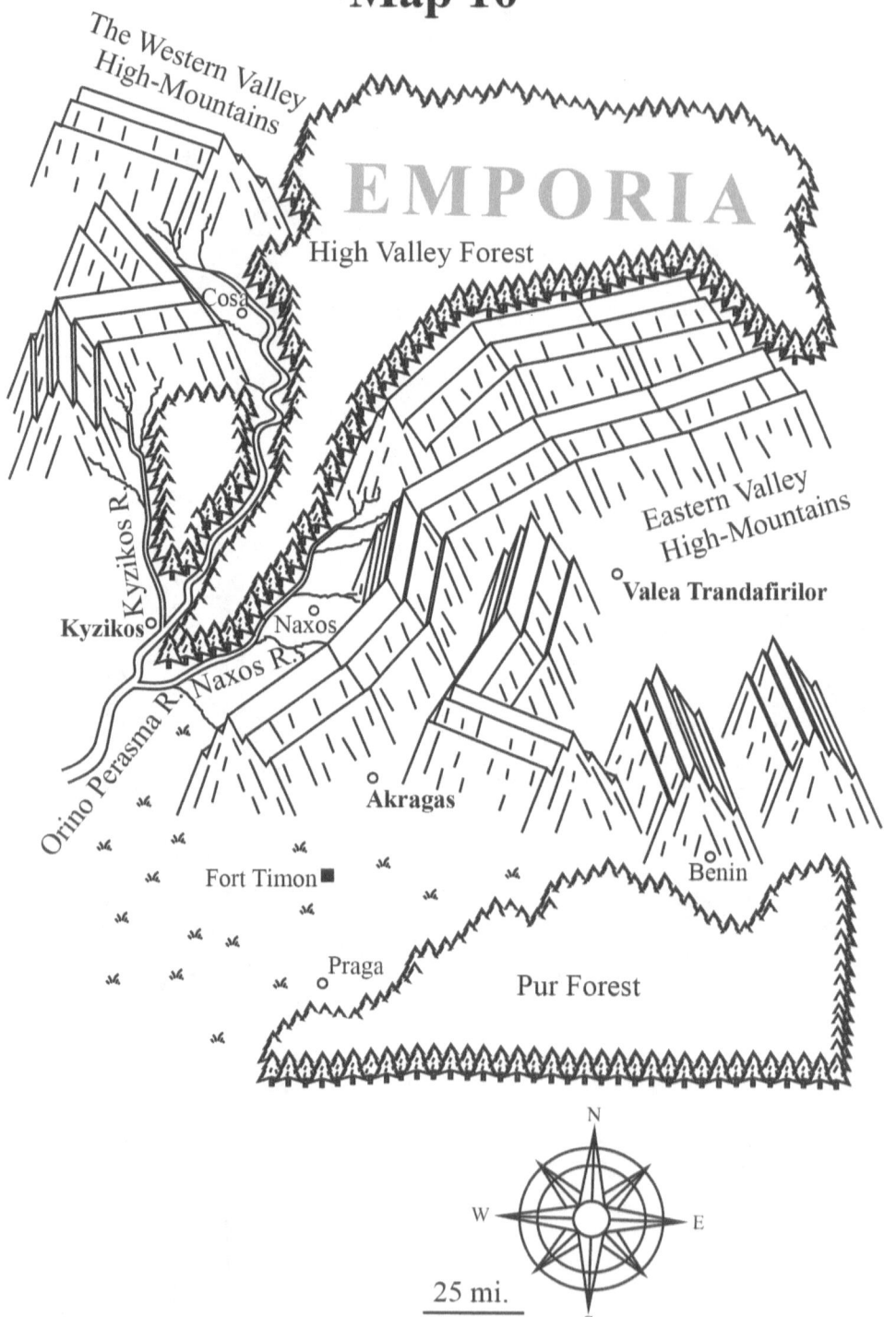

Luminarch
Map 10

The Western Valley High-Mountains

EMPORIA

High Valley Forest

Cosa

Eastern Valley High-Mountains

Valea Trandafirilor

Kyzikos R.

Kyzikos

Naxos

Naxos R.

Orino Perasma R.

Akragas

Benin

Fort Timon

Praga

Pur Forest

N

W   E

S

25 mi.

Luminarch
Map 11

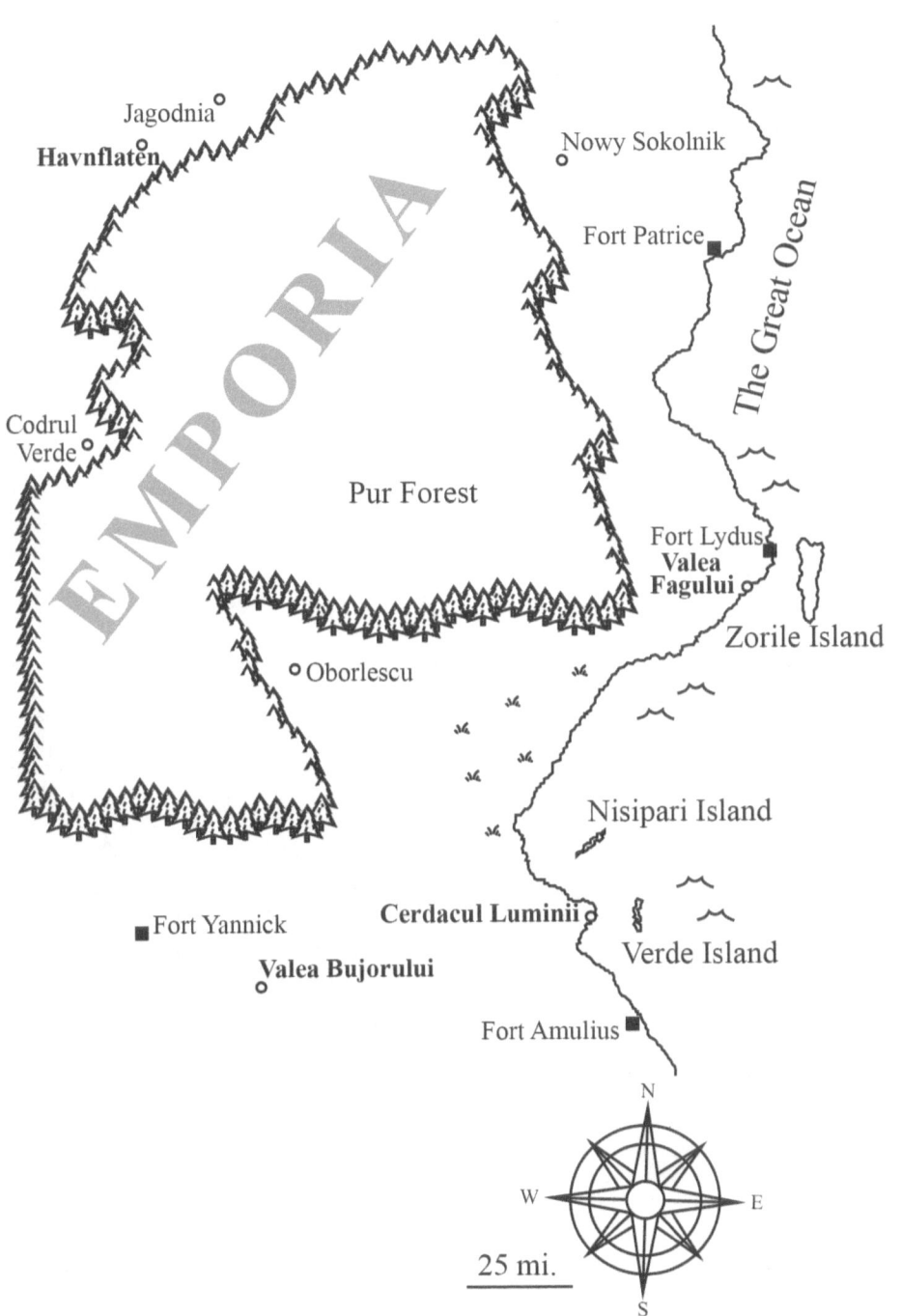

Jagodnia

Havnflaten

Nowy Sokolnik

EMPORIA

Fort Patrice

The Great Ocean

Codrul
Verde

Pur Forest

Fort Lydus
**Valea
Fagului**

Zorile Island

Oborlescu

Nisipari Island

Fort Yannick

Cerdacul Luminii

Verde Island

Valea Bujorului

Fort Amulius

N
W   E
S

25 mi.

Luminarch
Map 12

Montblancette Forest

○ Nordstrandelon

Vigne Fleur ○

○ **Montclairon**

EMPORIA

Fort Philip ■

KENDE

Hargitafalu

Verdeszegi ○

○ Arany Viorica

Honor's Water

Ficsorul Mare ○

Great Lake Mtns.

Vaugeois Island

Briseval ○

○ Csernoborosk

Fleuris Forest

Belleville

Vaugeois Strait

Fleuris Mtn.

Loire Mtns.

Fleuris Port ○

Ode R.

✪ **Aranykert**

The Southern Sea

Loire ○

Castel Nouvelle ■

Loire R.

VAUGEOIS

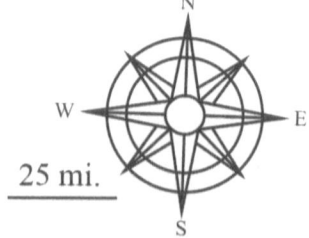

N

W — E

S

25 mi.

Luminarch
Map 13

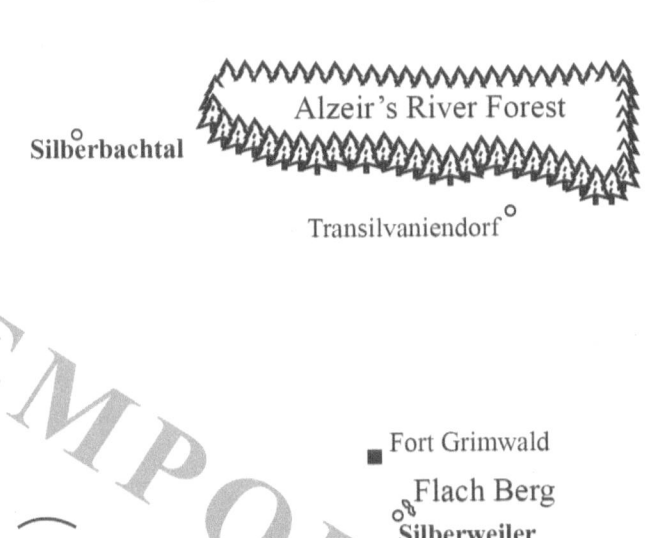

Alzeir's River Forest

Silberbachtal

Transilvaniendorf

Fort Grimwald

Flach Berg

Silberweiler

Neuhafenburg

Fort Ludger

Felsig Hills

EMPORIA

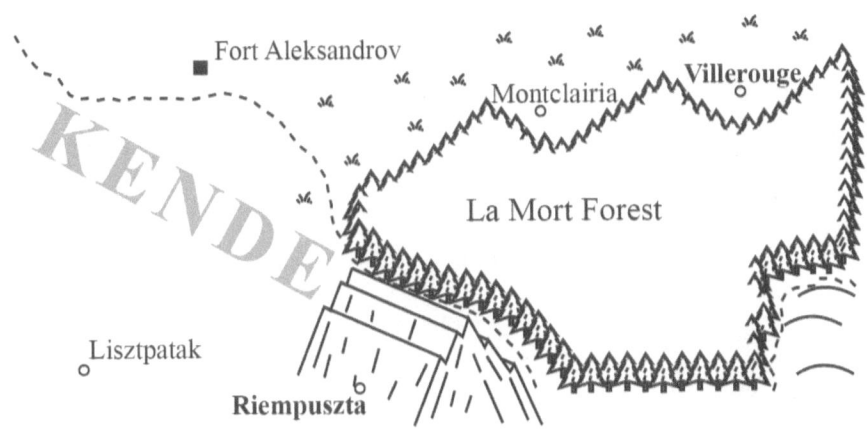

Fort Aleksandrov

Montclairia

Villerouge

La Mort Forest

KENDE

Lisztpatak

Riempuszta

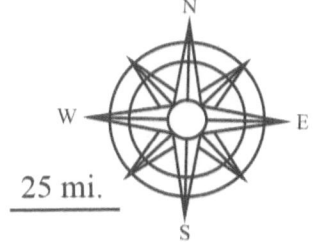

N

W   E

S

25 mi.

Luminarch
Map 14

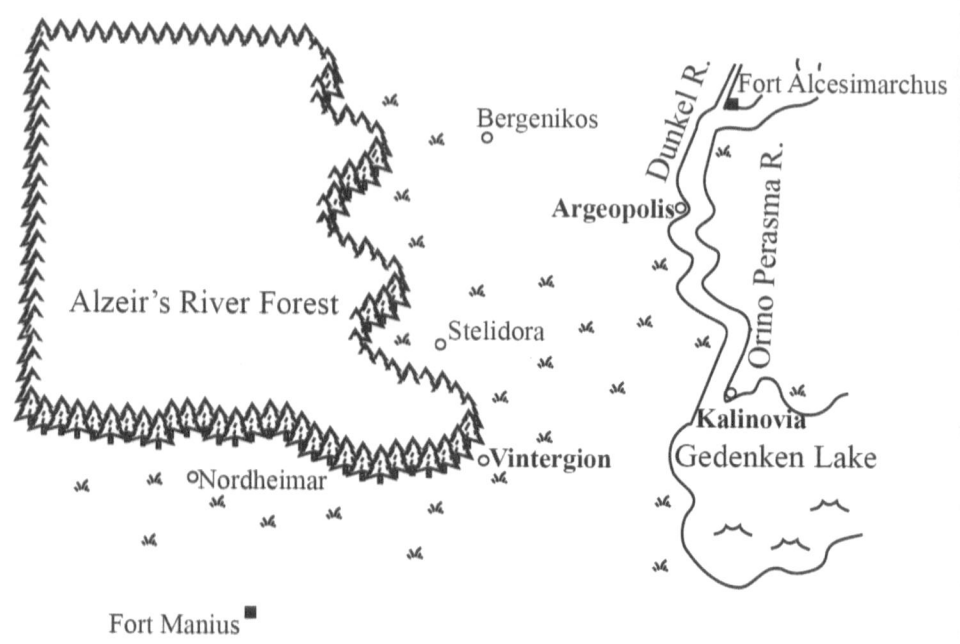

Bergenikos

Alzeir's River Forest

Dunkel R.

Fort Alcesimarchus

Argeopolis

Orino Perasma R.

Stelidora

Kalinovia
Gedenken Lake

Vintergion

Nordheimar

Fort Manius

Skynthos

EMPORIA

Bellevigne

La Mort Forest

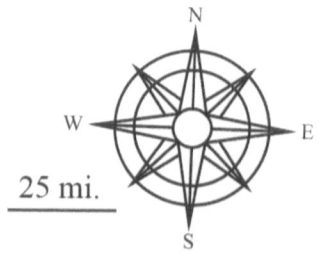

N

W   E

S

25 mi.

Luminarch
Map 15

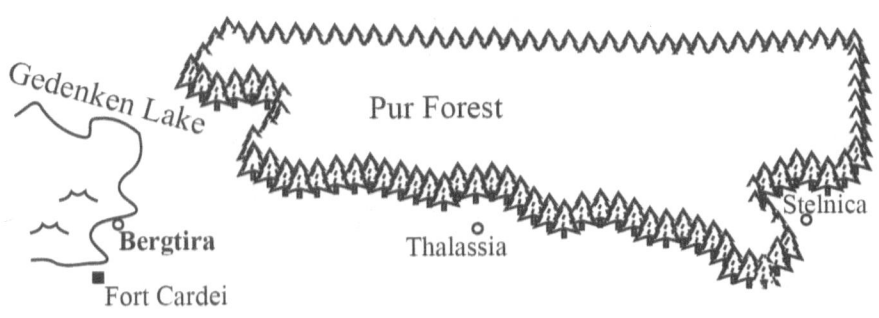

Gedenken Lake

Pur Forest

Stelnica

Bergtira

Thalassia

■ Fort Cardei

■ Fort Isidor

Veranopolis ○

○ **Heliodora**

EMPORIA

○ Floreni

Fort Lascar ■

■ Fort Oppius

Valea Lunii

Oamenii Nordului R.

Muntele Argelia

Lake Kennedy

Fort Troy

VARENIA

Verde ○

Oamenii de Sud R.

■ Fort Seaghdh

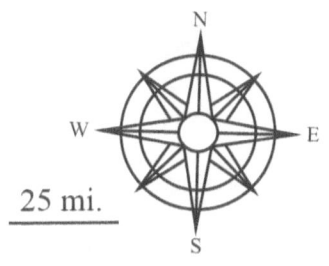

N

W   E

S

25 mi.

Luminarch
Map 16

EMPORIA

VARENIA

Melta

The Great Ocean

Floritoru

Brivas

Oamenii Nordului R.

Aquincum

Burrium

The Varenian Mtns.

Fenthia

Brathas

Fort Tane

Castle Hake

Byblus

Piatra Verdea

Noreia

Oamenii de Sud R.

Puteoli

Fulginiae

Hadria

Dunarcani

La Mort Forest

Procul R.

EMPORIA

INSAMIR

VARENIA

N

W   E

S

25 mi.

Luminarch
Map 17

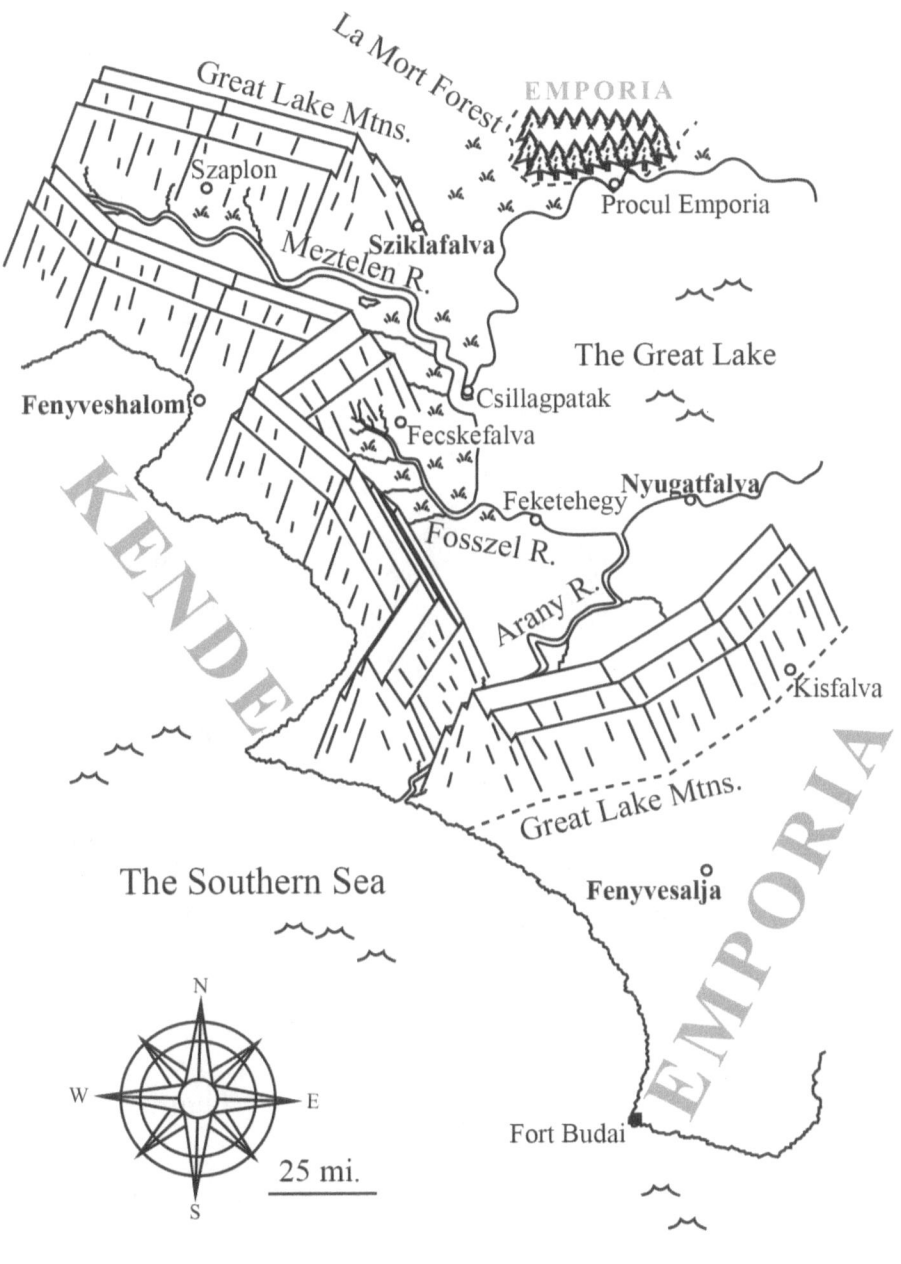

Luminarch
Map 18

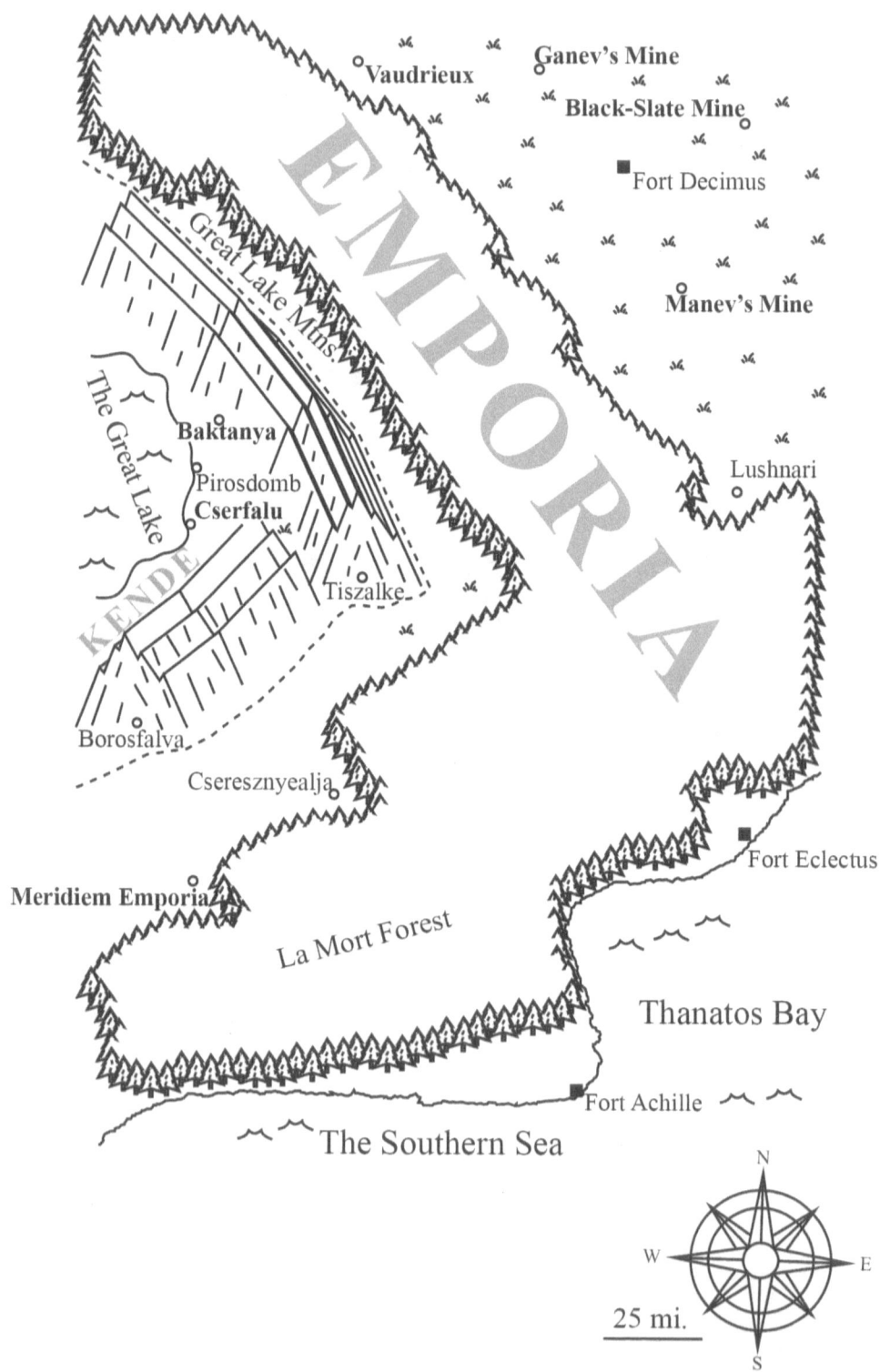

Luminarch
Map 19

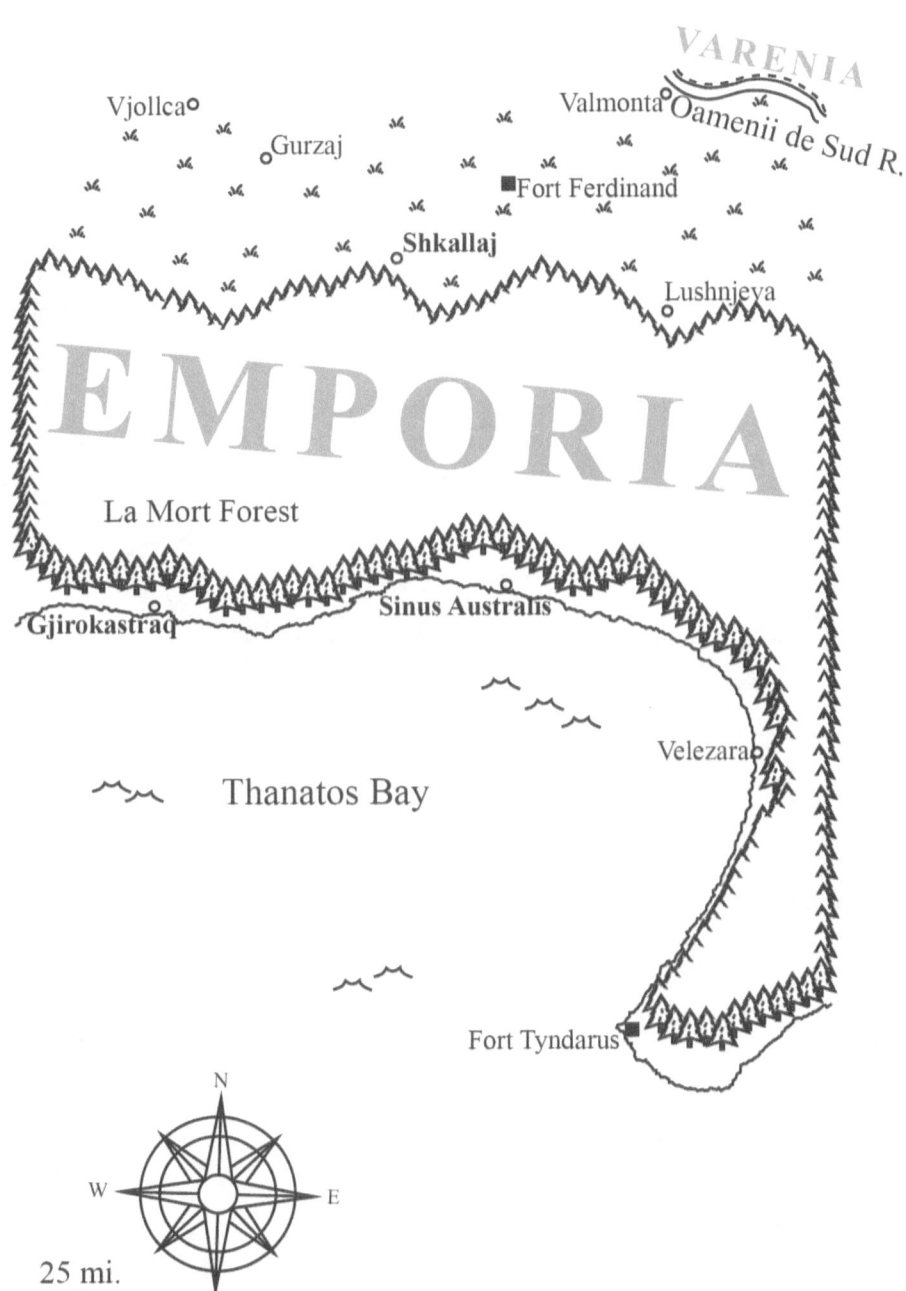

Luminarch
Map 20

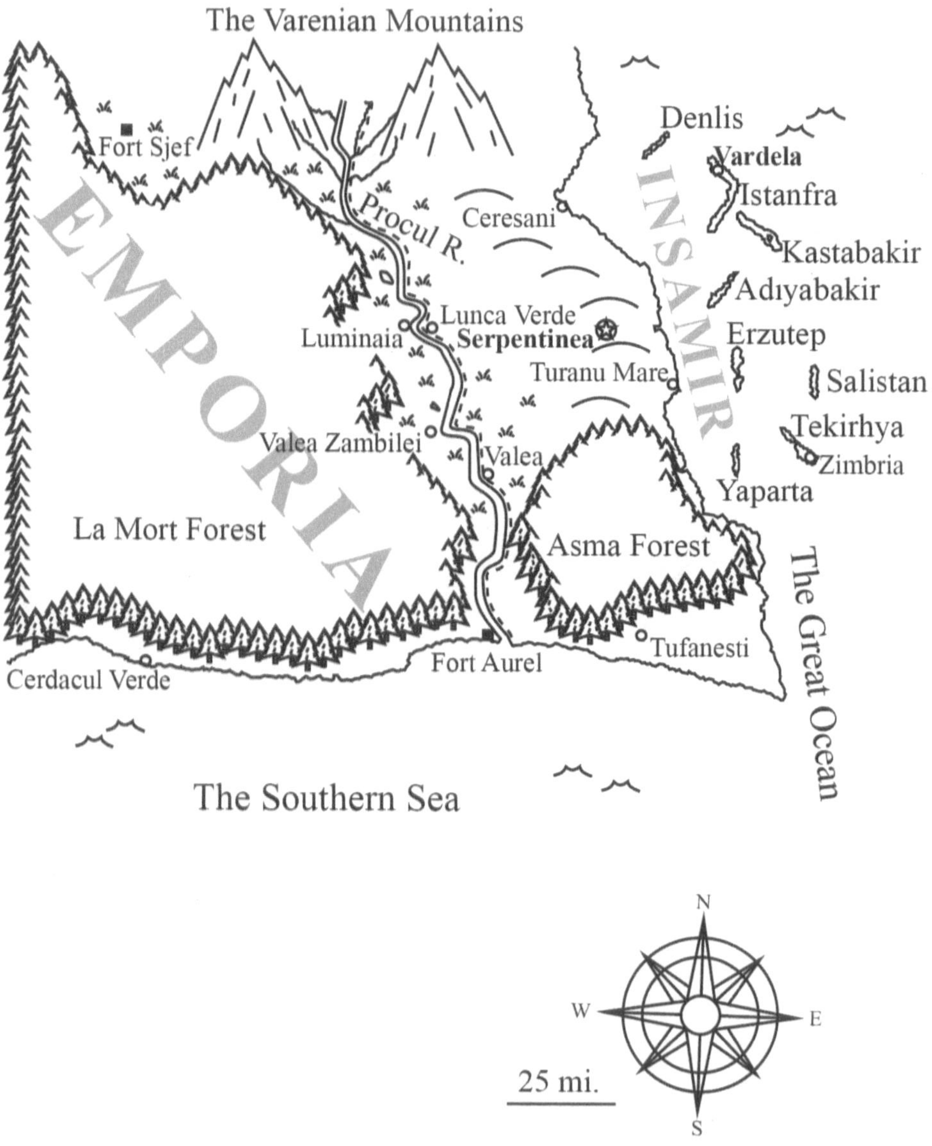

The Varenian Mountains

Denlis

Vardela

Fort Sjef

Istanfra

EMPORIA

Procul R.

Ceresani

Kastabakir

Adıyabakir

INSAMIR

Lunca Verde

Erzutep

Luminaia

Serpentinea

Salistan

Turanu Mare

Valea Zambilei

Tekirhya

Valea

Zimbria

Yaparta

La Mort Forest

Asma Forest

The Great Ocean

Cerdacul Verde

Fort Aurel

Tufanesti

The Southern Sea

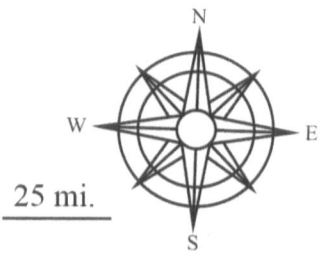

25 mi.

Luminarch
Map 21

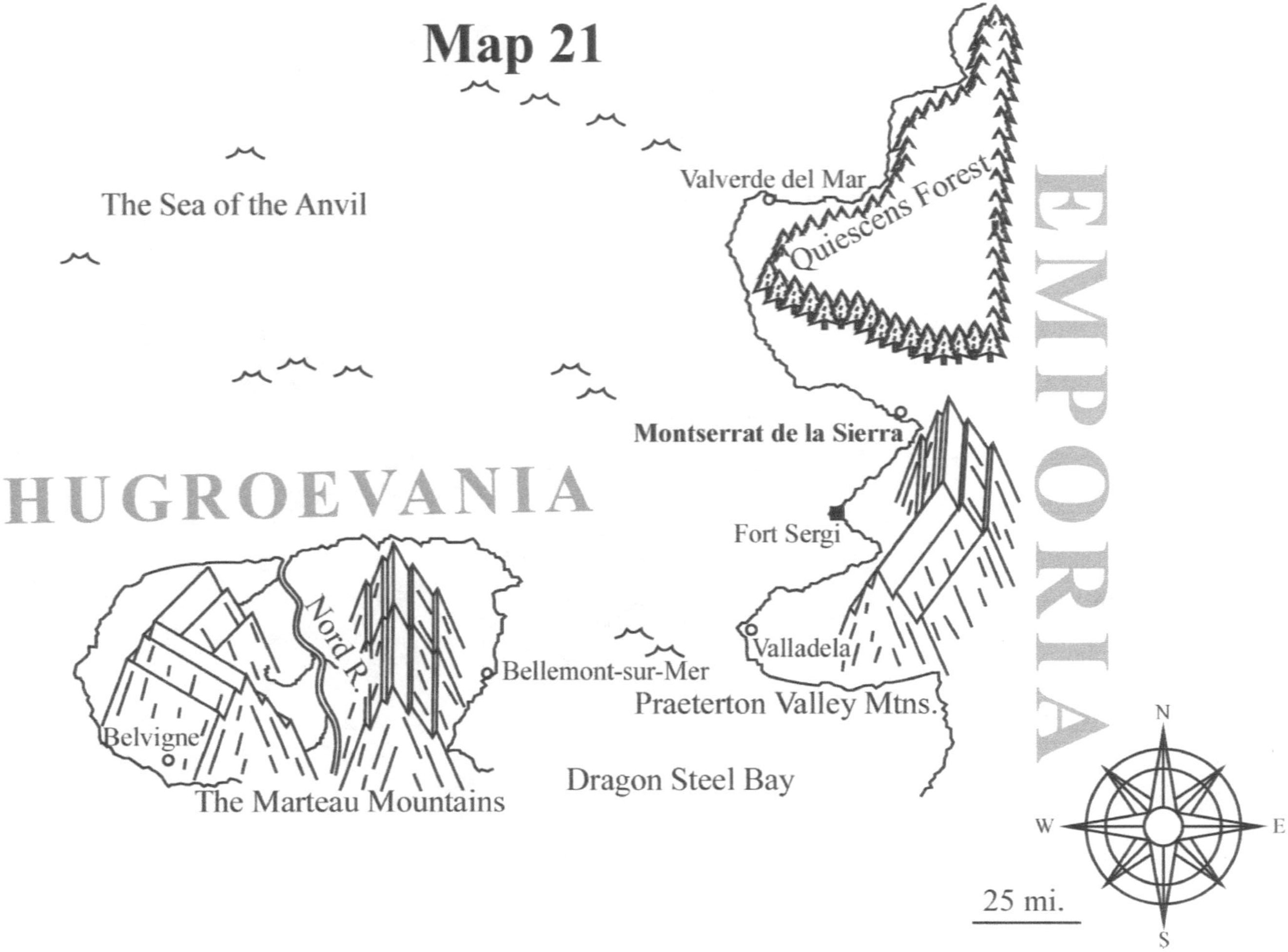

EMPORIA

HUGROEVANIA

N E S W

25 mi.

The Sea of the Anvil

Valverde del Mar

Quiescens Forest

Montserrat de la Sierra

Fort Sergi

Valladela

Praeterton Valley Mtns.

Dragon Steel Bay

Bellemont-sur-Mer

Nord R.

The Marteau Mountains

Belvigne

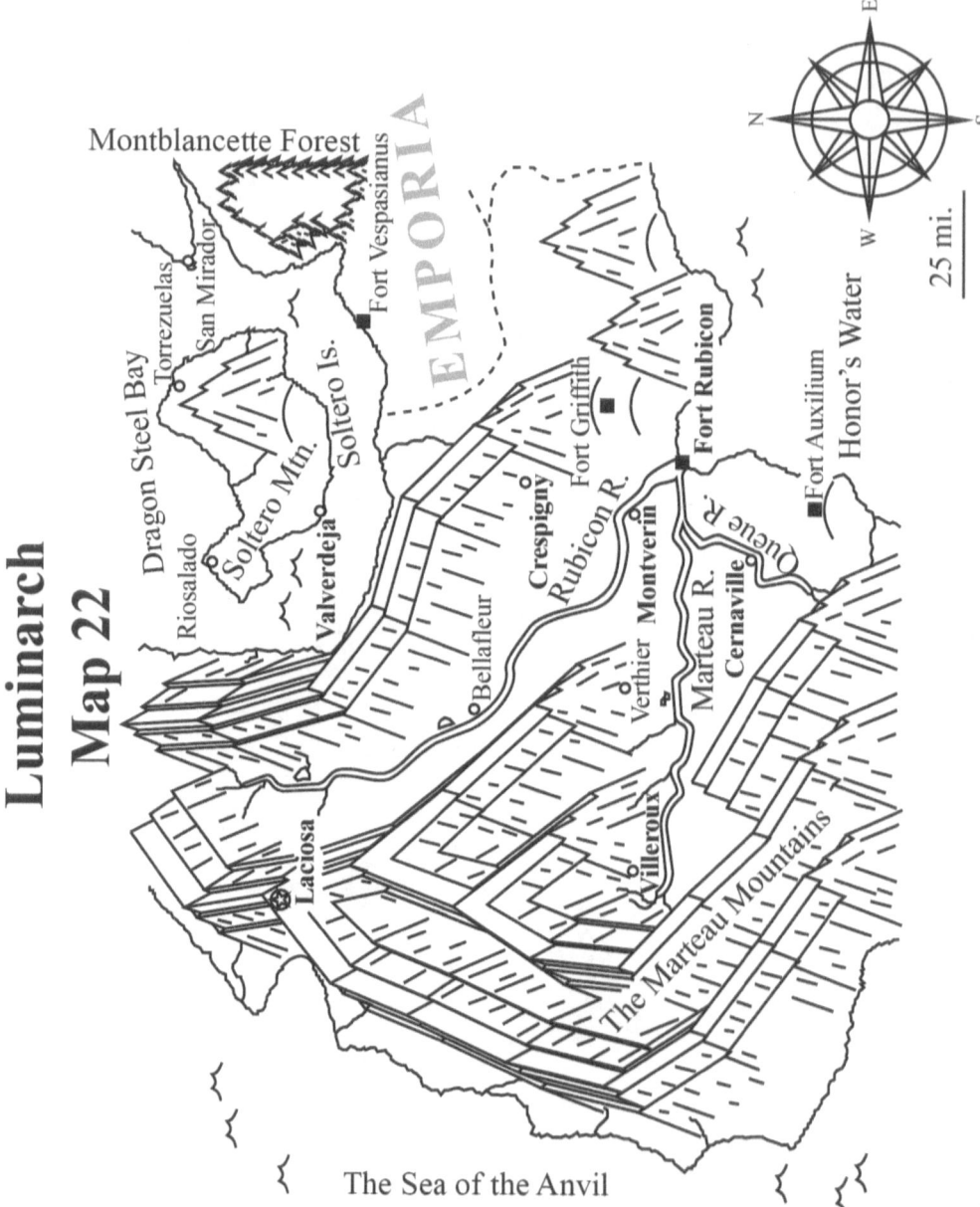

**Luminarch
Map 22**

Montblancette Forest

EMPORIA

Fort Vespasianus

Dragon Steel Bay

Torrezuelas

San Mirador

Soltero Mtn.

Soltero Is.

Riosalado

Valverdeja

Bellafleur

Crespigny

Rubicon R.

Fort Griffith

Fort Rubicon

Verthier

Montverin

Marteau R.

Quene R.

Cernaville

Fort Auxilium

Honor's Water

Villeroux

The Marteau Mountains

Laciosa

25 mi.

The Sea of the Anvil

HUGROEVANIA

Luminarch
Map 23

The Marteau Mountains

Valperrin

Cielmont

HUGROEVANIA

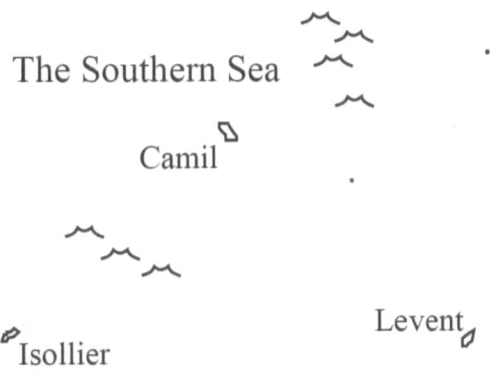

The Southern Sea

Camil

Isollier

Levent

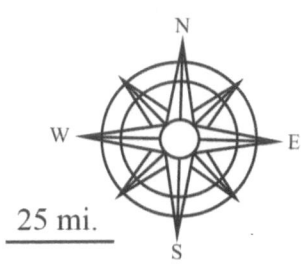

N

W   E

S

25 mi.

Marsh Island

The Ice-Plane Ocean

IARTHARLAND

Schootport

Granford R.

Schootport R.

Agivey R.

Bann R.

Edentry

Landbeek

Granford

Edentry R.

Arney R.

The Western Sea

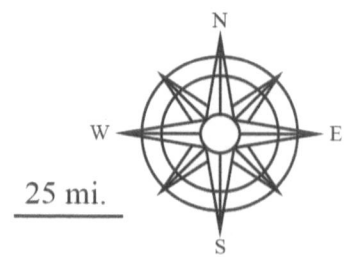

25 mi.

Senka Island

The Senka Ocean

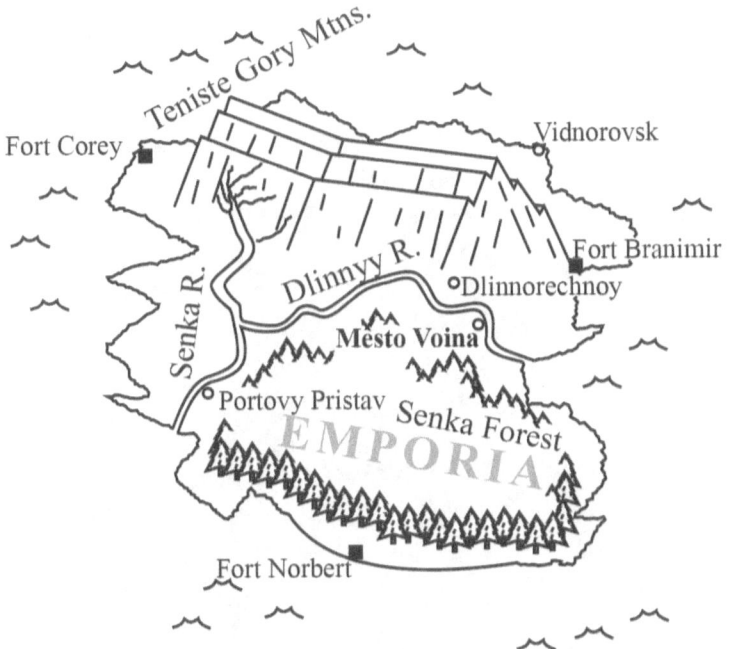

The Senka Ocean

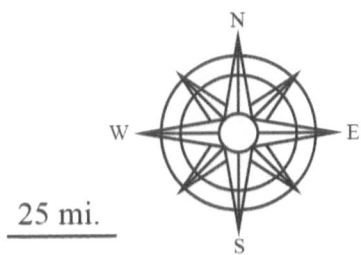

25 mi.

Velum Island

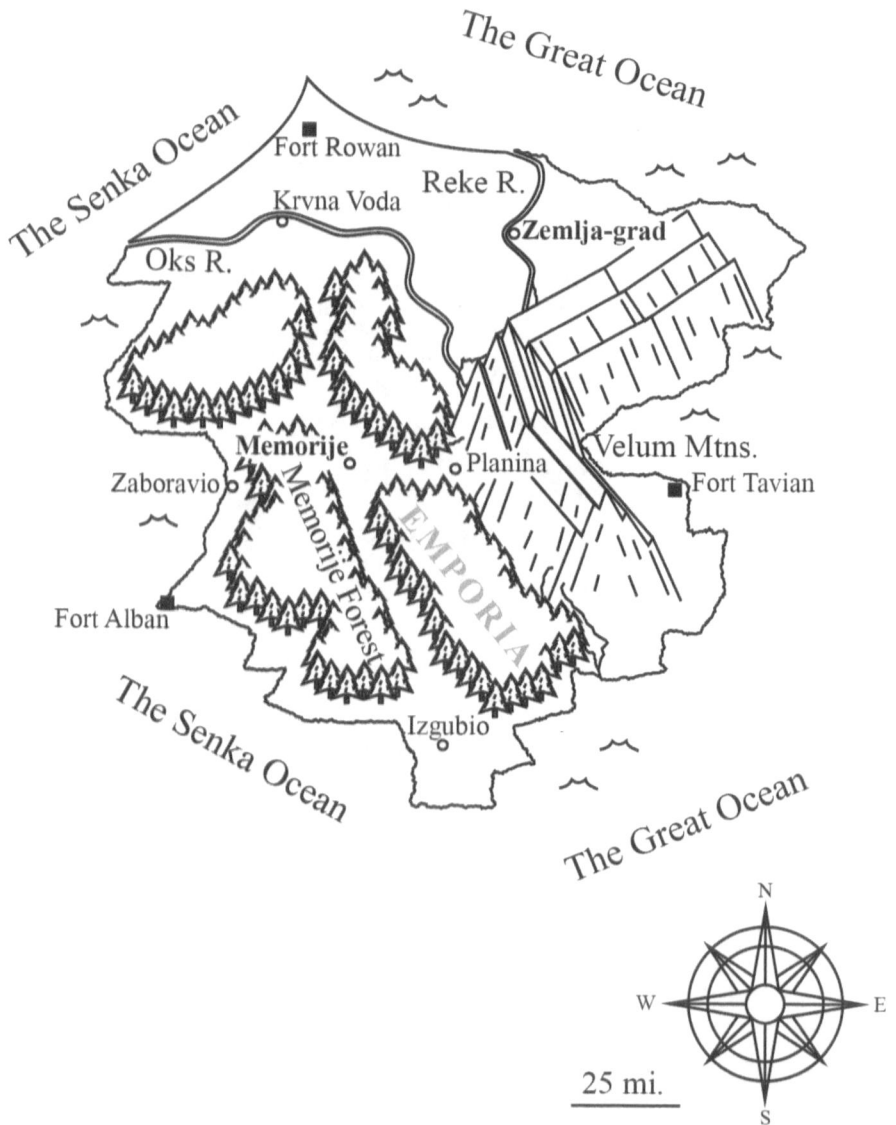

CONTENTS

PROLOGUE

The Assassination Attempt

Day 17, Emponar, Year 2123

Yeva hung in place outside a window to a corridor of the Emporian palace, at the heart of her enemy's empire. It was dark out, before the sun came to lighten up the world.

She was an elf, as were all her companions on this mission. They were all War Dancers, a special soldier to the race of elves. No matter how many attempts the other races tried to replicate, they were never close to the skill of the elven War Dancers.

Elves were naturally faster and more precise in their actions. As dwarves were naturally strong and largely non-fatiguing, taking longer to fatigue than other races. Dragons were, well, dragons and that should be enough to get the point across. Humans were the lacking race in Yeva's mind.

They were not strong like a dwarf nor were they fast and precise like an elf. They weren't dragons either, but in some way and fashion they had created the largest empire in history and were still looking to grow ever more.

The freaks weren't afraid of anything it seemed. She had seen Emporians clash head on with dragons like the psychopaths they are, without wavering.

It was tenacity she presumed. The will to keep going even though it seemed impossible to do. To swallow doubts and to push on. It was unnatural, to her anyway. All things should fear something else.

Her and her companions were chosen from among the best the Draken Confederation and Ludy Dvukh Chelovek had to offer. They wore no colors, but black.

Just like all War Dancers they had two thin, curved short swords sheathed on their backs as their weapons and wore light leather armor with woolen gambeson to keep them warmer in the cold of the approaching winter. Their strength was put in their speed and agility. Their swords had engravings upon them as decoration. All engravings were different on all others swords. The engravings represented a War Dancers journey and achievements.

Yeva had chest-long blonde hair that was bound up in a braid that fell around her left shoulder. She was slender in frame, but not short.

Beside her was Ivanovich, from Ludy Dvukh Chelovek just as her. He had black hair with a small slender, but long, braid of hair that fell over his right shoulder.

On her other side was another elf. She did not remember his name, but remembered that he was from the Confederation. She didn't care too much for him, only Ivanovich. She was looking at him and had been for… she didn't know how long, but he looked into her eyes then and smiled warmly.

She needed that, it was nearing the end of the harvest season and the wind was blowing, not too hard, but it was chilling. Banners hung from rods and floated in the breeze. Flags were attached to poles atop towers and other high points around the palace that also hung mostly limp, but lifted up slightly by the wind. The design was a silver Emporian shield with two silver swords crossing behind the shield and the tips pointing downwards upon a carmine red backing.

"Art thou prepared?" A voice asked her. She snapped out of looking at Ivanovich to notice that it was him whispering to her. His eyes searched hers for an answer as she came to.

"Verily," she whispered back. They both had Ludian accents as was the accent from the free Kingdom of Ludy Dvukh Chelovek.

Voices came into earshot from inside the corridor and heads looked up at the windows they sturdily gripped onto. A small hook was latched into a groove in the concrete and ropes were attaching them to the hooks that held them in place so they did not exert themselves while waiting.

The ropes tied around their waist and they propped themselves up with their legs and knees. They were not far from the bottom of the window ledge.

They had been scouting and preparing for this ever since they had reached Emporenna, capital of Emporia. They were there to assassinate Emperor Vaminus Rubicon.

Orders: Assassinate the Emperor, therefore landing a significant blow to the Empire and making it where it would be too hard for the Empire to counter strike because it would be winter by the time they had recovered.

This was to cover an extraction for a rebel force on Senka Island which had information on Emporian strategy. Excellent plan, to her anyway.

The voices came closer as well as footsteps. As the voices grew louder, they became discernible.

"How is the Britone front?" A man asked with a Praetorian accent. This voice would most likely be the Emperor.

"As well as it can go," another voice said, but deeper. Not much deeper, but noticeable. It sounded as if it was harder, more used. He also had a Praetorian accent. She guessed that this voice was Prince Andronicus Rubicon.

He was the younger of the two princes of Emporia, she had heard tales of the prince's accomplishments and was impressed, yet repulsed. He had achieved many victories, but he was brutal, very brutal. Most battles that he fought he won decisively.

"'As well as it can go'.That frontier never seems to end. For hundreds of years we hath fought there while seeming to go nowhere. We push forward, they push back, repeat," said Emperor Vaminus.

"If it accounts for anything, we are not losing. We push northward across the eastern Senka Ocean. Upheaval on those islands have subsided substantially," replied Prince Andronicus.

There were more than two foot falls sounding, indicating that there were guards, a good many. Steel clinked as they walked down the corridor. It began to sound as if they were almost there.

She and all the rest of the War Dancers, when the time was right, would spring up into the corridor and get to the physical part of their mission. Andronicus would be an obstacle that she was sure they could handle, and then when they did, he would be dead too. A spark of heated joy swept through her at that thought.

"Thou wouldest be bearing thy crown, Father," said Andronicus.

"The thing is but a weight that I doth not wish to bear at the moment," Vaminus huffed.

"Thou knowest the plan, thou knowest what could happen."

"Thou art but paranoid, I think. Why, thou art all ways in that armor now as if thou go to battle some demons in the dark." Wearing his armor, that changes things. She looked at Ivanovich then and he looked back. The same expression on his face that she felt on hers.

Worry.

Fear.

Her heart beat louder and a spark of doubt sprouted in her mind. Could they have known they were there? Could they have expected them from the beginning? Impossible. They were too careful.

"I am wholly concerned..." Andronicus abruptly stopped speaking.

"What?" Vaminus asked.

Everyone in the corridor had stopped and Yeva felt as if her breathing was louder all of the sudden.

"Concerned for thy safety is all," Andronicus finished. She heard shuffling of booted feet and one pair of foot falls, and then the corridor was filled with the sound of many walking.

"There are all of these guards about me, more elsewhere about the palace. For Emporon's bloody sake thou art with them. I doubt anything shall ever happen to me at this moment," said Vanimus, more of a complaint than a regular response.

War Dancers along the wall prepared themselves and began to fidget slightly as Andronicus spoke, "Unexpected things happen at unexpected times, Father."

Ivanovich slowly reached over his shoulders for his swords on his back and gripped the hilts with his hands. Yeva did the same, as did the rest of their companions. Although it was cold in the night air, sweat found its way down her brow.

"It's the middle of the night, Son," pointed out Vaminus.

"As I..." Andronicus stopped again. All of the others stopped as well. Then one pair of footsteps continued walking.

"Wha..." Vaminus started before cutting out as well and the last footfalls ended. Another pair started, heavier than the other and slower, more cautious.

The footsteps sounded as if they were right next to the windows. Then a carmine and silver feather helmet plume, in a pattern similar to zebra stripes, popped out of one of the windows down the line and jerked back inside.

Yeva let out a deep breath as she and all of the War Dancers unsheathed their swords and jumped into the windows, undoing their ropes that held them to the wall, just as Prince Andronicus finished crying out an alarm, "TO ARMS!"

Yeva alighted upon the window bottom as guards nearest that window turned towards her. One guard lunged with his shield in front and knocked a War Dancer out and sent them plummeting to the ground far below. Yeva jumped over the guard in front of her that was fixing to do the same thing to her as the other guard did to her comrade.

As she jumped over the guard she slashed with both of her swords. Sparks flew and metal grated against metal as her swords met with the helmet. The guard staggered into the wall and to the ground under her blow, scrambling to get his helmet off and holding his head.

Another two guards were pressing towards Ivanovich, trading blows. She darted towards them and sank one of her swords through the gambeson cape and the mail near the shoulder blades with a powerful thrust.

The man let out a gasp, which sounded similar to a grunt, as he fell off of his feet and to the ground. The other guard heard the crash of steel on stone and quickly shifted his body to glance over to where his fellow had once been. He saw her and began to back up.

She moved next to Ivanovich and followed the guard as he moved next to the other guards. The corridor was filled with short barks of orders and shouts from the Emporians that were hardly audible to her ears. The grunts and clashes of steel rand around them as well.

As she watched, her eyes fell upon a larger figure. Prince Andronicus. He grabbed one of the blades of a War Dancer with a mailed hand and wrenched it out of the War Dancer's grip as he moved into the guard of her comrade and thrust his sword into his chest. Andronicus pulled his sword free and moved onto his next target.

Calls were ringing through the corridors and more Emporian guards rushed to the skirmish. They had to move quickly.

Quicker.

She moved forward with the grace of her training and sent a flurry of blows at the guard before her. Ivanovich did the same. The guards blocked the blows with their shields and shuffled back. She kicked at the bottom of the shield and the guard faltered. She took the moment to move one blade as a distraction and the other over the shield to stab into his less protected neck. As her blade went down, another guard moved his sword into her path, parrying her blade before it struck.

She moved back and the guard she was about to kill saw and darted for her shield first. She sidestepped the assault and the other guard moved to aid his companion and attacked her ferociously. She deflected and parried blow after blow as she slowly backed up and to the right to move around the guard.

Ivanovich finished off his guard with a thrust through the throat and engaged in the rear of the two guards pressing her. He used the pommel of one sword to hit the back of the helmet of one, concussing the man and making him stagger to his knees.

Then he thrust his other sword through the mailed section of the guards armor. Steel links broke as the thin, needle pointed sword stabbed into his lower back. The guard stiffened and fell towards her from the power of Ivanovich's attack.

She moved to the side and he fell to one knee and regripped his sword that almost fell from his grasp and began to stand back up to turn around to face them. Blood flowed from his wound. They didn't give him the time he needed to turn around and Ivanovich ended his life by thrusting his sword into the man's neck.

She nodded her thanks and they moved on looking for their target. He was being rushed into a side corridor by several guards. He was extremely calm for this situation, standing tall and imperious in his fur lined, carmine and silver clothing. They both ran for him.

Then, almost out of nowhere, Andronicus was in front of them blocking their path. His face guard was covering his face and his longsword was dripping with blood. Much of his upper body was splattered and sprayed with the blood of her comrades. He loomed over everyone else in the corridor, standing at about nine feet tall with a broad chest, arms and legs. They themselves were about six and a half feet each. He was an extremely large man.

They attacked him.

Yeva threw herself down low as Ivanovich went high. Andronicus stood there as if he planned to stand there and let his plate armor take the hits. Just before they struck, he pivoted on one leg as the other rushed towards her, making contact with her and sending her into the wall by hitting her with one arm.

He then beared down on Ivanovich with a flurry of attacking swings. He knocked his swords away, then grabbed the collar of his leather armor with the same hand and launched him to the other wall. She stood up just as another War Dancer assaulted him from the flank with no avail. That was the chance they needed. She dashed for the door that Emperor Vaminus was led through and Ivanovich picked up his weapons and followed.

As she looked back at him, she saw Andronicus cut through the throat of the elf that attacked him and turned around to watch them go. She looked away and forward.

They followed the sound of shouting as they ran through the corridor. They turned a corner to find that four others had followed Vaminus. As they approached, one of the guards was hit on the pauldron and then his shield was kicked, sending the man backwards to the ground.

Andronicus turned towards two guards being beaten back by three War Dancers. He moved towards them and before any of the assassins knew he was there, he grabbed one by the neck from behind and struck another with a downward strike in between the neck and the shoulder, cutting into the body.

The elf within his grip tried to free herself with no success. He pulled his blade free of the dying elf and plunged his longsword into the belly of the elf woman in his grasp. The third elf saw this and backed away swiftly, the two guards following.

He turned again to find a guard with blood running down his gauntlet, which was grabbing at his face and another without his weapon using his steel vambrace and shield to block the blows from his attacker.

He must end this swiftly. There was no time to delay. Andronicus moved with lightning speed towards the elf and, with his longsword in one hand, slashed down from near his head to the other side of his body. His blade skimmed the elf's leather vambrace when the elf evaded away.

As the elf went to face him, he grabbed the elf by the shoulder and squeezed and used his entire body, brought the longsword into the elf's belly and rammed his blade into his belly up to the cross guard. A weak gasp came out of the War Dancer's lungs and the air inside them escaped him.

Andronicus pulled his blade free on an angle and opened the elf's belly. He locked his eyes onto another and charged her.

He held his longsword with both hands and swung for her neck. She sensed him and his blow nicked the back of her neck and she attempted to whirl away.

He left his longsword in his left hand, stepped forward and grabbed her long, braided hair with his right and pulled towards him. She grunted and he kicked out her leg and she began to fall to her knees. He then positioned his knee behind her and pulled down on her hair and raised his knee at the same time.

His knee connected with her spine and he heard a crack. Her lower body then went limp and he let go of her hair and she fell to the ground.

He moved onto the next. He swung his longsword and the elf deflected it, or more like dodged it. As Andronicus looked into his opponents eyes, he saw fear. So much so that he could smell, taste, and hear it resonating from the elf like the stench of a wet dog.

Andronicus swung again and again, forcing his enemy back. None of the swings were met by the elf's swords.

He fainted an attack with the hand that held his sword and, with his other hand, lunged forward, and landed a clenched fist on the elf's cheekbone.

The elf's jaw shattered and he staggered back, blood streamed and dripped from his mouth. Andronicus moved at him again, grabbing the elf's throat with one hand and punching him in the gut with the cross guard of his sword. While he squeezed his hand around his throat, he punched again.

The elf was struggling fruitlessly to get away, but he wouldn't let go. Andronicus punched again and again and again, squeezing tighter and tighter. With every punch, more blood spat from the elf's mouth.

The elf stopped struggling and went limp. He dropped him and turned to the door that his father was ushered through. He saw his guards standing to attention about him.

He opened his face guard, pointed at one half and said, "Ye, clean up this mess," and they saluted with fists to their chests. Steel clinked as vambraces and mailed fists hit hard against steel plate and mail. He began striding to the open door and said, "The rest of ye soldiers, follow me."

Yeva moved through the doorway that Vaminus went through. He stood on the other side of the room, next to doors that led out. He had five more guards about him.

Lachlan, the head of this operation, had left two of their companions in the corridor behind to slow down the rush of guards that were coming their way.

Vaminus banged on the door and yelled, "Open this door!" Men began shouting from the other side saying, "Open it!" "Hurry!"

"It's jammed! The bar is stuck!" "Out of the way!"

"MOVE!"

The doors began to shake. They had to move swiftly to catch him before the doors opened and more guards got in the way, allowing him to flee further into the palace.

All within the room seemed to know this, because the guards fell into position around their Emperor and created a half circle shield wall. One man was barking out orders and she noticed that his helmet, unlike the others, had a carmine crest upon it that was parallel to his shoulders and arced with his head, the ends pointing downwards towards his shoulders. There was a silver strip on the top of the crest. A centurion.

"Hold the line!" Shouted the centurion with a Rabian accent.

Lachlan must have come to the same conclusion as he charged the centurion and attacked. The other three War Dancers followed, attacking any one of the last five guards about Emperor Vaminus. The guards all planted their shields and placed their swords flat against the top of the shield, braced their stance and waited for them to engage.

They clashed with blow after blow, trying to pin the guards down underneath them.

After a few seconds, one guard fell, then a War Dancer, then another guard. Yeva continued to attack her opponent with attacks all over his body. She battered the rim of his shield, barely nicked his helmet, swatted at his sword and hit at his pauldrons, trying to get a clear shot for a weak spot in his armor.

His face, the mailed neck, armpits, inner elbows, wrists, any of the mailed sections on his torso that were between steel plates. The mail on the back of his legs and near his ankles, or even his helmet. His guard held strong against it all.

Then Lachlan hit the centurion in the side of the neck with the pommel of one sword. The centurion gagged and staggered backwards and his shield arm dropped and left his body open to attack. Lachlan moved in close and slid one sword into an eye and the Emporian fell limp and dropped his sword as he dropped to the ground, with a grimace of pain on his face.

Lachlan then moved onto the guard she was battling. He thrust his sword into one of the sections of mail between plates on his back and the guard arched his back, gasped, dropped his sword and fell to the ground.

Then Lachlan moved to kill the Emperor and traded a few blows before more War Dancers joined in and overwhelmed the Emperor, not that the Emperor was likely to last much longer against Lachlan anyway. It ended with one of Lachlan's swords through his heart.

Andronicus ran down the corridor hearing the clash of steel and iron. One of the Imperial Guards saw him and turned towards him, saluting.

"Whither be my father?" Andronicus asked as he reached the guard.

The guard pointed down the hallway where a score of other Imperial Guards were huddled, trying to get past something and said, "His Excellency be down that hallway, two War Dancers are stalling the men," he had a deep Praetorian accent.

"Move!" Andronicus shouted at the guards before him. They looked back, saw him, and parted like water upon a rock, tapping the guards in front of them to get them out of the way. He moved swiftly down the corridor and to where the two War Dancers were giving ground and killing or wounding Imperial Guards. The ratio of ground given to casualties made was significant with only three casualties in the corridor.

The Emporian men parted before him and the two War Dancers saw him then. Covered in the blood of their comrades and moving swiftly towards them, they took an involuntary step back and one ran as the other backed up slowly, both with dread befalling their faces.

He closed his face guard and attacked the one that stayed behind with multiple blows. The War Dancer continued to fall back. Then he knocked the elf's swords away and grabbed his shoulder, pulling the elf over, throwing him into the wall and out of his way and knocking the air out of him.

He moved past the stunned elf and left him for the guards to take care of. They did. Guards flooded around the elf and killed him. Other guards moved past as the guards did their work and moved on behind Andronicus.

He lifted his face guard and spotted the other elf that ran off and the elf looked back with growing horror and fled faster. He seemed younger, maybe it was the fear pulsing adrenaline through his body. He followed at a quick pace, or as quick as he could go, and the guards at his back followed him. Andronicus turned a corner and saw the young elf open a door and hustle inside, shutting it behind him.

The door shut as Reece, one of the War Dancers they left behind, slid to the floor in front of the door. His face was pale as fresh snow and sweat rolled down it. The doors near where the late Emperor lay were still being pounded upon.

"He's coming. He's coming," he panted out, voice shaking as if there was an earthquake. He continued, "Prince Andronicus is coming! Our end is nigh!"

A chill filled the room then as they all stared at the young War Dancer.

Andronicus ran down the corridor towards the door. As he got nearer to it, he closed his face guard, picked up his pace and lowered his shoulder, grabbing his longsword by the hilt with one hand, around the blade with the other hand and condensing his body. He squeezed his blade tight and made contact with the door.

The door slammed open. What felt like a body against the bottom of the door was flung across the room as the door was splintered and nearly torn off of its hinges. He raised his head and eyes slightly and searched the room through the eye slit of his helmet, his eyes locking onto the first figure that he saw clearly, no silver nor carmine red.

An enemy.

He raised his longsword above his head with one hand and brought it down upon the head of the War Dancer in front of him standing in stunned silence with one round swing.

His sword nearly sheared through the skull stopping just short of three quarters of the way through, the skull was nearly shattered from his blow. He grabbed the shoulder of his slain enemy and yanked the sword free with some effort.

The doors across the room were opening with a loud crack and Great-swordsmen came through, greatswords in hand and unsheathed. The guards behind him flooded into the room as well.

As he looked around he saw six corpses on the ground near the opposite doors and realized that the doors didn't open in time and he was too late. As he looked around some more he saw that there were three more War Dancers still standing and he moved towards one.

He and a War Dancer clashed.

One of the War Dancers that were near the opposite door was cut down by a Great-swordsman with a basic attack. A swing with the greatsword from near his right shoulder, stepping forward with his right foot and planting it as the greatsword cut into the neck and completely sheared through.

As Andronicus clashed with one of the War Dancers, another War Dancer joined in to fight him.

He stepped to the right and batted down the swords of one and with the broadside of his longsword, he smacked the elf in the face also with the broadside of his sword. The other attacked and he parried the attacks and flung his head forward, connecting with the nose of his attacker as blood flew with a crunch.

Emporian men filled the room now and only the two that stood before him still drew breath. Guards spread in a half circle and then Andronicus lunged forward and knocked the swords out of the hands of one with a combination of attacks and kicked him in the belly, sending him towards the wall. He then faced the other, who he had bloodied the face of was also moving to attack him and he disarmed her and sent her flying into the ranks of men. They grabbed her along with the dazed elf and had them pinned and on their knees in a second.

Andronicus lifted his face guard, walked over to the six dead corpses and saw his father. Dead. Darkening blood oozing out of his chest and across the stone floor. He kneeled near the corpse and studied it further.

"Clean this up," said Andronicus as he regarded his slain father. He stood and turned to where four guards held the two remaining War Dancers in place, looking at him. He turned to the roomful of guards and soldiers and barked, "The rest of ye soldiers, return back unto thy posts," he looked at the four holding the elves still and said, "Ye four stay hither and hold them." He then turned to a random soldier and said, "Receiveth my brother."

With a chorus of salutes, they all went about their orders. The nine corpses within the room were orderly strewn about the ground, the three elves were secluded from the six Emporians. As their filth should be.

A guard came through the door and saluted him.

"What is it?" Andronicus asked, looking at him.

"There are two living perpetrators remaining where the initial contact was made. What is it that thou wishest to be done with them, Thy Highness?" The guard asked, standing to attention. His accent was Rabian.

"Cast them into the dungeons until further notice," replied Andronicus.

The guard saluted and said, "It shall be done, Thy Highness," and strode out of the room at a quick pace.

Androncius then turned to the two prisoners in front of him and saw something around the elf woman's neck. He wiped the blood off of his longsword on his carmine cape, sheathed it at his waist and walked closer to her and grabbed it.

It was a small ornate chain.

He pulled it up and broke its chain on the back of her neck as she glared at him with hatred, blonde hair strands poking out of her braid. The soldiers behind her held her head still as she squirmed underneath their grip. The guards had dropped their shields and sheathed their swords so they could hold them. Once he had the necklace off he looked at it with interest.

He looked closer at it and delicately grabbed the half circle with his other hand. He opened the small half circle all the way, with much difficulty, until it made a full circle. It depicted one of the moons and read the inscription inside:

"My dearest, Ivanovich. My life, my love, my whole".

He shut it with a quiet click and looked at them both. The elf woman still stared at him with hatred and the other seemed to as well. It was then he noticed a similar looking chain upon his neck as well. It was more concealed than hers, but it was still visible.

The prisoner was rolling his shoulders as much as he could. Then his black hair covered it. His gaze was flickering between him and near to where the necklace was. Andronicus moved closer to him and reached for the necklace. The elf flinched away and began to writhe and grunt.

One of the guards cupped him over the head, not enough to knock him out, but enough to daze him enough to contain him. A sharp inhale came from behind Andronicus and he turned his head to see the elf woman staring at the elf with concern and then back at him and the guards about with hatred. Just a flicker of concern.

He reached for the necklace and grabbed it, the elf began to try to writhe again so Andronicus just grabbed the amulet of the necklace and yanked. The small chain broke with a tug and he looked at the two necklaces side-by-side. They were the same, at least on the outside. He looked back at the two captives for a moment, thinking.

"Interesting," Andronicus murmured loud enough to be heard within the section of the room they were in. He looked back at the necklaces in his hand and then back at the two prisoners and said, "I shall strike a covenant with thee. If ye tell me whom authorized this assassination, I shall give ye a well kept cell and good meals for a year, then I shall release ye to go whitherto ye wishes."

"And if we doth not?" The elf asked, who Andronicus supposed was Ivanovich. He looked at the elf for a moment, then back at the elf woman. Blood was still streaming down her face from her nose and dripping onto the floor.

Andronicus looked back at the necklaces and replied, "If ye doth not, then I shall hath it beaten out of thee or allow thee to rot in a rat infested cell until ye come to thy senses and tell me."

They glared back at him with untold and growing hatred, or was it fear that was veiled by angled eyebrows?

He raised an eyebrow in question and amusement. They kept quiet, only glaring at him. They were similar in that fashion, he could give them that.

He thought back to when the elf was hit on the back of the head, the look on the elf woman's face. Then about the two necklaces in his hand. He thought for a moment and then made his decision.

"If thee art to tell me not, then, so be it," he said. He directed his gaze upon the highest ranking guard in the room with him, which was a Veteran. This rank was indicated by a steel spike on the top of his helmet. The spike was centered on the helmet, was four inches long and was decently thick. Large enough to be seen from a distance away.

"Veteran, beat her until he speaks," he gestured at the elf woman and then the elf. He continued, "Bid what he says unto me when he says it."

"It shall be done, Thy Highness," the veteran said in a Britonic accent. He saluted and turned to look at the elf woman and up at the guard that held her and gestured up with his head to indicate to lift her up. Andronicus left the room then, heading for his brother's chambers.

The guards pulled her to her feet and she began to do her best to free herself as the veteran moved closer and raised a fist. He punched hard at the face, then at the gut and the gut again then the face, alternating between both his hands.

Blood began to run from the elf woman's face a little faster with every punch. More and more cuts began to form. Blood came from the mouth in drops and streams and her jaw could possibly not be considered a jaw anymore.

The elf began to writhe again, more desperate this time screaming, "NO! NOO! STOP! NO!" Almost a feral scream.

Andronicus turned into another corridor where his brother, Servius, was walking his way with three score men at his back. His face was taut with concern. His black hair was nearly a complete mess, his dark blue eyes looking darker, being sunken due to being awoken in the middle of the night, Andronicus was sure. He wore a carmine trench coat with a double column of silver buttons from the waist to the lower collarbone. Silver threads trimmed the edges of the coat with silver couplings.

"Thou art a bloody mess," Servius said, striding towards him.

Andronicus looked down at his blood-covered armor and back at Servius saying, "And thou look like thou hast slain all of those whom thou hast loved."

Servius smirked and asked, "As we speaketh of those whom we love, whither be Father?" They went to shake hands and Servius thought better, looking at Andronicus's bloodied mailed hand.

Andronicus understood.

"He hath fallen. He was slain in the west-wing painting galla," Andronicus answered.

Servius inhaled long and deep, his eyes down-cast. Servius was older than Andronicus by three years, but Andronicus towered over Servius, who was about six feet in height. Andronicus was much taller and larger in the chest, shoulders, arms and legs. More of a soldier than his brother, his brother being more of a politician.

Servius looked at Andronicus's hands again and his brow pinched in confusion before he said, "What is in thy hand?"

Andronicus held his hand before his face and looked at the necklaces and said, "Love letters."

Servius stared at him blankly, held between laughing and mourning the fall of their father.

"Well, didst thou catch the assassins?" Servius inquired, his arms stiffly by his side.

"Felled most of them, four remained alive at the end. Two in the dungeon, two being interrogated."

"Interrogated?"

"Yea, asked them who sent them. They hath chosen to deny my generosity."

Servius stared at him for a moment, looked at the necklaces in his hand and asked, "Was it something... persuasive."

"I believeth it was. They love one another, I think, and I hath ordered some soldiers to beat one until the other speaketh."

Servius nodded slightly. "Verily, while we wait upon an answer, shall we speaketh?" He asked.

Andronicus looked down at his armor and back up at Servius with a raised eyebrow.

"Clean it later. There is something I wish to discuss with thee first," said Servius.

He turned back to the three score men behind and ushered them off to their previous duties. They all saluted and marched off back to their posts or beds.

Andronicus and Servius walked off to a small lounge with just four chairs and small tables next to each of the chairs. An honor guard of thirty guards for each of them. Andronicus spotted a mirror and looked at himself. In his bloody armor and helm.

His forehead had a film of sweat on it, at least the part that could be seen anyways. His eyes were hazel with a tint of blue within. He had a thickening beard.

He tore his eyes from the mirror and to the tables and chairs. Servius sat down on the other side of the lounge from Andronicus and leaned back in his chair.

Andronicus didn't sit, it might stain the furnished chair, or break it. Instead he stood tall behind the chair across from his brother. Servius sat and Andronicus stood there for long minutes before Servius spoke, "Are those crafted of gold?"

Andronicus thought for a moment and said, "I doth not knoweth. I could test their strength."

"Nay, but hand them unto me. I shall find out later."

Andronicus agreed with that and he repositioned the necklaces and tossed them to his brother. It wasn't a good toss, but it was good enough to reach Servius. He picked up the necklace that he failed to catch and said, "Was this part of the plan that thee and Father spake of for the past few months."

"Yea, but nay. This assassination attempt was, but not Father being slain," said Andronicus.

"So, doth the plan goeth forward still?"

"Verily," Andronicus inhaled and continued, "I now go unto Senka Island, to prepare for the offensive."

"Departing before my coronation?" Servius asked, spreading his arms in innocence.

"Verily," Andronicus chuckled softly and continued, "I shall be departing upon the morrow. We shall hath to move quickly against them."

"What about our connection in Bergsee?" Servius asked as he fingered the jewelry. He opened them and read the inscriptions inside.

"She speaketh not unto me, therefore, she be not our connection, she is thy connection."

"Be not so depressed. I doth not blame her for not reporting unto thee."

"I blame her not either. I was harsh on her… cover."

"At the least it worked, and still works. Anyway about it, she reported that King Alfred is still adamant about not joining the Draken Confederation. Relations between Bergsee and Brandland art high, and still growing."

Andronicus nodded saying, "I suppose that thou couldst attempt to diffuse relations between Emporia and one or the other, perhaps both, and attempt for peace speakings before I begin the assault."

"Verily. By the time winter comes to an end, I shall obtain an answer."

"Surely. I shall rest before I ride in a few hours," Andronicus had his hands on the top of the ornate chair carvings and nodded his head to Servius and turned to walk away.

A guard briskly walked into the room and saluted and bowed to Andronicus and Servius and reported, "The prisoners hath spake, or, the prisoner. He claims the assassination was collaborated between all of the factions of the far north," his voice was thick with a Soltero accent.

"Very well," responded Servius .

"Thou art dismissed," Andronicus told the guard. Servius nodded.

The guard saluted once more and walked off. Andronicus turned to look at Servius and said, "Farewell. I bid thee a good coronation."

"How bad is, or was, the mess?" Servius asked, looking and running his thumb over one of the necklaces.

"I hath set men to clean it up. Servants shall be required after for a more thorough cleaning," replied Andronicus.

Servius nodded and said, "For a surety. Farewell, Brother," he looked up from the necklaces and at Andronicus as he said the words.

Andronicus walked out of the room and made way for his chambers. He would need to clean his armor before he rested.

Imperial Guards saluted him as he passed and bowed at the waist. This was the proper way of things in the Empire. They would be bending the knee to his brother before long now. As they did to Andronicus's father.

As he approached his chambers some guards and servants saw him. The guards saluted and bowed and the servants simply bowed deeply to him and one asked in a meek servant voice, "Is there anything we can doeth for thee, Thy Highness?"

"Yea, aid me with mine armor."

"We shall."

They opened the door and the servants and Andronicus walked in. The door closed behind him as four guards stepped in after. Andronicus angled his head so that the servants could get to the leather straps that held his helmet on his head, there were four. One on the front of his shoulder and one on the back, two on each shoulder. They were attached to his plate armor.

The servants undid the straps and Andronicus reached for his helmet and pulled it off. Underneath was a gambeson coif underneath a mail coif that protected his neck and padded his head from his helmet. He handed his helmet to a servant and he took it. As he did, a servant unclasped his cape and removed it.

Andronicus spread his arms and lowered himself to one knee and two servants pulled his upper body armor off, over his shoulders and head. Underneath that he wore a woolen gambeson tunic. Mail covered his shoulders and most of his chest, leather straps that were attached to the mail that grew out from the armor of his arms and looped around his neck and attached to one mailed piece to another. A belt held up a pair of armored leggings.

He stood back onto his two feet and removed the mail coif from his head. Then another servant began undoing the leather strips. He worked on one arm armor, undoing the strap that attached it to the other and then the strap that looped around his neck. After that the servant took the arm armor off by sliding it off of Andronicus's arm. It fell loose once his arm was no longer within the armor.

The servant then moved to the other arm and worked with the armor. The torso armor that the two servants had taken off was made of overlapping steel plates that were four inches in width and wrapped around his body. The plates that were level with where his arms would be were separated from one another so that the arm can fit through the armor. Same with where the neck would be. Faulds were attached to the bottom of the torso armor.

After the arm armor was removed, Andronicus removed the gambeson coif from his head. It could not be removed before the arm armor for it was part underneath them.

The next armor to be removed was the armor leggings. A servant undid the belt holding them up and then undid a few leather straps that held the leggings together as another servant worked on removing his boots. The boots overlapped the leggings to just above the middle of the shin.

Plates overlapped like on his torso armor, from just more than half way up the thigh and down to the knee. A poleyn covered the knee, then the overlapping plates resumed for the grieves and down to the middle of the shin where the boot started and continued the design, though the plates only covered the front of the legs. The top of the boot that covered the top of his foot was similar in this design, only that the plates attached to mail sections and both plates and mail sections were half an inch in width.

The boots overlapped the leggings. The boots were removed by opening small door-like covers that covered the leather straps that held the boot comfortably to his leg. The straps were undone and loosened and the boots loosened on his legs and were taken off.

Underneath where the boot overlapped with the leggings was mail. The belt that held the leggings up was undone and his leggings began to be removed. The steel plates went all of the way around the leg and covered it completely.

Andronicus looked for a bench and found it right behind him. The servants had moved it there as this was unfolding. He sat down on it once the armor was past his mid-thigh. The servants finished removing the armor and they laid it out neatly.

"Clean mine armor. Once done with the task I hath set to thee, place it within a travel bag. Then rest thine eyes and bodies. We shall be departing as soon as it be possible after some of it," ordered Andronicus .

"At thy behest, Thy Highness," the servants said and murmured, bowing to him as they did.

They took the armor with them to clean it and left Andronicus alone in the room with the four guards. He looked at them and said, "Depart from me. Stay nearest the door."

"At thy bidding, Thy Highness," one guard replied and they filed out of the room, closing the door behind them.

Andronicus removed his gloves and placed them on a desk within his room, then wiped his brow. He then ran his hand through his brown hair. It wasn't long, but it was in need of a cut. Now that the adrenaline was leaving his body he felt tired and wore down. There was a slight ache in his shoulder that he used to break down the door in his rush for his father. He rolled the shoulder and yawned.

PART
ONE

Chapter One

A Plan for Better Meals

Day 02, Rainmoon, Year 2142

The sun was reaching the western horizon and was ready to set the day to rest. The sky was clear but for small clouds that dotted the skies above Edvin's hideout.

Well, it wasn't necessarily "his" hideout, but he partially owned it in a manner of thought. He and his band of miscreants. The band wasn't really his either, but he was a part of it.

He sat on a rock that faced north, which was the direction of which the mouth of the hideout faced, and he pelted the ground with a handfull of small rocks. Picking one out of his hand at a time and lightly throwing it at the soft surfaced dirt, not much farther down the dirt was rock hard. Occasionally he would look up at the half hidden pathway that led up the side of the mountain.

The Hideout was located in The Swirling Mountains almost directly between Silvertoppen and Virvlande Begskant, closer to the latter than the former. It wasn't high into the mountains, but it wasn't any closer to the flat ground either. They were still a good distance from the main road between the two cities.

The wind was relentless and it made him feel miserable. Blowing hard at times then randomly stopping and starting strong again. It, and the sun low in the sky that stung his eyes, gave him a headache.

A bastard-sword leaned against another rock near to him. His garments consisted of dark brown, mostly stained by dirt and mud, wool. It was about half weathered with age and use. Over his tunic was a ring-mail shirt of black steel, not dragon steel, but regular steel. His gauntlets lay near his sword.

The sword itself was of no great value, but for it being a sword made of steel. Its crossguard was long, thin and circular. It ended in two enlarged spheres, one at each end of the crossguard. The hilt wasn't done well either and the pommel wasn't made of metal, but of a dark embroidered wood; which was cracked as well. It was within a dark brown leather sheath.

His gauntlets were made of studded leather, dark brown in shade, and had wool on the inside.

He wore his vambraces, but owned no other armor besides what he wore and what was next to him.

His vambraces were of the same make as his gauntlets, dark brown studded leather with wool on the inside.

Edvin's hair was blonde and fell to his shoulders. His eyes were a light blue and he had no facial hair. He had sharp features on his face. His hair was bound up with a strip of black cloth behind his head. When he stood, he was just under six feet tall.

He looked up from his rock doodling at the small, mostly covered by foliage, path that made its way up the mountain side. A figure climbed up the path, carrying a medium sized pack with him. Edvin watched him as he neared.

He was an elf with blonde hair as well, but his hair was not as long as Edvin's. His eyes were a dark blue and he was slightly taller than Edvin when they stood back-to-back. The features of his face were also sharp and strong.

The clothes he wore were stained with dirt and stained green by plants. He wore a cloak over his tunic and trousers that were stained the same color as the rest of his clothing. A sword sheath hung from his right side. A round shield was tied around his torso and was on his back.

He continued up the slight slope until he was almost right before Edvin. Edvin leaned back to look up at him.

"Good evening I pray," said Edvin. He had an Eirikish accent.

"We needeth to find ourselves a different spot to look out from. I saw thee from quite the distance off," said Valto, the elf with the pack, panting. He also had an Eirikish accent.

"Hmm. Perhaps behind these rocks here?" He gestured to behind the few rocks, one of which he sat on.

"Why art thou here instead of there?"

"It is more easy to see the path here instead of there."

Valto studied the two places, then walked around to behind the rocks and looked out over the path and the sloping fields that it traversed through.

"Surely enough," he paused and continued, "I knoweth not where Svartgeirr nor Tilda may be. How long hast thou been here?"

"Since…" he looked up as if to remember when he had arrived there and continued, "high sun."

Valto nodded and said, "I'll ensure that someone relieves thee."

"Many thanks."

Valto nodded with a smile and walked off for the hideout entrance, which wasn't too far away. Meanwhile, Edvin stood, picked up his gear that lay on the rock next to him and set it on the other side of it. He then sat down on the other side of the rock and leaned against it for a moment.

He changed his position multiple times, finding the best spot behind the rocks. By the time someone had exited the hideout, he had found what he thought was the best spot to look out from.

The one who exited was a dwarf, whose name was Ragnar, who had blonde hair that fell to just past his shoulders and was loose upon his shoulders. He had a great beard that lay upon his broad chest. His eyes were gray and he had a unibrow that shadowed them.

He bore a sword at his hip and a round shield on his back. He also bore a cap helm, a helm that only covered the back, top and sides of his head, that had no ornamentation. He wore a gray gambeson coat and trousers. He had no other armor other than that.

"Best go within. Supper hath been made and it shall lose its warmth at some time," said Ragnar. He had a Gaetan accent.

"It surely shall. My thanks to thee. Hast thou eaten?"

"Yea. A good meal to quench my hunger and fatigue," he said and he planted his broad hands on either side of his belly, which was quite round, but not quite bulbous.

Edvin laughed, stood and, while still chuckling, said, "I believeth that this spot here is best for looking out over the way up here. It may not be, but I say this so that thou may not need to squander too much of thy time in searching for a good spot."

"I thank thee for this."

Edvin gathered his things as Ragnar set his things down next to him. Ragnar also carried some small bundles with him that carried snacks within them.

Edvin walked up and into the mouth of the cave. It wasn't too large, but large enough for a dragon to fit into. The entrance couldn't be seen too easily from anywhere but a certain angle due to rocks and foliage.

He entered into the cave and wound his way through the cave as it widened as he went inward. Small crooks and crevices spread out into the walls of the main cave.

A light streamed, flickering forth from further within the cave. He made way toward it, walking up and down slopes in the cave floor. Voices rang out from further within.

Chuckling, one said with a tender voice, "And thou would doest but that."

"Nay, I should not," said another voice that was a little louder and bolder in speech.

"Yea, thou wouldst," said the tender voice.

Someone inhaled deeply and said, "Think what thou wish, but, yea, I say that thou art wrong in it."

Edvin walked around a corner to where three figures were. One elf, one dwarf and one dragon. The elf was Valto. The dwarf's name was Aksel. The dragon's name was Reider.

Aksel had stark red hair that fell around his shoulders. His beard was braided down his chest and half way down his belly. His eyes were blue and gray.

Reider had mainly midnight blue scales with scattered, both singularly and in patches, mud brown scales. The scattered scales were on his lower left jaw and on his right shoulder. Two patches were on his thorax, one near each front leg. His wings were midnight blue as were his horns and eyes.

He was about twenty-five feet long from head to tail, about fourteen feet tall to his back and nineteen feet to the top of his head when it stood erect so to speak.

"Wish for some food, Edvin?" Asked Aksel. He had the bolder voice. His accent was of Gaetan as well.

"Verily," he said, walking towards his sleeping quarters and set down his things by where he slept. He then walked toward where the other three were.

Aksel got a plate of food ready as he neared. It was ready before he got there and he took it. He sat and started eating it. The plate consisted of beans in some form of a gravy.

"Someday, we shall need to gather another form of food. These beans in gravy art now stale in my mouth," said Edvin.

"That is exactly what I was speaking about. We hath need for more meat in this group," said Reider, straightening up a little bit more. He had the tender voice. He had a Bergsian accent.

"And where is this place where we shall gather more meat? Whom is it that will gather it? Not I, lest thou allow me to find which is greatest," said Aksel.

Aksel was essentially the cook of their band of outlaws. All others did other things, but all listened for jobs to employ in. They needed the money and the food. Reider supplied the water, enough at least for them to survive gleefully with it.

"What thou sayest is greatest is many days away, and in possession of the Emporian Empire. Verily, we are able to move ourselves within their borders without being sought after, but, how is it that we shall come by this food which thou speakest of? The very moment we taketh what we seek, the Imperial Legions shall hound us down just as quickly as we can hath faith to leave their lands," said Valto.

"Is this what ye all were speaking of before I approached?" Asked Edvin.

"Yea, it is, but, nonetheless, I believeth that it can be done, and shall be done if we act. Valto is but faithless in this matter. What say thee?" asked Reider.

Edvin didn't speak for a couple seconds before saying, "I do believeth that it is within our power to doeth so, but I also believeth that it shall come with great risk."

"So thou hast taken the middle grounds, as thou hast done before many of times," said Reider.

"Yea, I doeth," admitted Edvin, taking another bite of his food.

"But thou must trust in me that, if we doeth this thing, I shall maketh the greatest meal all ye hath ever so tasted before. But nay, all ye hath tasted it before, for I hath made it before with all ye. Doth thee remember this time of which I recall?" Aksel looked at Valto when he asked the question.

Valto looked at him for a moment before he said, "Yea. I doeth."

"I doeth as well," said Reider and Edvin, though, not exactly in sync.

"Then doth all ye not wish to hath that same memory return freshly to all ye minds?"

"Yea, I doeth at least," said Valto.

"Then we shall hath a voting when all hath returned hither from whither to they hath gone," claimed Aksel.

"I agree," said Reider.

"Verily," said Edvin.

"Yea, I too say verily, it shall be done then at that time," said Valto. He continued, "I doth needeth the time before then to think of my vote."

"Yea. Me as well," said Edvin as he finished his food and he added, "Though, I doeth believe where I shall be placing my vote then."

"It is not as bad as thy claim with thine attitude, for I hath made it and it shall not hath been anyway better than that," claimed Askel.

"Therefore, I am sure that we shall needeth to embark upon this quest for better food," said Edvin.

Valto sighed and said, "Therefore, I suppose that it is in our best interest to wait for…" a clammer of noises and voices, voices mainly, sounded loud into the cave and an elf and a dragon stepped in, the elf first.

The elf's name was Svartgeirr. He had jet black hair, which was very odd to them all when each of them had first laid eyes on him, and the angled face of an elf, with the pointed ears. His eyes were a deep dark blue and he stood about six and a half feet tall.

The clothing he wore was the regular mud-stained brown as the rest of their clothing. A short sword hung in its sheath at his hip and a medium bow was unstrung and was in a sheath of its own on his back. There was also a quiver of arrows strung to his back, both angled up to the right side of his head.

The dragon's name was Tilda. She was almost all white but for several, only a few compared to the rest of her scales, were a reddish brown. These scales were scattered down her thorax and underbelly for the most part, some were on the front and left side of her neck. Her horns were white as were her wings, which also had some small stripes of gray in them, so small that they could only be noticed at a close distance.

She was twenty feet long from snout to tail, was eight feet tall to her back, and was twelve feet tall to her head when it was up. Her eyes were an icy blue with tints of gray in them.

Tilda looked up and said, "He must be reprimanded. Aksel, give not him any food, or if thou doest, giveth him the worst portion." She had a Drakish accent.

"For the others to arrive," Valto finished his previous thought before the chaos unwound.

"I did not doeth anything that she claims. I did not," argued Svartgeirr. He had a Zemlian accent.

Tilda huffed and made one bound away from him before she turned back around to watch. She sat there as well.

"I doth not cook such a bad meal as that. Only shall such a meal of which thee speaketh of be made when am I compelled to cook thee!" Aksel ended on a high note and Tilda looked at him, half in shock and half in disgust.

Edvin laughed at the comment. Valto shook his head, chuckling softly. Reider remained silent.

"Saveth me thy pride. What thou cookest is not so good as thou may believeth," said Tilda.

"And so the subject is brought to attention. We needeth the votes of ye two. Aksel wishes to traverse unto the lands of Emporia to scavenge some foods from there. He saith that he knoweth of where good meats can be found. What…"

Tilda cut Reider off and said, "I accept the offer to gather food of any sort that shall be better than what we hath eaten yesterday. It was too hard to swallow."

"Allow him to complete his speech. He was not done," said Svartgeirr.

Tilda stared at him and said, "If we doeth this thing, he is to be offered none of it."

Edvin chuckled and said, "He shall deserve it. I agree to goeth upon this quest for eatable food."

"Before we delve too far within this vote, we shall receive Ragnar for the vote," said Valto.

"I shall receiveth him," said Tilda.

She turned around for the exit and Valto quickly said, "The post can not be left unguarded."

Tilda sighed and said, "Yea, I knoweth this. I shall taketh his post until he hath voted and is able to return."

"Very well. What sayest thee, Svartgeirr? About the matter of this quest to Emporian lands," said Valto.

"I am, in all ways, prepared for a good journey and some action if that's included," he added the last part with his left hand shielding his mouth from the right side, the back of his hand was towards his mouth. It wasn't a whisper, but he acted it out as if it should have been a whisper.

Tilda scoffed, and shook her head as she left. Reider said, "I agree to this quest as well. I sayeth this for everyone's information."

"Yea, I knoweth that well," said Valto.

A moment passed and Ragnar walked in and said, "So, thou needest something from me?"

"Why doeth I feel that thou knowest what it is?" asked Valto.

"Because I do. I shan't pass over an opportunity like this. So, when are we departing for Imperial lands?"

Valto sighed and Reider said, "He didn't wish to go on this quest. He was against it."

"Ask Aksel. He is the one who wanted to go to start. Doest thee have any information on this topic?" asked Valto.

"Nay. How am I supposed to gather any information on this quest when I am here all day, every day?" asked Aksel, motioning with his hands.

"So, to start, let's gather information beginning tomorrow. Or, what is everyone occupied with on the morrow?" asked Ragnar.

"I'm staying hither at the hideout all day," said Svartgeirr.

"I was planning to goeth to Endes des Flusses on the morrow. I could change that plan," said Reider.

"I shall travel to Vacker to gather any information there," said Valto.

"I'll go with thee," offered Reider. "That'll be great," said Valto.

"Me and Ragnar were traveling to Varmvatten and Kulman Kaupunki at tomorrow's first light. I'm sure that we can gather information while we are there," said Edvin. Ragnar nodded in agreement.

"Gather something good whilst thou art there. Good as in food to partake in," said Aksel.

"Surely," said Ragnar.

"Now, I suppose I'll ask Tilda what she plans to do for the next month or so," said Valto.

Chapter Two

Departing Homeward

Day 08-09, Rainmoon, Year 2142

Adelhelm was watching the storm clouds pass on over the rest of Bergsee and Brandland, moving eastward. The smell of fresh water filled the air, and with every breath freshening his lungs making him want to keep breathing the smell in and to never stop.

He was on a cantilever facing north with open sides to the north, east, and west. To the south was a door in the mountain that led down and to the camp that he was at at the moment. On the other side of the mountains that he was currently on was the Drache Strait. He wasn't really on the other side of the mountain range from the strait, but was simply on the other side of a peak that blocked his view from the waters.

He was sitting on his haunches, the morning light peeking over the clouds from the low sun behind the clouds in the sky reflecting off his crimson scales. Or at least the crimson scales that cover the majority of his body, covering most of his tail as well as most of his main body and wings, excluding his underbelly. The scales on his neck being shared between crimson and burgundy scales, stretching up to his head and snout. The crimson dominating the left side of his neck and head and burgundy was the same on the right. Amber scales covered the minority of his body, mostly of his underbelly scales. His eyes were carmine and his horns were crimson.

His tail was curled about his talons. His body was a stark contrast to the gray and red stroked stone around him. It was cold, though not for him. All dragons that had fire dragon blood in them had the possibility of having the effect of a fire dragon. Their blood temperature was higher than all other living animals, much higher. He was normal on that scale, some fire dragons hatched with less heat and others may hatch with greater heat, defections really.

He turned his head around to the sound of movement behind him.

"How art thou fairing this morning, Thy Highness?" asked Wilma. A dragon that had steel gray scales and extremely dark gray, basically black, scales covering her right shoulder and right side of her head said. The extremely dark scales were dragon steel, just as the steel gray scales were iron.

"Well enough," he breathed in deeply before asking, "doth thou hast anything that thou is looking forward to? I'm sure it's thy last day hither for a time."

"Verily, Thy Highness. It is my Father's hatch day tomorrow, I was planning to surprise him by the early return."

"I pray that all goest well for thee," he said, still smiling at what she said.

"I thank thee, Thy Highness," she bowed her head to him.

"Is Elric awakened? Hath he risen yet?"

"I shall obtain thine answer quickly, Thy Highness," she bowed and left to find out what he wanted to know.

Elric was a prince from Bergsee and Adelhelm's friend. A friend he was to Adelhelm, but Adelhelm didn't like how lazy he was. He was upset most of the time too.

Adelhelm understood why Elric was upset as much as he was. It had become a part of him by now. Even then, it was disappointing to Adelhelm. He knew he couldn't entirely comprehend Elric, but was still disapproving of how he reacted to it all.

A moment later, a dragon bounded over to where he was and sat beside him and, with a Bergsian accent, said, "So, thou art departing for home? Abandoning me hither with Elric for me to deal with?"

The majority of Wilhelm's scales were marian blue and half wrapped around the length of his body like a swirl. It swirled with navy blue. A small diamond-like shape of a green so dark it almost seemed to be no different than his marian blue scales. His eyes were an icy blue and his wings were light blue.

"I hath dealt with him enough for the past few months. I needeth a break from him," joked Adelhelm.

Wilhelm chuckled and asked afterwards, "Art thou departing today?"

"Yea. Preferably within the next hour or two. Whether Elric arises or not."

"Very well. Doth thou thinkest that thou wilt miss the sea? Or, the Strait at least?"

Adelhelm barked out a short chuckle and said, "Worry not, I still hath a good amount of the water still within my mind. I can still feel it."

They laughed and, after a moment of laughter, Wilhelm said, "Perhaps, with some more time, thou'll turn into one of us."

"What, and be cold in the winter? Nay. I think not."

"Feeling the cold isn't such as that. It's worse."

Adelhelm laughed. As he was laughing, Wilma walked up and around to the other side of him than Wilhelm. She bowed her head and said, "Thy Highness."

Adelhelm looked at her and calmed his laughter to say, "What hast thou discovered, Wilma?"

"His Highness, Prince Elric, does not wish to be awakened at this time and to be left alone until he sees fit to arise himself."

Adelhelm half scoffed and said, "That's so stupid, he's…" he sighed and said, looking at Wilhelm, "Be ever not alike to thy brother in this way, or god help me I shall beat that lack of sense out of thy mind quicker than it had found its way in. I would doeth this to Elric, if only he had half a mind to learn from the beating."

Wilhelm sat up more straight, although he was already sort of sitting straight up, and said, "It shall be done, Thy Highness."

Adelhelm chuckled, turned back to Wilma and said, "Art thou and the rest of mine army prepared to depart?"

"Yea, Thy Highness. We can depart as soon as thou wishes," Wilma sat up straight to attention when he spoke to her.

"Good. Make preparations to depart sooner rather than later." Wilma bowed her head and walked off and Wilhelm began to speak.

"Woah, woah, woah. Thou art departing now? Thou art not waiting for Elric to make sense of himself?" Wilhelm asked the question as if it was in concern for Elric's being, but was really because he wanted to speak with Adelhelm some more before he left. Adelhelm supposed this to be the reason behind the question.

"I wish to see my family again. I hath not the will to wait here for Elric to come unto his senses and awaken. My soldiers also wish to see their families again as well as I. I am also certain that my Father would not hath me wait here either, but to return to him and to be by his side."

Wilhelm nodded and said, "Verily, thou speakest true."

"We shall meet again, some day in the future. Be patient until then.

Wilhelm exasperated an eye roll and, with a mocking bow of his head to Adelhelm, he said, "Yea, I shall do this, Father."

Adelhelm chuckled and mockingly said, "I knoweth that the power to do this thing is within thee."

They both sat there, watching the clouds and the landscape around them as Adelhelm waited for Wilma to return.

Wilhelm was looking up at the storm clouds that were moving northeastward and asked, "Thou hast not had too much of the rain water, doth thee?"

Adelhelm looked at him curiously and asked, "What?"

"Earlier, when thou hast said that thou hast had enough of the sea for a time, what of the sea in the skies?"

"Oh. Thou must understand this, the seas in the skies doth not smell, nor doth they taste, bitter of salt and other runoffs as the ocean doest. It is a smell and taste that I may never forget."

"I doth not seem to give mind to the smell, nor the taste. I simply avoid drinking it. The smell isn't as bad as thou places it."

"Interesting advice. Next time the water springs off of the hull of an Imperial ship, I'll remember to hold my breath until I turn as blue as thee."

They chuckled, Wilhelm first and Adelhelm followed. When the next moment passed, Wilma returned and said, "Thy Highness. Thine army is prepared to depart."

Adelhelm looked back at her where she stood near the path way inside the mountain, nodded and said, "Let us depart then." He turned back to Wilhelm and added, "God bless thee until we meet again."

"I pray for thee as well," Wilhelm bowed his head in respect and Adelhelm did the same in return before he left that cantilever. Wilma stepped out of his way and followed him to the flight platform, where his army awaited him.

When they arrived, Adelhelm found his army together and ready to move at his command. All doing their own thing, either by themselves or with some friends. Whether it be resting until he arrived or messing around with one another. Telling stories to one another and making invites to meet back in their homeland on their time off from the front.

Several noticed him, not anywhere near the majority, and they sat straight up and bowed their heads to him. All others noticed eventually, but not at the same time. More of if some rocks were tossed into a body of water and the ripples went outward from where they struck. That was how the noticing of his presence was spread amongst them.

"We hath not been hither long, but it has been long enough to aid our ally in the previous battles against Emporia. It is time we returned home to our families. To our fathers and our mothers and other loved ones. I pray that ye all hath rested well over yesternight. We shall not be stopping on our flight home," said Adelhelm unto them.

They bowed their heads to him again and all began to move to be in their flight formation. Adelhelm's Wing-guard were arrayed and ready to take off the moment he was in position. He surveyed them, nodded and turned around to ensure that Wilma had taken her position in the formation before he unfurled his wings and took off. His Wing-guard followed and behind them, so did the rest of the army.

They flew for a time, over much of the mountains that were Bersgee. Around Berggabel, where they stopped for a moment as he passed a routine inspection from the garrison from the city, and continued over The Feuer und Wasser Gulf and into Brandland territory.

It took around two hours to finish the flight. They were halted outside of Firetop city for another inspection before continuing onward to the capital.

16

Once they landed, Adelhelm and most to all of the others were slightly short of wind. They would recover quickly and could even go on for another few hours before having to stop, but they had reached their destination. Or, at least Adelhelm and several others had. Many lived outside of the city.

Adelhelm turned to Wilma and said, "Take parole and ensure that all are accounted for."

She bowed her head and said, "At once, Thy Highness."

Adelhelm took off again and left for the palace. He arrived shortly after and waited until the guards saw who he was and bid him past. He entered the palace and took a deep breath in. A deep breath of warmer air than what was down near the straight, or anywhere else other than the far south. Firetop was given its name for the volcano that it was situated near, and partially atop of. And the most important factor, no salty air.

He trotted inward into the palace. His first goal was to see his mother, though he didn't know exactly where she was. He passed many guard patrols, who bowed their heads and said, "Thy Highness," to him when he passed. Though he didn't know exactly where she was, he had a good guess of where she might be.

After a moment of traversing the palace, he stopped in a corridor and thought for a moment. He looked around at the walls and other passageways that led to other parts of the palace.

He stood still for a moment as he tried to remember which way to go. He squinted at each way around him until he saw a figure down one pathway and doubled his eyes back at the dragon, who had subsequently doubled her gaze back at him and well.

"Adelhelm! Thou art home at last, again," she said in a Brandian accent and bounded towards him.

She was almost completely covered with maroon scales, a few spots of bronze spotted her side underneath her maroon colored leathery wings and the back of the neck. Her eyes were carmine and her horns were maroon.

"Yea, I am. And how art thou, Adalgisa?"

She sighed and said, "Bored and with nothing to do." "That's the definition of being bored, 'being with nothing to do.

17

"What? No it isn't. Well, not exactly," she halted before him. Adalgisa, his younger sister. Adelhelm was forty feet in length and eighteen feet to his head, twelve feet to his back. Adalgisa was nine feet to her back and thirteen feet to her head. She was twenty five feet in length.

"I'm sure it is."

"I'm sure it is not. Needeth we seek a dictionary to discover who is correct?"

"Nay, not now at the least. Surely… surely thou hast proven thy point, but now I must be off to find Mother. Doth thou knowest where she is?"

"Verily. Follow me," she said and turned around to where she had come from.

Adelhelm followed her and asked, "Needeth I follow thee? Why not bid me where she is?"

"Because, I am on my way to speak with her as well."

"I see. So, what hast thou done whilst I hath been gone?"

"Hast thou not heard me earlier when I said that I was bored? With nothing to do?" She looked over her shoulder at him.

"Well, what about before thou became bored? Surely there was something that thou hast been doing in all this time."

She slowed down and they walked side-by-side down the corridor. After they were perfectly side-by-side, in the case of speaking with one another that is, she said, "There were things hither and thither for me to doeth that were interesting. However, those opportunities depleted until there wasn't anything for me to do."

"Oh, thou poor soul. Whatever would thou doest in this situation?"

She glared up at him for a second before saying, and still keeping the glare, "Boredom is not something to be trifled with. It is a dangerous field where one may become lost so deeply in thought that many thoughts that should stay undiscovered are discovered and they are not very pleasant, may I add. I'm sure that thou doest it all of the time, but I am not thee and I cannot deal with such things."

Adelhelm looked at her for a moment in silence. After that, he asked, "And what thoughts art thou speaking of?"

"Hmm?" She hummed out her question.

"Anything that thou art willing to share?"

"Nay. I must leaveth these thoughts to die deep in my mind, where they came from."

"Shall it not be that they shall only fester more, deeper in thy mind?"

"I hath thought of this, and, yea, they shall die there."

"However..."

"Therefore, nay," she cut him off.

"Oh. Harken unto thee. 'Doeth things my way. The way that is my way, and most importantly doeth not anything that isn't my way, for that way wouldn't be my way.' I'm sure Mother would approve," said Adelhelm and she started laughing.

She stopped walking and covered her face with her wings as she chuckled. Adelhelm stopped with her and looked around at where they were.

They were in a corridor of brown rock and dirt. Lit sconces lined the walls, and not much farther down, the corridor ended with two large doors. A few guards were posted at the doors in sentry position. Where they were sitting with their tail curled in a wide loop around their talons, their chests pumped out and wings partially unfurled. Staring straight ahead at one another.

"I didn't need thee after all, Adalgisa. This is the first place I would hath looked for Mother. The Royal Gardens. She practically lives in there," said Adelhelm, basing what he saw off of memory. He looked closer at the guards until he recognised one, Fabian of the third class.

"Thy Highness...es," said Fabian after a small hesitation, bowing his head.

Adelhelm strode towards him and asked, "Fabian, is Mother within?"

"Verily. Somewhere in there," said Fabian. His voice was brisk and had a Brandian accent. He continued to sit unmoving like a statue. He was nearly complete with tangerine scales with a small amount of yellow scales. He had bright orange wings and his eyes were a bright orange as well with tangerine horns. He was slightly smaller than Adelhelm.

"Very good. We need to speak with her," said Adalgisa now that she had recovered. "Open the door."

19

"At once, Thy Highness," responded Fabian. The two guards nearest the doors opened them. Adelhelm and Adalgisa walked in, side by side. The doors closed behind them.

The Royal Gardens occupied a large cave near the outside of the mountain. There were large steel grates in the ceiling of the cave, allowing the light of the sun to seep through and onto the trees and plants. By dragon standards, many plants were small, by human standards they would be quite large. Or at least decently sized.

There were trees from all regions of the Earth divided in sections. Pines and all the different kinds were sectioned together and within that section they were sectioned into their different types. Underbrush of pine forests grew in their organized sections of their own.

Fruit trees of all different fruits were sectioned according to their fruits, even though the fruits were too small for dragons, his mother kept them anyway.

All sorts of herbs were sectioned accordingly.

Flowering plants of all colors and sweet scents were organized by their colors in sections accordingly.

All trees and underbrush plants from tropical regions of the Earth were there. All trees were organized accordingly as well as the underbrush was sectioned accordingly.

There was no grass within the Royal Gardens. There were no vegetables nor were there fruits from any plant other than trees.

The Gardens were irrigated by servants, water dragons mainly. Birds flitted from one tall tree top to the other. Some flew in and out of the grates above. Many were chirping.

"Come, Adelhelm. Mother's this way, I think," said Adalgisa.

Adelhelm followed in silence for a moment watching the trees and plants. Dew was on many of them from the storm last night.

"Art thou sure she's this way? I think she's..."

"Shhh. Harken," Adalgisa cut him off and they stopped there. "Is this peace and silence I hear?" She wondered. She looked back to see Adelhelm looking at her lamely, his face contorted into a 'Really?' look.

"What?" She asked. He started chuckling and she turned towards him a little more and demanded, "Speaketh." He shook his head back and forth as he chuckled. "Thou art breaking the silence." This time she turned fully around to face him.

"I hath harkened unto it. However, it's quite hard to harken unto it when thou art near."

"What?" She asked.

"Thou knowest what I said, or art thou too busy speaking to harken to me?" He said and she looked at him with shock.

She stood up straight like she was accepting a challenge and said, "Doth not mistake me for thyself."

"Myself? Thou art the one that interrupts me more often than not."

"I doth not interrupt thee that much. And do not act as if thou art innocent, thou interrupt me too. This is not a one sided discussion."

"Yea, thou doest interrupt me so. Thou hath interrupted me six to seven fold more than I hast interrupted thee. Thou hath interrupted me two fold by this time and we've only been nearest to each other for nigh on fifteen minutes."

"Oh, that's what I'm missing. I should hath done it five fold by now."

"Verily. Let us find Mother before that occurs though."

A bird began to chirp loudly nearby and Adalgisa said, "My apologies Brother, but thou shalt find Mother on thine own. I shall be following thee around, thinking of ways to interrupt thee more so that I may meet my quota of interruptions. Therefore, feel free to speak openly."

"Oh I'm not dealing with thee. Thou art half spoiled," he said and started walking again.

"Half spoiled?! I am not half spoiled," she said and the bird chirped loudly as she spoke and walked side-by-side with him. She continued, "I am a perfectly raised princess of Brandland. Mother hath even congratulated me on my manners."

"Not ever did I saith that she didn't. Therefore, what I meant was that I giveth thee too much leeway. I shouldn't let thou interrupt me at all."

"But thou art too good of a big brother to do that though, therefore, it's all well," she smiled pleasantly at him and he stared back at her lamely.

"I knoweth this. I'm such a great big brother to thee. What would thou doest without me? Art thou not ever so happy that I was there when that dignitary from The Draken Confederation came by?"

She huffed and the bird chirped again, this time it was joined by others and she glared up at the sound and it quieted almost immediately. She looked back at him and said, "That is such a bad memory. Why wouldst thou bring that subject to light?"

"I'm not certain, only one of those times where thou became ever more indebted unto me. All these things I doeth for thee."

"Well, I attempt to repay thee, but thou only fumble every chance. All of the many chances, too, may I add."

"That's not my fault. I fumble with them not. I, if anything, make it better. Well, wait, thou doth not even doest anything in those situations."

"Doest not doubt me. I helped thee find Lioba Grenze, remember?"

"Yea. Verily I doeth remember that well. I thank thee for her.
She was beautiful."

"Oh, thou art welcome for that, how long wast thou courting her? Three months perhaps?"

"Five months, which I am glad she lasted that long beneath Mother's criticism."

"As am I."

"Only long enough to maketh me believe that she was the best. Long enough for her scent to taketh hold of my nostrils."

"Oh, how horrible."

"It is. It's tormenting me."

"Poor brother." Adelhelm scoffed.

"Adelhelm, thou art home," said a female voice from down a pathway in the greenery. They stopped in place. Adelhelm looked over Adalgisa and she turned around to look. After Adelhelm saw that it was their mother, he walked around Adalgisa a little so that he did not have to look over her.

She was mainly bronze scaled with tints of gold here and there on her front legs and thorax. Her eyes were gold as well as her horns and her wings were bronze. She was standing in a pathway between two different tropical trees. It looked like they were mahogany and sapota trees, but Adelhelm wasn't sure.

"We were looking for thee," Adelhelm said as his mother inspected one of the trees.

"Well, here I am. Though, I doeth wish to know what ye two were speaking about. I hath rarely ever heard ye two agree with anything outside of being watched by me or thy father," said Caitlin. She came from a branch of the royal line in the Kingdom of the Cladaigh an Iarthair. Her accent wasn't as thick as it was before, but it was still noticeable. She was the same exact size as Adalgisa, nine feet to her back, thirteen to her head and twenty five feet long.

"Verily. Thou art correct about that Mother. We were arguing. I finally bent and allowed Adelhelm to have his way," said Adalgisa with a form of benevolence and sadness mixed together in some way. Adelhelm faltered and looked at her with surprise.

"Adalgisa. What were ye arguing about?" Asked Caitlin.

Adalgisa looked from Adelhelm to Caitlin, containing her smirk so that Caitlin couldn't see it. Adelhelm looked from Adalgisa to Caitlin in bafflement.

Caitlin turned her gaze on Adelhelm and asked, "What happened? Adelhelm, what was said? Thou look like thou wast not expecting Adalgisa to speaketh. Is there something thou art hiding?"

"What?" Adelhelm chuckled out and continued, "She's lying. I didn't say anything."

"It sure sounded like ye two were speaking with one another. Therefore, it would seem that thou art deceiving me at this very moment," accused Caitlin and Adelhelm looked at her in disbelief.

"But-but Mother. Verily, yea, we were speaking with one another, but we weren't arguing. Only taking part in a discussion between brother and sister," said Adelhelm.

"Verily. I knoweth how discussions between siblings can be like. I had a few of them in Cladaigh an Iarthair. I also knoweth how siblings may jest around with one another endlessly. Though, sometimes it's not a jest. Therefore, if thou art not willing to tell me. Then I'll ask thy sister about it," said Caitlin and she turned to look at Adalgisa. Adelhelm was speechless about what was happening.

Adalgisa came closer to Caitlin and Caitlin held her wings out and comforted Adalgisa, who was looking more and more depressed by the second. "Tell me, darling, what was said?"

"I only wished to lead him to thee after he had returned and he simply disrespected me immediately," she said and seemed to shrink with meekness. Adelhelm's amazement grew with her every word. She continued, "And he made jokes about me and looked down upon me," Adelhelm started chuckling softly to himself and slowly shaking his head, looking downwards. Adalgisa went on, "Then we arrived here and it only got worse and…"

"Thou needest not say any more. I hath heard enough," she said and looked at Adelhelm with a serious look. At this, his smile went away and he no longer had a pleasant feeling about this. She continued, "Adelhelm, what doth thou hast to say about this? Besides laughing that is."

"Wha-what?" He half whispered.

"Thou heard what I said. Answer my question, if thou wish to take part in this verdict," demanded Caitlin.

"What she said is not true, or, it is, but not wholly. Yea, I made jokes, but I didn't disrespect her so. And if so, I didn't intend it," he stated.

"He's lying," said Adalgisa. Adelhelm looked at her in astonishment and then took a double take to see that she was sniffling and her eyes were glimmering in any light that hit her eyes directly.

Caitlin raised an eyebrow at Adelhelm and asked, "Surely."

"What? Mother, believeth that not. I would never doeth such a thing, or things to hear her speaketh of it," pleaded Adelhelm. "Thou wouldn't? I remember a time that thou would," replied Caitlin.

"But that was twelve years past. Eleven perhaps, but, nonetheless, a long time past. I can say that I hath changed. Even thou hast said that I hath changed from that behavior."

"Thou can say anything, that doth not make it true and if thou changed once, thou can change again," said Caitlin. She squared with him as she spoke.

"That is true, but I'm not lying. I speaketh the truth," said Adelhelm.

"If thou art speaking the truth, then tell me the whole truth. So far, thou hast but denied what Adalgisa hast said. So, tell me the so-called 'truth'."

"Verily. It started when Adalgisa and I saw each other within the palace. Somewhere near the... Main Eastern Hallway. We exchanged greetings and then I bid her tell me where thou was. Granted..." he started chuckling softly as he spoke, "I did look down upon her, but I didn't disrespect her. Then we left to find thee here. Previously, we were talking about how she interrupts me so much. Therefore, that's my side of this," as he was saying this, Adalgisa had to be shushed by Caitlin multiple times before he had finished.

"I don't interrupt him that many fold. That's how thou should knowest that he is being deceitful," stated Adalgisa.

"Nay, Adalgisa, thou doest interrupt him that many fold, however many fold that is anyway. Though, Adelhelm, I don't entirely believe thy story either," Adelhelm was about to object, but Caitlin held up a wing to cut him off and added, "Therefore, I shall make a compromise. Adalgisa, thou shouldst know that thou hast failed in attempting to use a petty reason for a reason."

Adalgisa thought to object, but ended up only opening and closing her mouth and backed down. Caitlin continued, "And Adelhelm, thou shouldst not laugh at thy sister as thou didst and if thou art to use the fact that she interrupts thee, then thou shalt not allow her to interrupt thee to start."

Adelhelm nodded solemnly and said, "Yea, Mother." "Now, Adelhelm, apologise to thy sister."

"What? But..." Caitlin silenced him with a glare and he looked at Adalgisa and Adelhelm said, "I apologise." Caitlin nodded her approval and looked at Adalgisa.

"I accept thine apology," said Adalgisa with little contained smugment. Adelhelm looked from his sister to his mother to gauge her response of the tone to see that Caitlin didn't seem to care, or hear it.

"There. All is better now. Now, Adalgisa, I should like to speaketh to Adelhelm privately for a moment and, if thou wouldst like to, we may speak after" said Caitlin and shooed Adalgisa away with a small flick of her wings. Adalgisa obeyed and trotted off into the foliage, leaving Adelhelm and his mother to themselves.

After a moment of silence, Caitlin gently held Adelhelm with her wings and smiled at him.

"Mother, is there some sort of jest that thou hast not said? Thou art bloody near beaming like the sun on a summer day," said Adelhelm.

Caitlin scoffed and asked, "Can a mother not be proud of her son? Tell me, how was thy time in the Strait?" She hugged him.

"I-the same as it usually is. Slow most of the time and then even slower for most of the rest. Though, that's not the usual question thou bids me for first. Nor doth thou ask it with that amount of enthusiasm."

She pulled out of the hug and said, at first mockingly, "'The same as it usually is'? I heard that it was thee that turned back the Imperial fleet from its advance. That isn't the same as it usually is."

"That wasn't a fleet, or, verily, it was a small fleet attached to a legion. Only about fifty ships and not all of them were even First Rates either. Many were Second Rates and Vanguard ships. The legion was on a bunch of transports. Weak, last minute ships that sink when a big wave strikes them," he gestured with his wings as he spoke.

"Hmm. That's not how my brother told it. He sent a message of how thou pushed them back off of the flank and…"

"Mother," said Adelhelm underneath her voice. She continued.

"How thou, thyself, led the attack…"

"Mother…" Adelhelm tried to get her to stop, but she continued.

"And how thou placed all of those high-snouted generals and commanders from the Confederation into shame. Again."

"Verily, that much wasn't exaggerated, but nonetheless, he over exaggerated it all. It's not like I was alone in that endeavor. Elric was with me."

She wrapped a wing around him, hugged and said, "Either way. Thou acted and the world beheld of how great of a mind thou art again and placed those Confederate scum in their place. Below thee," she squeezed him and tapped her snout to the left side of his face in a kiss.

"Yea, surely I hath annoyed both the Empire and the Confederation once again with mine actions. I wonder who shall be targeted by both of the top two world powers. Perhaps it will be a race to get to me first," he joked.

"First of all, the Empire hast become acclimated to it, I'm sure. And second, I shall not let that happen to thee too. Not three of mine offspring. I shall be damned by al-mighty god before I let that happen," she broke off the hug and looked at him seriously.

"I-I was only jesting Mother. I didn't mean it in that way and thou shouldn't say such things that loud in the open. I hath noticed that..."

"I hath noticed that I doth not care about their pathetic opinions anymore. Not after Wilhelm. Even if god did curse me to lose three of mine own, then I shouldn't rest until I hath settled the payment. Whether through heaven or hell, I should taketh my revenge. I shall not lose thee too, Adelhelm. Thou art most likely to be my last son and I couldn't bear to see thee die too."

"Mother, thou art filling me with sorrow. Please, don't speaketh about that anymore. It pains me to see thee like this."

"Thou art correct. It isn't good for me to speak that way, but... Adelhelm, thou hast been struck again?" She was looking at his thorax, where it joined with his right leg. He looked down as well to see and sighed.

"It isn't that bad. It was only a scratch."

"A scratch shouldn't hath removed some of thy scales. Look at it, it's so... uncouthly. Portraying a scale pattern like that. Thou already possess several others on thy body..." She looked at his face and continued, "And thou hast that pattern to prove my point."

Adelhelm reeled in shock to her comment and said, "'That pattern'? What doth thou mean by that?"

"I mean that it looks like a stain of some sort. Like someone threw a load of paint on thee and it took to thy scales because thou didn't wash it off. It's probably exactly what happened, even though thou deny it."

"I'm not so sure, Mother. I think that it's grown on me," said Adelhelm, finishing his sentence with a pose that showed off the right side of his head and neck to Caitlin, clearly proud of his pun.

Caitlin scoffed and said, "Please, don't do that in public. Not even as a jape, I shouldn't be able to take it well."

"Worry not, Mother. I'll be sure to include these new scales as well. I shan't let any go unappreciated," she sighed and he chuckled and wrapped one of his wings around her and before he could wrap the other wing around her, she wrapped one of her bronze wings around him. "I shan't do anything of the sort."

"Oh, I'm so appreciative of thy concern," she announced lazily. He half laid his head on hers. She scoffed and said, "Thy father does the same thing. I knoweth not why I hath but one child that took after my size. All of ye others took after thy father."

"It's not that bad," he said and she looked up at him with a look that said 'Really'. He started chuckling again.

"Very well, go off to thine own business. I hath a daughter to speaketh with."

"Verily, I shall. Take pleasure with thy plants, Mother." "I shall. Now get out of here. Go and knowest that I love thee," she placed a kiss on the side of his face again. The left side where the crimson scales were. She made it a point to do such a thing. Even if she was on his right side, she would maneuver over to tap his left side.

"I love thee too, Mother."

Caitlin started walking off to where Adalgisa bounded off too. Adelhelm looked around him and did his best to remember which way was the quickest way out.

"The quickest route is that way, Son," said Caitlin, pointing with her tail. Adelhelm nodded and trotted off in that direction.

"I thank thee, Mother. I was about to remember that."

"Oh, surely thou wast. Farewell," she waved a wing at him in farewell.

"Farewell, I'll see thee during supper," said Adelhelm, waving his farewell too and left. After a moment of trotting around the Royal Gardens, he found the doorway he was looking for, or at least the doorway he thought he was looking for.

Chapter Three

Time For Family

Day 15, Rainmoon, Year 2142

Adelhelm landed on an outlook that faced northwest, over most of the land of Brandland. The rock there was the same as most of the exterior rock around the mountain. Black and dark gray.

He stared at a dark wooden door that was embroidered with iron. The sun was reaching near early evening, late afternoon. Four guards stood sentry before the door.

The first guard had steel gray scales with small accents of dull gray scales near his snout. His wings and horns were steel gray and his eyes were dull gray. He was nearly the same size as Adelhelm, slightly taller though.

The second guard had mostly steel gray scales as well, except for some small patches on his tail. His wings were steel gray and his horns and eyes were a darker gray. As were the patches on his tail. He was such a similar size to Adehelm that it seemed that they were the same size.

The third guard had solely steel gray scales, but was the smallest of all. She had steel gray horns, eyes, and wings.

The fourth guard had a large patch of very dark gray scales that stretched from her thorax and down her left side. It then went sporadic around the main patch. The rest of her scales were steel gray. Her horns and wings were steel gray, but her eyes were a silver gray. She was slightly larger than the third guard.

"My Father wishes to see me?" Adelhelm cleared with the guards.

"Verily, Thy Highness. He hath been expecting thee. He's inside," a guard said.

"Very well."

"We'll bid the King that thou hast arrived. Wait here, Thy Highness," the guard responded and turned around and gestured to the door with his head.

A guard near the door slightly opened the door and poked his head in. Adelhelm could hear the voices, but couldn't distinguish between words. After a brief moment, the guard removed his head from the doorway and opened the door completely. The guards stepped out of Adelhelm's way and he strutted forward into the study. The door closed behind him once he entered.

Light came from sconces from the walls. The walls were gray stone and fine dirt covered the floor. A stone ledge jutted out of the ground where his father was sitting and looking down at the stone ledge. Adelhelm faced his father and asked, "Thou wished to see me, Father?"

"Verily. I wished to speaketh with thee a long time ago. Was my messenger troubled in the task of seeking thee out?" His Brandian accent was deep, but not too deep. Only deeper than a regular tone of voice.

The majority of his scales were crimson. His underbelly was blood red as well were his eyes. His wings were carmine. His horns were amber. He was eighteen feet tall to his head, twelve feet to his back and thirty eight feet long.

"I'm not certain. Though, I was moving about the palace recently. That may be the cause of the delay," said Adelhelm.

Giovanni looked up from his desk and up at Adelhelm for a second before he sighed and, with a chuckle, said, "As always," he stood and asked, "How was thy time in the Drache Strait?"

"Near the same as before. We repelled the Imperial fleet and secured the waters again," said Adelhelm. Giovanni stared at Adelhelm for a moment and Adelhelm realized that he was staring at his right side. "Verily, I suppose it was not the exact same. I should need to be missing my scales on my left side for that to happen."

Giovanni burst into a chuckle and said, "That's the truth," his chuckle died down and he asked, "How was Wilhelm? Uh-Wilhard's son."

"Well. I think. I didn't spend much time near him, but for the time we were near each other, he seemed the same as always."

"I see. That's good," he paused for a moment and continued, "Well, I heard of what thou achieved. I'm proud of thee."

Adelhelm smiled and he felt his heart fill with pride at his father's words and said, "Many great thanks to thee, Father."

"Well, now that thou art hither. I wish it of thee to do some things for me."

"Anything. Or most anything."

"I want thee to travel unto Windig Cirque. Visit Windtop, Flache Spalte, Juwelenstadt, Cirque Mund and Flussbasis," Adelhelm nodded and Giovanni continued, "Meet with the nobles and the Chief Mayors. Word has reached me that there are odd tales originating from Windig Cirque. I want thee to diffuse the situation."

"Surely. May I beseech what the tales are?"

"Verily. There art missing persons reports. Mysterious killings and vanishings. People from there are being called mad for strange tales they are telling to any that will harken unto their voices. I hath sent soldiers to diffuse this, but none of them, if not one or two, hath been seen again. I want thee to go unto there, to place another mind to it. A mind that has a voice and stature that carries authority."

"I understand. How long hath these reports been being reported?"

"The first report that I can connect to these cases is eight years ago. Then, there weren't many of these cases. So few that they seemed to be normal, but now, the amount of reports has spiked upward and continues to grow. It gives me concern for public order there."

Adelhelm nodded for a moment before saying, "Very well, I'll depart tomorrow, as the sun rises."

"Nay. Stay here for another week or two. If thou departs as early as tomorrow after thou hast barely returned, thou'll break thy mother's heart. Besides, Wilhelm may not be with us for that much longer. The doctors are saying that he won't last much longer," said Giovanni and the pride in Adelhelm's heart fled all at once and he noticeably deflated. Though it wasn't much, his father noticed and said, "Please, stay for a time. Thou art always gone and I'm beginning to feel that thou art avoiding him. Go and see him sometime whilst thou art hither."

"I shall, Father. I... shall," said Adelhelm, finishing with a sign.

"Good. I promise thee that it shall be good for thee to see him again. He used to always make thee smile and, verily, be happy, so to speak."

He deflated a little more and nodded saying, "Yea. That he did."

He remembered when Wilhelm wasn't sick and dying. Memories of when they would play together and have good times together. His eyes were downcast from his father's eyes.

"Say thy prayers for him. Perhaps god will grace us with his life," said Giovanni, placing a wing on Adelhelm.

Adelhelm looked up into his father's eyes and nodded. "Good. That is all I wished to say. Thou art dismissed." Adelhelm nodded and said, "Surely."

He turned around and shook himself as if to get the feeling of depression off of himself.

He straightened a bit and said, "I'll see thee for supper."

"Surely. I'll see thee as well."

"Farewell until then Father."

"Farewell, Son," said Giovanni and he smiled at Adelhelm and Adelhelm left for the door that he had entered. Two guards sentried the door inside the study. One had white scales, no other scales. His wings were white and his eyes were an icy blue. His horns were white.

The other had dark blue scales with accents of brown. His wings were blue and his eyes were brown. His horns were brown.

The first one opened the door and Adelhelm exited. The door shut behind him and he stood for a second before unfurling his wings to take off. He bent his legs and jumped off.

He beat his wings and flew down past a couple peaks. He rushed through the air, feeling the wind flow through and past his horns and down the length of his body and he smiled.

Flying always gave him a thrill. He beat his wings harder and faster, gaining speed by the second. After only a few seconds of this he remembered where he was going and he turned to the right and down.

He flapped his wings and slowed as he landed on a balcony with a slight thud. He furled his wings in and turned from the view to the mountain side where a door was placed in. Two guards sentried the door.

One had orange scales for her underbelly and everything else that wasn't the back of her head, neck, her back itself, and the upside of her tail, which was all white. Her wings were white and her eyes were a tangerine orange. Her horns were orange. She was thirty feet long, sixteen feet to her head and eleven to her back.

The other had dull gray scales on her front legs, thorax and the front of her neck and lower jaw. Her wings were crimson as was the majority of her scales and her eyes. A couple patches on her tail and back were a bright yellow. Her horns were carmine. She was the same size as the other.

They bowed their heads and, both in Brandian accents, said, "Thy Highness."

"Ulrike, Silke. Good day, isn't it?" He trotted up to the door and they opened it for him without a word.

"As it is after most storms, Thy Highness," replied Ulrike, the second guard.

"That's the truth," he said with a small chuckle. He entered the room, stopped just inside the doorway, turned his head around and said, "I doth not wish to be disturbed."

"Surely, Thy Highness," complied Silke, the first guard.

Adelhelm nodded once and they closed the door. The space inside was lit up slightly by holes in the rock above, though there were still shadows in the far corners. The room was quite spacious, reaching high and in an almost circular formation. It was more like a half square, half circle shape.

He crossed his room to another door that was nearly on the opposite side of his room. He reached the door and opened it slowly. A head popped into view as he opened the door and then he opened it farther.

"Thy Highness," the guard that saw him first bowed his head as he said those words. The other guard was more behind the door and looked around the door to see for himself.

"Thy Highness," said the second guard and bowed his head as well.

The first guard had light blue scales with water iron scales, scales of steel gray that shone as if there were rainbows within. His eyes were green and his wings were blue. The second guard had complete dull gray scales with wings and eyes of the same color.

"Not one being is to disturb me," said Adelhelm.

"It shall be done, Thy Highness," said the first guard and Adelhelm nodded once in agreement. He backed away from the door and the guards outside shut it for him.

He turned around towards his room again. There wasn't much, a table-like structure like what was in his father's study. A large area with a lot of soft, uncompacted dirt that was surrounded by a stone ledge that sort of held it all in one place, all though Adelhelm didn't think it was going to go anywhere.

There were unlit sconces on the walls. The ceiling slanted with the slope of the mountain side. Though the holes in it didn't face south, and more east, a good amount of light split in through them.

He began to pace, thinking about what his father had said. About Windig Cirque and the reports that is. He did his best to keep his mind off of his brother.

Different scenarios played through his head about how he was going to accomplish this task, perhaps a way to sneak out to Windig Cirque without his mother noticing, or another way where she agreed with him and allowed him to leave. That was the better option there.

His mind mimicked conversations that he could have with her, what he would say and what she would say in return. How he could convince her to be alright with him leaving for a few weeks again.

While he thought of these conversations, in one of them, she brought up the topic of Wilhelm, his brother. How Adelhelm should stay there and not leave for as long as she could hold him there. He slowly stopped pacing and he lost his focus as his thoughts spiraled towards Wilhelm. The memories he had with him.

After a brief moment of that, he shook his head and abandoned that part of his mind for some other time. He did not know how long he had paced, but noises began to threaten his chain of thought.

He heard something, some sound, coming from the door to the palace. It sounded like voices, but he wasn't sure. He hadn't broken out of his thoughts yet.

"Thy Highness, Prince Adelhelm," a voice sounded through the door. Adelhelm stopped pacing again and looked at the door.

"What is it?" He asked. He didn't sound angered, or he didn't think he did. He did his best to hide the fact that he was at the very least disappointed.

"Her Highness, Princess Adalgisa is requesting to speak with thee," the voice begrudgingly said.

Adelhelm thought for a moment, debating whether or not it was worth it to stop his thinking for her at this time or not.

"Nay. I doth not want to be disturbed," he said.

The voices resumed outside the door, "He is not to be disturbed. Prince's orders."

"Verily, thou can neglect that order. I need to speaketh with him," said a female voice in return.

"Mine apologies, Thy Highness, but it must wait until His Highness is allowing visitors again."

"I must say something unto him. Art thou determined to deny me mine entry? A Princess's command?"

Adelhelm had had enough by this point. Adalgisa had won her victory at last.

"Permit her," said Adehelm.

"At thy command, Thy Highness," said the male voice.

"Now, step aside quicker. I'm entering," she said and that's when he heard the door open. He stared at her.

"Leave, and return to thy task of not letting anyone else disturb us," said Adalgisa.

"It-as thou commands, Thy Highness," he said and the door closed and the light from the corridor went away. Adelhelm was staring at her with a look that said, 'seriously?'.

Adalgisa smiled at him and said, "Good evening, Brother. How goest thy day?"

"MMmm. Decent to say the least."

"I thought thou wast resting. Thou wast awake until late yesternight."

"That affects me not as it affects thee."

"Oh, I suppose thou thinks that thou is better?"

"Is that a challenge?"

"I thought that thy words were the challenge."

"Nay. I was simply speaking the truth."

"Very well. I only wished to knoweth how speaking with Father went," she said.

He didn't respond for a moment before he said, "What?"

"How was speaking with Father?" She said louder, more clearly.

"I heard what thou said..." he briefly paused and continued, "but why doth thou wishest to know?"

"I don't know, but I wish to know."

"Why would I tell thee? It could be a secret." "'Could be'. Not 'is'."

"Then at least give me a reason to. Not only, 'I wish to know'."

She sighed and thought for a moment before saying, "Very well. I wanted to knoweth what the two of ye were speaking of. Art thou departing again for a time? How long shall thou be staying hither if thou doest depart?"

He inhaled deeply before saying, "If thou needest know. I am to depart on a diplomatic-type mission to Windig Cirque for Father. I'll be hither for at least a couple weeks."

"Thou art remaining hither for a couple weeks? At least? I thought that thou wouldst depart as soon as thou couldst."

He exhaled and mumbled, "I wanted to, but Father wishes it not. He wishes that I remain hither for at least a couple of weeks, for Mother's sake."

"I see. It is understandable."

"That isn't all that thee wished to know, is it?"

"Nay, it isn't. It's that Lamberta and I were speaking and I thought that thou should join us. Moreover, she also wanted to speak to thee as well.

"Hmm. What about?"

"Oh, the usual thing or two. We critically judged multiple other dragons, ladies of mountain-holds that is, and spoke about the Empire and everything else."

"Nay, nay. I meant, what did Lamberta wish to speak to me about?"

"Uh-why should I knoweth that?"

"I'm only wondering. If it is truly important and if I truly needeth to go."

"It was important enough to her. She said that she had come up here to speak with thee and that she was turned away."

"That is understandable."

"What? What's understandable?"

"That she was turned away from speaking with me."

"How is that understandable?"

"Because I told my guards that I wasn't to be disturbed. That obviously wasn't enough to stop thee though, so what's the point of it all?"

"Why would I let something like that stop me?"

"Because there is usually a reason someone doesn't want to be disturbed when he says that he wishes not to be disturbed."

"I'm not sure why that was, but whatever the reason, doth thou still not wish to be disturbed?"

"Verily, nay."

"Good, now come. Lamberta's in the Lower-Eastern Lounge Cavern," she sort of made some form of hop towards the door. He chuckled at her and followed her to the door. She slowed down so that they walked side-by-side and began talking.

"So, I'll tell thou up to the point where Lamberta and I had stopped speaking. When I had come up here to gather thee," she said.

"What? Or, nay, speak on," he said.

"Good. What we were, and shall be speaking of, is any tidings we had discerned from Emporia's northern frontier. I had heard that King Nikitovich had gathered all the Ludy Kamnya that could gather to his side. I think it's smart. This way he can coordinate all the soldiers he can against Andronicus. Lamberta thinks that it's not as smart."

"Yea, I agree."

"With who?"

"Lamberta. All it does is confine all resisting Narodi to one place where High Prince Andronicus can crush them all at once. I'm, in a way, convinced that he's letting them through with purpose."

"That is exactly what Lamberta said. There is only one thing though, it's that they are all within the mountains. Secured within a natural fortress. I truly don't think that Emporia can take it. Especially if King Nikitovich has the aid of the rest of the free factions of this world, plus the Confederation's help."

"The Confederation's help means nothing."

"Let me rephrase mine argument. The Confederation's distracting border with Emporia."

Adehelm bobbed his head up and down in acceptance and, raising his voice, said, "Open the door," and the door opened. He and Adalgisa walked through silently. The door closed behind them and Adelhelm turned to Ulrike and said, "Tell the others that I am no longer within my room and retrieve two guards from inside."

"At thy command, Thy Highness," she complied. Ulrike didn't go within his room, but around to another, smaller ledge and through another door. A moment later she came back out and two more guards followed her out.

The guards exited from the doorway a moment later, led by Ulrike. She reclaimed her position by his door and the other trotted up near him. They bowed their heads to them once close enough.

Adalgisa had unfurled her wings and had just lifted off of the ground. Adelhelm did the same as she waited for him, hovering in the air. The two-guard escort had lifted off after them as they saw them leaving.

After a moment of flying towards their destination. Adalgisa slowed enough so that they could speak and be heard and Adelhelm slowed with her.

"I challenge thee to a race," challenged Adalgisa as they flew near to where their destination was in front and beneath them. Adelhelm looked down at the mountain and back at Adalgisa with a smile.

"Art there stakes in this race?" He asked.

"I had none in mind. I was only thinking of boasting about how much slower thou art than I."

"Oh, verily. So cocky for one who hast been humbled before and is close to being humbled again."

"Oh please, I beg of thee. Thou must hast gaps in thy memory, I hath never lost to thee and I will never lose to thee."

"Very well then, I shall prove thee wrong. Say when."

Though neither Adelhelm nor Adalgisa were looking back, the guards behind them looked at one another with the same expression towards one another, a look that said, 'Not again.'

Adalgisa looked down, back at him and down before saying, "Start!"

She pulled in her wings and angled downward with her snout. Adelhelm did the same. The guards dived as well. Just a second after beginning the dive, Adalgisa began to slow for her landing and so did Adelhelm just behind her. They dived at about thirty degree angles.

They both slowed to land and Adelhelm took his chance and folded his wings just slightly, to fall faster. As he dropped past Adalgisa, she saw and did the same, but by then he was in enough the lead.

Where they needed to land was in a large cave mouth that led into the mountain slightly, like a gaping mouth in the face of the cliffside. Stalactites protruded from the top of the cavern and stalagmites grew from the bottom in some places. They both picked up and shot into the cavern and high-speeds. Adelhelm was still leading with Adalgisa nearly head to head with him. Not long after they had darted into the cave mouth they prepared to land.

Adelhelm found a good stalagmite to land on. He aimed for it. Adalgisa turned to land somewhere else near to where he was going to land. The guards behind were following quite well. Adelhelm slowed a little more before reaching out for the stalagmite and grabbed it. His claws dug in the farthest he could force them as they scratched the stalagmite.

He pivoted on the tapering column as he came to a stop.

During this, Adalgisa hit a flat section of ground and bounded up and landed again and ended up finally stopping about two-hundred and fifty feet farther down. After Adelhelm had come to a complete stop, he looked up at the escort that had followed as well as they should have. He nodded and waved a wing at them to go and they did.

As Adalgisa came to a complete stop, they looked up and found one another. Adelhelm had looked up first, but Adalgisa found him first and she spread her wings and gave a shout of victory.

"I won," she said as Adelhelm looked at her.

"Nay. I don't think thou didst," answered Adelhelm.

"Yea, I did. Thou only didn't see."

Adelhelm was about to reply before another voice cut in saying, "What are ye two doing?"

Adelhelm looked in the direction of her voice and said, "Attempting to catch Adalgisa in a lie."

"I'm not lying," chuckled Adalgisa.

"Lamberta, did thou seest who landed first?" Adelhelm asked.

Lamberta was curled up with her tail underneath her fore legs. There was a clay tablet laying in front of her that she must have been reading before he and Adalgisa had disturbed her.

Most of her scales were a ruby red, the inside of her fore legs and her neck and thorax were shared between bronze and golden scales. Her wings were ruby red, but her eyes were a carmine red. Her horns were ruby red as well. She was about thirty-five feet long and fifteen feet tall when standing.

"What doth I receive if I tell the truth?" Lamberta asked. She had a Brandian accent.

"The humbling of our kindly sister. She was very confident that she would triumph over me, though she also denied that I had won her in other races as well. To sum it up, she was too cocky for her own good, much more, our own good," offered Adelhelm.

"Adelhelm had not spoken of the stakes. See, if he loses, I'm going to hold onto the victory for at least a week, but it better be for longer. Thou can share in the revelry with me if thou wishes," Adalgisa offered as well.

"Adelhelm, thou hast never said what I would get from telling the truth," said Lamberta.

Adelhelm raised an eyebrow and said, "Adalgisa shall be humbled, and we three would know of it. So, when she decides to attempt to over stretch her bounds, we would hath evident cause to have her quietened."

"I shall not stand for this, Lamberta, tell him that he hath wasted his words. I knoweth that I landed first," said Adalgisa, standing a little taller and imperious. She had trotted a little closer to both Adelhelm and Lamberta. Adelhelm landed nearer to Lamberta, only about fifty feet away from where she lay.

"Well done," said Adelhelm and after a few seconds added, "Thou hast given a command to Lamberta instead of an offer. I wonder what she'll think of that." Adalgisa squinted her eyes at him.

Lamberta thought about that for a second before saying, "The truth is that I didn't see who landed first, I wasn't watching, but I did hear the landings."

"Go on," urged Adelhelm.

"I think I heard a scrape first, then a thud," Lamberta offered up.

"That would hath been me," said both Adelhelm and Adalgisa at the same time. They looked at each other for a moment.

"The thud? Yea, that wast thee, Adalgisa," said Adelhelm after the silence.

"Nay, I landed on a stone patch there. See?" Adalgisa pointed with a wing at a patch of stone not far from where Adelhelm still clinged onto the stalagmite he had landed on.

"But, how would me landing on this stalagmite result in the sound of a thud?" Adelhelm asked.

"Obviously it was thy tail hitting the ground," said Adalgisa with nearly an all knowing tone, though, Adelhelm would've known if his tail hit that hard. It would've hurt and above all, he would have felt it hit.

Lamberta lay there, her head resting on her tail as she watched the conversation unfold. Adelhelm looked at her for a second and back at Adalgisa and quickly back at her. It seemed that she was taking a lot of interest in this. She looked at him and they locked eyes. Adalgisa was looking between the two of them.

"I think thou doest know who landed first. I think thou wast watching," accused Adelhelm.

"Thou thinkest too much," Lamberta responded.

"What?" Adalgisa was puzzled and asked no one in particular.

"But I am correct with this thought though," Adelhelm said to Lamberta.

"I could lie," said Lamberta.

"I knoweth this, but will thee? I'm positive that I landed first, almost without a doubt, but that shan't matter. What would thou hast of me?" Adelhelm asked, resigned.

Lamberta smirked and said, "Is there anything thou hast to offer that I should wish of thee? That is the true question."

"Surely I have more than him. Surely," said Adalgisa, gesturing at Adelhelm with a wing.

"Perhaps, but I'm thinking otherwise," Lamberta replied to her.

Adalgisa sat on her haunches and asked, "Well, what doth thou hast then, Adelhelm?"

"He has time that he can spare in a conversation with me," Lamberta replied in his stead.

"Yea, I'm sure I do." Adelhelm let go of the stalagmite and stood on the ground. His forelegs had gotten tired from clinging onto the stalagmite.

"So do I," said Adalgisa in a voice of complaint and continued, "Thou wished to see him earlier, but couldn't because he was too busy."

"Yea. Indeed he was," Lamberta confirmed.

"But no longer. I do hath an apology to offer thee as well, if thou art willing to accept it," said Adelhelm.

"I shall. I did see Adelhelm land first. He had clung onto the stalagmite before thou had hit the ground, Adalgisa. He only spun around on that stalagmite like a ballerina," confessed Lamberta.

Adalgisa chuckled and Adelhelm looked at Lamberta and mocked a chuckle himself. After Adalgisa had chuckled a moment more she stifled her amusement, sniffed with disdain and said, "Very well. Be this way, if thou must."

"I must," said Adelhelm with a wing touching his thorax and bowing his head slightly.

Adalgisa scoffed at him and said, "Thou art unbearable enough to maketh me think of other things."

"And what things would those be?" Adelhelm asked.

She looked at him a second and said, "I hath been thinking that the sun has reached its position in the sky that indicates that supper is near."

"Verily," said Adelhelm.

"Shall we gather in the dining hall then?" Lamberta asked.

"That is what I implied," said Adalgisa.

"Very well. It is probably best that we gather there sooner rather than later," said Lamberta.

"I agree," said Adalgisa.

"I doth not think that thou knowest what thou agrees to, Adalgisa," said Adelhelm.

"Why is that? Or, I mean, what doth thou mean by that?" Asked Adalgisa.

"Remember the last time thou wast late, Adalgisa? Mother was furious," said Lamberta.

"Verily. I remember well enough to recall that thou had laughed at me."

"Nay. Thou recall it wrong. I was the one who had laughed at thee. Lamberta is princessly enough that she was able to contain her amusement," said Adelhelm.

Adalgisa looked at him, unamused by the recalling of the memory. Lamberta smiled as she remembered what exactly had happened and said, "He speaks true. I now remember it all. I also remember that Mother was as amused by thine actions then as Adalgisa is now."

"I remember that as well. She brought Father into it," said Adelhelm.

Adalgisa looked at her and back at him saying, "There is no semblance of allies in this family. It's all but a free-for-all."

Adelhelm laughed and Lamberta said, "Verily, it is."

"Verily. No one is safe hither. Not even when I was courting someone, did they always take my side. I always attempted to take theirs though, but they never really made their own side. It makes me wonder, if one belonged to me as a wife, whether she'd join my side, join one of thy sides, or choose her own side by that point," said Adelhelm.

"She wouldn't side with thee. She couldn't. Not for long anyway," said Adalgisa.

"Now I'm curious. We should get thee a betrothed, Adelhelm, and figure a way to take Mother and Grandmother off her back long enough for her to get climatized and ye two to marry. I wish to see what would happen before I get married off," Lamberta announced.

"Now, don't be too excited. We all know that there is no way any of us, one at a time or all three of us at once, could hold Mother back from attempting to persuade me that I should cancel the courtship. And persuading is a very light term for how she enlightens me on what she wants me to know and act," said Adelhelm.

"Father would possess such an ability. I'm sure of it," said Lamberta.

"I'm not so sure of that. I mean, it's completely possible, but the thing is, I'm not so sure that he would comply," said Adelhelm.

"Why not?" Lamberta asked.

"I hath no idea. I only feel that he wouldn't. Primarily because he is married to Mother," said Adelhelm.

"Thou art correct. It is impossible, unless Father arranges the marriage himself," said Adalgisa.

"The only problem with thy statement. The only way for Father to arrange a marriage, Mother would most likely hath to agree to it. That's the problem," said Adelhelm.

"'Most likely', keywords, Adelhelm. He could make the decision without Mother's approval," said Lamberta.

"Yea, and Mother would not care much for the decision, nor for my wife," Adelhelm replied.

"And if Father made that sort of decision without Mother's approval, then Grandmother would chastise Father to no end," Adalgisa said.

"This is true. Very true," said Lamberta.

"Enough about this talk. What about the talks of food we had earlier?" Asked Adalgisa.

"It passed on for a moment, but now that thou hast brought the topic back to attention, we should go. Food is great. Especially food hither at home. Let me tell ye, food on the front is nothing compared to the sorts of food we eat hither," said Adelhelm.

"I'm thinking that thou hast told us this before, but I may hath forgotten whether thou hast or not because of how trivial it is to know," said Lamberta. Adelhelm looked at her.

"Trivial? Well, I suppose it is to thee, since thou art never going to go anywhere besides palace to palace and plaza. Thou art allowed to stay hither where it's nice and cozy and dry," Adelhelm mocked. Adalgisa looked at him flatly.

"Are we going to eat or simply stay here to continue bickering?" Adalgisa stood and aimed for the doorway when she spoke.

"Bickering? Thou almost sound like Grandmother when thou hast said that word," said Adelhelm as he walked across the room, towards the door.

Lamberta laughed and said, "Thou doest! Adelhelm, that was very accurately described." She continued chuckling.

"Well, Grandmother is amazing, so that's a compliment," said Adalgisa, defending herself.

"I wasn't saying that Grandmother isn't amazing. She is. I was simply agreeing with Adelhelm in his statement of the obvious," said

Lamberta with an aloof expression on her face. Adelhelm and Adalgisa chuckled.

"Enough banter. Let's go," said Adelhelm as he approached where he and Adalgisa had entered.

"It's not very smart for all of us to go with each other at the same time, is it?" Lamberta watched Adelhelm as he turned around to look at her.

"Perhaps. I'll go first," he turned to leave again.

"Wait," Adalgisa called out. She trotted up to Adelhelm and Lamberta walked closer.

"What?" Adelhelm turned his head around and looked past one of his unfurled wings.

"Only this," said Lamberta. She made a quick bound towards Adelhelm as he looked at her. Adelhelm grunted as she shouldered him backwards into Adalgisa's way. She then took off with a grin.

Adalgisa shuffled away from Adelhelm as he regained his balance.

"What art thou doing? Tackling me?" Adalgisa asked. She trotted to get past him.

"Not a chance at that," said Adelhelm as he blocked her path. "What about her?" Adalgisa gestured at open air to indicate Lamberta.

"She won't get much farther," said Adelhelm. "Oh, whatever. Thou couldn't catch a flea."

"What? A flea? No one can catch a flea. No one can see a flea."

"I know, I know, but Lamberta's getting away. Or she's getting farther away, or ahead, or closer to her destination, or our destination."

"Stop, only stop. It would simply be the dining hall and I'm leaving," said Adelhelm bounding towards the exit to take off.

"Only after me," Adalgisa tackled him with more effort than she let him see. They both rolled onto their talons and Adelhelm came out of the roll facing Adalgisa. He gave her a look.

"Oh really? Not very likely."

He looked around to make sure no one was looking and then shoved Adalgisa back. She stumbled back and regained her balance. He quickly turned around and took off before Adalgisa could properly react. It wasn't long before he cleared the mouth of the cave.

He beat his wings harder and gained altitude, slowly rotating towards the Royal Dining Hall. There were little clouds in the sky and the sun was near the western horizon, painting the sky and ground in oranges, reds and yellows.

It wasn't long before he was gliding in to make a landing. He landed, stirring up dirt. Eight guards were positioned by a double doorway that led into the Royal Dining Hall. They all bowed and said, "Thy Highness." Adelhelm nodded his dismissal.

He walked towards the doors and the guards opened them for him. He entered and Adalgisa landed behind him, elegantly as she, as a princess, was required to. Before Adelhelm was Lamberta, who was inspecting a tapestry. She looked at him as he entered, then looked past him at Adalgisa.

Within the Royal Dining Hall, there were sconces that held blazing torches. Tapestries hung from the walls and a large table occupied the center of the hall.

"What took thou so long?" Lamberta asked mockingly.

"I wanted to give thee a head start. If I didn't, then it would hath been too easy. It took a little longer than I expected, Adalgisa here wanted to give thou a little extra time to get here," Adelhelm gestured with his wings as he spoke.

She sighed and said, "Very well, thou hast lost. Sit," she waved a wing vaguely towards the center of the dining hall.

Adelhelm sighed as well and said, "Yea, at thy bidding," walking over to his seat to sit.

Adalgisa circled the table as well to her seat and said, "Adelhelm, if thou doest that again, I shall tell Mother."

"What was that?" Lamberta asked, looking at Adalgisa. Adelhelm started chuckling.

"Very well. I shan't do it again, Thy Highness."

"What happened? Adelhelm, thou didst not do anything un-royal-like to our sweet, sweet sister, didst thou?"

"He did the utmost unruly thing known unto this earth," said Adalgisa, looking indignant.

"I shoved her and took off to chase thee here," confessed Adelhelm. Lamberta guffawed at him and started chuckling.

"It's not funny, it's insulting," said Adalgisa.

"Why? Why didst thou shove her?"

"She thought she could tackle me. It was simply in self defense," said Adelhelm.

"That's not true. We had an entire conversation between the two incidents," argued Adalgisa.

"It was a delayed reaction," said Adelhelm. Lamberta laughed and Adalgisa stared at her.

"How dare thou laugh. It is not amusing," said Adalgisa, looking at Lamberta in astonishment.

"What?" Asked Lamberta.

"It's insulting to me. I can not believe that he would doeth such a thing to me."

"Taketh some humor in it. Besides, he's only our brother, it's not like what he does actually affects us," said Lamberta with a smile and shaking her head.

Adelhelm shook his head, smiled and stood up, walked around the table and both Adalgisa and Lamberta watched him walk.

"Where art thou going?" Adalgisa asked him, unmoving.

"Only over here," he said as he approached a double doorway. There were no guards on the inside of the dining hall and the doors he was walking towards were a different pair of doors than he had entered through.

"And what's over there that has caught thine interest?" Lamberta asked.

"Only a thought," Adelhelm assured her as he neared the doors. He opened one door slowly and sort of peaked out. A guard on the other side of the door was looking back at him. They made eye contact for a brief moment, the guard giving him an odd look before Adelhelm opened the door farther and the guard finally recognized who he was and bowed her head saying, "Thy Highness."

The other guards turned to look at him, then looked back forward quickly, then back and forth twice before making a decision. They bowed and said, "Thy Majesty."

Adelhelm was confused a little before he caught on. "What art thou doing, Adelhelm? Thou art looking like a fool," said Adalgisa.

He turned his head around to look at her and mocked, "Be patient, Young One. I..."

"'Young One'?!" Adalgisa exclaimed. "What doth thou mean by that?"

"I mean that thou shouldst wait a little longer when I say to be patient," said Adelhelm as he went to turn around again to look out of the doors, or door since he only opened one.

"What he actually meant by that is that thou art young. Hence the title, 'Young One'," said Lamberta.

Adelhelm rolled his eyes and sighed. He opened the door more and saw his mother standing there, staring at him. He froze and said, "Mother. What a surprise."

He said the words loudly for his sisters to hear, though they still managed to not hear it.

"What?" Adalgisa asked. She waited a second before continuing, "Wait, I wasn't speaking to thee."

"But I was speaking to thee. And pointing out the obvious too."

Adelhelm swallowed and gave his mother a smile. She looked at him with cool eyes and asked, "What's going on? Is there... anything I would like to hear, Adelhelm?"

"Uh, well, perhaps. Or..." Caitlin pushed him with her wings. He didn't try to stand his ground and simply backed out of the way and entered the hall. Adelhelm followed enough to get out of the way of the door so it could close. The guards obliged.

Adalgisa scoffed. Lamberta didn't react. She was only looking directly at Caitlin who was looming near Adalgisa. "Thou shouldst mind thine own business for once. I only want to speak to Adelhelm peacefully and thou shove thy way into the conversation," said Adalgisa.

Adelhelm slowly approached Adalgisa, attempting to pass by Caitlin's perspective as a peaceful entity. She whipped out a wing into his way and gave him a sharp glare. He stepped back and Lamberta said, "So, where's Father? He's usually here by now."

"Why wouldst thou ask me that? How should I knoweth the answer to such a question?"

"She wasn't asking thee," said Caitlin. Adalgisa jumped and turned her head around in a blur.

"Mother... Hello," said Adalgisa with a warming smile.

"Hello, Adalgisa," she looked up from her and at Lamberta and said, "I knoweth not where he could be."

"Oh, then, why the sneaky entrance?" Asked Lamberta. "It all started when I found Adelhelm sneaking about the palace entrance to the Dining Hall," said Cailtin.

Adelhelm walked around Caitlin and back to his seat. Caitlin grabbed one of his front legs with her tail, still watching Lamberta. Adelhelm stopped in his tracks.

"Thou should knowest, Mother, Adelhelm insulted me earlier and didn't apologize," Adalgisa confessed.

Caitlin looked at Adalgisa and asked, "Is that true?" Caitlin's grip on his leg loosened for a moment and Adelhelm thought that he could sidle away and to his seat, but Caitlin's tail tightened again when he moved the leg she had a hold of. He stopped again.

"Verily," said Adalgisa.

"It's not as bad as she makes it out to be. He only shoved her," said Lamberta. Caitlin's mouth opened a little bit and Lamberta added, "After she insulted him that is."

Caitlin's astonishment grew some more. She looked at Adelhelm and simply gave him a look that asked the question.

"I apologize," said Adelhelm.

Caitlin looked at Adalgisa and asked, "What did thou sayest to him?"

"Nothing. I said nothing to him," said Adalgisa. Caitlin's grip on Adelhelm tightened and she had jerked his leg towards her, sort of pulling it out from under him, when Adalgisa had spoken and it tightened more when she spoke again.

"Or I did, but nothing like what thou may think," said Adalgisa.

Caitlin took a deep breath in and inquired, "And why is that?" "I only complained, that's all," said Adalgisa.

"Complained? About what?" Caitlin asked, her tone slightly more gentler than before.

"I-I-I wanted to win a race against him to here," Adalgisa conceded.

"I'm confused. Thou wanted to win a race? How is that connected with thy complaining thou spokest of earlier?" Caitlin asked. Adelhelm had slowly leaned towards her as she spoke, she turned her head around to look at him and asked, "And what is it with thee?! Can't thou hold still for a few minutes?"

"I can, but I only wanted to sit at my designated seat at the table," said Adelhelm as he pointed at his spot with a wing.

Caitlin looked at his spot and back at him and said, "Art thou serious? Thou couldn't simply sit down over there?" She looked and pointed at where he used to be at the start of the conversation, then looked back at him. He couldn't see the spot because Caitlin was in his line of sight towards it.

"I could hath done so, but I wanted to sit over there," He gestured to his seat at the dining table again.

Caitlin sighed and said, "Very well. Go ahead, thou son of mine," and she let go of his leg and pushed him away from her with her front legs.

"I giveth thee my thanks, Mother," he said and wrapped his wings around her and hugged her. Then he broke the hug, though still staying close to Caitlin.

Caitlin chuckled and whispered, "Go to thy seat." She poked at him with the bend of her wing. Then she added in a normal voice, "Thy Father shall be here shortly."

The King did arrive shortly and they ate as joyfully as could be. As far as Adelhelm could tell, his parents loved it when they got along. Especially after Wilhelm had gotten sick, or more accurately poisoned. First of all, the sickness was out of place. It was rare for dragons to get sick. Though when they did, it was severe. Most dragons that actually got sick would die from the sickness. After they had eaten, they conversed with one another some more before going their separate ways. The King left first and the Queen left with him. The others dissolved not long after and went their own ways.

Adelhelm went to the balcony outside his room and watched the sun set complete. He looked over the city below. He didn't think much, only watched and enjoyed the silence. This was his usual custom and the guards were used to it. They kept vigilance, but whispered to one another as they waited for him. He didn't mind as long as they stayed quiet, or quiet enough that he could easily block out their conversation so that he may enjoy the tranquillity.

The sun set behind the mountains and the valley of The Dark Husk Mountains. The beauty of the sun and the shimmering tributaries within the valley, changing and giving way to the beauty of thousands of stars above. Once there was barely enough light to see details, he stood and turned for the door.

The guards had finished speaking and had nothing else to talk about and they opened the door for him, saying, "Thy Highness". He nodded his thanks and response and entered. The door closed and the room was covered in near complete darkness.

He couldn't actually see anything, but there were a few vague shapes though they might have just been what he thought he was seeing. He opened his jaws slightly and blew out a continuous plume of yellow, orange and red fire that illuminated the area so that he could see for a brief section of his chamber and what surrounded him.

It was his own chamber, but he wanted to make sure he was not going to run into a wall. He had done that once recently and found that he didn't like it.

His eyes glowed slightly and it seemed that his thorax did as well. With only a second or two of breathing the fire, he found where he wanted to go and he stopped his fire breathing. He was tired, well not fatigued really, but he usually fell asleep early so he was ready to sleep again.

He walked around the bed-like area and then onto the slightly elevated ledge that it was on. Once he was where he wanted to be, he laid down and shifted a few times as he got comfortable. As he shifted, some dirt went up his nostrils and he sneezed and shook his head slightly. He lifted his head up off of the ground and finished shifting before he laid and relaxed his head again.

He relaxed his wings to fall to the ground around him. He used one wing as a sort of blanket. His tail lay around him, the tip near his head. He stared at it for a moment before closing his eyes. The feeling of closing his eyes slightly burned yet filled him with ecstasy. He lay in his chosen position until he fell asleep.

He was standing on a ledge looking out over a clouded abyss. A bright light shown far below, showing through the bleakness. Adelhelm found that he envied that light, it was warm and he was, oddly, cold.

Wind was blowing where he was and with every minute, the wind gusts got stronger. He couldn't take his eyes off of the light. His breath was a heavy steam with every exhale, his breath was also warm before the cold wind blew it away.

He was able to take his eyes off of the light long enough to look around for a way down, looking for any obstacles below that would be in his path of flight.

A strong gust of wind unsteadied his balance. He stumbled a little bit before he was able to recover. The wind was blowing in his face, his eyes, forcing tears to run from his eyes. They blurred his vision, he tried to shake them away, but they would come back.

He looked away from the wind to stop the tears, only to see the gray bleakness turn to black. Black tendrils reached out and claimed more of the space around him. He shielded his head from the wind with a wing as he looked down at that warming light.

It was still bright.

He looked back at the darkness and then back at the light. He stepped off of the ledge and opened his wings. Not completely open, but open enough to slow his descent and ready to unfurl completely or to be folded back in quickly.

His weight pulled him down, though the wind still blew him wherever it wished to.

There were no obstacles, but the light never seemed to get any closer. He flapped his wings, though still keeping them half unfurled, to control his descent.

The air around him became colder as he went. The gray continued to turn to black around him. The darkness seemed to want him. To consume him. The light seemed so close, yet so far away.

Unreachable.

The cold was beginning to become unbearable. He felt as if he was turning to ice from the inside out.

Another ledge appeared out of the gray and he stiffly landed on it and furled his wings in tight against his body, they were numbing up.

He looked from the light to the black closing in around him then up to the ledge he left, but the ledge wasn't there to be seen and far, far in the distance, was a dim light. Such a dim light that it seemed minuscule to all other things around it.

He turned away from it and back down at the bright light below. He winced at an aching pain that bloomed in his thorax. He looked down as if to see what was in pain. He was expecting to see something, but at the same time he wasn't. His breath caught as he saw his crimson scales turn to a white-blue. The pain worsened as his eyes snapped open.

His head shot up and he breathed in deeply and exhaled, shaken by what had just happened. He looked at his thorax to see crimson scales. When he looked at his thorax, he saw his forelegs. They shook as if he were shivering vigorously. He felt that he should be in pain, but he wasn't.

He looked around his room. It was dark except for the light that came from the moons outside.

He repositioned a bit, tucking his forelegs beneath him as if to hold them still, and relaxed back down to sleep. He was tired and he struggled to keep his eyes open for any longer, though he wasn't completely sure whether he wanted to go back to sleep or not. The dream, or nightmare, he had just had was still fresh in his mind.

His lungs felt as if there were a heavy burden upon them, crushing them and making it hard to breathe. After enough time, he fell back into sleep.

He awoke again in pitch darkness to an unknown fear. He did not know why he woke, only that there was something that he did not want to confront. Something that made him afraid. He stood slowly and shook the tiredness from his body and stretched. He came out of his stretch and took a step and hit into a wall and stumbled tiredly back and took another step away to shake his body again. He illuminated his scales, casting shades of red and yellow shades of light across his room. He blinked the tiredness from his eyes and took a step and then another.

"Open the door," he said once he knew that the sleep was cleared from his voice. The door to the inside of the mountain opened slightly and he walked up to it and it opened all of the way and he unilluminated his scales.

"Good morning, Thy Highness," the guards said in turn and Adelhelm contemplated telling the truth, but only nodded and walked out of his room.

One guard had pinkish-red scales that covered the majority of her body and her wings. Other spots over her body were covered in orange scales, her eyes were a bright orange.

The other guard was almost completely covered in cobalt blue scales. Her wings and eyes were a forest green. The small amount of scales that weren't cobalt blue were midnight blue and her horns were midnight blue. The first guard went to a nearby door to rouse some more guards as an escort.

"Nay. I'd like to go alone this time. I'll stay within the palace," said Adelhelm. The guard stopped before she reached the door and Adelhelm added, "Mark my words for they are the truth. I shall stay within the palace grounds. I go to see my brother."

The guard nodded and resumed her position at the door. The other guard whispered something in her ear and disappeared through another door to inform the other guards, the guards that were outside on the balcony, that the prince was no longer within his chambers. Adelhelm didn't stop to look, only walked purposefully for his destination.

After walking for several minutes, and passing several guard patrols, he arrived. Two guards sentried outside the entryway and bowed their heads and said, "Thy Highness," to him as he stopped before the door.

One guard was completely white and had icy blue eyes.

The other guard's front legs were white, most of the rest of his scales were iron scales. His wings, as well as the small amount of scale that weren't white or iron, were scarlet red. His eyes were amber in color. His horns were crimson and he was about thirty feet in length and about sixteen feet tall.

"Open it," said Adelhelm and the guards obliged and he went through. The room was lit up by sconces on the walls. It wasn't a large room, but near the center was his brother, curled up and seemed as if he were sleeping. He was sleeping in a way, only for a better word, he was in a coma. Dying.

His scales were carmine, almost every one but for the inside of his legs and underbelly, which were two different scales. Bronze and yellow, a fiery kind of yellow if that can be imagined. Though his eyes were not open, Adelhelm remembered what color they were. Bronze. He was more like their mother in that way.

Wilhelm was thirty two feet long, sixteen feet to his head and ten feet to his back.

Is this what Adelhelm had feared when he woke, what had woken him from his sleep? Was it the bad dream? He didn't know, and he really didn't know if he feared it or if he hated it and cursed it. He thought it was more of a fear as of this moment rather than a hatred and regret. He decided that he would face this fear right now.

He walked up next to Wilhelm and laid down, his front legs were tucked beneath him and he curled his tail close about him. He stared at him for a moment, a long moment in fact.

"Why?" Adelhelm half whispered, technically to himself, but more to Wilhelm. He continued, "I ask 'why' to so many things. So many, but why thee? Why this?" He was slightly gesturing with his wings. "Why?"

He paused for a moment before continuing, "Thou should hast seen what had happened today. And heard what was said," he got up to pace around as he spoke, "Thou should hast seen how Adalgisa tried to tackle me. She learned that from thee," he pointed his tail at him and continued, "I only wanted to make that clear. So, back to the topic. Or, more on, onto the next topic. Mother tries to pin the teaching of that behavior on me. I know it was thee. Thou art hither almost all of the time. Or-or... eh."

He stopped pacing and looked at Wilhelm. He shook his head slightly and continued pacing, saying, "Anyway. Uh..." he sighed and said, "Why am I here? Why do I even come back? To suffer? This is stupid."

He stopped pacing as he stopped speaking and looked at the door. He turned for it and started walking with determination. He stopped at the door and looked down at the ground, taking deep breaths in and out. He looked back at his brother and wilted. He slowly approached Wilhelm, laid down near him, and looked at the ground. He stared at the talons of his front legs and said, "What hath happened to me, Wilhelm? What hath I done?"

He looked from the ground, and his talons, to his brother and stared for a second before saying, "It should hath been me, not thee. Perhaps things would be different. I-I hath... become something wrong, or-or I am becoming... something wrong."

His brother's breaths were so small and quiet. So strained and tired. Adelhelm could see his skeleton. So thin.

"Thou must return to us," said Adelhelm, but when Adelhelm looked at Wilhelm's boney back he said, "Or perhaps it is best that thou pass soon."

He stared at the ground before his brother and unfocused. Memories played in his mind and time passed without.

Caitlin walked into the room and saw Adelhelm lying there next to Wilhelm. She smiled slightly and said, "Good morning, Adelhelm."

Adelhelm didn't hear anything though; therefore, he didn't respond. She cocked her head in confusion and asked, "Adelhelm? Art thou awake?" Again, he didn't hear anything, nor did he respond. Caitlin approached him and laid a wing on him. He reacted to her wing touching his wing and his focus, or his lack of focus, was broken and he looked up to see his mother there, standing near him.

"Hello, Mother," said Adelhelm.

"Could thou not sleep?" She asked.

"I did," he said and looked back at Wilhelm.

"The guards say that thou hast been within for at least a couple hours."

"Perhaps, I hath not been keeping track of the time."

"Adelhelm, the sun hath not risen yet. It's not expected to rise for another two and a half hours. That would mean that thou hast been awake most of the night."

"I went to sleep early, I'm feeling well enough," he said and she looked at him with a concerned and slightly annoyed look. He looked up at her and said, "Truthfully. I'm well."

"Art thou certain? When the guards saith that thou hast been here for a time, they also said that they heard voices within and that they decided not to interrupt. When I walked in and called thy name, thou didn't react. Thou lay there still as stone and I know that thou feel as if it was thy fault that this happened, but it wasn't."

He looked away from her and said, "It was."

"Nay it wasn't. Yea, the food was meant for thee and the food was poisoned. How wast thou to know that it was poisoned? Thou wast only generous and thou wast not wrong for it. It wast not thy fault."

Adelhelm looked up at her, but his words never reached the back of his throat and were locked back away in the back of his mind. He looked back at his dwindling brother. She sighed.

"Hast thou at least broken thy fast?" She asked.

"Nay. I hath not."

"Very well. Leave thy brother to rest and come with me. I would like to eat with thee," she said and half wrapped her wing around him in a hug and he stood to go with her.

Chapter Four

The Traitor

Day 20, Rainmoon, Year 2142

Violeta briskly strode down the hallway towards two large mahogany doors. The hall was made of granite with stained glass windows of a variety of colors, the sun was shining through them from the east. It was the third hour of the day, the sun crested the horizon less than an hour ago.

Today was supposed to be her day off, but no longer. Duchess Estela had requested her to come in this day due to urgent business. Violeta did not know what this urgent business was about, but if Duchess Estela thought that it was something of import, then so did she.

Guards stood either side of the door. They stood in glistening plate armor, which consisted of a broad and smooth breastplate, great helms with plumes of yellow and cobalt blue. Smooth rerebraces, vambraces, cuisses and grieves.

Cloaks of yellow and royal blue. A yellow 'I' encompassed by two yellow arcs on a royal blue field made the coat of arms of the Offices of Intelligence of the Kingdom of Libertadia. They were equipped with standardized halberds with large heavy blades at their top. They also had sheathed swords at their hips.

They saluted with their arms outstretched at an ascending angle in front of them, their hands were overturned, their palms facing upwards as if something was alighted upon them. She nodded to them and strode to the doors, which they had opened for her. She walked through and into the room beyond. After she crossed through the door frame, the guards closed the doors behind her.

The doors shut with a thud and multiple heads looked up to see who had entered, all that looked stood straight and saluted her. Boots snapped against the stone and all others looked up from what they were doing and saluted as well. She nodded sharply to them and walked to her office. They returned to their tasks and conversations.

The room was large, reaching twenty-five feet tall, one-hundred and fifty feet in length and seventy-five feet wide and open, when it wasn't filled with people. Elves and Dwarves worked within. One of the short walls had a world map on it. A large table was situated near the center of the room, closer to the opposite side of the room than the world map upon the wall. The table was also covered with a map of the world. Smaller tables were situated around the large table with magnified maps of continents. Other smaller tables held maps of factions.

No humans worked within the room, they were frowned upon for what Emporon the Butcher had done in forming Emporia and what they were still doing. The emperors of Emporia were tyrants, all of them. They owned too much land for their own good, and the five kingdoms that they had oppressed for hundreds of years.

Beating them and using them like pawns on a game board. Those poor innocent people. It was clear that Imperial Emporia needed to be stopped, the question was how. Everything they tried, or most everything, would not work.

Brute force failed, at least eventually, and spies would work, until they were caught that is. Some spies weren't caught, but that was rare within itself. The reason the great kingdom of Libertadia had not fallen was due to the Emporian fleets not being able to cross Anvil's Sea; all of the water dragons that could fight were spread throughout the sea. Fleets also patrolled and would come to battle against the Empire.

Not that there weren't any humans within Libertadia, but they didn't and would never hold any station of true stature. They were servants underneath all. There were different stations of being a servant, some of honor. Most were servants under nobles, barons, lords and royalty of Libertadia. Violeta had a few servants of her own. They were subservient and loyal, as far as she knew anyway.

She entered her office and closed the door. Her office was situated on an elevated platform on the far side of the map room from the large world map on the wall. The side of the office that faced into the room was open, allowing her to see the entirety of the room from her desk.

A knock on the door came soon after she had gotten comfortable within her chair.

"Enter?" Violeta asked before the voice could announce itself

The door opened to a young elf woman with black hair and a slightly pointed face. She carried a tray with cups of a steaming liquid. She strode towards Violeta and offered a cup.

"Good morning, I pray, madam," said the elf woman, handing the cup to Violeta's outstretched hand.

"My thanks to thee."

"I pray that thou doest not give heed to mine asking, but I thought that today was thy day off, madam?"

"I was called upon. Go, gather mine officers and bid them to me."

"By thy command, madam."

They both had a Northern Libertadian accent. The elf woman left the room, closing the door behind her. Violeta sipped at the steaming cup. Warmth bloomed throughout her chest as the hot liquid flowed down her throat. It was Inniberra tea, and they did well on making it.

She watched the room before her bustle around and about their tasks as she waited. It wasn't long until the door of her office was knocked upon.

"Enter," commanded Violeta.

The door opened and three figures stepped in. There were two elves and one dwarf. They saluted and she nodded in return and they took their seats across the desk from her.

"Madam," they all said accordingly, all with Northern Libertadian accents.

"Bid me thy reports. Herberto, thou shalt begin," said she and pointedly looked at the elf to her far left. He nodded. He had dark brown hair and brown eyes with pointy features. He was six and a quarter feet tall and had brown eyes.

"The battling on Britone continues as before. Still. Magister Hermann is still idle in Fort Habstrast," he said. This was not the best of news, most news about Emporia wasn't good, but it could be a lot worse of news.

"Any ideas as to what he is waiting for?" inquired Violeta. "Orders it may be, we are not certain. It may be reinforcements."

She nodded and turned her gaze upon Calista, the other elf, who was sitting in the center. Calista had dirty blonde hair that fell to the middle of her back with sharp features and high cheekbones with brown eyes. She was six feet tall. Calista was not a Libertarian name, but she was born within the great kingdom.

"More Emporian fleets are moving near the coast of Luminarch. There were two large fleets, amassing around fifteen hundred ships total, we believe," reported Calista.

"Where are the larger fleets sailing?" inquired Violeta. "North, I believeth they are destined for Britone." "Whither are they now?"

"One is near the northern coast of Varenia, and the other is but to the south of Insamir's southern coast. Both hath begun from Thanatos Bay."

Violeta huffed. Then she turned her eyes to the third officer, a dwarf. He was shorter, like all dwarves and had long, almost ragged, black hair. His long black braided beard and mustache hung nearly to his feet when he was standing. He had slightly tanned skin and deep blue eyes. They locked eyes for a moment before he spoke.

"Nothing approaches from the west," he said.

Violeta raised a deep brown eyebrow at him. He stared back with unrelenting discipline.

"Edmundo?" She asked.

"What? It's the same as it hath been in all ways. I thought that I was but giving thee a chance to guess," he replied.

"Verily?"

Edmundo nodded. She looked over at the main room and pursed her lips and after a short moment she noticed something. An entire crew was not there. One table of the room was not attended by intelligence workers and was left mostly bare.

She stood slowly as she saw a dwarf approach the table and pick something up and walk off with it the way she had come. A look of absolute puzzlement was played across her face as her eyes followed the dwarf woman through the room and to a door that led out of the room. She pointed at it and asked, "What's happening?"

They looked in the direction that she was pointing.

"Duke Javier and Duchess Estela hath seen it fit that this crew is to be investigated for… treason," announced Edmundo. Calista looked at him and then averted her eyes downwards. Violeta looked at him and back at the room through the pain of glass that separated the two rooms.

"Treason?" She said, incredulous.

"Yea. What they are suspected to be charged with, I knoweth not, but I knoweth that they are being questioned. Intensely," replied Edmundo.

Violeta looked at him and then at the other two and asked, "What do ye two know?"

Herberto inhaled slowly and said, "I knoweth nothing more than Viscount Edmundo here," and gestured at the dwarf with one hand. Violeta looked at Calista until she answered.

"This is all that we were told," said Calista. Violeta looked from them, to the abandoned table and to where the dwarf woman had left.

"Well, then, goest back to thy crews," said Violeta. They all stood up.

"Err, not thee, Edmundo. Not yet," Violeta added before they began to walk out. Calista looked at Edmundo and he returned the look. Herberto and Calista briskly saluted and strode out of the room. Violeta watched them go and, once the door had shut, she looked down at her cup of tea. Still slightly steaming, almost half gone. She sat down and turned her chair to face the map room, propped her feet upon a wooden stool and picked up her cup of tea.

She was asked to work today, but she was still waking up from her dreamy sleep. She looked down into the tea within the cup and saw her reflection, slightly. Her brown hair was loose and some of it spread over her shoulders. A little bit was hanging straight down and she saw it in the corner of her eye which was brown. She tucked the stray strands behind her ear and looked up at the bustling room before her. She was six and a half feet tall when she stood up. Edmundo had sat back down by then and had laced his fingers together.

"What else doth thee knowest?" She asked, still looking at the main room. Edmundo shifted in his chair for a more comfortable position and relaxed with a sigh, also looking at the empty table.

"I knoweth what I hath been told," he replied. That irritated Violeta. Most of what Edmundo usually said irritated her. He irritated her.

"I am certain that thou doest know what thou hast been told. Now, I bid thee, speakest it unto me. Thy superior."

He stroked his beard and said, "Thou art my superior, verily, but Duke Javier is also my superior. And I'm certain that the Duke is more superior than thee."

Violeta leaned back slowly and rested against the back of the chair she was sitting in. She still wondered why Dutchess Estela had requested her at the map room that day, but she was still certain that it was important. Maybe Duchess Estela wanted to tell her about the investigation and what was happening. She sipped at her tea as she watched the mesmerizing scene playout before her. She would get up and go over the crews later, when she felt that she wouldn't mishear half of the voices that talked to her.

It took as much effort as she could muster just to listen to the three officers. Even then, she thought of what Edmundo had said and if there was some hidden message. She couldn't think of any, she didn't need him now, but he was right about nothing ever happening in the Eternal Sea. For years they had thought that Emporia would strike from behind, but it never happened. Matter of fact, they never attacked at all unless they were attacked first.

She wanted to know what the tyrant, Emperor Servius, was thinking, and most of all she wanted to know what Prince Andronicus was doing, where he was, who he was laying waste to. She wanted to hope that he was dead, but such news would spread quickly. The whole world would most likely rejoice at the death of that man, or more like a monster.

"What doth thou knowest of Prince Andronicus?" Violeta asked.

"He is still near the Ludy Kamnya Mountains," Edmundo shifted in his seat again and continued, "It is completely possible that the Kingdom of Ludy Kamnya shall fall before the new year, but not likely. Emporia takes conquests slowly, but surely."

"That shall be all. Thou art dismissed," said Violeta after she had nodded her head.

"Verily," complied Edmundo. He stood and strode out of the room. Her thoughts drifted off as the time passed by.

A knock sounded in the distance with a voice, "Madam Violeta?", as she sat there, her eyes unfocused. The knock sounded again as well as the voice, "Madam Violeta?", and she blinked this time and realized that it was her door that was being knocked upon and her name being called.

"Huh? Enter," said Violeta as she turned her chair to face the door and placed her cup on the table and the door opened. An elf woman with black hair that fell to her back and blue eyes stepped in and, well, was more in the doorway than all of the way into the room.

"Duchess Estela wishes to see thee immediately," she said, which was what Violeta was waiting for. Violeta stood and walked around her desk and to the door.

"I thank thee for telling me," said Violeta. The elf woman nodded her head and stepped out of the way and Violeta walked through the door and waited as the elf woman closed the door and led her to wherever Duchess Estela was. Violeta was sure that she'd get her answers there.

After moments of following the elf woman, the elf woman opened an elf sized door and led Violeta through. Inside was a large room that was attached to a balcony where sunlight touched the floor directly. The room was largely empty but for a large table and stone carvings of dragons were near the walls. A massive clock hung above the door that Violeta had been led through. The other elf woman continued to lead her to the balcony and Violeta was annoyed, only slightly. She could find her way to the Duchess by herself well enough, but she allowed the elf messenger to lead her there anyway.

Out on the balcony, two dragons commuted with one another. One was ten feet to the back, sixteen feet to the head and thirty five feet long. The other was nine feet to the back, fourteen feet to the head and twenty eight feet long.

The larger was covered in golden and silvery scales. Her wings were a swirling mixture of blue and silver, as were her horns.

The smaller of the two had dull gray scales covering the entirety of his torso as well as his head. His wings were golden as well as his tail and the parts of his legs that weren't the steel gray of iron. They spoke loud enough for Violeta to hear. Both had Northern Libertadian accents.

"Thou shalt speak to thy father about this," the larger of the two said.

"Yea, but he hath told me to speak to thee about it," the other replied.

"Hath he seen her?"

"I believe so. Yea, he hath seen her."

"Hath I seen her?"

"Verily. Her name is Ana. Ana Riovana." "Oh her. Yea, she is very beautiful." "Then thou wilt allow it?"

"Hath thy father allowed it? If thy father hath allowed it, then I see not a reason in denying it."

"He hath allowed it. I thank thee, Mother," the smaller hugged his wings around his mother and parted almost as quickly and his mother fondly stroked the side of his head with her wing. She noticed Violeta and the messenger and looked back at her son.

"Go now. I hath business to take care of."

"Verily Mother. I thank thee," and he moved off. Almost bounded off that is. The messenger and Violeta took his place and they bowed low to the Duchess.

"Duchess Estela, Countess Violeta," the messenger said obediently.

"Thou hast done me well. Depart from us now," said the Duchess. The messenger complied and bowed deeper before leaving. Duchess Estela looked at Violeta and gestured with a wing to come closer. Violeta obeyed and they walked off a little ways before the Duchess stopped, sat on her haunches and said, "I would suspect that thou art wondering why thou art hither today."

"Verily," Violeta partially lied. She thought she knew, but didn't quite know yet.

"That would be because there is a traitor in our midst. A spy of some sort."

"This I did not know."

"Verily, we think that we hath found a good lead to the traitor, but are not certain. Doth thee knowest why I hath bidden for thee to see me?"

"I supposed that it was to speaketh to me of this."

"Yea, a portion of it. I wish it of thee to find out who the traitor is and exploit them. Root them out for me and my husband."

"By thy bidding, Duchess Estela."

"Good. Thou shalt not report to anyone but me in this matter. No one else. Is this understood?"

"Yea, Duchess Estela."

"Thou shalt not withhold anything from me either. Speaketh to me everything thou discovers of this treachery."

"At thy bidding, Duchess Estela," said Violeta. She was beginning to be annoyed by this folly. She would do this thing. Why did Duchess Estela seem to doubt her so? She would do this and prove herself to Duchess Estela.

"That is all I needeth from thee this day. Thou art allowed to return home and resume thy time off. And another key, I doth not wish to begin this investigation before the week after this week. Am I understood?"

"Understood, Duchess Estela," said Violeta and Duchess Estela smiled warmly at her, glad.

"I thank thee, Countess Violeta. There are obvious reasons why thou art of the rank thou hast been given. If thou doest this well, I shall do my best to promote thee for it."

"Many thanks, Duchess Estela," said Violeta, who was pleased with this. She would do this task with greatness.

"That is all. Thou art dismissed to return home now. Please go home, thou hast been such a great officer throughout this past month."

"I thank thee, Duchess Estela. I taketh this task with great honor," said Violeta. Duchess Estela smiled again and Violeta turned around and left.

She returned to her room only to find someone to tell that she was going back home. She did.

She approached the closest figure to her, Viscount Edmundo and said, "I shall not be hither for the remainder of the day. I am departing for mine abode."

"Verily, Countess. I bid thee a good remainder of this day," he replied. She nodded and left for her home.

Chapter Five

The Emperor

Day 26, Rainmoon, Year 2142

Servius sat at a rectangular table in his study room, looking over sheets of paper. Reports from all over the Empire filled the table in front of him.

The room was large and mostly rectangular except for the domed ceiling. A chandelier hung from the ceiling and sconces on the wall, emitting light throughout the room. Six guards stood near the door. More guards patrolled the corridors outside the room and officers occasionally checked in on the six guards in the room. The smell of melted wax filled the air.

A cup filled with water was on the table within Servius's reach. He wore a trench coat of carmine red with a double column of silver buttons from his waist to his lower collarbone. The coat was trimmed with thick silver threads along with silver couplings. He wore a circular crown of silver with cube-like protrusions from the top that went all around the crown. The crown of Emporia.

"Legate Hartmut reporting to His Excellency, Emperor Servius Rubicon, of the public order and maintenance of the client state of Hugreovania. Public order in the valley is well and becoming better by the day. There are still minor discontents, mainly on the coasts to the west, but nothing of import, Thy Excellency."

Servius nodded to himself and placed the report to his left on a stack of read reports and picked up another sheet with his right hand from a stack on the unread letters and reports. Servius began to read off the next sheet. It caught his attention and he hurriedly held it in two hands and read carefully.

> *"Thy Excellency, Prince Adalbert has passed on. I am sure that this is another action of the Draken Confederation, but I'm not completely sure. King Wilhard's suspicion grows by the day as he thinks of the deaths that hath been befalling his children. His suspicion is that the Draken Confederation is attempting to narrow his possible heirs down to one that will accept a confederation with them. I worry that they will succeed in this. They are not far away from accomplishing this if this is their goal. Even if it is not their goal, it will eventually become it, I believe."*

Servius sat up straight at this news. He didn't know that his informant could worry. He thought that Andronicus had stripped that trait from her.

Back on topic. This was not great news. Even though King Wilhard's suspicion was focused on the Draken Confederation, he would most likely also have some form of attention on Emporia as well. The Draken Confederation could twist this to seem like it was his actions, not theirs. That would strip him of any possibility of peace between Bergsee and the Empire.

He didn't think that Bergsee, under any ruler, would ever join the Draken Confederation. That was better than nothing. He had not sent a diplomat to Bergsee for fifteen years and with this news, it might not be best to send another for a time as well. Servius was thinking that after those years ideals may have changed, but he still had to be careful and delicate with this.

He reached for his cup of water that was apparently empty. He remembered that he drank it all just before. He looked at the nearest guard, who was a legionnaire, not that there was any indication of rank for Servius to see, but that Servius heard his rank earlier. Primis' and legionnaires did not have any identifying marks like other ranks did.

He picked up his cup and tipped it, the top toward the man and said, "Legionnaire."

The guard looked towards him and down at the proffered cup and walked towards him and collected the cup and walked back to the door and opened it. He poked his head and left arm out of the door. When he stepped back in and closed the door, the cup was gone and he returned back to attention at the door.

He waited for a moment before the door was knocked upon and a guard opened it slightly. He then opened the door enough for a servant to enter, carrying a pitcher and his cup. The servant had taken the pitcher to refill it. Apparently, he had drunk the last of the water while she was gone.

She had long blonde hair, almost a white, and light skin. She set the pitcher and cup in their customary place on the table, really where there was no paper near him, and bowed to one knee.

"Thou art dismissed," said Servius.

"At thy bidding, Thy Excellency," she said and left the room. Servius reached for the cup and another page. The last page. He took a swig from the cup and held the page up to his face. He put the cup back down and began to read.

> *"Thy Imperial Excellency, I, Praetor Balint of Senka Island Province, regret to inform thee of yet more civil raids…"*

Servius inwardly groaned. This man along with this province was already on Servius's nerves. One would think that they would just be content with what had been given to them. This part of all of the reports was supposed to be at the forefront of this task. How on earth did it get at the back?

> *"… along the borders and roads out of the Senka Forest. With this report, I should wish to ask of His Excellency that four shipments of food be sent in earnest."*

Servius stared at the words for a long moment before taking in a deep breath and laying the report down to his left with disdain. There had been 'civil raids' there for, well, since he could remember.

He took the report from Praetor Balint and placed it at the top of the stack. He looked at a small stack of letters and reports that had come in today. Many of them were only reports of movements and progress. Others were invitations and letters. He looked around for a pen and placed one atop the stack.

He picked up the small stack of papers and put them down on a cleared portion of the desk. He drank what was left in his cup of water. He put the cup back down, picked up the separated paper along with a blank sheet of paper and pen he had just set down. He scanned over the report from the praetor and began writing on the blank paper:

> *"Praetor Balint of the Province of Senka Island. Thy request shall be granted. More men shall be sent to thy command, but this rabble must be destroyed. If this issue persists, thou shalt be stripped of thy station and I shall find another to take the governance of the Province of Senka Island. Emperor Servius Rubicon of The Emporian Empire, Emperor of Emporia and her client states."*

He finished and folded the paper into thirds, opened the top right drawer and picked out an envelope. He opened it and placed the paper inside and closed the envelope. He flipped the envelope to face up and wrote:

> *"Message for Praetor Balint of the Province of Senka Island."*

He closed the drawer, flipped the envelope back over and reached for a tray with a red candle that was mostly burnt down, red wax pooled at the base of the candle. A wax seal stamp with the imperial sigil on its base lay next to the tray. He picked up the tray and poured some wax on the envelope, he put the tray back down and picked up the stamp. He stamped the wax to the envelope and placed the stamp back down.

He then picked up another paper and began to write:

"Master Jamie, I charge thee with the task of transporting five shipments of provisions to Senka Island and the inventory of such. Before thou dispatch these shipments, report to me.

Emperor Servius Rubicon of The Emporian Empire, Emperor of Emporia and her client states."

He then folded the paper into thirds and grabbed another envelope and placed the folded paper into the envelope and put it back onto the table face up and wrote:

"Message for Master Jamie of the Imperial Provisions Reserves."

He would write up a draft for a proposal of peace with Bergsee another day. He stood with the envelopes in hand and walked toward the door and the guards saluted and bowed their heads and fell to one knee as he approached.

"Legionnaire, bid servants take the pitcher back to the kitchen and get me a messenger in the east-wing garden balcony," said Servius.

"At once, Thy Excellency," the guard responded in a young tenor voice with a Praetorian accent. He was shorter than Servius, but not short. His eyes were a dark blue on his light face.

He bowed again and turned on a heel as the other guards did as well. They all moved out of the way of the door and one opened it as well. Servius walked out of his study and into the corridor. The guards followed him into the hallway, as did more that were prowling outside the study. The sound of boiled leather padding the guards' steel boots thudding upon the stone floor filled the corridor. More guards were stationed around the palace and as he and his personal guard marched through the corridors they saluted and bowed their heads and fell to one knee. As was proper.

These men weren't just regular soldiers that were given the station of guarding the palace. They were a whole other class of soldier than the swordsmen in city garrisons, armies and fort garrisons around Emporia. They wore carmine capes of gambeson, trimmed with wool, that tied around the neck and fell down the shoulders and back. The bottom of the capes hung just above the ankles. The sigil of the Imperial Guard dawned upon the front of their left shoulder holding their capes around their necks and shoulders, a silver crown that stood out from the steel of their armor.

Each man had a sword at his left hip and a mace along with a half-gallon sized water skin at his right and all soldiers of Emporia, whether they were Imperial Guard or manning a garrison or marching with a legion or sailing the vast seas, were all trained to use their right hand as their sword hand. Their dominant hand. Even if they were born and raised using their left hand, they were later trained to use their right. As was proper.

All of the Imperial Guards he and his entourage passed stood at attention with their hands clenched in a fist and held at their heart, saluting him as he passed. They would also kneel to him. As was proper.

They were all equipped with large rectangular shields; or tower shields; same as all other Imperial Guards, Swordsmen, and Spearmen. The shields bowed towards the man that held the shield, encompassing the soldier a little farther. They held the shields perpendicularly with their forearm and hand, one strap was near the inside of the elbow and the other near the wrist. Their hand clenched a handle on the shield. They held their arms at ninety degree angles, their upper arm was parallel with their torso.

The shield was forty inches in length and three feet in width. The front of the shield was covered with V-shaped lips that pointed at the center and went up and outwards to the edges of the shield. These were to help deflect arrows. A steel boss was at the direct center of the shield. The shield was made of a sheet of interlocking wood; five sheets of wood, which were two millimeters thick, were checkered upon one another. One sheet placed vertically and the next being placed horizontally and then repeated. A paper thin sheet of dragon steel covered the outside of the shield and was painted carmine in color. The shield was then rimmed with a paper thin band of dragon steel. The V-shaped beads were painted a silver paint.

They walked through a courtyard. The sun was high in the sky, just east of noon. Pathways were squared with one another through squared off gardens of trees and underbrush. Only good looking underbrush was maintained in these small garden spaces. A fountain was in the center of the courtyard, tall and elegant.

Pillars held up cantilevers with rooms atop them, some balconies. Underneath the cantilevers were doors and Imperial Guards patrolled there. Occasionally a pair of guards walked through the courtyard. When Servius came near any Imperial Guards, they saluted with fists to hearts and kneeled as the regular.

Their armor was made of steel plate and mail that were separated into sections; the top section was a steel plate, the next section was mail, repeat. All the way to just below their navel. Then it was attached to faulds that came down to just above their knees.

The faulds were long steel strips, one inch in width, attached to each other by leather. Their rerebraces and vambraces were similar to scale armor, but were more square or rectangular plates. The top plate was on top of the plate below it and so on. An angled couter was worn on the elbow. Cuisses, and greaves were the same in design as the rerebraces and vambraces. Angled poleyns were worn on the knees. They wore gambeson armor underneath their main armor. Not only as cushioning against the weight of the heavy armor, but also to keep them warm in the cold and add extra armor. Though it kept them warmer, it did not have too much of an effect when the temperature itself was warm.

He and his entourage made it to the other side of the courtyard and entered into the far east-wing of the palace. As he walked down the corridor he fixed his couplings and his collar. Then he stroked his beard and ran his hand through his hair. Alternating the papers he held from hand to hand.

He approached a door with four guards posted at it. As he approached from afar, they turned from looking at one another and stood at attention at the sight of him. As he neared, they saluted and bowed and kneeled.

"Open the door," ordered Servius.

"At once, Thy Excellency," one responded.

He opened the door and the other stood to the side. Servius turned to a guard of the rank of Tribune behind him and said, "The usual, Tribune."

"At once, Thy Excellency," he responded with a salute and a bow. The crest on his helm that was parallel to his shoulders and had a stripe of silver on the top and at the center between the top and the base of the crest. Servius walked through the door as the tribune issued orders to his men. Six guards followed him in and the door shut behind them. Imperial Guards stood guard all around. They all turned to see who had entered and saluted and went to one knee to his presence.

A man stood to the side of the door. He went to one knee and bowed his head and said, "Thou hast requested me, Thy Excellency."

"Yea. Taketh these messages to the communication office and have them take them to their proper recipients," said Servius, offering the messenger both envelopes.

"Immediately, Thy Excellency," the messenger said as he bowed at the waist again and took the envelopes and headed for the door. The guards opened and closed the door as the messenger passed through.

Servius turned to the balcony and searched. It wasn't long before he found what he was looking for. He strode towards the balustrade and rested one hand on the banister and wrapped one arm around his wife's shoulders and kissed her on the cheek.

"How wast thy morning?" She asked. Her voice was sweet and soft. Her accent was that of Corinos, but it was slowly becoming unnoticeable.

"It could be better, but let's not trouble upon trivial things. Hast thy morning been well, my love?" Servius asked. "The sunrise was beautiful. Didst thou watch it?"

"Nay. I was in my study, away from the rising sun."

The air was still this day. Banners and flags hung limp on towers and walls. His wife's name was Tryphosa. Her hair was black and fell to the middle of her back in long curls and locks and her skin was light in color. She was shorter than Servius by nearly half a foot and her eyes were green.

"Is Validus in his studies?" Servius asked.

"Verily. Thou wouldst speak with him. All he thinks of his battle and glory. Nothing else," said Tryphosa, leaning against him.

"That's not all bad. It is a great thing to seek glory in battle." "He listens not to most anything else. He speaks about Andronicus and the front as if he would will himself there if he could."

"I'll speak to him about wanting only glory, but I will not speak to him about withholding himself from it. I'm sure one day when he's older and of age, he would love to be tutored by my brother on the front."

"Please don't let him do that. Thou knowest how dangerous a battle can become."

"If he asks, I shall not forbid it. Besides, Andronicus shall be there with him. By that I mean that there would be no worry."

"I'm sure thy late father would say the same."

Servius inhaled and exhaled before saying, "My father knew the risks the same as my brother. My brother shall also knoweth the risks, and he hath learned. I'm sure of it. I shall speak with Validus about keeping his mind open and being a wise man instead of a foolish man."

"Is that the best that I'll receive from thee?"

"Yea, it may be that thou wouldst course him into wishing to stay away from the fighting, but that is thy discussion with him. Not mine."

"Surely. I thank thee for that much."

"Shall we go see him now, I hath nothing to do for the moment?"

"Yea, I hath seen my share of nature for this morning. The rest shall wait for the sunset."

They turned from the balcony and started back the way he had come. The guards opened the door for them to pass through. The guards that followed Tryphosa around followed them as well as his own guards. The corridors rang with the sound of marching soldiers. It was glorious to be heard.

They reached the courtyard he had passed through earlier and walked along the outer path, along the pillars and cantilevers. Guards that walked that path also saluted and kneeled before them once they had gotten out of the way of him and those who followed. Tryphosa walked by his side through this.

"It is New Sun Day in Varenia and Insamir in a month and a half. Doth thou wishest to go there and watch the celebrations? I was planning to spend about a week there for the holidays. Or holiday.

They celebrate it on different days. Quite convenient," said Servius as they walked together.

"It's not as if they would dare share the day with one another. It would start another war between them," she answered.

Servius chuckled and said, "Verily, there would be. It is why I must attend both holidays and give both kings my gratitudes and blessing. I think it would be good if thee came as well. That would spark happiness in their hearts. Maybe as well as the hearts of both the populations."

"I shall go if thou wish it of me. Though thou mayest need to introduce me to the higher class of Varenia and Insamir if I were to go."

"That could be arranged," said Servius as they entered into the palace main. Guards saluted and kneeled to their passing. He continued, "I wish for Validus to go. Therefore, he'll be stuck hither, and thither, until after then I can do that much for thee."

Tryphosa sighed and said, "So let it be done."

"Fear not for him. Yea, I grant thee, it is dangerous, but if he will learn and grow and be wise. Then there is little to fear."

"Little?"

"Yea, little,. There is always the possibility that an unfortunate occurrence may... occur, but that is a little possibility to be sure."

They continued walking through the palace until they reached their destination. The guards standing near the door and within the hallway saluted and kneeled as they saw him. Servius gestured to the door and ordered it open. The guards complied.

He and Tryphosa and a few guards entered the room before the door shut. Inside the room were two desks and sconces that burned from the walls where there weren't any books near. Bookshelves near covered the walls and where the sconces were placed were thick sections of stone between the bookshelves.

In the room were two people. One was near one desk and the other was sitting at the other desk. They both looked at them as they entered and the one sitting stood up and the other person kneeled to one knee and bowed. The one that kneeled spoke first.

"Thy Excellency," the man said in an older and wizened voice with a Praetorian accent. The other simply stood and waited his turn. Servius turned to the speaker.

"Master Veraxus, leave us for a moment," commanded Servius.

"At once, Thy Excellency," the man stood and made way to the door. Servius and the others had stepped out of the path to the door. The man had slightly wrinkled features. He had brown hair that contained streaks of gray within and a smooth shaven face. His eyes were a deep blue. He wore silk clothing of carmine and silver threads. The main thread was carmine with silver stripes near the shoulders and designs atop the shoulders as well.

As he left, Servius turned back to the other man in the room. The other smiled at him and strode towards him. He was of a height with Servius and looked very similar too. The main defining features were a younger face and a different taste in fashion. The younger wore imperial clothing, a carmine and silver silk clothing that was inlined with wolven furs. He also wore a cape of carmine and silver also inlined with furs.

"Father," the young man said. He reached out with his right hand and arm. Servius did the same and they grasped arms and wrapped the other arm around each other. Validus looked just like Servius, but younger. His facial hair was almost finished coming in full. The last of the stragglers withering away into smooth and refined hairs. He was six feet tall.

"Son. How goest thy studies?" Servius asked as they finished their embrace.

Validus grinned as he said, "Well enough."

Tryphosa waited patiently as Validus moved from Servius to her and said, "Mother."

They embraced and kissed each other's cheeks in greeting. Tryphosa had to stand on her toes and Validus had to lower himself for it to happen.

"For what do I owe this pleasure?" Validus wondered as he grinned at them.

"Thy mother," said Servius, paused, turned from Validus to Tryphosa and continued, "Love, leave us if thou wouldst. I should like to speak to Validus personally."

Tryphosa nodded and stood on her toes to place a kiss on his cheek before leaving for the door and exiting. Servius turned to his son and gestured to go further into the room near the desks. Validus complied and they walked towards the desks, he went to the desk he was near before and Servius walked for the other desk.

"What was it that thou wished to speak about, Father?" Validus inquired.

Servius turned a book around and looked at the cover which read, 'The First Great War: Part One'. He looked at the top of the book and saw a bookmark.

"Thou saith, 'well enough', hmm?" said Servius.

"Yea."

"What hast thou been studying?"

"The very book that thou art fingering," Validus gestured at the book. Servius looked at him and back at the book. He opened the book at where the bookmark was and picked up the book to read where they were, though Validus answered before he found it out. He said, "We had barely begun the fall of The Great Montefort, very interesting."

"Ah, the fall of The Great Montefort. I think I remember this battle. It was where King Napplemon took his last stand. A terrible last stand if I remember correctly."

"Yea. A man can learn much from the histories. Especially when the people in the histories commit stupidity."

"Yea, thou wouldst learn from all of thy predecessors." "As I do."

Servius turned from looking at the desk, which was covered with books, placed the book back down and turned to face him.

"Thy mother is worried that thou wishest to go to the front in Drakenmor when thou art... prepared enough perhaps?" Guessed Servius.

"I suppose that she would hath probable cause to worry. I intend to do exactly that. As for being prepared enough, that is slightly true. It's mostly because she has begged of me to stay this long," confided Validus.

"Well, I told her that if she wanted to change thy mind, that she would hath to speak to thee and do her best. I, though, should wish for thee to come with me and thy mother to Varenia and Insamir for the New Sun holiday."

"Surely," said Validus.

"Very well. After then, thou mayest go to the front if that is thy wish."

Validus nodded and said, "As thou wish it of me, I shall."

"Excellent," said Servius as he smiled at Validus and strode for the door and continued, "Be clear minded in thy studies. I'll see thee later."

"For a surety, Father. I bid thee a great day."

Servius reached the door and the guards opened the door as Servius turned around and said, "I bid the same to thee, Son."

Validus was sitting in the chair, leaning forward with his fingers laced before him on the desk. Servius turned back to the door and stepped out, the guards followed. The master was standing to the side, patiently waiting. Servius looked at him and he looked up from his thoughts and bent his knee.

"I thank thee, Master Veraxus. Thou art allowed to continue thy teachings," said Servius.

"The honor is mine, Thy Excellency," said Veraxus, bowing to him. He walked into the room. The door shut behind him. Servius looked at his wife and made for her. The Imperial Guards that were his personal guard formed up behind him as he walked. She smiled at him and he smiled back.

Chapter Six

The Storms Pride

Day 01, Elvenar, Year 2142

"I hath brought that report for thee, Thy Highness," a dragon with marian blue and brown scales said. His eyes were light blue, his horns were marian blue, and his wings were brown. He was fifteen feet to his head, ten feet to his back and twenty five feet long. He had a Varenian accent.

"And that is..." Valerian urged after a moment of waiting. He too had a Varenian accent. His scales were royal blue with accents of cobalt blue on his shoulders and the inside of his front legs. Accents of midnight blue were at the base of his horns and in two stripes, one down each side of his face to his nostrils, his horns were midnight blue as well. His wings were royal blue and his eyes were cobalt blue. He was sixteen and a half feet to his head, eleven feet to his back and thirty three feet long.

"The mission was a success. Noble Bogomil has passed." "Good. Speak no more of this..."

"It shall be done, Thy Highness."

Valerian stifled a growl. He wasn't finished before the idiot complied. "Thou art dismissed," he said.

"Surely, Thy Highness," the dragon bowed and left. Valerian exhaled slowly, containing his irritation. He turned around and left the small room that they were in.

He could still see the informant leaving, ever so casually. That irritated him even more.

"Bad tidings?" Teadora, his courtier, asked with a Varenian accent. He looked at her.

She had silver scales with two stripes of rose red scales reaching from her eyes to her wings, one down each side of her neck. Her wings were silver as were her horns. Her eyes were gold. She was sixteen feet to her head, ten and a half feet to her back and thirty feet long.

"Nay. It was good tidings."

"Truly? It doesn't look like it."

"It was," she looked at him, almost disappointed. He sighed and said, "Why must it be him? What was wrong with Trandafir? She did her job perfectly. With no complaint and didn't act as if she were amazing in her feats."

"She was too good."

"That doesn't make any sense. It was her job to spy, but for me."

Teadora sighed and said, "He's not that bad, only give him a chance."

"I hath done so. I am. He's only an idiot, or at least acts alike to one. An extremely stupid one. What made thee think that he's better than Trandafir?"

"Please stop saying that name," she said. Valerian conceded and nodded.

"Let's walk," he gestured with his head and she stood. They walked side-by-side through the Varenian palace in Puteoli. The stone was mostly dark gray with veins of a lighter gray in some places.

"Thou..." Valerian sighed and said, "thou don't like Tran..." he shook his head and continued, "mine old informant, so, why doest thou like this new one?"

"His name is Traian, for one, and I like him because he is someone who shan't betray us."

"But, is he not a spy? If he's exquisite at his occupation, wouldn't that mean tha..."

"He is someone we can trust. Trust me with this. Please," she pleaded, giving Valerian a pleading look. Valerian looked at her, sighed again and nodded. He looked forward again and she said, "Besides, he is very good at his occupation, if that was thy concern."

"That wasn't my concern. That was part of the foundation of my concern. My concern was that if he is as good as thou sayest, wouldn't that mean that he is not much different than Trandafir?"

"It's that name again."

"My apologies, but it is only easier to say her name than to say, 'mine old informant'. Why doest thou dislike the name?"

She looked at him for a moment before saying, "I'm only concerned for thy safety, that's all."

"Mmm," he hummed. She stepped closer to him to where their wings touched. He looked at her and she smiled warmly at him. That made him smile back and he stopped, she stopped with him and he tapped his snout to hers. "Thy beauty never ceases to captivate me."

Her smile broadened and she tapped her snout to his snout and she asked, "Shall it ever?"

He chuckled and said, "Perhaps not."

"Perhaps?" She did her best, which was very good, to look betrayed.

He chuckled louder and said, "What's wrong with what I said?"

"What doest thou mean by, 'perhaps'?"

"I suppose I mis-spoke. Nay, it shan't ever leave thee," he said. She dropped the facade and smiled again. After a second, he said, "We've stopped in the middle of the corridor, blocking the way."

"Then that's the way it shall be."

"Oh, surely," he said with a chuckle. There was a moment's silence and Valerian remembered what he had asked her earlier, and realized that she hadn't actually answered. "Yea, thou art beautiful, but thou never answered my question from earlier."

A look of confusion came upon her face and her eyes searched for what it was that she was missing. "What doest thou mean? I did answer thy question. Thou asked why I disliked thine old informant."

"I did ask that, but I also asked what made thou trust... Traian so much. Where didst thou find him?" He asked. He had forgotten the name there for a moment.

She didn't answer for a second before saying, "Why doest thou ask?"

"I'm only curious where thou found such a good spy."

"It was a... A-uhh thing my mother wanted me to do," she said. Teadora had averted her gaze forward and down and she looked back up at him once she was done talking. Valerian had watched her and he didn't believe a single word she had said.

Not that it wasn't plausible, or that it couldn't be true, but that he just didn't like it. Therefore, he kept the thought and feeling to himself.

"That's an odd thing. It was my mother that had me get in touch with my previous informant as well. Motherly love I suppose."

She snorted and said, "Obviously."

A dragon bounded into the corridor that they were in, looked both ways, spotted them and trotted up to him saying, "Thy Highness. King Victor wishes to see thee immediately," and the dragon bowed to him.

The dragon had white and midnight blue scales competing for his body. The white controlled his front side and most of his right side. The midnight blue scales controlled the rest. His wings were a dark blue shade just lighter than midnight blue as well as his horns. His eyes were an icy blue.

They had stopped and Teadora looked at him with contempt. "I knoweth that. Tell my father that I shall see him shortly," said Valerian.

"Verily, Thy Highness," the messenger bounded out of their way to do as he ordered.

Teadora watched him go as they started walking again. Valerian watched her and said, "Why doest thou look at servants so? What hath they ever done to thee?"

"They... they're servants," she replied, innocent.

"That they are, but what wouldst thou do without them? What could thou doest without them?"

"I could still live my life without them. I don't need them to stay alive. I'm a dragon, and much more, a Varenian. Some human or something may need servants to live, but me? Nay."

"Is that so?"

"Verily. Why else would I saith it if it weren't so?"

Valerian shrugged his wings with a smile. After a moment of silence, Valerian said, "I should speak with my father. I hath been delaying it for hours now." He looked at her. She looked back and sighed.

"Surely. Go, go. I'll find something to do whilst thou art speaking with thy father."

He smiled at her fondly and she returned the smile. "I'll see thee then," he reached his head over and tapped his snout to hers. They held the contact and eventually began rubbing their heads together, purring softly. Valerian broke the contact and said, "I pray a good day upon thee until then."

"I shall. Now, thou shouldst be with thy father by now. I'll be in my room, if not, I'll tell my guards where I'll be."

"So I should," he stepped away and began to walk towards where his father should be, or at least where he thought he should be. Teadora went her own way.

He trotted through the palace and passed a guard patrol. They bowed their heads and said, "Thy Highness." He continued past them and for his destination.

It did not take long for him to reach his father's study. Six guards were posted by the door.

The first guard was completely steel gray scales with steel gray wings and horns. His eyes were a bright gray.

The second guard had amber scales for the majority of his scales. His back, horns and wings were orange. His eyes were bright yellow.

The third guard had steel gray scales with two stripes of water iron scales, starting from the tip of his snout and ending with his front talons. His wings, horns and eyes were steel gray.

The fourth guard had cobalt blue scales that contested with steel gray scales. The cobalt blue scales dominated the center and majority of his scales and the steel gray scales covered his head, part of his neck and most of his tail. His wings were royal blue as was his eyes. His horns were steel gray.

The fifth guard had blood red scales with accents of steel gray near his lower jaw, on his back near his wings and on his left front leg. His wings were blood red as were his horns. His eyes were brown.

The sixth guard was complete in scarlet scales with small stripes of steel gray on his sides and underbelly as well as a few on his thorax. His wings were scarlet and his horns were as well. His eyes were steel gray.

"Thy Highness," the lead guard said as he bowed his head to Valerian.

"Thy Highness," the other guards said, quieter than the first guard had said it, and bowed their heads to him as well. They all had Varenian accents, as they should.

"Is the King within?" Valerian asked as he stopped before them.

"Verily. He's been expecting thee for some time," the first guard replied.

"Let him know I'm here now."

"At once, Thy Highness," the first guard said and turned to look at the sixth guard.

The sixth guard turned around, opened the door slightly and poked his head inside. Valerian waited for a moment until the guard pulled his head out of the door and it closed. "His Majesty says that thou must wait."

"Wait?" Asked Valerian incredulously. "Yea, mine apologies, Thy Highness."

"Don't apologize to me about it. Tell me why. Hath he not been waiting on me?"

"He didn't specify anything, Thy Highness, he said only that thou must wait."

Valerian sighed and sat, curling his tail loosely about him. The guards made eye-contact with the one across from them. Valerian stared at the door.

It was made of mahogany and was banded with dragon steel. It was a regular door other than those features. The doors in Varenia, at least the palace doors, were made of mahogany, but were rarely bound with dragon steel.

As time passed, his eyes unfocused as did his mind. He got to thinking of his conversation with Teadora, which led him to other conversations that he had with her. All of the problems she had had, and still has.

He thought of why she hated Trandafir so much, or why it seemed that she hated her so. She had never given a reason why and when he asked her, she evaded the question. Whether it was by asking her own question, answering the wrong question, so to speak, or just didn't answer at all.

Nor did she ever give him a direct answer when he asked about Traian, granted, he never asked about him too much. He had thought about this many times before. He was beginning to become suspicious, very suspicious.

He blinked a few times, refocusing his attention onto the present. Nothing had changed. The door was still shut, guards still sat in their customary positions and avoided eye-contact with him.

He glared at the door. His father was really going to make him do this? Sitting there like a fruit that had fallen too far from the tree.

More time passed silently as he waited for his father to let him in. He knew, or at least was very sure about it, that his father wasn't doing anything, but was being petty at the moment.

He had to wait on Valerian, therefore, he was making Valerian wait on him. It was becoming irritating to Valerian.

After another few long moments, the door opened and his father looked at him and said, "Enter, Son."

Valerian stood and trotted forward into the room. He closed the door behind him once he entered.

There was little light within the room, no light torches. Only the light that streamed in from the outside and underneath the doors.

The darkness did not inhibit Valerian's sight, but it seemed as if there was as much light in the room as there was on a cloudy day.

There were empty nooks in the walls where thick leather parchments should be, but weren't. King Victor sat by his desk-like structure and watched him.

He had sapphire blue scales with two patches of dark green scales on the outside of his front legs. The patches stretched from where the wing attached to the body to the middle of his foreleg. His wings and horns were queen blue and his eyes were the same dark green as the patches of scales. He was seventeen feet to his head, twelve feet to his back and forty feet long.

"Thou art late," said Victor with a Varenian accent. "I know, I…"

"Why? I told thou that I wanted to see thee today, two hours ago, and yet thou wast not here."

"I apologize, I…"

"I don't want thine apologies, I asked thee a question."

86

"I was speaking with Teadora and became distracted. That is the reason as to why I am late, besides, it wasn't two hours ago, it was one hour ago."

Victor snorted and said, "Either way, thou wast late. How didst thou become distracted?" Valerian went to speak, but Victor continued, "Never-mind that, no matter how thou became distracted, it must not happen again. Thou can't become distracted as King."

"I understand."

"Doest thou? I seem to remember thou saying that a few times before and yet it still happens. Doth that not strike thee as an oddity?"

"Surely. Though, I doeth say that I understand. Not that it shall never happen again."

Victor paused for a moment, then said, "Good point. Only, attempt not to become 'distracted' again."

"I do attempt that, it's why it's distracting and makes me late."

"Don't fail in attempting it as if thou art some Brandlandan or something of a lesser sort similar to it. Thou art a Varenian." "I shall do my best, Father."

"I knoweth that thou wilt. Now to the reason as to why thou art here. The Emporian fleet is sailing north for the Drache Strait. I want thou and an army to go with it. More accurately, The Emperor hath requested of me to send an army with the fleet. I want thee to lead it."

"When do I leave?"

"In a few days, be prepared. Listen to what the Magister hath to say. He is a cunning man and thou can learn things from him. He is also steadfastly patient. If thou follow his orders, then thou wilt gain his favor. Don't ask stupid questions either. Only know that if thou don't follow his orders, he can become ruthless."

"I understand."

"Good. I hath much faith in thee with this, Valerian. Doest not fail me."

"I shan't."

"Good. That was really all I wished to speak with thee about. Go and do whatever it is until I call for thee again."

"I understand."

"So thou doest. Get out, thou art dismissed if that's what thou wanted thou to hear before thou finally left," he said, shooing Valerian away with his wings.

Valerian stayed where he was, only moving his head backwards and eyeing his father with a questioning look. After a second of the look he turned around, keeping his gaze on his father until he had turned fully around.

"Oh, I won't be there for supper this evening. Expect that," said Victor.

Valerian turned his head around to look at his father before nodding and saying, "Very well." Valerian opened the door and walked out, shutting the door behind him.

"Thy Highness," said the guards. Valerian trotted past them and for a destination that he had not yet had in mind. He thought as he made his way through the palace and made up his mind. He was going to see his cousin. First though, he would tell Teadora where he was.

She made it a point to know where he was, or where he was going. He didn't know why, but she wouldn't stop asking and complaining about it until he finally gave in and did as she asked.

He wandered through the palace until he arrived at Teadora's room. Two guards were positioned outside the door.

The first guard had blood red scales with accents of steel gray scales in a scattered pattern on her left side and a little bit on her right side. Her wings were blood red and her horns were as well. Her eyes were carmine red.

The second guard had reddish brown scales with several spots of dull gray scales; one on her head between her horns and others were oval-like formations down her sides. Her wings were a dull gray and her horns were reddish brown. Her eyes were steel gray.

They were speaking with one another before Valerian turned the corner that led to the room. They sat at attention as he approached and, once he was close, said, "Thy Highness."

"Is my lady within?" Valerian asked as he slowed, getting nearer.

"She has decreed to not be disturbed, Thy Highness," said the first guard.

Valerian looked at her for a second then at the door. He then asked, "Does that exclude me?"

"She did not specify anything other than that she was not to be disturbed, Thy Highness."

"She isn't sleeping is she?" "I'm not sure, Thy Highness." "Did she sleep well last night?" "I believeth so, Thy Highness."

"Could thou seest if she is sleeping or not? I deeply wish to see her for a brief moment."

The guards looked at one another for a split second, worry showing on their faces. The first guard turned to open the door and Valerian said, "Never-mind that. I suppose that it is better to not take the risk. I only ask that when thou seest her again, or when she emerges from her room actually, that thou shalt tell her that I am with my cousin."

The guard relaxed visibly and the first guard said, "It shall be done, Thy Highness."

"Good."

The guards bowed their heads and Valerian trotted off for his cousin. He knew that he was somewhere within the palace, or at least the city. He hoped it was the palace.

He trotted past a cave opening and a female voice called out, "Valerian!"

Valerian stopped, back tracked to the opening and looked into the room, which was a lounge area. Stalagmites and stalactites protruded from the floor and ceiling of the lounge room. It was a minor lounge area, so it had no real name.

Within the lounge area were two dragons.

The first had admiral blue scales that covered most of her body. Sapphire blue scales covered her underbelly and thorax as well as a diamond shape between her eyes and horns. Her wings and eyes were admiral blue, her horns were sapphire blue. She was seventeen feet to her head, eleven and a half feet to her back and thirty five feet long.

The second dragon had dull brown scales with tan scales that ran down her back, back of her neck and sides. Her wings were brass as were her eyes. Her horns were tan. She was fifteen feet to her head, ten feet to her back and twenty seven feet long.

The first dragon motioned with her wings for the other dragon to leave saying, "Go. I wish to speak with my brother privately."

"At once, Thy Highness," the second dragon said, bowing her head and trotting to leave the room. Valerian had no interest in speaking with his sister, so he turned to leave as well.

"Valerian! Come back here!" His sister called out. Valerian half ignored her and sauntered off.

A padding sounded behind him and before he could turn around to look, a young dragonet jumped onto his tail and began running up his back.

At first, he was turning his head around casually, expecting to see his sister. Now he snapped his head around to see the little dragonet, which was now in the middle of his back.

He snapped his head back, clamped his jaws around the body of the dragonet and lifted it off his back. He held her in an awkward position; her wings were unfurled yet pinned to her sides. She squirmed in his mouth as he turned around and trotted back to the opening.

He stopped in the entryway of the lounge area and gave his sister a look. The dragonet had been trying to bite onto his lower lip, with success, while growling. It sounded like a playful growl only because she was still young.

His sister looked back with a relaxed expression and said, "Thou can either speak with me or spend the rest of thy day tempering that storm thou hast got in thy mouth."

Valerian didn't move for a second, inhaled deeply, and trotted into the room and next to his sister. He shook his head, releasing his lip from the dragonet's mouth, and dropped her on the ground next to her mother.

She hit with a dull thump, landing on her talons. She stopped for a moment, getting her bearings straight, then looked around, saw him, and darted for him. She was about the size of Valerian's head, even longer so.

His sister's right front leg snaked out and snatched her. "Control her, Veronica, or something," said Valerian, back stepping away from the two.

"I control her, enough," she held the dragonet down with her front talons, she had a Varenian accent. The dragonet continued to squirm to get out of the grasp. Veronica growled low and the dragonet stopped and relaxed, looking abashed.

"Good," said Valerian. He turned to leave.

"Whither to doest thou think thou art going?" Veronica asked.

"Out. I hath another destination in mind," Valerian said as he trotted to the exit.

"I'll send her after thee again."

Valerian stopped, turned around, looked at her and asked, "Again?"

"Again. As I said earlier, I control Lacramioara, enough," said Veronica as she shifted her hold on Lacramioara and she shifted tentatively.

Lacramioara had royal blue scales with small stripes of admiral blue that patterned down her sides. Her wings were cobalt blue as were her eyes. Her horns were royal blue. She was three feet to her back, six feet to her head and eight feet in length.

"Nay. I don't think thou possess that much control over her," said Valerian, taking a few more steps away from her.

Veronica looked down at Lacramioara and said, "Go play with Uncle Valerian. Quickly."

With those words, Lacramioara licked her chops, looked up at Veronica, then at Valerian and ran after him. She flapped her wings quickly and gained altitude. Valerian heard and turned his head around. Lacramioara latched onto his face, her wings batted against his ears and he reeled back.

Veronica chuckled. Valerian whipped his head back and forth and half threw Lacramioara off and to the ground. She rolled a couple times and stopped on her talons.

"Veronica, can I speak with thee in approximately one hour? Perhaps two? I want to speak with Constin," exasperated Valerian. Lacramioara crouched and pounced for him. She landed on his foreleg and clamped onto it with her talons and teeth.

Valerian reached down to pick her up and off his leg as Veronica said, "Constin? He's not hither."

Valerian pulled Lacramioara off with some effort and plopped her down in front of him. She tried to get up and attack him again, but held her down with his front talons. She squirmed more to get out from under him. He laid down and asked, "He isn't?"

"Nay. He was, but he left this morning."

"He did?"

"Verily. I wished to see him, speak with him, but I couldn't find him until some servants and guards said that he had left early this morning."

Lacramioara had stopped squirming and began to squirm again, more vigorously this time, and whining slightly. Valerian looked at her and lifted his talons. She got to her talons and stood, clawing and biting at his right front talon.

"Lacramioara, come here," said Veronica. Lacramioara didn't hear, or didn't care. Veronica sighed and said louder, "Lacramioara."

This time she stopped and looked at her mother. Veronica motioned with her right front talon and Lacramioara looked at Valerian. "Go," said Valerian, gesturing with his head. Lacramioara gazed at him longingly then bound over to Veronica.

"Good job," said Veronica as she cradled Lacramioara and tapped her snout to her dragonet.

"So he's gone then," said Valerian.

"Yea, therefore, let us speak. When art thou to be married and have a little dragonet?"

Valerian shrugged his wings and said, "Whenever I get to it, or something."

"I hath forgotten that thou sayest that so much."

Valerian thought for a moment before realizing what she meant and said, "I suppose I doeth so."

"Therefore, what doest thou mean by, 'Whenever I get to it'?"

"I meant what I said and I said what I meant. I knoweth not."

"Thou art courting someone at this moment, art thou not? Marry her."

"Well, hear this, is it odd that she would want to speak with me after I hath finished a task, only for me to find that she is sleeping or something?"

"What doest thou mean?"

"I mean, we were speaking earlier and I needed to see Father; he wanted to speak with me; and she said that we could speak afterward. When I hath finished speaking with Father, I went to her room, where she said that she would be, and found that she was unavailable. Apparently she was sleeping, which I still don't believe, but I decided to let it go. Isn't that odd?"

"How long wast thou gone? Speaking with Father that is," said Veronica as she half played with Lacramioara.

"Ten minutes at the most, it may have been fifteen."

"Perhaps she was tired and wanted some rest. Give her only a little space to herself, Valerian."

"I doeth. She wants this and she wants that and another thing over there. It's almost as if she wants me to change my life for her."

"How so?"

"Doest thou remember Trandafir?"

"Verily. Continue."

"Well, she wanted her removed from my service because she was 'too good at her profession'. I don't see how that's a bad thing when the person in question is on thine own side. Therefore, she had her replaced by someone else. She said that she was only concerned for my safety, so I thought that I may as well let her taketh her victory and continue on with my life."

Valerian looked up from his doodling in the dirt to see Veronica looking at him with a mixture of concern and confusion on her face. After a moment Valerian asked, "What?"

"That is odd, Valerian. I may hath been pushy with my husband, but not with something like that," she said, shaking her head slightly and slowly.

"So, too much space?"

"Perhaps, too much space in the wrong direction. That is extremely odd that she would do that," she smiled at him and added, "Let's put our minds together with this and figure it out. I hath not had this sort of fun for some time now."

"Sure, but I'm leaving on campaign in a few days, so I won't be able to help very much after that."

Lacramioara popped her head over Veronica's foreleg, looked at him longingly and struggled to say, "Va-an."

It was a little squeak and Veronica said, "It's Uncle Valerian to thee."

Lacramioara looked up at her and back at Valerian and gave a little whine. Valerian sighed and said, "What was that for?"

"Thou art near a second father to her, Valerian. Is it a crime for her to be saddened by thy departure?"

"Nay, but I'm not leaving yet," Valerian finished and Lacramioara whined again. This time she climbed over Veronica's foreleg and ran over to him. "I must go. I'll return another day," said Valerian as she neared. She climbed up his front leg with some effort and reached over to his head. Valerian didn't react in time and she latched onto his left ear and began pulling. It didn't hurt too much, but was still painful.

He chuckled softly and swiped her off with his front talon of the corresponding side. She hit the ground and bound to her talons and went after him again. He crouched and chomped playfully with her.

Lacramioara bounded to her right, reared up on her hind legs and pounced for him. She landed her front talons on his lower lip and clamped on to it. He opened his mouth and she reached up to bite his upper lip, but she let go of his bottom lip to reach it.

He closed his mouth, gently, and her grip on his mouth loosened and she fell off. He pinned her down with his front talons and laid down as she bit onto one of his claws.

Veronica was smiling and she said, "Couldst thou distract her whilst I speak with Father? I'll get Sorana to get her as I'm speaking."

"Verily," said Valerian as he played with Lacramioara. "I thank thee," said Veronica as she stood and left.

Lacramioara shifted and stopped suddenly, watching Veronica leave. Valerian let her watch. Lacramioara whimpered and Veronica stopped, turning her head around and said, "Stay here, Dear. Wait here for Sorana."

Veronica finished and left. Lacramioara tried to follow her, but Valerian stopped her with a talon, picked her up by her tail with his mouth and pulled her closer. She roared and growled at him and tried to follow Veronica again.

"Nay, Lacramioara, thou must stay here with me," said Valerian and blocked her path by unfurling a wing. Lacramioara stopped and looked at the wing, beginning to whimper. Valerian nudged her with his snout and she stopped for a moment. He nudged her again and she attacked him this time.

She climbed onto his face and bit onto one of his horns. He shook his head back and forth, throwing her half off his head.

She clung to the side of his head, gripping onto his horn and ear on his right side. He rolled to his left and onto his left side. Lacramioara was growling softly.

He lay on his left wing with his right wing furled near his body, slightly unfurled in royal posture. His mouth was open and nudged Lacramioara around. Every once in a while, he closed his mouth playfully.

They played with one another for some time before the dragon that had left before, the one Veronica had shooed away, entered and bowed saying, "Thy Highness."

Lacramioara stopped, looked at her and Valerian said, "Look who it is. Who is it?" Lacramioara hummed with content. Valerian laughed and said, gesturing with his head towards Sorana, "Go with her."

Lacramioara looked at him and whimpered, taking quick breaths in and out.

"Young Lady," Sorana bowed her head to Lacramioara and she looked back at her, blinking. Valerian watched for a second, then nudged Lacramioara with his snout to get her going. She snorted with dissatisfaction and looked at him.

He smiled at her look and said, "Go on. Doest not act like I hath not played with thee for the past half hour or so."

She half growled half hummed and took small steps backwards, looking between them both. After a moment of this, she suddenly turned and tried to burrow herself underneath Valerian's right front leg. She half hid between his front legs, pressing against his thorax.

"Lacramioara," Valerian looked down at her. She looked up at him and whimpered at him. "Thou must go. I'll see thee tomorrow," he smiled down at her gently. He lifted his right front leg and bent it in, exposing her.

She stepped away from him with a small step and seemed to deflate. He gestured with his head for her to go to Sorana. Lacramioara made a jump toward Sorana and walked the rest of the way.

Sorana crouched and lowered her head next to the ground. Lacramioara stopped, looked at Sorana and, looking as sad as she could, she looked back at Valerian.

"Enough of that. Go on, all shall be right," Valerian gestured with his head to go. Lacramioara grumbled and went to leave, stopped and decided to jump onto Sorana's neck and onto her back.

Once she had taken her spot, Sorana bowed her head to Valerian and said, "Many thanks, Thy Highness."

Valerian nodded his head to her while Lacramioara curled up on her back. He watched them go, shifting to a better position to lay.

Chapter Seven

Most Is Quiet On The Northern Front

Day 06, Elvenar, Year 2142

The sky was slightly cloudy on this day in the north. The wind was a simple breeze in Fort Virgiliu. Silver and carmine streamer banners flapped feebly atop wall towers.

High Prince Andronicus was standing in the top room of the command tower of the fort, looking across the landscape outside the fort. It was mainly flat with a little amount of hills that were small enough to be missed on a first glance. Tall grass swayed with the breeze, flourishing the best they could from the small storm that had come through almost two weeks before.

The courtyard below was bustling with movement. Garrison soldiers marched in formation and practiced different formations. Moving from one formation to another formation. Soldiers with horns patrolled the walls. Fort Virgiliu was built like all forts, or similar like all forts. Some forts would look the same, but were not really ever direct copies to one another.

Walls surrounded the buildings of the fort. The central tower was near the direct center of the fort, like all other forts. There were two towers for every fort gate. The gate would be directly between the two towers that guarded it. The gates were made of wood, but were cased and reinforced by dragon steel.

Wall towers that were built into the walls were spaced out at every one hundred thirty feet. When the distance between a gate tower and a wall tower was within one hundred thirty feet, the difference was split between the two towers nearest the tower that was too close to the gate tower. The walls and towers had roofs to cover the tops of the walls and towers. Streamers were mounted upon the towers, but not the walls. At the top of the wall towers and gate towers were scorpions. Two scorpions faced outside the fort and two faced inwards with one facing to its left and one facing to its right. This was the same with every wall and gate tower in the fort.

The walls stood at thirty feet tall and the wall and gate towers stood at sixty feet tall. The central tower stood at one hundred feet tall, towering over all other buildings in the fort.

At the very top of the central tower was a large scorpion; in other words, a ballista; designed to kill dragons. It was called the fort ballista.

In all forts, there were three bell towers. In forts the main signal for battle were ringing bells. They were spaced out around the fort. The bell towers stood at seventy feet in height. The bells were made of brass and the mouth was five feet in diameter. The main flag of the Emporian Empire was mounted atop the central tower and was large enough to see from one and a half miles away. The command tower was near the center of the fort and stood at eighty-five feet tall.

Barracks, feast halls, strongholds and stables filled the rest of the surface of the fort. One building led underneath the fort where there was an extremely large supply storage. Supplies included ammunition for the fort ballista, the scorpions in the wall and gate towers, arrows for LongBowmen and arrows for the Crossbowmen. Food of many variations were stored below, as well as water.

So much rations that forts could last for a year and a half before the stores were empty. Five cohorts guarded the storage space from any perpetrators that would mine their way into the storage space. Most barracks were home to Emporian foot soldiers. There were four total cohorts of cavalry with two barracks designated to their numbers. Each barracks were two stories with the ability to house five hundred men in each story.

One large barracks, one larger than the other barracks, was designated to messengers. All long range messengers, any messenger that carries a message outside of the fort, were wind dragons since they were the fastest moving creature on earth.

Any soldier/messenger outside of being an Emporian were auxiliaries, essentially anyone that wasn't a human. Auxiliaries would never earn citizenship from Emporia, because they were not Emporians to begin with.

In order to know a friend from a foe was that dwarves and elves flew their factions banners below Emporian banners and dragons had silver and carmine tassels tied around their horns with key words as another security precaution. Though it might not work in the first place, it was still an attempt to stop spies and saboteurs.

Andronicus was looking for the return of the messenger he had sent out for Legate Dragomir. He was supposedly on his way towards a mediocre village that had risen in rebellion against Emporian rule. The dwarves of the falling Kingdom of Ludy Kamnya were being inspired by their young King Nikitovich. The mountains of Ludy Kamnya was where the bulk of the fighting was taking place.

Though the Emporian Empire was constantly winning the young king in battle and had the mountain range surrounded the best that could be done, more and more dwarves around Ludy Kamnya flocked to his calls by the day. Many were caught on their way there, many more somehow found their way into the mountains.

There were four infantry cohorts in the courtyard below. There were two cohorts facing the other two cohorts, all four were in a shield wall formation and were inching towards each other. Tribunes were shouting orders to their cohorts, urging their men on. The objective of the exercise was to stay in formation while under pressure. It wasn't long until the four cohorts met and began to push one another. Tribunes shouted out encouragement to their men to stay in formation and to push with all their strength.

Exhausted soldiers rested nearby and watched. Centurions also encouraged the men in their centuries to hold firm against the weight. They did not use any weapons, just their shields and put their entire weight behind their shields and pushed. The second row pushed the first row and the third pushed the second and so on. Each cohort was twenty men in depth and twenty-four men in width. The standards that held the banners of Emporia and the number of their cohort as well as the name of the army or fort garrison they were in were in the rear of the cohorts. The cohorts compressed against each other and men shuffled their feet and grunted in effort.

Andronicus looked back up at the open sky above and beyond. It had been hours since he had sent the message out, but he understood that it may be difficult to find a specific legion that was on the move. Andronicus waited patiently all the same.

After Andronicus was done scanning the skies once more, he looked back down at the two thousand men continuing to push and hold their formation under the pressure. They were doing well. From a first glance it would seem like it was one giant blob, but upon closer inspection one could see the crease between the four cohorts.

One main crease went down the center where the two sides had come together. Another crease was less visible, but still definable. Only definable by deliberately separating the two cohorts that were side-by-side. That crease was harder to spot and to continue to see.

A horn blew and officers began to shout out the order to halt and slowly the two pairs of cohorts fell apart from each other. Each backed away slowly from one another in an ordered retreat. After they were back at their starting positions, they halted and held formation and waited for another horn to be blown. A few minutes later, the horn blew. Soldiers rested their posture and followed their tribunes out of the center of the courtyard.

Andronicus looked back up at the sky once more and finally saw the messengers returning to the fort. He looked back down at the courtyard below. Some of the soldiers that could see over the walls and buildings were looking up at the approaching dragon.

It was just past midday now and the wind was picking up slightly, becoming a stronger breeze by the moment. It was warm in the north during the summer, or warmer than it was in the winter and when one felt the cold of the northern winter winds, one would feel much warmer in the summer and feel much better about it. What really defined if it was cold or not was whether one could see his own breath before his eyes.

Andronicus did not bear his armor this day, but stood in his gambeson under armor, which was in six pieces; leggings, a tunic, two gloves and two boots with thin leather pads at the bottom of each boot which were padded for extra comfort. The gambeson he wore was carmine inlined with silver threads.

The insignia of the House of Rubicon, two silver swords crossed with the tips of the swords pointing downwards behind a silver Emporian shield on a carmine backing. In this case it was only the two swords and the shield on his tunic.

It wasn't much longer after the dragon landed that a knock came to his door. He was still standing at the window, looking down at the courtyard. Two cohorts had been presented with blunted weapons and were in formation and ready to start the melee. He looked at the door before saying, "Enter."

The door opened and a soldier stepped in and closed the door behind him. He was wearing his armor, but not his cape. His helmet was on and at the top his helmet was a carmine crest with two silver stripes in it, one at the top and the other between the top and the base of the crest. The indication of the rank tribune, depending on whether the soldier was in a legion or garrison.

The soldier saluted and bowed at the waist.

"Speak Tribune Semtimus," ordered Andronicus, turning from the window to face the tribune. Tribune Semtimus straightened and moved his arm to his side.

"Auxilery Danut has returned from his run. Legate Dragomir is near Komsodar. He shall reach Korontsy within the month," said Tribune Semtimus.

Andronicus would have wished it to be sooner, but the rabble in Korontsy would not be going anywhere and will be dealt with nonetheless. Andronicus inhaled and said, "Very well. Thou art dismissed Tribune."

Tribune Semtimus saluted, bowed at the waist, opened the door and walked out, shutting the door behind him. If Legate Dragomir was near Komsodar, that would make sense as to why veteran auxiliar Danut took so long. He would just need to be patient until the time Dragomir arrived. Andronicus turned back to the window and looked down at the courtyard to watch the melee progress below.

Korontsy was a town, not quite a city, nearly directly between both Forts; Adi and Virgiliu and the city of Kamennoye Serdtse.

From where he stood, he couldn't make out details of the melee, though he could hear it clearly. Men grunted and communicated with their in cohort comrades.

Andronicus couldn't really see the center of the combat, but could see the edges. A soldier lifted his shield to block a strike from a soldier of the other cohort. The soldier then swung and struck the shield of his attacker. The strikes went back and forth until more men joined the fray and Andronicus could no longer see the engagement clearly.

When a soldier was hit with a stunning or dazing blow, they would lift their sword above their heads in a reverse grip and would get out of the combat as quickly as possible to avoid any more beatings. Many would yield to a well placed hit anywhere on his body. They were given orders to not strike too hard in an attempt to avoid lasting injuries.

Below a soldier tripped and another soldier from the other cohort shot in for the attack. He stepped quickly up to the soldier who had fallen and was in the process of standing back up. He lifted his practice sword and brought it down, almost gently, upon the back of the man's neck. The attacker then took a stance to defend himself from the beaten soldiers' comrades that had originally come to save the soldier. The beaten soldier finally got up, looked at the two fighting before him and walked out of the fray.

The edges of the formations usually frayed, though it was a key prospect to get rid of the fraying on the edges of Emporian formations.

Andronicus tore his eyes away from the skirmish and walked to his desk. There was a map on one wall that portrayed the world map. Another map was on another wall. The world map was on the wall directly behind where his desk was facing the door.

The other map was a magnified map of the Drakenmor front specifically, only where Emporia had captured and her borders. This map was on the wall to his left. The window that he had been looking out of was to his right when he was sitting at his desk and facing the door. He sat at the desk and laced his hands underneath his nose, and rubbed at his half bushy mustache and thought.

He sat there in thought for a time before his door was knocked upon and a voice sounded, "Thy Highness, thy dinner is prepared."

Andronicus furrowed his brow and looked out his window. The sun was setting. Andronicus shook his shoulders and readied himself.

"Enter," he said firmly and the door opened to a servant carrying a platter of food. He placed the platter down upon his desk and bowed and dismissed himself from the room. The food consisted of two slices of warmed breath with butter and mashed potatoes with gravy with a cup of water. The food was steaming with warmth and the water was cool. He ate with calm thoughtfulness. The food filled his stomach with warm satisfaction and the water balanced with it.

He finished and he pushed the platter away and laced his fingers on his desk. He wanted to push the dwarves past their limit, but he also wanted to wait until all of his enemies were before him.

The Ludy Kamnya were bottled in with no way out, a siege in other words only on a larger scale. While he waited on the Seventeenth Legion to reach their destination, he plotted on how he would best conquer the mountains. He had quelled the majority of the unrest in the conquered regions. He believed that the rest would melt away after Legate Dragomir was finished with the rebellion in Korontsy. Though, he would have to wait nigh on one month for his results. He would sit there for another time before he left for his room and slept.

Chapter Eight

The Champion Wolf

Day 13–14, Elvenar, Year 2142

Eivindr Wolf sat in gray darkness and oiled his great-axe in sullen peace. He was a dwarf from the northern coast of the Draken Confederation. Or was it western? He wasn't too sure of that. It had been a long time since he had been outside his quarters, training grounds, the carriage he would travel in and the arena's in major cities all across the Draken Confederation.

He wore a woolen shirt, that was almost a jacket, and woolen trousers. A wool cloak hung upon a peg on the wall. All were a ginger red color, the same as his hair.

He had a mustache and beard, both were braided together and came to the tip of his sternum. His hair was a mohawk with shaved sides, the mohawk stood three quarters of a foot tall upon his head. His eyes were an icy-blue.

He, reasonably, did not have his woolen gloves on as he oiled his great-axe. His woolen gloves were also ginger red in color.

His great-axe was near as tall as him, to the top of his skull not hair. The handle was made of a Drakenwood limb and was engraved with intricate carvings of the history of Eirikland. The pommel was made of dragon steel and was molded into the shape of a snarling dragon's head and was rather long and large in comparison to regular pommels.

The axe itself was double-bladed and each was a foot and a half in height, three-quarters of a foot in depth, from blade to where the axe-head was attached to the shaft. Each face of one axe-head had a different engraving and the face of the other axe-head that faced the same way of the previous axe-head mirrored it.

The great-axe lay upon his lap as he sat on a bench. Then the door opened and light flooded into the room. Though the room was now mostly lit by outside light, Eivindr was still in the shadow of a corner. The door was in fact three different sizes of doors in one. The smallest size was the appropriate size for dwarves. The next size larger was for elves. The next size of door was the entire door and was large enough for dragons. The door for elves had opened.

The light was bright to Eivindr's eyes, which were used to the dimness of the dark. The elf that had opened the door stepped inside a small amount. Darkness then retook the room where the elf's shadow fell. The elf stood for a moment as his eyes adjusted, scanning the room. Eivindr's eyes had readjusted quick enough, so he could see who it was.

The elf's name was Hallvard Dungeon and was his manager in a way. Hallvard was a guard in service to Lord Edvard and Lord Edvard would coordinate matches for Eivindr and Eivindr would fight the matches for Lord Edvard, though Eivindr didn't have a choice in the matter of match or whether he wanted to fight for him. Eivindr was a convict.

A prisoner who was given the offer of wasting the rest of his life in a cell, which wouldn't have been very long nor very lovely, or he could fight in the arena's to try and possibly earn himself redemption for his crimes and be pardoned. That wasn't going to happen though as Eivindr could see it. He would spend the rest of his life fighting and killing for the entertainment of the Draken Confederation, or any of those who could afford to watch.

"A match is for thee, on the morrow. Less than two hours before the sun reaches the horizon," Hallvard finally said to Eivindr.

He wore a hauberk with plate pauldrons, boots, greaves and vambraces. A great helm with dragon wings attached to the top of the helmet was strapped to somewhere on his armor near his right shoulder. The armor and helmet was steel lined with dragon steel. A rather heavy metal to make armor of, but very effective. He also bore a longsword at one hip.

"Pray I ask who?" Eivindr inquired.

"Thou may, though thy prayer shalt not be answered wholly. Only know that he was captured in a battle, so know that he is no civil prisoner."

"I'll be ready to fight."

"As thou must," said Hallvard, then he stepped out of the room and the door closed.

Hallvard said 'a battle', though Eivindr knew that the elf knew nothing of battle. Hallvard, unlike Eivindr, had never been in a battle before. Not a true battle anyway, Eivindr knew. Eivindr thought of who it could be by race. When he heard the word battle he thought of the Emporian Empire, though it could be a rebel force that had most likely been crushed.

Though there was no way one could have fought against the Emporian Empire and had come away more ignorant than before. Eivindr had fought Emporian soldiers on the battlefront, and they were no cowards.

Images played through Eivindr's memory. The din of battle rang softly in his ears. He sniffed, rubbed his beard and put the great-axe aside. With his free hands, he rubbed at his eyes and willed the memories away and one name came back to him. Magister Hermann.

Magister Hermann was the leader of the Emporian forces that Eivindr had fought. When Eivindr thought of the battle, he wanted to rage, it was the last battle he had fought in.

He was a Major in a Confederation army and the orders given to his General were to assault an Emporian fort. They were stationed in Britone and the fort was called, 'Fort Habstrast'.

The orders made sense when they had first been relayed; Assault and besiege Fort Habstrast as another army assaulted the city of Long-Grass and in return the forces in the fort could not reinforce the city's garrison. The smaller settlements and villages around the city and fort were also going to be raided before the main attacks. It was a small offensive.

It was said that the garrison of Fort Habstrast was low at the moment, the majority was lured out by raids. It was to be a decisive victory, until it was discovered what was actually happening. It was discovered that the raids were quelled by the fort garrison and the garrison of the fort was in return held by Magister Hermann and a new legion from Luminarch.

That news had shocked some doubt into the ranks, though it wasn't enough that it couldn't be controlled. They marched on Fort Habstrast anyways, against the judgement of all officers in the army.

When they reached the fort, it now had to be quicker than was planned. They couldn't be encircled by Imperial reinforcements if they wanted any real chance of winning and living for another day. They assaulted the fort with siege machines that they had constructed on their way to battle. Siege towers and artillery. Walls were cracked and towers did as well under the relentless siege, but the Emporians inside the fort were unwavering.

They loosed flights of arrows upon flights of arrows and scorpions shot bolts at their siege artillery. The fort ballista shot and destroyed their siege towers one by one. When dragons came in range of the scorpions or the fort ballista and they were either killed or turned away by the fort artillery.

The Imperial battle bells rang with a song of darkness and death. Eivindr had led a push through a damaged and newly cleared section of wall that was destroyed by a catapult before it was obliterated by fort artillery. Only one of seven siege towers had made its way to the wall and only wasn't destroyed there because it was behind the wall and its roof, hiding from the fort ballista, most scorpions and fire arrows.

He and his soldiers clashed with Emporian Swordsmen. The Emporian Swordsmen formed a shield wall in the breach. Banners on standards were held high above the combat. He wielded a great weapon with one head being an axe head and the other was a narrow spike, similar to a pickaxe's pick, and a long shaft. He and his dwarves battled hard with the near impenetrable Emporian formation.

Shields were split into and armor was dented and scrapped as they fought in the crevice in the wall. He had battered a man's shield back into his helmet and slammed the neighboring man's helmet with the back swing. By the time his weapon had returned next to him, the gap he had created was filled in with more Emporian soldiers. The Emporian in front of him swung his mace and Eivindr stepped back from the attack. He then pivoted his weight and swung furiously at the shields that he could see.

Around him dwarves and men fought with all their strength. A dwarf brought his great warhammer around in a great swing at near the center of a shield and knocked the man holding back into the ranks of men behind him. Not long afterwards the spot was refilled. Another dwarf was bashed into by an Emporian shield and was knocked to the ground. The Emporian darted forward with his mace and swung it down upon the dwarves helmet. It impacted and the helmet was caved in and blood ran out from inside the helmet and pooled on the ground.

Flights of arrows darkened the sky when the arrows went soaring past over-head. Eivindr attacked the shield wall and this time knocked an Emporian to the side and back swung his great weapon into another Emporian and back swung his great weapon back into the initial man, with the pick pointing towards his target. The pick punched through the armor and into the man's upper arm and struck the bone.

The swing stopped with a jolt and he couldn't actually hear though he could pretend to have heard the bone snap. The man was knocked back into his comrade as Eivindr wretched his weapon free in time to parry a strike from the nearest enemy to him.

Horns were blowing as men and dwarves fought and died with the occasional dragon that was found by the fort ballista or scorpions. The bells rang loud and almost clear over all the shouting, roaring, screaming and weapon clashes.

An arrow nearly found its mark as it skid off of his helmet. He and the rest of his dwarven knights fought and died with Emporian heavy infantry there in the breach. One could barely take a step without stepping on the dead or dying.

As Eivindr rested and his fellow knights clashed with the enemy, he could see caved in breast plates and helms. Helmets that were removed in the fighting as well as broken arms, legs and necks. Blood at times would be splattered upon armored hands and arms that held the weapon that did the deed.

Emporian capes would poke out of the bodies that covered the ground as well as green plumes of his fellows. Near to him there was a white spot among the dead that turned out to be a bone that had shot out from a man's neck.

He shook the memories out of his head and stood and picked up his great-axe. He started for a wall with a stone ledge that jutted from the wall. There was a pedestal on the ledge that he placed the great-axe upon, gingerly and with fervour.

His weapon had been gifted to him by the son of the lord whom he fought for, The Honourable Haldis Vangar. Eivindr almost found it odd, but he didn't dare question a lord nor his son.

His stomach grumbled, reminding him that the sun was setting and that he should eat. He rubbed his mustache and turned for the door. He rolled his shoulders and reached for the door handle that belonged to the door that was his height. The dwarven door.

He opened the door to a hallway with two sentries at every door. The two at his door looked at him exit and looked back, staring forward. They were elves in mail halberks and a barbute helmet.

They held a spear and shield with a sword sheathed at their side. Their shield had a steel boss and the area around the boss and a thin plate of dragon steel. The shield was oval in shape and stretched from the guard's knee to shoulder. The guard's arm held the shield perpendicular to the length of the shield.

He walked past them and turned left, towards where the mess hall was. He walked down the hallway and found himself standing before another door with another two sentries standing before him, guarding the door. They wore the same armor and bore the same weapons as all the others. They watched him approach and admitted him once he had gotten there.

He opened the door and stepped inside, closing the door behind him. Twenty others sat in seats at tables. The tables weren't long, but round with the ability of seating five at a time. The tables and chairs were made of rough cut wood and were prone to giving their occupants slivers.

Some looked up at who had entered and back down at their food once they saw him. He made his way to one side of the room where the food was served. He picked up a tin tray and a servant scooped some slop onto his tray. It was a creamy color with beans within, white beans.

Eivindr could see them. Eivindr much rathered meat instead of beans and heated milk turned into half jello, but at least he had food to eat.

When Eivindr fought and won, he got the reward of eating meat. A few good thick pieces of ham, a steak, sausages, and many other types of meat. Since he didn't fight though, he got this jelly. When he lost, well, he would most likely be dead. So, he didn't know what he would have if he somehow survived losing.

He took his food and sat at a table where another two were sitting and began eating. An elf and another dwarf. The elf was thick armed and thick legged. He had black hair that was cut short, as well as his black beard. A scar ran across his left jawline. Two of his fingers were cut short at the first knuckle. His eyes were sunken and were blue-gray.

The dwarf was also black haired and black bearded. His hair was cut at three inches from his scalp and stood straight up, being flat on top. His beard was also cut three inches from his face. A brown streak split his beard into two down the center of his chin and his eyes were brown-green. He was also thick armed and thick legged.

Eivindr didn't pay much attention to the others until he thought back to when he was looking at them. He stopped eating and looked back up from his food.

"Ye are new," said Eivindr to the two. They looked at one another and the elf nodded his head and swallowed.

"And thee?" He said in a gruff voice with the accent of Zemlian.

"I hath been hither for a time," replied Eivindr. A long time at that, or not too long. Not as long as others, but longer than most.

"How long?" The dwarf asked in a Ludian accent, which surprised Eivindr. The Ludy Kamnya dwarves were mostly under imperial control. Some found their way across the border, most stayed where they grew up. Eivindr swallowed a spoonful of the bloody rat retchings before he spoke.

"Close to ten and four years now," answered Eivindr. It wasn't very long in terms of imprisonment, but it was quite long in arena fighter terms. He took another spoonful.

"I don't suppose it would be proper or wise to share names. All they shall become are more names that shall belong to the dead soon enough," said the elf. He scooped some slop and ate it with difficulty.

"Well thought," Eivindr replied, then continued, "Thou art from Ludy Kamnya, art thou not?" The dwarf looked up and nodded his head. "Pray I ask when thou left thy homeland?"

"Only two years passed," the dwarf replied. Eivindr grunted. "How was living under Emporian rule?" Eivindr asked after another swallow of food.

The dwarf shrugged and said, "It was better than this, but no better than before they conquered my hometown. They would bring food when the thane of the town asked. The Emporian's would serve out the food orderly, but if thou crossed them in but the slightest way or if they thought that thou crossed them. They could be harsh."

"Thou hast ran away because of something they did?" Eivindr asked. The dwarf nodded and it was really just then that Eivindr saw that the dwarf was quite young. Eighteen years perhaps, maybe younger. Eivindr took pity on him and said, "I hath been appointed to a match tomorrow and if I win, I'll share some of my winnings with thee. Perhaps it'll give thee but the slightest bit of light in this dark world."

"Winnings?" The elf asked.

"Yea. When thou fight, thou shalt win or thou shalt lose. To win means that thou shalt, or should, receive a good meal. If thou lose it shall mean thy death," said Eivindr, he then scraped some of the scraps off the tray.

"I knoweth not how to fight," said the elf.

"Me neither. I'm but a poor farmer's son," said the dwarf. Eivindr looked at them in confusion.

"If neither of ye knowest how to fight then why did ye choose to fight in the arena's?" Eivindr asked.

"I didn't get a choice. I was but walking around the countryside when a troop of riders came and asked me questions of where I came from and who I was. I answered truthfully and they bound my hands and feet and took me away without another word. They brought me hither and left me in a cell," the dwarf pushed out. He sounded scared near to his death.

"I thought I would be a servant of some kind. They never said anything about me fighting. They said that I would simply serve Lord

Edvard Vangar," said the elf. He leaned a little closer and whispered, "I think they lied to me," and the elf nodded once in contempt.

"Nay, they're only waiting on thee," said Eivindr, setting down his spoon.

"Verily?" The elf asked, surprised.

"Nay! Thou wast lied to and if thou wast born with the ability to think and still obtained that ability, thou wouldst keep thy mouth shut and wouldn't complain to them about it. It'll only get thee lashed," said Eivindr, reprimanding.

"Why would they do that though?" The elf's mind was now in knots. It made Eivindr want to laugh, but he didn't want to be too harsh on them.

"Because they need fighters and thou wast of a lower birth than other prisoners and no one would care if thou wast cut to ribbons in the arena for the pleasure of the high-born," said Eivindr. The elf wilted and looked back down at his food. Eivindr was done with his food though and he stood and walked with his tray to the same wall the food was served and at the very end of the wall of food, where other used trays were placed.

He placed the tray down with the others and strode for the door. There were no guards on that side of the door, only the outside of the mess hall door. Eivindr thought that a stupid idea of whoever had thought of it, most likely Lord Edvard.

He exited and closed the door behind him and strode down the hallway to his quarters or cell, whichever one would prefer, most likely the one who was living within them. He thought that the sun was down and darkness was closing around the remaining light of day. He would sleep and in the morning he would practice for the fight.

He entered his quarters and strode for his sloppy thing of straw called a bed. He undid the buttons of his wool shirt and pulled it off and once he had reached the bed, he sat upon it. He laid the wool shirt on the ground. Underneath his wool shirt he wore a thin thread small shirt that would make wearing the wool shirt more comfortable.

He undid the laces on the linen shirt, but left it on. He pulled his boots off, they were made of wool with leather soles. Once he had removed them, he set them near the bed in an orderly fashion and he turned around to face the bed. Then he removed the leather bands that tied his beard and mustache hair together and braided and threw the leather cords upon his woolen shirt. He unbraided his facial hair so that it was loose. He grabbed the rough wool blanket and lifted it so that he may get underneath it.

He lay upon the bed as his body now felt the energy leaving him. He yawned and did not cover himself fully with the blanket. It was not winter yet, only summer. Then he slept.

He woke and shifted from his shoulder to be on his back and looked up at the ceiling above. He inhaled and yawned, throwing his legs off of the bed and shook the sleep from his head. He sat there on the edge of the bed without thought, blank. He looked down at his linen shirt and he laced the shirt back up and reached for the wool shirt and the leather cords fell off and to the ground.

The air was cool on his skin. The morning air where no sun was reaching. He put the wool shirt on and buttoned it up the front with the wooden buttons. After he had that done he moved on to his boots. He stamped them onto his feet and laced the boots tight. He yawned and stood. Today he would warm up for the fight later, but first he must break his fast. He ran a hand down his beard. First he would braid that though.

He knew how to braid his facial hair by instinct and muscle memory. Once braided he held the braids with one hand and bound the braids with the leather cords. The leather was worn and was quite old as well. Once braided and bound in place, he let his facial hair fall against his chest.

He stood and made his way to the door for his food. He opened the door and light from the hall outside temporarily blinded him. The sudden transition from darkness to light was not entirely comfortable. Once he could see enough to move around without looking like he was drunk he walked out of his quarters and shut the door.

The guard held a spear in one hand and a round shield in the other, both gilded with dragon steel. His armor was the regular hauberk with a sash of gold and scarlet linen. His helmet was open faced with a piece of metal that covered his nose and a cloak. The cloak was gold and scarlet with a hold door as the arms. The guard looked at him and when he spoke he had a Gaetan accent, "Fight today, correct?"

"Yea. Art thou off duty then?"

"I wouldn't miss it," the guard looked to the nearest guards and quieted his voice so that only Eivindr could hear before adding, "I hath heard that thine opponent is an Emporian. Great-swordsman I think."

Eivindr looked at him with an expression of half shock and half excitement. "Seriously?"

The guard nodded and said, "I hath also heard that many shall come to watch and the talk around the house of Lord Edvard is that there is a bet on thy fight between him and his son, The Honorable Haldis Vangar. I knoweth not what the bet is, but it has been the talk around hither. It has made them bitter to one another. If they weren't already bitter to one another to start with."

"I thank thee for telling me these things."

"Like always," the elf guard nodded and then said in a little bit of a louder voice, "Better go eat, it's not going to be there forever. And thou better not lose this evening, I hath placed a bet on thee," and the guards around that heard the words chuckled as well as Eivindr.

Eivindr moved on and walked down the hallway. He reached the door and the guards stopped talking for a moment and opened the door for him. He passed through and the door closed behind him. He walked for where the food was as he did all the days before. He got his food which looked the same as the day before, leftovers most likely, and a slice of low quality bread.

He sat down at a table that was unoccupied and began to eat his slop in peace. Not long after the door opened again and closed as well. Eivindr didn't look up and ripped a piece of bread and chewed on it. Not much longer after that two figures sat down at the table he sat at. It was the elf and dwarf from yesterday. Eivindr looked up as they sat and began eating their food. After acknowledging their appearance, he got back to eating his food.

"So, thou art fighting today then," said the elf. Eivindr looked at him for a second before responding.

"Art thou fighting today?"

"I knoweth not how anyone could fight when eating this slop," the elf complained.

"I do. It's called thou fights or thou dies more feebly than most. And let me tell thee now. They don't like seeing feebleness."

"Why? What would they do? Skin me after I was dead?" The dwarf challenged. Eivindr liked that retort. It was entertaining.

"Perhaps. Though that wasn't what I was thinking they would do. I was thinking that they might look to thy family to repay them for the disgrace."

"My family?!" The elf's voice cracked.

"That is what I barely said."

"Well I'm no coward, for sure," the dwarf claimed.

"Good! Keep that spirit well," said Eivindr, patting the dwarf on the shoulder. He finished his food and stood. He took the tray to its designated area and strode out of the room and into the hallway. He walked for his quarters.

Once there he strode for his great-axe upon its pedestal, glorious and splendorous in every way. Once he was standing before it he stopped and looked at it, thinking. He stood there for a while as his thoughts spun around what his life had come to and what he did. He thought of things like this often, but pushed the thoughts away when the time came. He did the same here.

He sat on a stool that was near the with his weapon and stared at the great-axe for a moment before he reached for a book that was upon the table and a charcoal pencil. There was no title on the book, only a plain cover made of dried, cracked, old leather that felt as if it were going to fall apart any time now. Perhaps by the next touch. He lay the pencil down within his reach and near the edge of the table.

He held it in his hands, only staring at it for a while. He waited until his eyes adjusted to the dark.

He opened the book to somewhere near the center. There was writing on the page he opened to and he flipped through pages to a page that had no writing upon it. He stopped on the first page that was blank and flipped back to the previous page and read what was on the page to remember what spot he was on. He then picked up the pencil and began to write within the book, which was now on the table.

He wrote for one page in the book before he stopped. He had made it a point to himself to only write one page a day. He got the book after he won his first arena fight. Every time he won, and anyone else won they would receive a certain amount of coin that they could use to their desires. It could be saved up to pay their crime debt, or they could spend it somewhere else. Like how he spent some on the book. He had bought the book for multiple reasons. He wanted to make sure he remembered how to write for the remainder of his life and how to read as well. He also had always wanted to write a book.

Once he had finished writing, he shut the book and placed the pencil on top of it. He sat there staring at the book for moments. He found himself thinking a lot more than usual and he knew the reason. It was because of what the guard had said. 'I hath heard that thine opponent is an Emporian. Great-swordsman I think.'. An Emporian Great-swordsman.

That was a rare occasion, capturing an Emporian Great-swordsman, they usually went down fighting and died in those cases. From what he remembered of fighting them. They fought like cornered rats, but with calmness and clearness of the mind and would slaughter most that came near them. He would have to be careful for the next fight, though he might not. So, not so much so like a cornered rat, but with enough skill and ferocity to literally kill a dragon, or two, or three. He knew that any Imperial soldiers that happened to be captured were not treated well, or they weren't treated well most of the time.

He never saw any Imperials during his time as a prisoner, but he did when he was a free dwarf. The Imperials he saw were ruthlessly treated like rabid dogs. He did not like Emporians, but for the rest of the Emporian Empire did not deserve such treatment. Not even Emporians that were prisoners deserved to be treated in such a way. He thought that no one should be treated in such a way.

He sat there until he blinked noticeably and shifted on the stool and decided to stand and get to his practicing. He put his wool gloves on and then walked to his great-axe and lifted gingerly off of its pedestal and, within his quarters, began to practice and warm up.

Hours passed as he practiced his forms and attacks and defenses off and on. Taking breaks every once in a while to breathe and drink water.

Before he knew it, the door to his chambers opened and a figure poked its head in and said, "Time to go."

Eivindr agreed and he brought his great-axe with him to the door. The guard stepped out of his way and he walked out into the hallway. The guard held his hand out and Eivindr gave him the great-axe. The guard took it and Eivindr was escorted to the prep rooms near the arena, where the contestants, or fighters, would wait for their turn and get prepared for the fight. All guards wore the cloak and arms of house Vangar.

After a time of being escorted by a few guards, he was shown into a narrow room. Basically a hallway that led away from the main hallway.

Inside the narrow room was a bench with two others sitting upon it by one wall and chests lined the other wall. The two within the room didn't look up as Eivindr entered, one guard following him into the room. The guard then led Eivindr to a chest and unlocked it with a key. The guard then left and Eivindr turned around and the guard handed him his great-axe who nodded once at him and winked as he shut the door. It would seem that he was betting on Eivindr as well.

Eivindr could make many rich this evening and leave others poorer than they were when they entered that day. His mind was then drawn to what the guard had said earlier that day. Something about a bet between Lord Edvard and The Honorable Haldis. What could it be? It didn't really concern him, but he still wanted to know.

He approached the chest to get his customary items. A mail hauberk and an open face helmet that had a long section down his head that allowed his mohawk to poke out of the helmet. There was a ledge where his mohawk would protrude through his helmet. He leaned his weapon against the chest and slid the hauberk on as well as his helmet.

As he was doing this, the door opened and an arena guard, similar to regular guards but for the coat of arms upon their cloaks which were forest green and black. The arms upon the cloak was an eagle that held a scroll in one talon and olive tree branches in the other. Its wings were half unfurled with its beak pointed one way, showing the side of its head. The coat of arms of Eirikland. All arena guards were enlisted directly into their kingdom. In this case, they were soldiers of Eirikland.

One of the others stood and walked towards the guard and the open doorway and the door closed behind the fighter. The way the fighter walked to the door, he almost made it look like the walk of shame. Which was quite accurate all things considered.

He may die out there for all Eivindr knew. After Eivindr had his hauberk and helmet on, he looked down into the chest to see a coat of the house Vangar. He lifted the coat over his head and shifted it onto his body. He then picked his great-axe up and sat on the bench, not too close to the other fighter, and leaned on his weapon as he waited.

Crowds roared, cheered, booed and chatted with one another as fighters fought and died on the sands and dyed the ground red with their blood. After a few minutes, another fighter entered through the door from the main hallway and prepared for her fight. Not much later, the door to the arena opened to the same guard and the fighter that was there before him stood and strode for the arena. The door closed behind him. The crowds continued their raucous and their gambling.

He stayed in his spot, unmoving, as he waited for his time. It seemed like hours passed as he waited. Though when the guard came for him, it felt as if not enough time had passed. The guard cleared his throat and Eivindr stood and walked towards the door. The guard shut the door behind them and they were in a corridor with torches on the walls. Within the corridor were more guards, several more guards, and one reached his hand out for his weapon. Eivindr complied.

They fell in around Eivindr and escorted him to the arena. They all had oval shields. At the head of the formation was a guard that wore plate armor other than a hauberk. The guard wore a great helm with wings that shot straight up, like two horns that protruded straight up from the top of the helmet.

They bore no spears, but had sheathed short swords on the small of their back. Steel clinked and the corridor was filled with the sound of marching leather and steel boots. Before long they were standing before a portcullis where light poured through the gaps. It was bright at first, but Eivindr was able to get used to it quick enough. Outside, in the arena, a voice sounded loud and clear for all to hear.

"Now be prepared for a known dwarf. A dwarf who hath been with us for fourteen years and perhaps for a longer time yet. A post soldier who hath differed to pay his debt in blood and death and scars. Welcome in, Eivindr Wolf!"

The crowd then erupted. It would seem that he was a favorite for today. The portcullis began to open and the guards parted between him and the entrance to the arena sands, creating a half-circle behind him. The guard who had taken his great-axe offered it back to him and he took it and walked out into the light and sand of the arena.

The crowd noise became more absolute once he cleared the tunnel. He knew what the crowd wanted. He held his great-axe in two hands and lifted it above his head and gave a battlecry that could almost be heard above the thundering of the crowd. The crowd grew louder at his action and he pumped his arms up and down and continued his battlecry.

It was hard to see anyone in the stands above, but that didn't concern him. He didn't care who was watching. He only knew that he would not die easily today.

The crowd died down and the speaker spoke again saying, "Now, for the contestant. An enemy to our great nation. A great enemy to the world of freedom. An Emporian captured in battle and brought hither for justice. It is hardly justice for only one to pay one's debt when there are millions and hundreds of millions of debts to be paid, but we do our justice fairly and surely. Across the arena comes the criminal to face his fate. Shall justice be done this day?"

The crowd erupted in agreement and the portcullis across the arena from Eivindr opened and a figure in Emporian armor stumbled out and staggered his way to the center, harshly escorted by a few guards who jeered and jested at his behalf. One guard held the man's weapon. Eivindr already stood in the center of the large arena leaning on his great-axe with the head down. The walls were at siege wall height.

A speaker, not the main speaker, stood in the center as well. Once the Emporian had finally reached the center, facing Eivindr, he swayed but was able to keep his feet beneath him. His weapon was then forced into his hands and he held it. His armor was immaculate, though it wasn't shining it was still splendorous. It was dirty and scratched. The carmine straw plume was tattered and stained. His cape was muddy and was ripped near the end and was clasped around his neck with a simple small steel stake, like a large pin. That wasn't right, Eivindr knew.

The armor was made of overlapping steel plates, the top overlapped the one beneath it and so on. This went down to just below his navel and then turned into faulds made of leather and steel strips. The rerebraces, vambraces, cuisses, and greaves were done in a similar fashion akin to the torso armor. His helmet was on and his face was exposed to a boney featured face. Then it clicked completely in Eivindr's mind. The poor man was famished. Starved and mistreated so severely that there was no way that he could even put up a fight.

"Are there any words to be shared before this event begins?" The speaker asked. It was loud and it echoed throughout the arena. It did not hurt Eivindr's ears, but it felt that it should. An amulet hung around the speaker's neck, who was an elf, that held a white piece of what looked like rock in a metal band. The metal was unknown to Eivindr as was the white rock like piece. Both Eivindr and the Emporian stared at one another for a couple seconds before Eivindr reached out his hand to the Emporian and spoke.

"To the victor," he left the rest unsaid.

The Emporian hesitated for one split second, looking at him with partial curiosity before reaching out his hand and grasped Eivindr's and finished, in a rasp, with a thin smile, "The spoils."

They nodded to one another and they parted as the speaker said, "And with that, let the match begin!"

The crowd cheered and booed and jeered at them. Eivindr hefted his great-axe and once they were near twenty paces apart from one another, the Emporian unsheathed his greatsword. Once the greatsword was out of its sheath completely. The sheath was taken from him rather forcefully.

Once he was done with that, he grabbed his greatsword with both hands and pivoted on his right foot. His greatsword held high near his right shoulder and he looked on at Eivindr. The speaker had left by this time and the main speaker announced, "Begin!"

And with that Eivindr approached his quarry with weariness, though he wasn't afraid as he thought he should be. He couldn't be afraid of such a weakened man. He doubted that the man could swing his weapon more than once, maybe twice.

The Great-swordsman stood as if he were a statue as Eivindr approached. Nothing moved but the man's head and eyes as Eivindr shifted around him.

Since Eivindr was fond of his life, he was not going to do the foolish thing. Which was to charge the man. Weak or not. Famished or not. Eivindr did not doubt that with one blow his days would be numbered.

Eivindr didn't know much about fighting Great-swordsmen but that of what he knew about fighting anything. To wait until it was fatigued enough to gain the upper hand. He approached slightly, barely getting within the greatswords range and trying to provoke the post soldier. The man didn't even flinch. He only stood there, watching and waiting for his time to strike.

By this time, only a few seconds had passed and Eivindr knew to not keep the crowd waiting, so he did the foolish thing and charged well within the range of the greatsword. And within the blink of an eye, they were swinging at one another.

Eivindr held his weapon close to his body so that he might try to deflect the blow from the greatsword. It didn't come. The Emporian stepped back and away from Eivindr, which was unexpected. The man only stood and stared. The man's eyes were now focused on something on or near Eivindr.

Eivindr circled around to get to the man's back and the man didn't turn, which Eivindr thought as odd or stupid, so he took quick steps in to strike, but the man pivoted on his right foot and swung his greatsword at Eivindr's throat with great speed. Eivindr ducked and rolled and by the time he was back on his feet the greatsword was coming back towards him.

The Emporian had swung with much of his strength and had let the momentum of his swing twirl him around in a circle. Eivindr swung his great-axe up and it struck into the greatsword and sent it over his head as he leaned away from it. The sound of the two weapons hitting was akin to the sound of a gong being struck and it rang out like one too.

Eivindr had recovered his footing when he parried the attack, but the Great-swordsman was still recovering. Eivindr took that chance to strike and swung his weapon above his own head and, with a mighty swing, he brought it around to hit the Emporian's chest. The Emporian gathered what strength he could and back stepped and got just out of the range of Eivindr's swing.

The swing had so much power behind it that Eivindr struggled to stop and the Emporian took his chance at him and swung his weapon low at Eivindr's legs. It occurred to Eivindr that he wore no leg protection but for his woolen pants. Eivindr stepped back but was too slow as the greatsword cut through his pants and opened his leg.

The cut wasn't deep, but it was noticeable enough to make Eivindr hesitate to step on it. It didn't hurt too much to put pressure on his leg so he pushed the wound out of his mind and focused on his opponent. The Emporian had recovered his footing and held his weapon in two hands in the same posture as he had before at the beginning of the fight. This time Eivindr circled to his left, so in retrospect he was standing in front of the Emporian.

The man only moved his head and watched Eivindr move. He was conserving his energy the best he could, but his energy wouldn't last for much longer and Eivindr was sure of that at least. He was wrong about how many swings the Emporian had within him and he was afraid to guess again.

Eivindr stepped slightly within the Great-swordsman's range and when the man didn't move at the slightest, Eivindr attacked. He brought his great-axe up above his head as the Emporian took a small step with his right leg and swung his greatsword at Eivindr. The two weapons clashed and, as Eivindr had it play through his head, his swing was stronger and followed through.

The Great-swordsman's swing was knocked back and he was forced to pull his left foot off of the ground to stay on his feet. Eivindr let the momentum of his previous swing induce another and his great-axe swung around and struck the Emporian in the lower back, near the kidney, and the crowd cheered loudly.

There was a grunt of pain from the Emporian spun from the blow and he fell to his knees and he arched over and retched. As Eivindr watched, the bile fell out of his mouth and mingled with the sand beneath. The armor where Eivindr's great-axe had struck was bent and had caved into the man's body.

The Emporian held himself up with his arms, but his strength was leaving them and he slowly crumpled to the ground and lay on his back, breathing heavily and labored and the crowd cheered again. Eivindr took pity on him in some way, maybe because of how the man was treated and starved before he was thrown in the arena to die.

Eivindr and he made eye contact as Eivindr approached to kill him. Eivindr raised his weapon and the Emporian seemed to know what was next and he nodded the best he could. It wasn't until now that Eivindr realized how young the man actually was. Early twenties it looked like, perhaps younger than even that.

He only looked like a boy, only just turned into a man. Eivindr took greater pity on him then. How the man fought in his last moments, probably knowing that he was already dead before he had even been rushed onto the sands. Then trying to accept his own death.

The Emporian's eyes were still open and as Eivindr's great-axe rose above his head and the Emporian closed his eyes and had a small smile upon his face and the great-axe came down upon his neck. The great-axe pushed through the mail coif and cut until it hit a bone in the neck. There was no other sound but the crowd as the blood poured out from the body, pulsing to get out and into the sweaty air and the crowd cheered louder.

Eivindr pulled his weapon from the neck with a harsh tug. Guards approached him and one held out his hand and Eivindr gave him the bloodied weapon. The guard had a grin on his face and another guard or two had sour looks. They escorted him from the sands, but they did not take him to the correct exit. Maybe he was wrong, but he was sure that it was another. Other guards cleaned up the dead Emporian and prepared for another match. The portcullis before Eivindr opened and he walked through and into a dimmer place than the arena.

Inside the corridor there were more guards, but these guards wore a different coat of arms. It was a ruined gatehouse. The towers broken and crumbled and the gates broken and shattered. He hadn't seen it before, but yet it looked familiar to him. The colors were a very dark gray on crimson. There were eight of them and they were lounging around and were still getting up. The guard who had Eivindr's great-axe handed the weapon to one of the guards who had the odd coat of arms.

"Here it is. Here he is," the guard that had escorted him with his great-axe said.

"Well respected," said the guard who received the great-axe. They nodded and parted. The guards with the ruined gatehouse on their chests now stood near him and chatted quietly and Eivindr was confused. "Thy helmet and armor."

Eivindr removed his armor and gave it to the guard. "Come with me, Little Wolf," the head guard said. Eivindr looked at him with a raised eyebrow and followed the guard's direction. Half of the guards fell in around him and marched him through the corridor and the other half stayed where they were. The crowd in the arena roared their approval at something or someone as a guard opened a door and walked through. Eivindr and the rest of the escort entered after.

Inside the side corridor there was only one figure which Eivindr did not expect to see. An Emporian. He stood erect near one wall and looked down at something in his hand. He didn't look up when they entered nor did he seem to care. He was a Great-swordsman. He didn't wear his helmet, but it was on the bench beside him. A plume of carmine and silver dyed straw went perpendicular to his shoulders.

The plume was largely carmine but for two silver stripes that went through the plume, one at the top and one that went through the center of the plume. Both went lengthwise through the plume. Everyone who had entered gave the man a wide berth as they went through the room. What was extremely odd was the clasp that held the man's cape around his neck. It was a silver crown. The man's hair was covered by his coif of gambeson and another coif of mail. He had a black beard that had a brighter patch of hair at the very point of his chin. His greatsword leaned against the wall. Eivindr stepped out of the room and followed the guards as they continued to lead the way to somewhere.

They led him up stairways and through corridors and they passed multitudes of guards with different coats of arms. Many he knew, many he didn't. They also passed servants and the such and Eivindr was done with being confused and asked, "Where are we?"

124

"Going?" The head guard said in a questioning tone. He had a Gaetan accent.

"Yea."

"That would be… uhhh… uuhhhmmm… Someone help me out, please."

"To the honor able, honOble. Nay, it's…" Another guard tried to speak and another laughed as another, the last that hadn't spoken, then spoke.

"Honorable," said one that had an Iarthairian accent. "Yea. Honorable. That's it," the stutterer finished with a Norden accent.

"I can finish it from here. We are gathering at the pavilion of the Honorable Haldis Vangar who hath requested thy… uuhhh… presence. Presence, verily, that's it," the original guard said.

Eivindr was more confused now than he was before he had asked the question. He looked up at them and one looked back down at him and grinned. Eivindr eyed him and looked away.

"Thou art frightening him," one guard said, who was behind him. He had a Finnidal accent.

"What? Me? Nay. I couldn't do that to the Little Wolf. Nay," the guard who had grinned at him just now. He had a Norden accent.

"We're here. Now sshh," the head guard said. The others all hushed and the head guard knocked on the door he stood near. A second later the door opened slightly to another guard and then opened all of the way and Eivindr and his escort walked through and the door shut behind them. The sounds of the crowd became much louder as Eivindr exited the corridor.

They had entered through a small door apart from the dragon door. Dragons guarded the door and elves guarded the door Eivindr entered through, dwarves also guarded the door. Eivindr's escort then escorted him through the back of the pavilion and to the front where the crowd was louder. It became harder to hear anything but the crowd.

The escort stopped and the head guard approached a dragon who, unlike the others, didn't really lounge, but was still as stone as he watched. The head guard approached and stood in a position where the dragon could see him. The dragon looked and lowered his head to near the head guard and the guard said something and the dragon said something that Eivindr couldn't hear either. The guard nodded and walked back to Eivindr and said, "The Honorable Haldis is requesting thee to join him for the rest of the events for this evening."

Eivindr complied and was led to a seat next to the dragon. Now that time had passed, his leg began to ache where he had been cut and he yearned for respite. He sat and the guards departed.

The dragon who was apparently Lord Edvard's son, The Honorable Haldis, was a mixture of scales. Gray, brown red and a very dark gray that was nearly black but for a certain sheen that made the difference between it and black and was unmistakable.

The gray scales covered small patches on his tail and back. The brown scales covered most of his body and his wings were the same color. The red scales, scarlet, were all on his back, one solid column down the length of his spine. His horns were brown as his wings. He was eighteen feet to his head, thirteen feet to his back and forty three feet long.

The dragon obviously had metal dragon blood because the only dragon scale that could be that dark was a type of metal that only dragons could produce.

Dragon steel.

It was a rare scale to have and an even rarer metal. The rest of the scales became almost irrelevant as Eivindr looked at the dragon's thorax where the dragon steel scales were. The dragon's entire thorax and most of its neck was covered with the scales. The crown of the skull, technically a horn between the two main horns of the dragon's head that was stout like an obtuse triangle but was covered in scales, also was covered with dragon steel scales. Only male dragons had crowns, it was an identifying trait. It was large, but not large enough to see from a distance. Another identifying trait was that the two main horns of a female dragon were closer together, but that was harder to notice.

Eivindr looked down at the blood stained sands at the fight that was taking place. It was two elves, or that is what Eivindr thought, that were pitted against one another. One had a long sword and the other had a short sword and a dagger.

One would think that where Eivindr sat that he would not be able to see the fight, but all of the stands were magically enhanced to be able to see. Wind magic that bends the light to help one see farther.

The fighter with the dual weapons parried a strike from the other fighter and slashed with the other weapon, her knife, and opened a wound at the unprotected ankle. The fighter with the longsword crumbled to the ground with a scream, the other fighter attacked and slashed open the neck, the bowels and the face with multiple strikes and the fighter with the longsword died screaming in pain. The crowd erupted in cries of joy, excitement and delight for the pain that the fighter had felt in his last moments.

Haldis' mouth tightened and he turned to a nearby wind dragon, or a dragon that had a decent amount of wind scales, and said something. A second later the crowd noises quieted noticeably and Haldis turned his gaze on Eivindr as Eivindr was looking around and that was when he realized what happened to the sound. Eivindr looked up at the dragon who was studying him.

"Art thou famished?" Haldis asked. His Eirikish accent was barely distinguishable under his raspy voice. It sounded as if it hurt to speak, so much so that Eivindr almost thought that his own throat was damaged. Haldis' eyes were dark like his dragon steel scales. Deep voids of darkness. Eivindr thought that he should probably tell the truth, it's what Haldis seemed to want. He hoped.

"If it pleases thee."

"It does," said Haldis as he turned and searched. He found who or what he was looking for and beckoned. A serving elf woman appeared and bowed to him. She had medium brown hair that fell past her shoulders with deep brown eyes. Her skin was light with a slight tan to it. "Gather my guest whatever he would wish to eat."

The elf woman turned to Eivindr and bowed her head slightly and asked, "What wouldst thou like to eat, Master Eivindr?"

That was wrong. He was no 'Master', but he wouldn't say anything about that. He didn't actually know what he would rather eat when he thought of something and asked, "Anything?"

"Anything," said Haldis.

"Then I would hath some spare ribs."

The elf woman bowed her head and Haldis smiled just slightly. Eivindr absently rubbed his leg gingerly and Haldis noticed and made a motion as if he finally got something that he should have gotten long ago and said before the elf could leave, "And get his leg temporarily bandaged." The elf bowed again and left at a quick pace. Haldis looked at Eivindr for a second before he spoke, "I should guess that thou art wondering why thou art here. Art thou?"

Eivindr could almost swear that speaking hurt him every time he spoke. After a quick second, Eivindr said, "Verily."

"I don't knoweth if thou heard, I would think thou hast heard, but to be sure. Hast thou heard anything about the bet between me and my father?"

"Yea, though, I don't knoweth what it is." "Was. I won the bet. Thou wast the bet." "What? What doest thou mean?"

"I mean that whoever won the bet won thee. Thou wast the pot, that is probably a better way to saith it. A clearer way."

"So, what was the bet?"

"The bet was how long it would take thee to win thy match and how thee would finish the fight," said Haldis and he took a deep breath. It would appear that he ran out of breath and continued, "Rather specific, but nonetheless. My father wagered that thou wouldst kill the Emporian in less than fifteen seconds, I thought not. He also thought that thou wouldst kill the Emporian with one blow, I thought not."

Half way through, Eivindr began rubbing his neck as if it was his voice that sounded in such a way. He wondered what had happened to cause that. "So, it would appear that thou hast won. In both ways."

Haldis smirked and shook his head and said, "I didn't doubt for one moment. My father isn't the best at judging the ability of soldiers. Especially Emporian soldiers."

"So, what happens now?"

"What happens is that thou now fight for me."

Eivindr blinked, not knowing what to say for a moment before he asked his question, "So I belong to thee? No longer Lord Edvard?"

"Exactly," said Haldis, looking at the sands where there was no fight at the moment. Eivindr was a little confused at that.

"Was there a fight already?" Eivindr asked.

"Nay. Not since the fight that thou watched the end of. We're in an intermission. An intermission takes place every ten fights. The watchers like to hath their discussions every once in a while without missing a single fight that they hath paid to see."

Eivindr understood and he nodded in understanding. A servant, not the same elf that had come before. In fact, she didn't look like an elf and that would be because she wasn't an elf. She was a human and that was something that Eivindr didn't expect to see. A serving human serving a dragon directly? She approached Eivindr with some white linen and stopped just before she reached him and bowed her head and asked, "Shall I bandage thy leg, Master Eivindr?"

Again with the master, but he would swallow that for now. He did not want to make a scene and look like a complete degenerate. Instead he said, "Verily."

She bowed her head and knelt by his leg. He propped it up on a table that was apparently meant for him and she began her work. She had dirty blonde hair with medium blue eyes. Her skin was mostly without tan.

"The next fight is the last," said Haldis as if the human wasn't even there, but still watching the human woman bandage his leg with interest.

"I hath never been in a night ending fight nor hath I seen one. Is it something special like I hath heard many say it is?"

"Verily, it truly depends on thy point of view on the word 'special'. It is special because it is different than any other fight."

"How so?" Eivindr asked as he tried to keep his focus on Haldis and to seem like he did not mind that a human woman was bandaging his leg. Haldis didn't seem to care. He only watched the human woman finish bandaging Eivindr's leg with keen interest.

"The usual fight is one on one. The night ending fights are always different in some way. Two or more versus two or more. One versus two or more. A dragon versus a great elf, dwarf or human fighter," said Haldis. The human woman made sure that the bandage was secure before standing and bowing her head again to Eivindr. "Thou art now dismissed," said Haldis. She looked up at him and bowed, a little smile of happiness on her lips and left. Eivindr watched her go with curiosity. "Confused as to why she is here?" Asked Haldis.

"Yea. I thought that humans didn't serve dragons directly." "That's usually the case. Not because they are not allowed to, only that humans are looked at disdainfully. Treated with disrespect and cast aside."

"And thou don't seest them that way?"

"Nay. I like to think of myself as equal to my underlings. Why should I punish one for nothing and keep the other after punishing them for something they did? I don't like how humans are treated hither. It's rather hypocritical to me," he paused and took a deep breath.

He continued, "Once, dragons used to rule most of the world and I'm sure we were looked at in the same fashion as we look at humans today. Or maybe we weren't. After all, Emporians treat their enemies with respect and honor and can treat their prisoners the same way. Hast thou heard stories of how the Emporians mistreat their subjects? I simply find that quite inaccurate," he deeply inhaled again.

He continued, "If they did treat their subjects poorly, then how is their loyalty to the crown so high? Nonetheless, in the end, I won't treat any humans in my service poorly or harshly and I don't like how others treat them. I hath spent portions of mine accounts purchasing them. I hath made bets on them as well. Any way to get them, or most any way, I shall attempt."

He cleared his throat and winced and took a deep breath. The servant arrived with the spare ribs and laid the platter before Eivindr and he looked at it for a moment before he began to eat.

He had eaten half of the meal when a portcullis opened below and Haldis turned to the wind dragon and waved a wing at him. The sound barrier dropped and the sound of the crowd came back to full volume as well as the main speaker.

"Welcome three of our contestants for this final match tonight. The infamous Dancing Death. A War Dancer whose backstory we hath all heard and is fighting for her future as a possibly free person. And next to her are her previous partners in war, Essen Lisa and his twin brother, Tom Lisa. They hath joined her for this match and perhaps a well met reunion between three partners. Welcome!" The speaker finished and the light bent before Eivindr's eyes and the three War Dancers became clear.

The elf woman had shoulder length black hair and the others had light brown hair that was a few inches long atop the head. They also sported a goatee of light brown hair. The eyes were indistinguishable to him though. The two twins seemed the exact same. They wore light gambeson and leather armor. No helmets. Thin curved swords were holstered on their backs.

"Now, for their opponent. That's correct, only one, is another one of our great enemies. Another Emporian who hath been caught in battle, though, this one is different from our previous Emporian who had been defeated by Eivindr Wolf. This one is a tribune in rank. Superior to the veteran earlier, though still the same as any other. Evil and an enemy of justice. Shall more justice be served today?!"

The War Dancers below all raised their hands and arms and shouted. The crowd erupted in what sounded like confused excitement as another portcullis opened. It was the portcullis nearest to Eivindr so he couldn't see it at all, but it was where the Emporian stepped out and was escorted to the center of the arena where a speaker stood as well as the three War Dancers. Eivindr was as confused as the crowd seemed to be. This wouldn't be a very competitive fight. Guards escorted the Great-swordsman out. The same looking guards that had escorted him up to The Honorable Haldis. They at least wore the same coat of arms.

Unlike the young Great-swordsman that Eivindr had fought, this man took great strides and did not wobble on his feet. Every step was powerful and his armor was well kept. He saw the plume of straw and thought that it was the same Emporian he had passed on his way up here. He carried his greatsword with him all the way there. The guards around the Emporian gave the man respect.

The man reached the center as the crowd booed and jeered at him, he paid them no mind. Eivindr realized that Haldis was silent and watching intently.

"Is there anything to be said before the match begins?" The speaker that was on the sands asked the fighters. Right as he finished, one of the elves spoke.

"I shall rip thy heart out and feed it to a young human I know. I knoweth that she'll love it," said one of the twins. It was more spitting than speaking.

"Perhaps when thou art dead, thy body may actually do the earth some good," the elf woman said menacingly. The crowd cheered in agreement at the words that had been said. The speaker below was smirking as he looked from the elves at the Emporian.

"And with that, let the match begin!" The speaker backed away from them and made his way off of the sands of the arena. The contestants parted from one another and the War Dancers took spacing between themselves in a stance.

The Emporian unsheathed his greatsword and handed the sheath to his escort. One took it and the two guard units left the arena.

The Emporian below turned around and searched the stands and his searching stopped on Haldis. When Eivindr saw his face he knew that it was the Emporian that he had passed in the corridor.

The Emporian looked at Haldis and Haldis stared back and nodded slightly. The exchange went quick enough that it seemed that the Emporian's eyes never stopped and he looked back at the War Dancers before him.

The Emporian drew himself up and held his greatsword in his right hand, straight up and sort of braced the hilt with his forearm as he held it up near its larger handguard. He then closed face guard and held the greatsword with two hands in the same stance that the other Great-swordsman had. The War Dancers unsheathed their weapons and loosened their muscles.

"Begin!" The main speaker announced and the War Dancers closed in on the Great-swordsman who only stood there.

Wind magic enhanced not only their vision, but Eivindr could also hear things that were said below. "Hast thou fought War Dancers before, retch?" One of the twins asked. Eivindr didn't know which one it was, they were identical.

There was a second's pause before the Emporian answered, "Yea. I vividly remember his brains spilling onto the floor of the Imperial Palace. Hast thou seen it before?" The voice was muffled by the helmet but was still distinguishable.

The War Dancers continued their advance, but Eivindr felt it in his bones. When he saw the man's face, it wasn't a weak face. His voice wasn't weak either and the Emporian had just mentioned being within the Imperial Palace. Eivindr knew that the man was of the Imperial Guard, the best of the best of Emporian soldiers. He could now see that this was going to be possibly competitive, in the Emporian's favor.

The War Dancers continued their advance and encirclement and Eivindr had a sinking feeling in his stomach. He looked up at Haldis who was watching with great interest, but there was a smirk on his face. He saw what was happening as well. Eivindr looked back down at the fight.

The War Dancers closed in on the Emporian from three sides. While they were encircling the man, he was inching backwards, waiting for them to get a little closer together or a little farther apart. They attacked and the Emporian stepped to his left, turning and stepped towards one of the twins with his right foot and swung his weapon.

The elf tried to dodge but was too slow and the greatsword clipped the elf's cheek and drew some drops of blood. He used his momentum to turn around and face the other flanking elf that had dove into an attack and buried his greatsword into the War Dancers side.

The heavy weapon cleaved through the gambeson and boiled leather almost with ease and the elf was knocked off of his feet and half thrown through the air. He had dropped his swords and grabbed at the wound with surprise and the Emporian pulled his weapon from the dying body. The other twin looked on with surprise and the Dancing Death had recovered quickly and backed away before the greatsword came flying through the air for her neck.

With that, one elf was dead, or dying, and the other two were recovering. The crowd booed slightly. Haldis' smirk grew. And Eivindr just shook his head in disappointment. These War Dancers have not seen Great-swordsmen in battle. The Dancing Death might have, but her companions hadn't and they weren't helping.

The Emporian advanced with great strides, like speed walking, and the remaining twin shuffled away, but the Dancing Death attacked and exchanged a few blows with the Emporian then backed away and the

Emporian looked at her for a moment before regaining his stance and attacked her.

She did her best to either stay too far away or too close for the Emporian to make a proper strike. The other War Dancer recovered and saw his chance and took it. The Dancing Death kept the Emporian's attention while her companion closed in. He slashed at the legs and tried a finishing thrust at the neck, but his mistake was not making that his first move. The Emporian backed up into the War Dancer and knocked him off balance. The Dancing Death took her opportunity and tried to pommel strike the head.

The Emporian shot his left arm up and deflected the strike and threw himself forward and his helmet connected with the cheekbone of the elf woman and threw her off balance and he quickly turned around and grabbed his greatsword with two hands again and knocked away another attack and made his own attack.

The elf woman recovered her balance quickly, but not quick enough. The Emporian left his greatsword in his left hand and grabbed the collar of the elf and and head butted him, concussing him. The Emporian threw the concussed elf away from him and turned around to find the Dancing Death nearly on top of him. He had grabbed his weapon with two hands again and swung at the elf woman's waist. She had to throw herself away from the blade and from the Emporian.

The Emporian advanced on her and swung at her unrelentingly and drove her back farther and farther. Every time she tried to get around him and to her concussed and weary companion, he got in her way and forced her away from him and towards the wall. The elf woman saw that she was being forced into a corner and knew that she needed to get out.

The concussed War Dancer was getting up, shaking his head and was weary on his feet. The elf woman attacked the Emporian but that only served for the Emporian to grab one of her blades and ripped it from her grasp and continued his advance on her.

Eivindr could see that she was beginning to panic. He would be too if he were in that position. The elf regained his steadiness and looked around, saw that his companion was being pushed back and then found his swords. The Emporian pushed the elf woman back farther and was almost to the wall.

The elf woman made one last attempt to get free of her predicament and paid for it as the Emporian slammed the broadside of his greatsword into her lower leg and struck her feet from beneath her. She cried out in pain and the Emporian finished her off with a thrust into her chest. The blade pierced her light armor and knocked the breath out of her, or most of her breath.

The Emporian pulled the blade free and turned around to see the last War Dancer waver. He advanced and the War Dancer quaked with fear. The crowd urged him on, calling him a coward and to kill the Emporian. Only a few voices cried out though, many others were silent.

The War Dancer looked around and the Emporian walked towards him with his ever powerful strides. He held his greatsword with two hands and parallel with the ground. The War Dancer then made his decision and dropped his swords and begged for mercy crying, "I yield! I yield! Mercy! Please! Mercy!"

The Emporian stopped before him, boos came from the crowd. The man opened his face guard and looked up at Haldis and Haldis made a motion with his wing. The Emporian looked down at the pleading elf. The crowd called for the elf's death. The Emporian lifted his greatsword up in his original stance, up near his right shoulder and asked the elf, "Hast thou ever fought an Emporian before?"

The elf trembled, looking at the greatsword and shook his head and with tears rolling from his eyes choked out, "Nay. Nay."

"Thou lies," declared the Emporian and with that the Emporian stepped forward with his right foot and swung the greatsword at the elf's neck and with a lucky strike, sheared through the neck and the elf's head parted from his body that fell to the ground and twitched violently. The crowd half cheered and half spoke disappointed. Blood pulsed from the sheared neck and after a moment of laying on the ground the pulses became less noticeable and the blood more just flowed out of the neck.

Guards approached the Emporian wearily and afraid. The man looked at them and the guards who had escorted him out into the arena seemed to have no fear of him as they walked up to him. The Emporian grabbed his cape and wiped the blood off of his weapon. The guards handed him his sheath, sheathed the greatsword and looked at it for a moment. He then handed the weapon to one of the guards who had their hand out and allowed them to escort him back into the corridor. The crowd began to disperse and the guards of the arena cleaned up the bodies.

The Emporian's armor had a little blood on it. Eivindr watched him exit the arena and looked at his platter, which he had emptied and looked up at Haldis to see him smiling.

Chapter Nine

He From The Far East

Day 20-26, Elvenar, Year 2142

Harsh Sarkar lay in a dory with two other bodies. They were most likely dead, or close to it, Harsh was sure of it. They hadn't moved in days, or a day, or hours, maybe only one hour? Harsh couldn't tell. He couldn't tell whether he was even alive or not.

The sun was beating down upon him, making him sweat and forcing his eyes shut. There also seemed to be no clouds through the entirety of the great blue sky. Harsh couldn't feel any wind blowing, though he was laying within the edges of the dory.

They had quit rowing what seemed forever ago, yet it felt like he had just been doing it before. It also felt as if they had been at sea for a lifetime and the life he had lived before they had fled seemed like someone else's memories.

He licked his dried and cracked lips. The back of his throat burned with dehydration. His dirty blonde hair was long and like a rat's nest. His gray eyes sunken into his skull. He had a shaggy beard of the same color as his hair.

The dory rocked and rolled with the waves of the sea. The last fish they had caught either didn't give him much nutrients or it was a long time ago. Harsh didn't know which it could be. All time was lost to him. All he knew was day, night and day, other than the time he spent sleeping, though he didn't know how much time he spent sleeping.

He felt like his muscles had been torn and stretched while he had slept. Nonetheless, he still did his best to sit up and look around at the vast blue, splashing waves of eternity that seemed to never end. It never ended. He looked and looked around and saw only waves splashing against the small boat and afar from the boat. It seemed to him that one wave wasn't moving, then it looked like it moved. He put it out of his mind until it looked like it didn't move again. He just slumped back down and closed his eyes to rest again.

He opened his eyes and licked his lips. And rolled onto his side and tried to sleep again. The boat rocked and woke him up again. This time he decided to sit up from his dreamless sleeping and look around once more and noticed something almost immediately. The sun was being clouded by a cloud. Not a thick cloud, but a cloud.

He sat up a little bit firmer and looked around the boat. The other two bodies were still unmoving, as far as he could tell and there still wasn't any land in sight. Just water and more water. He licked his lips and shifted his weight to his other arm to continue looking. Just more water and more water. Then he thought he saw something, a wave that didn't move. He rubbed his eyes and blinked and rubbed his eyes again and looked closer. A strand of hair flopped down over his eye as he was squinting in the direction of the unnaturality of the horizon.

He began coughing and he moved his hand to cover his mouth and coughed dryly and violently.

Once he had finished his coughing fit, he looked back out at the seas around him and saw what he thought was land. The feeling of extreme relief and happiness flooded over him. The pain of his hunger and thirst left him for a small moment of respite. His head pounded and was caught between the extreme anguish and astonishment that land was now in sight.

Harsh fell back down and rested and did his best to restore his strength. He had closed his eyes and fell asleep without him noticing. Next he woke the boat was pivoting on one end of the boat and the other was slightly rocking. Harsh sat up the best he could, the pain of hunger and thirst had returned.

It seemed that everything on his body was in pain and aching. The back of his throat had constricted and his bottom lip was bleeding. He licked his lips and tasted the blood, though he didn't have enough spit in his mouth to spit it back out nor enough to swallow it. Once he had propped himself up against the side of the dory and saw something other than water for once. It was what looked like dirt.

He grabbed the rim of the boat and pulled himself painfully across the boat and to the other side of the dory. He went from one side to the other, length-wise. He crawled over the bodies without noticing or registering them as bodies.

He reached the other end of the boat and reached down with his hand and found that his hand did not break through the surface and he scooped up a partial handful of dirt and brought it up to his eye level and slowly dropped the dirt from his hand. His breath almost caught in his throat and then his breathing got more deep and rapid. He looked up to the sky and whispered a prayer so silent that it was simply his mouth opening and closing.

He had prayed many times during their desperate journey of escape from their enemies. He turned around to the others in the boat and shook them with what strength he had left. Neither of them stirred. He shook them again, nothing happened. Harsh began to fear the worst.

"No. Please, no," he whispered so quietly that it was almost incomprehensible. He spoke the common tongue, or at least the common tongue of Chimantia.

He continued to shake them feebly with his weak arms. The strength had left him and he slumped onto the body he was nearest and rested. He pushed himself off of his fellow escapee and flopped over the side of the boat and onto the wet, muddy shore. Nats swarmed off of the ground and buzzed all around him.

He lifted his head and began to crawl his way further inland. His hands squished the mud that he laid them upon. He used his hands and forearms to pull his body over the mud and onto short, thick grass. More nats burst from the ground with every movement of his.

He was covered in mud and his head felt as if it would explode at any moment, yet he still crawled on. His hands grasped chunks of grass and pulled. Every time he pulled his body forward with his arms, a hammer pounded the inside of his skull. He reached a rock that jutted out of the ground and he clung onto it and pulled himself up onto it and tried to look around. His vision was blurry and made it hard to see anything. He hugged the rock and closed his eyes. When he closed his eyes, his eyes burned with painful pleasure. So much so that it made him want to open his eyes to get away from the pain, but also didn't and couldn't.

His eyes opened and the sun was reaching the horizon, shining into his eyes. He looked away from the light and studied the geography surrounding him. The landscape was made of grass that grew taller as it went farther inland and away from the tides. The grass started just four feet from the shore line. The grass grew to be near to half a foot in height at its tallest blade.

He decided to begin munching on the grass. If it didn't help his thirst, then it would at least quench his hunger slightly.

Flowers of many different varieties grew as well. Rocks were also in plenty all around. The spot where the boat he had traveled in had landed near one of the only spots where there were no rocks. Rocks small and smaller were strewn across the shore and large rocks and larger rocks accompanied them.

There were few trees in sight. He licked his lips and spied something that looked like smoke coming from a rock, or it may be that it was a home. He looked down and over at the boat and back at what he thought was smoke and licked his lips again. The building shouldn't be too far, but he still wasn't sure if he would make it.

He left his rock and grass and began to crawl. It was difficult. He contemplated if it was worth it and began crawling again. His head was beating like a drum and his throat screamed for water and his stomach clenched in hunger.

He crawled and crawled for the building as the sun fell behind the ground. The ground was getting colder every time he inched forward and the air was cooling as well. The mud made squishing and sucking sounds as his forearms and hands went up, forward, down and pulled his body forward another half foot, or less. The light was fleeing from the world and the stars were showing themselves to the world.

The moons were becoming more stark against the darkening of the evening sky. The sky was yellow, orange, red, purple and blue, and started from the west to the east. He strained to pull himself to the home, but his strength left him forty feet from his destination. He lay there, sprawled on the ground, dying. His head ached so much that he couldn't form a prayer to his gods. He closed his eyes and drifted away into darkness.

His eyes opened and were looking at something, but he didn't know what. He blinked and turned his head to the origin of light of where he was. It was a candle. He blinked again and looked around a little more and finally realized that he was in the room, laying on a bed with a rough woolen blanket laid upon him. He shifted and looked around again.

The room was small, or small in comparison of what he thought of the size of the bed he was upon. It was square with one desk in the room which was next to the bed and where the candle was. There was also a cup on the small wood desk.

His headache came back to hammer him relentlessly once he had lifted his head. He lay his head back down, squeezed his eyes shut and groaned in pain. He moved one hand to his forehead as if to gently comfort his mind.

The door opened and a dwarf, though he didn't know what a dwarf was exactly, walked into the room. He had a large brown beard that hung to his chest and brown scalp hair that came to his upper back between his shoulders. He wore thin, light wool leggings and tunic, but no gloves.

He wore socks of thin wool as well. All were worn, old and stained. He looked at Harsh and turned back around and shut the door behind him. Voices sounded beyond the door and were incomprehensible and muddled in with one another and a moment later it opened again and a different being approached him. Harsh opened his eyes and looked at the door the second time, once his head felt just a little better.

The being's scalp hair was brown with strands of blonde mixed within and was braided and banded with metal clasp-like rings and hung down to the being's waist and had no beard. After a quick analysis of the being showed that the being was a she and she wore light, white woolen leggings and tunic and socks. Her eyes were a deep green and her skin was light, or at least lighter than his own. His skin tone was light brown, more brown than light brown though. She held a wood bowl in her hands as well as a wood spoon. Whatever was in the bowl was steaming.

She scooped something out of the bowl with the spoon and proffered it up to him, steaming, and; in a Ludian accent, though he didn't know this; said, "Eat."

Something he didn't understand. His eyebrows pinched in confusion and he looked at the spoon and back at her. She gestured the spoon towards him again and said, "Eat, thou needst food."

Another chain of words that was incomprehensible. It was easy enough to understand what she wanted, but why couldn't he understand her. Did she speak a different language? He opened his mouth and she placed the spoon in his mouth and he closed. His headache was tolerable, but just barely. He swallowed the spoonful that he was given and the girl said, "Doth thee like the taste?"

Something that, alas, Harsh could not comprehend. He looked at her with confusion and she saw and paused for a moment. Then she put the spoon into the bowl and pressed all five of her fingers together on one hand and did an eating motion and then moved her hand down to her belly and made the motion of rubbing her belly. Harsh could understand that, he thought at least, and he shrugged. She nodded and offered another spoonful and he took it.

His headache was slowly degrading and whatever it was that was in the bowl tasted like some form of porridge, but Harsh wasn't sure. In the end it did taste good. The first few swallows tasted bland and it still slightly tasted bland, just not as much.

After he had finished eating the food in the bowl, the girl stood and grabbed the cup and tilted it towards him and said in her gentle voice, "Here is some water if thou needst it."

Though he didn't understand her words, he thought that he understood what she wanted. He looked into the cup and took it and inclined his head to her and she left the room, closing the door behind her. He looked into the cup closer and saw that it was water and he drank. The taste of the wood mingled with the water and gave it a flavor, or what Harsh thought of as a flavor. He wasn't thirsty, nor hungry, so he was supposing that he had been found and taken care of by these people. As he drank the water his headache was subdued a little more.

After he had drunk most of the water from the cup, he laid back down and relaxed. He thought of how he couldn't understand what the girl was saying, nor what the voices were saying outside the door as they spoke to one another. Then he realized how much thinking made his head hurt. He shoved the thoughts out of his mind and shifted in the bed for a more comfortable and closed his eyes to sleep.

He woke to the same scenery that he had awakened to what he thought would be the day before. Then he remembered prayer and that he had forgotten to pray before he had fallen asleep. He looked around the room to see if anyone was within the room with him before he prayed quietly.

He prayed in silence. He sat up enough to look around comfortably and saw the cup on the desk. He reached for it and found it full again and he drank deeply. A knock wrapped the door before it opened slightly. He looked at the door after he put the cup back down on the desk. It was the same girl as before along with another bowl with steaming food within it. Most likely the same thing as before.

She gestured with the bowl and said, "Art thou hungered?"

Another thing in what Harsh thought was her tongue since he could not understand it and was still able to speak his own tongue. He thought of the gesture as a question like, 'Doest thou want any?'. Harsh nodded and she entered the room and he removed his hands from underneath the blanket and cupped his hands to hold the bowl. She set it into his hands and the warmth spread from the bowl and into his hands. He inclined his head to her in thanks and she smiled in response and looked at his cup, saw that it was almost empty and took it with her when she left.

This time Harsh looked into the bowl to see if he knew what it was. Or if he could decipher what it was made of. It was a creamy color and was mostly creamy in texture. It had what looked like oats or some other type of grain. He stirred the food and reassessed his thought of grain. It was a grain, just wheat though. Maybe some barley. He guessed it was made of water, wheat, barley and something else that he could not identify. A simple dish, though quite good nonetheless. He picked up the spoon and began to eat the porridge.

As he was eating the door was knocked on again and the girl entered with the cup. She walked to the desk, put the cup down and she looked at him as he ate. He looked up at her and she gestured with her hand the same way she had the day before. With the five fingers of one hand pressed together and moved her hand to her mouth then down to her belly and made the rubbing motion. He smiled and nodded to her. She smiled back and inclined her head and he did as well. She left the room and shut the door behind her.

He ate the food until it was gone and he scraped what was left in the bowl. When he was contemptuous of his ability to eat as much out of the bowl he could, he placed the bowl onto the desk and drank some water. He drank until the cup was half empty and he put it back down on the desk.

He then wondered how long he had been sleeping before he had woken up. He felt his face, he was still gaunt. He moved the blanket and lifted the tunic he had on to see his skin pulled against his ribs and pelvis. The skin on his hands was also pulled to the bones. It reminded him of before he had left his homeland. The horrors, death and destruction he had witnessed. He had witnessed his own loved ones get killed by the demon's minions. The demon's followers. The line of thought made his mouth turn up into a sneer.

He shook his head and decided to test how well he could walk or at least move his legs. He threw the blanket off and sat up on the bed with his legs, apparently on the floor. That's when he realized that the bed he was sleeping on was really just a pile of straw laid out upon the ground. Although he suspected his bed to be made of straw, this still surprised him. He looked up at the ceiling that wasn't too far from his head. He might barely have enough room to stand in the room, which made sense since the people who had been taking care of him looked shorter than usual, or at least stockier than normal.

The desk was basically a box now that he looked at it clearly. There were no windows within the room either, the only light was the candle that flickered light throughout the room. So standing was out of the question, maybe he could kneel. He thought about that before he decided not to and laid back down on the roughly put together bed and threw the blanket over him.

It was warm near the candle and cold everywhere else. He supposed that was because of the dirt that never touched sunlight. He wanted to see what had happened to his companions, but knew that it would most likely be best to lay down and rest.

A headache still bothered him from time to time. His stomach still ached as well, though it wasn't an urgent pain like before. Before the pain was so regular that there were times that he wouldn't feel it until he moved and his body remembered that he was alive.

He thought as he lay there. He was sure that she spoke another language, probably the lot of them. He heard multiple voices, or at least tones through the door. If they spoke a language other than the language he knew, he would have to learn it. If he were to live here for the remainder of his life, he would have to learn as much as he could.

Laying there, he decided to begin the learning phase after he slept and had some more food. That made him think of before when he first woke up and the girl showed him the cup. She had said something then, something like 'wadur'. He thought about that for a moment and practiced saying it.

"Wadur. Wuhdor. Wa… wa… der… dur… wader." Harsh whispered to himself.

He practiced the 'W' sound a little bit and nodded to himself when he thought he had the right sound. He then proceeded to the next sound. The 'uh' or 'ah' sound until he found the sound that sounded right to him. Then the next sound and then the last sound, 'er' or 'ar' or 'ur'. He finally decided on which he thought was best.

He tossed around until he found the most comfortable position before finally relaxing and closed his eyes to sleep some more. Sleep came quick enough and he went into another dreamless sleep.

Harsh woke to something tapping or padding his shoulder. He looked up at an unfamiliar face looking down on him. It was another one of the dwarves. His beard and mustache were dark brown and were long and braided and bound by metal clasp-like rings. His scalp hair was also dark brown and was ragged and fell down to the middle of his chest. It hung loose and fell all around his shoulders and back. There were hints of gray and white strands within his scalp hair and facial hair. He had creases in his face, though Harsh could not see any true expression on his face or in his icy blue eyes. He wore similar clothing to the others and himself.

"Art thou well?" Asked the dwarf in a Ludian accent. Something that Harsh couldn't understand. Harsh rolled over and shifted to face him. This must be the father of the girl who had been bringing him food. Harsh inclined his head to him in thanks, but that wasn't what the being was wanting. Behind him the girl stood in the doorway. He turned back to her and asked her, "Was he able to understand thee, or thou him?"

"I don't think so. Everytime I said something he would get this confused look on his face," she answered and shrugged.

"But he's been eating and drinking."

"Verily," she nodded as she answered. And yet again, Harsh could not hear. Or he could, but he couldn't comprehend.

The supposed father turned back to him and looked into Harsh's eyes, searching. Harsh searched as well, though he didn't know what to search for.

The dwarf sniffed and said, "Then we should do our best to teach him. I want to learn whither he comes from. Why is he hither, and who the other two are?"

He stood on his short legs and gestured for Harsh to follow. Harsh swallowed and found his throat dry. He turned to where the cup was and reached for it and drank it dry. He placed the cup back down and moved to be on his hands and knees to get up. He couldn't stand up all of the way and crouching like he was was too much effort for him, so he sank back to his hands and knees.

His boney knees pained him as he crawled on them, but he continued nonetheless, wincing.

"Art thou certain he should be moving? He's still weak from famine," the girl said.

"He should get some sunlight and after that we shall begin to teach him to speak, or understand," the elderly dwarf replied.

He followed the dwarf out of the room and into another that looked like a kitchen or family room. Maybe actually a dining room, maybe all three. A long table occupied the center, or near the center, and counters and cabinets occupied the far end of the decently large room. A door was placed near the counters and a hallway led to somewhere else in the house. They made way for another door that was between two windows that had no glass within. A window also held a place in the kitchen.

"Selidova, get the young and tell them that it is time for their learning. Tell thy mother I wish to see her outside," said the elder.

"Yea, Father," the girl responded.

The elderly dwarf before him opened the door and exited, the girl turned down the hallway and out of sight. The father held the door open for him as Harsh crawled out of the house. Once outside he attempted to stand and succeeded. His legs were wobbly underneath him and for a moment he forgot how to walk. He looked down at his legs and tried to will them forward as he remembered they did once before.

He took one unsteady step and another. He spread his arms out to his sides for some more balance. The father stood by his side and gestured with a hand to a bench or chair and led Harsh to it. Maybe he wished for Harsh to sit and rest in the daylight. Harsh guessed it had only been two days since he had seen the sun, or was it one. It really depends on whether they fed him two times a day or only once.

"That's it. Walk," said the dwarf as he aided Harsh to his destination. After a moment of walking, his legs had gotten exhausted, but he was almost to the outcropping. He made himself walk although every nerve, muscle and bone in his body wanted him to rest and stop moving. Just a few feet. The dirt below him wasn't hard, as his bare feet could testify to after treading upon it. The grass was softer though. It felt as if it cushioned him.

He reached the outcropping and all but dropped into the cushioned bench. The cushion though was made of straw and didn't help much in the fall. Since he had hardly any muscle really anywhere on his body, it hurt. It felt as if he just tried to break his own bones.

He let out a sigh of satisfaction that he had made it, though it turned into a wince as a pulse of pain shot up his body. The dwarf sat next to him. The sun was out and shining like in the days he had lived peacefully with his family. His wife, his children. He hoped against most odds that they were well, but who was well after what had happened. He pushed those thoughts out of his head the best he could. He should think of how to live here, in this new world.

Harsh looked up at the sky. Clouds were evident, but they weren't many. The sun was up near the middle of the sky. Some birds flew around, circling and dropping down to behind a small rise that blocked Harsh's view of whatever was behind it. The air felt nice and warm on his skin. Not as warm as he thought it should though with the sun as high as it was.

A figure made its appearance from the rise as it climbed the other side and headed towards them. He/she looked at the abode and saw them sitting there and changed direction to meet with them. The father spoke, "Art thou done?"

"Yea, though crows are still looking for a meal and the stink is still around. We hefted the boat out of the water and onto the shore after we buried the bodies. All or most of the possessions we left in the boat," the approaching dwarf said. He too, had a Ludian accent.

He wore brown wool leggings and tunic, the same that everyone else wore. His hair was brown flecked with light brown strands and was long and fell loosely to his just past his shoulders. His beard was about three inches from his face to its end and was similar in color. His eyes were a blue that was noticeable from a distance.

Harsh had quit bothering to try and hear what was being said. Instead he just leaned back and took solace in the warming sun. The blanket and bed was warm too, but he rathered the sun's warmth. It was generous to him.

"Take the boat to the tackle shed for now," the elderly said. "Yea, Father," the other replied.

Harsh felt thirsty now and thirsted for more water. He also felt extremely famished and wanted nothing more than to eat more food. The other dwarf strode off back the way he had come. The door opened and another dwarf exited.

"Over here," said the father.

The new dwarf looked their way and walked towards them. Harsh saw that this was another girl, or woman actually. She looked to be of a similar age to the father beside him. His wife most like. She wore similar clothing to the rest of them. It seemed to Harsh that he had landed in an impoverished area of this land. Or at least an area with fewer options of clothes to wear. Her hair was light brown to dirty blonde. Her eyes were green.

"Thou asked to see me, Dear?" She asked as she neared. "Yea. I would like it if thou wouldst teach our guest to speak, or understand at least."

"Is that his wish?"

"Whether he does or not, I want him to. There are questions to be answered."

"Why not take him to the authorities? I'm sure whatever he has to say would be best heard by those who have the swords."

"Perhaps thou art correct. It may be best, but wilt thou at least teach him until I go into town again? This way he knows enough to know when he is being spoken to."

"I could, but remember. When thou goest into town next, we need all of the space and rations we can spare. Thou knowest this."

"Yea, I doeth. I hath only questions and I want them answered."

"I doeth as well. I shall teach him the basics. By then it might be time for thee to go for another load."

"I agree," said the father.

The father patted him on a boney leg to get his attention. Harsh snapped out of his stupor and looked at him. He gestured to his wife and Harsh looked blankly for a moment before shaking his head as if to shake the stupor off and swallowed.

The wife gestured for him to follow and said, "Come then. I'll teach thee the best I can."

Harsh didn't understand her words, but he thought he was getting better at charades. He looked down at his legs as if to give them a motivational speech to get up and push through the pain of walking. After a second of that, he used his arms to help push himself up. It was strainful and for a moment Harsh thought that he would be too weak. Perhaps he was too weak, the father helped him in his plight and helped walk him back into the house.

Harsh was focusing on his walking and for a second he stopped and looked back up at the sun. It filled him with memories of a dear friend that he had lost. He had watched him die as he did nothing to save him. His lips quivered slightly and tears wanted to form in his eyes, but he tore his eyes away from the sun and that's when he noticed that the dwarves were looking up at him. He thought that he had heard voices as he stared at the sun, but they were faded out by the memories.

"Could the lesson be taken out here today?" The father asked. "I suppose. I'll get the little ones out here."

"I don't know what he's seeing, but maybe it is something from his past. A memory good or bad."

"From the way he was staring at the sun, I would think it was good, but he was staring at the sun."

"In the end, I thank thee, Janna. For doing this for me." "I want to know what he saw then, there may be some wisdom in his mind that could be shared for all of us. Maybe he could teach us a little of what he knows once we understand one another," she said as they gestured and led him out of the sunlight and back into the abode.

Chapter Ten

Requisitions

Day 02, Manylight, Year 2142

Edvin and Valto stood in a mass of people. Mostly dwarves, but there were some other elves and some dragons. They wore gray cloaks that covered all but their feet, ending at their ankles.

There weren't many murmurs around the crowd that stood on the dry ground. The grass was trampled and the rocks were removed from the ground. Buildings were arrayed sporadically.

They were in a mediocre sized town called Westerhaven. It was near the border between Emporia and Brandland. They had entered Imperial land a few days ago and went south first. They found a good enough hideout as a base of operations.

"Next!" Shouted a man from the front of the crowd. Everyone in the crowd stepped forward to a few stands that were set up before the crowd. Emporian soldiers patrolled and watched the crowd for any who had ill intent. They also stationed the stands and gave provisions to those before them.

Edvin spied a man that was looking over the crowd. He scanned the crowd, his eyes darting from individual to individual. They made eye contact and Edvin held it until the Emporian looked away and unto another being somewhere else. Edvin smirked to himself for a moment.

"What's that about?" Asked Valto, looking at him. Edvin looked at him and said, "Nothing."

"Don't act as an idiot, I beg of thee." "I shan't. I swear."

"I don't give a damn what thou swears. Stop it."

Over the time of the day, they moved closer to the stands. The voices and conversations that took place near the stands grew louder and easier to hear.

"How many young?" Asked an Emporian, with a Praeterton accent, who sat behind the desk stand. He held down a piece of paper on the wooden desk and held a pen in his right hand. His eyes were light blue and he had no beard. He, and all of the other Emporians who were sitting at desks, wore their armor.

"Three," said a dwarf with a Ludian accent, who stood on the other side of the stand from the Emporian. He wore dirty and half torn clothes that were more like rags. His beard was black, tangled and extremely rough looking. His eyes were blue and his hair was black. His hair was cut to the base of his head.

"Three..." the Emporian said to himself as he wrote it down. He looked up from the paper and at the dwarf for a second and asked, "Clothing as well?"

The dwarf bowed low and said, "Yea. Verily. Please, Sir, please."

The man wrote it down as another Emporian leaned forward to look at the dwarf that was almost on the ground. He gave him a curious look at first, then huffed to himself in delight, smiling as he looked to a nearby Emporian and said in a whisper so that none else could hear, "Mountain Dweller finally found his rightful place hither."

The Emporian who had been talking with the dwarf leaned over his desk and looked down on the dwarf saying, "Thy requisition paper hath been filled, take it before I hath thee escorted to the rear of the crowd to wait again."

The dwarf quickly stood, bowed his head to the Emporian, and took the piece of paper and moved off with a mumbled gratitude.

The man got another piece of paper and said, "Next!"

Edvin and Valto stepped forward and the next person in line got their turn at the requisition desk.

She had ragged blonde hair that fell around her shoulders. Her eyes were light blue and she had a scare on her left cheek that ran from her temple to her chin. Her clothes were gray wool that was scuffed and worn. She was six feet tall.

Next to her was a small elven child that seemed no older than four years old. She was wearing similar garments, but she had a blanket wrapped around her shoulders. No one could tell that she was a she though. Her hair was dirty blonde and wasn't very long, only falling down to the base of her neck and her eyes were queen blue. She was about three and a half feet tall.

The Emporian looked up at her, then at the child that clinged to her left arm and back at her saying, "Name and request?"

"Kristine Fjord. Please, I needeth food and water for me and my child," said the elf woman with a Norden accent. Her voice was soft, but desperate.

The man looked at the child then back at his paper and wrote something down saying, "Food and water... Anything else? Perhaps a reason for that scar on thy face?"

"Wha-wha-nay. Nay, I only tripped and fell on a sharp rock. Only that happened," said she, shaking her head. She pulled a few strands of hair away from her face.

"MmmHmm. Therefore... nothing else? Clothing? Shelter?"

"Nay, please. I hath need for only food and water, Kind Sir," she said and she bowed low to him and ushered her child to do the same.

The Emporian eyed her and inhaled deeply before saying, "Very well. Take this and gather thy requisitions," and held out the paper to her.

"Many thanks. Many thanks," she said, taking the paper graciously and pulling her child with her.

The Emporian watched her go and after a moment, he turned slightly around, leaned back and whistled. An Emporian jogged up to him and leaned his head down close. In quiet tones, they spoke so that no one else could hear.

"What is it?" Asked the one who jogged up. He had a Britonic accent.

"That elf woman is hiding something. I believe it's information about these Border crimes," said the other.

"Verily, I'll watch her."

"Good," the soldier nodded and turned back forward to resume his duties. The other Emporian stood back up straight, watching the elf woman, and slowly walking after her.

The Emporian at the desk grabbed another piece of paper and said, "Next!" Valto and Edvin stepped forward before the desk. The Emporian looked up at them and asked, "Names and requests."

"I am Trond," said Valto, bowing slightly at the waist.

"I am called Ivar," said Edvin, making the same actions as Valto.

The Emporian wrote one name down and was about to write the second before he stopped and asked, "Are ye wishing to place separate requests or not?"

"Uh-both. Not separate requisition slips. One singular slip," said Valto.

"Very well," the Emporian wrote down Edvin's false name then asked, "Requests?"

"Food and water. For us for the next two weeks. There are others of us elsewhere at the moment and I wisheth to gather food and water for them as well. I pray to thee," said Valto.

The Emporian looked up from his paper and at Valto with a curious look. Looking at him as if he had said something utterly stupid. He started to nod slowly before asking, "Are ye two new hither?"

Valto blinked and looked at him oddly before saying, "Yea. What makes thee beseech me of this?"

"The cause was that thou hast asked for a specified amount. The supplies are given out in certain amounts depending on the amount of recipients and size of recipients. Thou shalt not ask for a certain amount of supplies."

Valto nodded saying, "I understandeth this." "Good. Now, how many ye are there?"

"Us two and five others."

"What are their kinds?"

"Two dragons, two dwarves and one other elf. All are full grown, but one dragon is smaller than the other."

"Wind dragon then?"

"Yea."

"Very well, anything else for thee?"

Valto looked at Edvin for confirmation and Edvin said, "Doth thou knowest whither we can purchase well made weapons? We needeth such things to ward off bandits and such. We are traveling far and across countrysides and un-patrolled lands."

The Emporian had looked up at him the moment he had asked for weapons and watched him intently until he finished. After he did, the Emporian contorted his face in thought for a moment before he said, "Thou may find the best made weaponry in New Dubovsky.

The city has grown greatly since Emporia hath taken the region. Peoples from across the Empire hath come there to live. I'm sure that there are many smiths thither."

"Many thanks for thine information, Sir," said Edvin.

"Yea, but, it is many miles afar as it is. I doth not think that thou shalt have need of the weaponry by then."

"We hath many and more travels afterward, we were to travel through that city, or nearby, during our travels anyway," said Valto.

The Emporian nodded slowly and said, "Very well. Only the food and water rations," he wrote down some more words before handing the paper to Valto and continued, "Take this to those wagons over there and they shall fill thy requisition."

Valto took the paper and said, "I thank thee. I pray that thou hast a good life."

Valto bowed his head to him and he and Edvin left. The Emporian watched them go, confusion clouded all his thoughts. He didn't know what Valto was up to, but he was sure that it couldn't be good. No one, other than other Emporians and some from the client states would ever say such a thing and they had Norden accents.

He shook his head and regained his posture as he restarted his routine.

Edvin and Valto walked towards a convoy of covered wagons that was guarded by what seemed to be about one cohort of Emporian soldiers.

They stood in a single line circle around the wagons as other Emporians moved about the wagons and inside of them, hauling crates in and out of the wagons. On one side, the closest side of the convoy, were several desks where lines started.

Edvin marveled at the amount of soldiers that were there. In the Draken Confederation, there were not nearly as many soldiers guarding a convoy of wagons. He had never seen the size of an Emporian cohort before. When he saw his first Emporian soldier in his armor, he was intimidated by the man.

Now, he was slightly frightened by the amount of Emporians that wore their armor. He knew that he shouldn't be frightened, which is why he wasn't terrified by it. If he and simply one Emporian were to get into a sword fight, he was sure he could win, but he really didn't want to find out the reality of his imagination, though.

Valto, though, had been in the Confederations armies and had fought in Britone for a year or so before returning home.

After he had returned, he was almost sent back out to fight, but ran away instead. Coming into Imperial land and seeing Emporian armor again had not surprised him, but still filled him with dread.

All in all, Edvin was relieved that Valto was not freaking out when he came too close to an Emporian. Even so, Edvin didn't want to know what Valto would do if an Emporian drew a sword upon him.

They reached the back of the shortest line there was. It was the same line that Kristine from earlier was in and they were, once again, behind her and her child.

Valto leaned close to Edvin and whispered, "What doth thou thinkest the Emporians wish from the woman? Thou sawest the way they watched her go."

"Something to do with some sort of scar upon her face, perhaps? The man didn't seem content with the answer she hath given him," said Edvin in the same tone.

"But why would that be his business anyway? It's not as if he careth about anyone else but another man."

"I knoweth not the answer. What brought up this chain of thoughts?"

"Chance, perhaps? I paid it no mind until I found ourselves behind the woman again. I wonder what the scar looks like."

Edvin looked at him funny and asked, "What hath that anything to do with... anything that we are hither for?"

"Nothing. I only wonder."

The child that still clung to the elf woman's arm, looked back over her shoulder at them. Edvin smiled at her and she grinned back at him. Valto's brow pinched in confusion and he looked at Edvin, who made a silly face at the girl.

She giggled at him then and Kristine looked down at her asking, "What's so fun that warrants that, Dear?"

She looked from them, up at her and said, "The silly one behind us, Ma," and she pointed at Edvin. Valto sighed and rolled his eyes. Edvin half averted his gaze.

Kristine never looked back at them and simply said, "Very well, but be quiet now. I need to speak with the Legion-man now."

"I shall, Ma," said the little girl and she resumed to hug her mother's lower arm and hand. After a second, she looked back at them again and Edvin made a curling motion with his hand and index finger to indicate that she turn back around. She did and not much later, the elf that stood in front of the mother and child took a small sack and left.

"Next," said the Emporian behind the desk. His voice was tender and he had a Rozwidlenian accent. He had dark green eyes and a short cut goatee of black facial hair.

Kristine and her child stepped forward and she handed the requisition slip to the man. He took it and read the writing, nodding to himself. After he read it, he said, "Very well. Wait a moment and we'll hath that here for thee."

"I thank thee," said Kristine.

Valto folded his arms as he waited. Edvin's hands were on his hips and he rocked slightly on his heels and balls of his feet.

The Emporian had handed the slip to a man behind him, who was looking curiously at Kristine. He left and the man that sat behind the desk puffed out his cheeks and fiddled with a pen. He hadn't looked up at her face yet.

He looked up slightly and saw the little elven child looking at him intently. He furrowed his brow at her and stopped fiddling with the pen.

Nothing was said between anyone there, except people in other lines. After a few seconds of stare between the two, the child and the Emporian, the child abruptly said, "Thou sound nice. What art thou doing hither?"

Kristine had lost herself in thought and didn't realize it until it was too late to stop the child. Edvin and Valto kept their straight face, Edvin with some effort.

"Forgive her, please Sir, forgive her. She's only a child," pleaded Kristine, holding her child closely.

The Emporian looked up at her, his straight face cracked when the child had asked her question, and asked, "What in the hell is wrong with thee? Why needeth I forgive her for she hath done nothing to me?"

"I-I only wished not to disturb…" She was cut off by the Emporian.

"By god woman. Allow the child to be free. She's only a child."

"Uh-uh, I…"

"Be but silent until thy requisitions art given to thee," he said and waved a hand at her. She had her eyes down since he had first responded.

It wasn't much longer before the man came back with a crate and a sack on top of it. Two more men followed him with two crates each.

Each crate was three feet long, three quarters of a foot crate tall, and a foot wide. They were made out of any wood, as long as each crate was made of the same wood and didn't have random boards of different colors making up the same crate.

The two carrying two crates set them down near the desk. The man, who was the man who had been sent to fill out the requisition slip, set his crate onto the desk and lifted the sack off of it.

The man sitting down took the sack and looked inside of it. After a brief moment, he tied it back up and, holding it out to Kristine, said, "Here be thy requisitions. Take it and go on with thy day."

"Many thanks. Many thanks," she said hurriedly and took the sack in one hand and rushed off with her child.

The man that had returned watched her hurry off and looked at his fellow Emporian and, in an Alzeirian accent, asked, "What's wrong with her?"

"She's a ground groveller. Acted as if her child simply speaking is a crime," said the Emporian at the desk.

"Ah. She's one of those people then. Idiotic freaks." "Verily," he inhaled and said to the crowd, mainly to Valto and Edvin, "Next."

They stepped forward up to the desk and Valto immediately asked, "What was the problem with her?" He asked it in a way that made him sound against her and with the Emporians point of views.

"Those sorts of people are only more difficult to deal with. They are taught all their life that we Emporians are cruel and vicious in any situation, and seem to neglect the fact that we have families too," said the man who was standing. His arms were folded across his chest, as far as they could be folded with his armor on that is.

"That sounds like a tale straight out of the Confederation. Hell, mine aunt used to tell me stories similar to that. How Emporians were monsters and were demons that had crawled up from the lowest pit of hell," said Edvin.

"Thou doest not believe them, doest thee?"

"Nay. Mainly because she would also abuse me from time to time."

"That's one way of knowing who to believe and who not to believe," the man at the desk said, chuckling. He then said after a second, "Hand over thy slip."

"Surely," said Valto as he handed the slip to the man. He took it and held it in both hands as he read it. His face became more confused the farther he read until he looked up at Valto and said, "Hast thou brought a cart for all these rations?"

"Nay. I had thought that we could carry it ourselves."

The man looked at Valto like he was crazy and said, "Thou cannot carry all this that thou hast asked for. It is too much. Why, one single ration for one of these dragons is almost the size of thee."

"I was not thinking of that. Doest thou possess a cart or wane that we may borrow for a day or two?"

"What? Thou expect us to gift thou a cart to haul this in? Nay. We hath not a cart to spare nor hath we the men to spare to guard the cart and return it hither. Thou shalt come back when thou hast a cart that thou may use."

"But, what of the requisition we hath made?"

The man picked up a paper and pen and began to copy what was written on the previous paper onto the new paper. Once he was done copying the requests, he signed the bottom of the paper and turned to the man who stood behind him and said, "Sign this here as a witness," and the man signed it. He then looked to Valto and said, "Taketh this pen and sign this paper with thy name, and the same for thy companion as witness for thee."

He proffered the paper he had just copied onto and they did as he bid them. He then proffered the other paper that had the two Emporian names and said, "Taketh this copy as proof of thy filled requisition slip. We shall keep this copy as proof that thou doest not lie. Return when thou hast a cart or more companions to carry such requisitions."

"Mine apologies for being such a burden unto thee. We hath not thought this journey completely through," said Valto as he took his copy of the requisition slip.

"Not all is thy fault. Thou shalt not hast even passed the requisition desks over there. Nonetheless, keepeth that slip and return when thou can haul thy requisitions."

"We shall," said Valto and they left. "Next," said the man sitting at the desk.

Valto and Edvin walked out and away from the large crowd. After they were well away from any Emporian soldiers, Valto said, "That didn't work."

"Nay. It didn't. At least we got the requisition slip," said Edvin.

"Yea. There is that much. Now, we've got to get the others hither to pick it all up. I wonder how that conversation shall go."

"We didn't need the cart. It was only a means to an end. An end that was to come quickly anyway."

"Truth be told."

Chapter Eleven

The Battle Of Korontsy

Day 07, Manylight, Year 2142

The sun rose in the east and the land became visible for as far as the eye could see. The Seventeenth Legion was now within striking distance of their target: Korontsy and the rebelling force within.

Legate Dragomir had charge of the legion and he would march them unto victory this day. The men of the Seventeenth Legion were tired of marching and were ready for a fight, their patience waning. They would have their fight this day.

The men of the Seventeenth Legion were still wrapping up their camp and would be ready for their final march towards this accursed city. Dragomir was sitting upon his horse, his bodyguard cohort was around him. All were clad in their steel armor.

Their armor was of the armor of regular heavy cavalry. Steel plates overlapping one another from top to just below the navel. The same with their rerebraces, vambraces, cuisses and greaves. Their helmets were on and their faces were visible. Large kite-like shields occupied their left hands that also held the reins to their horses.

Carmine capes of gambeson fell around their shoulders and down their backs and were clasped by the sigil of the Seventeenth Legion, which looked like this: XVII.

It was a pin that held the cape around the neck of its owner. The horse armor was a simple coat of mail. The horse's head was covered by a steel plate. The back of the neck was covered by the same singular coat of mail. Underneath the mail coat, there was a gambeson coat that kept the mail from the horse's hair. This was the same as all cavalry.

Atop the Legate's helmet was a carmine feather plume that ran down the length of the helmet, perpendicular to his shoulders, and atop the helmets of his bodyguards were that of straw dyed pure carmine that also ran down the length of the helmet, perpendicular to their shoulders.

When the tents for a cohort were pulled down and stored, that cohort would then stand at attention before Dragomir. They stood forty men long and twelve men deep, the officers stood at the front of their centuries and the standard bearers stood next to the tribunes of the cohorts. Century bannermen stood near their centurions.

The standards were banners near the top of long wooden shafts with the standard of the legion they were a part of. Therefore it would look like this: At the top was a steel plate that had the number XVII, indicating the legion the cohort was a part of, and was attached directly to the shaft itself.

Underneath that would be a small shaft of wood that crossed perpendicularly with the main shaft and held the Imperial banner. Underneath that would be the cohort's standard, which was another steel plate with an engraving of the cohort's number and was attached to another cross of wood. This was the cohort's main standard. The other standards were the same except that they were smaller by a considerable size.

The bannermen/standard bearers stood near their officers with the banners/standards in their right hand and an Emporian shield in his left. Horns were slung about their bodies. The bottoms of the shafts of the standards had a steel spike. The sun was within the second hour of its rising when the Seventeenth Legion was arrayed and ready before Dragomir.

The geography around them was low rolling hills. So small that they weren't really considered hills. They were about one hour or more from their destination and they would make that march soon. The tents were all stored in horse drawn carts and wagons and were left at their camp site. The legion consisted of six infantry cohorts, two cavalry cohorts, and two archer cohorts and then the legate and his bodyguards. The infantry cohorts were of three different infantry types. One Great-swordsmen cohort, two swordsmen cohorts, and three spearmen cohorts.

Dragomir sat on his horse as the legion stood still. He was in front of his bodyguard cohort.

"Today, we set out to end our march north. To quell a rebellion in the name of the Emperor of this great empire. We look forward unto our coming battle and our coming victory over these Rat-Beards who raise themselves higher than their station. We march to show these dwarves whose wrath they hath called upon themselves. We march to do the Emperor's bidding and to deliver his will. We march to return peace to the lands of the Empire. We march to the battle that I hath promised ye and to the victory that is owed to ye. Now! WE MARCH!" He pumped his right hand in a fist into the air and the Seventeenth Legion saluted and gave a shout.

Before long, the Seventeenth Legion was on the march in a single column. Dragomir and his bodyguards led at the front. Behind them was the rest of the legion in this order: Great-swordsmen cohort followed by the two swordsmen cohorts, then the three spearmen cohorts, then the two archer cohorts and then the two cohorts of cavalry. Those were followed by horse wains and wagons filled with medical supplies, water skins, water barrels and oil barrels.

After three quarters of an hour of marching, they were just another few moments from reaching the village of Korontsy.

Within the village, dwarves ran about from house to house and street to street. The legion was visible unto them. A force of red and steel gray. The dwarves within Korontsy were no warriors of note, but they still had their weapons and armor that they were able to craft in the town forges. One dwarf, the Thane of the village, shouted orders to the scrambling dwarves. "Get those baskets to that barricade! We don't hath much time, the Empire is upon us!"

"But, Thane Larionovich, we're all but farmers! We're goin' to die!" A dwarf in dark gray wool clothes, more like rags though, called out. The Thane looked at him.

"Don't doubt now! We can win this legion."

"How can we win death, 'cause that's what's comin' for us!" "Pray to the god of our fathers and their fathers before them and we shall win!" The Thane encouraged them. They still hesitated to get to their positions. "I shall stand next to ye all in this! I shall fight these invaders with ye!" This gave the villagers some hope and they started going to their positions and tasks quicker. The Thane constantly looked out at the horizon at where the Emporian legion was and at the others that were in sight from where he was. "Come on! Faster, faster!" The Thane shouted.

Legate Dragomir and the Seventeenth Legion overlooked Korontsy.

"Order the men to form up into the fifth battle formation," Dragomir ordered a bodyguard nearest him. The man had grabbed a horn at his side that was looped around his neck and lifted it up to his lips.

He waited a second, remembering and making sure that he would get it right, then he blew the horn in a series of six notes. The first note being slightly longer than the others, that were all the same size. The final note sounded and a few seconds later the legion that was marching in a single column then broke and moved to their cohort positions. Moments later the legion was in formation five of Imperial regulations.

The two swordsmen cohorts were front and center, flanked by two cohorts of spearmen. One on each side. The two cohorts of archers took the space just behind the swordsmen cohorts and behind them was the legate and bodyguards cohort. Behind them was the cohort of Great-swordsmen and the other spearmen cohort. The two cohorts of cavalry were in the very rear, behind the entirety of the rest of the legion.

They waited a little longer as the rebel dwarves finally got into what they might call a semblance of any form of a battle position within the village streets. There were barricades in the streets that the dwarven rebels were in formation behind and on top of. It looked like an abomination to all that was orderly. It was a task on its own to depict ranks in their formations.

A moment later, Dragomir turned to the hornblower of his bodyguard and said, "Blow the order forward."

The horn blew in one long and deep blow and with that, the Seventeenth Legion began to march closer to the village. The dwarves shuffled, fidgeted and shifted backwards away from the approaching legion. Hearts began to beat faster now and the dwarves began to breathe faster as the legion closed the distance.

"Hold this ground!" The Thane ordered from his position in the line of a ragged formation atop of a barricade.

Once within bow range, Dragomir gave his order, "HALT!" The hornblower beside him blew his horn in the same way he had to initialize the advance and the legion stopped. "Archers! Hail arrows!" He ordered loud enough for the entire legion to hear, and possibly the rabble within the village.

The tribunes of the two archer cohorts complied instantly and began to shout out their orders to their cohort, "String thy bows! Prepare to hail arrows!" They strung their longbows and stood at the ready, awaiting their orders.

Within the village, the dwarves did hear the order and began to fear greatly for their lives. Not many shields, arms and armor were made in their frantic preparation for a rebellion, but enough may have been made to arm enough rebels to hold their main street. They lifted up their shields in a loose formation, not bunching up yet still close. They lifted their shields to above their heads and hid behind them. The shield bearers were on top of the barricades and behind. Many dwarves huddled directly behind the barricades.

The tribunes of the Longbowmen looked over their men and, nearly in unison, shouted, "NOTCH!" The Longbowmen drew arrows out of their quivers at their hips and notched them to their longbows.

"DRAW!" The orders rang out amongst the Seventeenth Legion. The Longbowmen drew their longbows and aimed them slightly up, just enough to fly over the swordsmen before them and their fellow archers and loosed the moment they had reached their full extension.

The arrows flew through the air in a tide that shadowed the ground beneath the flight of arrows. Just after the arrows left the bow strings, the tribunes shouted, "NOTCH!" And the Longbowmen notched another arrow each.

The first flight of arrows whistled through the air and met the dwarves, many stuck into the ground or were embedded into shields, but many more struck their mark in legs, arms, stomachs, chests, necks. Since the dwarves had little to no armor to wear, many of the dwarves died or fell to the ground in pain, screaming, "MY LEG!" or, "NOO!"

as they watched their friends fall to the ground. The entire entity of dwarves faltered.

"DRAW!" Longbows creaked as strings were pulled to cheeks and released the strings and another flight of arrows flew towards the dwarven rebels.

"NOTCH! DRAW!: NOTCH! DRAW!: NOTCH! DRAW!"

The orders rang and the Longbowmen complied and arrows flew to take dwarves to their deaths. As dwarves fell, some brave rebels ran up to take up shields and protect themselves and their injured companions that were being slaughtered. Many died in this process.

After six volleys of arrows, Dragomir looked to his hornblower and said, "Cease."

The hornblower put his horn to his lips and blew out a long note like before. And with that the arrows ceased. The dwarves were nearly broken and Dragomir had the mind to break them entirely.

"Order the swordsmen forward and order the cavalry around the village," Legate Dragomir ordered his hornblower. The man complied and blew his horn in a complicated series of notes.

He blew three regular notes, then paused, then blew four notes of the same length. He paused again before blowing a long and deep note like before to sound the advance. And a few seconds later, the two swordsmen cohorts advanced.

The hornblower then blew his horn again and blew ten regular notes. He paused again. Then blew eleven regular notes and he paused again before he blew out one more blast; long and deep, but unlike before, it wasn't as deep, but longer; to sound an advance, and a few seconds after that note sounded, the cavalry rode out from the formation and around the village, one on each side of the village.

The swordsmen infantry got near to the village and the townsfolk wavered and many broke and began to run.

"Nay! Stand thy ground! Fight!" The Thane urged the villagers. Not many of the fleeing dwarves listened as they ran for their lives.

As Legate Dragomir watched, he sensed that something was wrong here. The village had risen up in revolt and he had thought that there were more settlers who had lived here, but there was too little an amount for this rebellion. There must be reinforcements on the way, somewhere.

He should have noticed this earlier, but was too eager in his will to crush the rebel force. He turned to one of his bodyguards and said, "Something is wrong. Get back to camp and get me a scout in the sky. Quickly!"

"At thy bidding, Legate," the man complied with a Praetorian accent and wheeled his mount out of formation and back for the camp. And galloped off. Dragomir looked back at the village.

The tenth cohort of the Seventeenth Legion was on the west side of the village and was waiting for any villagers that tried to flee from this battle. They all knew their orders: kill any and all rebels. This rebellion would be extinguished immediately. The eleventh cohort of the Seventeenth Legion was on the east side of the village and was doing the same thing with the same orders. The third and fourth cohorts of the Seventeenth Legion advanced into the village, the villagers wavered and backed away from the two Swordsmen cohorts.

The swordsmen cohorts neared and a couple dozen of dwarves pulled out hunting bows and shot at the approaching Emporians. "Shields up!" The tribunes of the two cohorts ordered and the men raised their shields. Arrows bounced and streaked off of the shields, many arrows broke and broke upon the shields. Every man that felt or saw the arrows strike and go astray knew that the arrows were not carbonized.

The Swordsmen got closer to the barricades and the dwarves fidgeted more. "Halt!" The tribunes ordered and the cohorts came to a shuddering stop. They still held their shields towards the rebels.

The front rank held their shields directly at the dwarves and the ranks behind held their shields up above their heads. "Light torches!" Came the order.

Dwarves heard this and stepped back in shock. The Thane then shouted, "Get off the barricades!"

Emporian soldiers in the back turned around and propped their shields up on the ground and their heads. They reached into satchels and pulled out sticks with linen wrapped around one end. Along with the torches, they pulled out small water skins that were filled with oil and a match book. They doused the linen in oil and lit the torches. They then quickly picked their shields up and made their way through the formation to the front.

The dwarves were filing off of the barricades, mainly jumping off. The dwarves that were huddled behind the barricades had to move first though. So, it took longer than it should have.

The Emporians that held the torches reached the front of the formation and the shields split for the torches and the soldiers threw the torches at the barricades. Many torches hit the barricades, some threw over, but some torches didn't reach the barricades. Though that was very few. One of the soldiers that had thrown it short looked at the torch in dumbfounded shock. A soldier next to him looked at him with an odd look.

"Bad throw," said the soldier who had thrown the torch. He had a Rozwidlenian accent. The others that heard chuckled. The barricades burned hot and bright. The Emporians hid behind their shields, as they were trained to do. Some of the rebels didn't get away from the barricades fast enough and were lit on fire. They screamed in pain, fell to the ground and writhed. Others came to help.

Seeing the dwarves turn their backs to his archers, Dragomir gave the order to shoot more arrows. The dwarves in the village didn't hear the order and did not react. More were loosed and hit dwarves in the back. After the first volley, the dwarves scrambled for shields and cover. Arrows hit dwarves in the neck with blood splattering out of the wounds in their necks and blood dripped from their mouths. Some arrows went straight through the neck, others struck the spine and stuck in the neck, breaking necks.

The tribunes of the two swordsmen cohorts called out an order to their men almost at the same time, "Shield Wall!"

The order was carried down throughout the cohorts. It was harder than usual to hear anything due to the raging of the fires. The soldiers in front held their shields out in front of them and waited.

"Advance!" The order came and the Swordsmen slowly marched forward towards the fires.

"Cease!" Dragomir shouted and his horn blower sounded his order.

"Cease!" The tribunes of the archer cohorts shouted out and the archer cohorts ceased their shooting. An archer missed his quiver and half threw his arrow at the ground, it slightly penetrated the ground and immediately fell over and lay on the ground. Archers who saw looked at him, side long in judgement. The archer quickly bent down and picked up the arrow and threw it into his quiver.

The Swordsmen neared the flames and in a quick burst, they charged the burning barricades and broke them down with ease. The barricades crumbled and the hot flames faltered. The fire got snuffed out and not even a smoldering coal or ash was left with any heat.

For clarity, the front and rims of their shields were covered with a thin sheet of dragon steel. It being a magical metal, it did not react the same as other metals. For this instance, the dragon steel was not affected by the fire. Instead, it affected the fire by absorbing its heat and sort of killing the fire.

The rebel dwarves had formed up a pathetic line of fearful villagers. The tribunes saw and ordered, "March them into the dirt!"

The soldiers gave their approval and marched in formation to deal death to the rebels. The rebel forces gave their own battle cries and pounded their shields with their weapons and chests with their fists.

"Attack!" Some dwarves called out and charged. Other dwarves saw this and followed. Rebel dwarves clashed with the Emporian shield walls and died for it. The inferiority of their armor and weapons compared to Emporian make showed as Emporian heavy infantry cut them down like wheat during harvest.

An Emporian's sword slashed through the neck of a dwarf and the dwarf fell backwards and into the mob of his fellows. Dwarven women fought as well and paid the price for it. Another dwarf fell and another and another. Emporian swords cut through necks and torsos and limbs and faces and much dwarven blood was spilt and the ground was soaked through with it. An Emporian centurion pivoted his stance and thrust his sword into the throat of a dwarf. The dwarf fell down to die. A dwarven scythe was swung down towards an Emporian Veteran's shoulder, but he raised his shield and blocked the attack.

Dwarven axes, swords, maces, all crudely made, and hammers held little to no effect on the Emporian shield wall. Many dwarves attacked the lower part of the shields as more dwarves attacked the upper part of the shields and many of them died in un-practiced attacks, weak and sloppy strikes that would glance off of the shields and leave the dwarves open to a swift counter-attack by the Emporian Swordsmen.

The shield wall pushed up through the streets and into the village proper. The Emporians stepped over and onto fallen bodies as they advanced at a snail's pace. The rebels were untrained and only served to loosen and warm up the Emporians, like an appetizer for a larger course.

The first rank of Emporians began to tire and the second rank readied themselves for swap places with the first rank. The men in the second rank tapped the shoulders of the men in the first rank softly, yet hard enough so that the soldiers could feel it through the armor. They then pivoted to their left to where they were all facing one way, perpendicular to their previous positions. The soldiers in the first rank planted their shields and hid behind them, letting the shields get hit by several strikes by the rebels.

After a second of this, the soldiers in the first rank pivoted to their right and back, just as the men in the second rank pivoted to their right and forward. With this, the second rank became the first, the third rank became the second, the fourth rank became the third and so on. The men of the previous first rank made their way to the back of the formation.

When they got to the back, a soldier in the back said, "Don't slay them all. I want some glory."

A few other soldiers chuckled. The men who came from the first rank and to the rear of the formation were drinking water from their water skins and were breathing heavily. The battle went on.

Back at the camp, spare soldiers wore their armor and did their best at playing cards. Several sat in a circle around a table as they played cards, many others stood near the edge of the mostly consolidated camp. All of the tents were folded up and stored in their proper wains and wagons. The horses were tied to deeply pounded in steaks with buckets of water near them so that they could drink at their will. The spare soldiers of the Seventeenth Legion mainly lounged and kept their eyes open. A wind dragon of the Seventeenth Legion circled about high in the sky and watched at large. The other two of them were on the ground. One walked around, stretching, while the other relaxed with the Emporian soldiers. All, or most, chatted as they waited for the rest of the legion to quell the rebellion and return.

"I'll draw," said a soldier with a Rabian accent as he threw down a card and reached towards a soldier who didn't wear his upper body armor, the torso and arm armor, and he drew a card and handed it to the original soldier.

"Taketh it, Risner," said the dealer with a Soltero accent and Risner grabbed his card and looked at it, leaning backwards so that no one else could see what he had gotten. It was a castle, but that isn't what he wanted. Matter of fact, that was the exact card he had just gotten rid of, only it was black instead of white.

"Not what thou wanted, is it?" The soldier next to him said with a Rabian accent.

"Take thy turn," said Risner.

"All thou needest say next time is, 'nay'." "Taketh thy turn, Raynor."

Raynor chuckled as he looked at his cards. Two metal dragons, both were gold, and two castles, silver and brown. His last two cards were a sailor and a farmer, he wanted neither. He grabbed the sailor with his off hand and tossed it onto the table and said, "Draw."

"Here," said the dealer, giving Raynor a card and putting the discarded one in a separate stack. It was another sailor.

"What?" Raynor asked in disbelief. This was the third time in a row he had gotten a sailor after he had traded one in.

"Not something thou wanted?" Risner asked mockingly.

"It may be that I overstepped my bounds then. I apologize."

"And that's bloody right."

A rider rode up to the camp and halted before a patrolling Spearman. The rider was from the Legate's bodyguard and he spoke, "The Legate hath requested a scout in the sky."

"We'll hath one up thither," said the Spearman and jogged off into the camp. The bodyguard rode back to the battlefield. The Spearman reached the center where the game of cards was being played and found a Great-swordsman and sallied up to him. He watched the man approach. Once the Spearman reached the fellow soldier he said, "The Legate hath requested a scout in the sky."

"At once," the Great-swordsman said and looked for the nearest dragon, who was laying down and relaxing. The Spearman went back to his post and the Great-swordsman ordered out, "Thou! I don't remember thy name, but the Legate wants thou up thither immediately!"

The soldiers had looked up at the voice, but only the dragon's attention was held.

"I'll be there in less than a minute," said another voice. The Great-swordsman turned to see another dragon bend his legs and unfurl his wings and took off. The dirt was stirred up from the ground and wind whipped Emporian capes around. One soldier's cape wasn't fastened around his neck and was blown into the face of a fellow soldier. A few soldiers laughed. The Great-swordsman nodded to the wind dragon that was flying for the skies of the battlefield and turned back to what he was doing. The other dragon that was laying down resumed his relaxation.

"Were any of ye scared that ye were almost given some work to do?" A soldier playing the game of cards asked, looking at everyone that was playing the game. He had a Purian accent.

One huffed and said in a Praeterton accent, "Nay. Playing with ye is almost too easy."

"Shut thy mouth," said another with a Praeterton accent.

"Can we not all only have reason with one another?" Another one asked with a Britonic accent.

"Not with thee," said Raynor. Others chuckled.

A Great-swordsman centurion walked by and looked at Risner oddly, or actually behind him and down at the player he was walking past.

Risner looked up at the Great-swordsman and noticed this and his brow furrowed in confusion. He quickly lowered his head to hear what the soldier was whispering and bellowed out a laugh. Risner turned around quickly to see the wind dragon there, watching the game. The dragon looked at him as if he were innocent.

"I'm done playing this game with thee, Assen!" Risner said as he stood and threw his cards at the table. Raynor looked up at him and behind him and saw what Risner saw and looked back down at his cards and over at the player across from him that the centurion had walked past and shook his head.

"What doest thou mean?" Assen asked.

"Thou knowest what I mean," he said, then looked from Assen to the wind dragon and said, "So doest thee, Hubert."

"Me?" Hubert asked with a Hugroevian accent. "Yea, thee."

"I can't even play the game."

"Thou needest not to be able to play the game to help another cheat," said Risner. The other players were laughing and chuckling.

"So art thou conceding?" The dealer asked. Risner thought for a minute.

"Nay," he said and came back to the table and picked his cards back up to the entertainment of those around.

The dwarves were spent and were trying to flee from their village, but they did not make it too far as heavy cavalry ran them down and into the earth with their lances and iron-shod hooves. The lances were alike to spears, but longer and thicker than what a spear would be. Then at the end, instead of a blade, it was blunted as to not penetrate the victim, but to simply crush their bones.

The two cohorts of Swordsmen were sacking through buildings and removing anything that could be of value. They were nearly finished by this time and would soon begin lighting the buildings on fire.

"Has that structure been checked?!" A centurion shouted out, pointing at a building that was half a shack half an atrocity.

"Recheck it anyway! Release any livestock that are penned up!" A tribune bellowed out to his men.

Cattle and sheep ran around and out of the chaos that was taking place within the village. Some of the villagers had not made it out of their homes in time and were questioned harshly about any valuables that they knew of. Afterwards, if they had revealed any valuables known to the Emporian soldiers, they were rallied up into the village square, or what they called a square.

As for the others that did not yield any unknown valuables, they were killed on the spot where they either lied or yielded already known valuables and wouldn't yield up any other. Since children did not know much, and were looked upon as mostly innocent in many matters, it was up to the adults to save them. One stash of valuables for one life. If it was the parent of the child being questioned, then the parent and children were spared. They would be questioned more thoroughly later. The villagers screamed, cried and held their loved ones.

The building was raided and the soldiers came out with nothing and rejoined their fellow soldiers.

"Quickly! Faster!" A tribune bellowed.

Outside the village, many of the rebel villagers were attempting to flee the field of battle, but they would not. The tenth and eleventh cohorts of the legion ran them down and into the earth. They pelted them down with balled lances, lances that had a small ball-like end. It wasn't a very bulbous end, more like only dulled, but they were very effective for the legions of Emporia.

Cavalrymen lowered their lances and charged fleeing dwarves, landing hits on the heads, backs and chests. Breaking bones and crushing bodies in their charges.

A cavalryman charged a running dwarf woman. He lowered his lance and leaned forward in the saddle. The dwarf woman looked back and saw him and turned around and raised one of her hands in surrender. The poor dwarf woman was carrying a small child in her arms.

The Emporian aimed his lance at her chest, where the child was, and made her cringe away. She did not get away though as the cavalryman's lance crushed the bones of the child and dwarf woman. The lance forced the two to the ground harshly.

The cavalryman pulled his lance up and linked with his fellow cavalrymen. If the dwarf woman wanted to live, then she should have never rebelled against the Empire.

Within the village, the captured villagers were being led out of the village. The dead were left to rot. "Light torches! Set the village on fire. Start from the north and we'll move out back from where we entered!" The tribune of the fourth cohort ordered his men. "Thy will be done, Sir!" The men sounded out. As they sacked the village, they wrapped the sticks within their satchels and any large sticks and boards that could be hand held. The linen was then doused with what oil the soldiers had and then were lit on fire. The men holding the now lit torches ran off to light any houses on fire that they could. Within moments, the northern buildings were burning.

Legate Dragomir's bodyguard had returned and Dragomir waited. The rebel forces here were all but destroyed, fleeing to their deaths. A thought struck him and he thought about fulfilling it, but decided not to. All would be well. He thought he heard something to the west, but wasn't sure. It sounded odd. He watched as the village caught fire and burned.

The sound came again and it was growing louder. Men around him looked in the same direction and his hornblower said, "Those are war drums, Sir."

"Reinforcements, as I expected, but why would they hath a war drum in their possession, lest they be formally enlisted, it shouldn't be," said Dragomir.

"Not any war drum, Sir," he paused for a second and added, "It sounds like a Confederate war drum."

"Confederate?! Impossible. There is a fort between here and their nearest border. We would knoweth it if they were here," he stopped as he thought for a second and added, "Lest, they marched through Ludy Dvukh Chelovek."

"It is possible, Sir."

"Turn the legion around to face them. Double time!" He ordered. The hornblower grabbed his horn and blew out one deep blow that held two notes, almost like two different blows, but he didn't breathe in before making the second note and the two notes were right next to one another. The notes sounded the exact same, but different pitches.

He made that blow once and then blew one more time that held three notes, but was lighter of tone and with every note, the pitch became higher like it was building up momentum. This indicated a left flank pivot. There was a moment's pause before the men of the cohorts moved.

"A left flank pivot?" A centurion asked the tribune of the third cohort. The men filed behind the tribune and formed up.

"To the field! Quickly!" The tribune ordered and the cohort marched for the field outside the village. The fourth cohort did the same, marching down two different streets. The third cohort on one and the fourth on the other. The village continued to burn and crumble. The living villagers were then killed.

The tribune of the eleventh cohort rounded up his cavalrymen by holding his lance near straight up and twirled it in a circle above him. Once his bannerman saw this, he raised his banner high and waved it in circles above his head and cavalrymen flocked to his position. He had heard an Emporian war horn blow out what he thought was a left flank pivot. Near where he was rounding the eleventh cohort to formation, the tenth cohort was forming up.

Corporal Durand flew high above the battlefield and watched. He saw the approaching blocks of soldiers and the legion that had pivoted to face the approaching army. Smoke from the village blocked out his view most of the time and he couldn't see anything really. He was about to warn Legate Dragomir about the reinforcements, but then the legion had pivoted. So he stayed up high and circled around. His scales weren't camouflaged with the sky. He didn't think that it was needed this time. Camouflaging could get exhausting after a while and he thought it best to stay visible to his legate, or at least try to.

From where he was, what he could see and had seen, he thought that the dwarves slightly outnumbered the Imperial legion. The cavalry were returning to formation behind, to the north, of the village and the Swordsmen were moving out of the village. Burning it as they left. He didn't see anything other than that. He continued to keep his vigilance though, not letting his mind wander off. It could get hard at times.

He thought he saw something in the corner of his vision and he looked up to see another dragon charging. He was too late. The dragon hit him and quickly tore out his throat. The dead body fell downwards towards the ground.

Dragomir watched as banners and dwarves crested the small rise that they were behind. His Swordsmen had exited the village and were marching back to the large of the legion. They would not take long to reach the rest of the legion. The tenth and eleventh cohorts were somewhere off near the village.

Within the next minute, the third and fourth cohorts had returned to the legion main. The Swordsmen were given a moment's rest as Dragomir looked to the sky for his scout. He couldn't see anything, but there was much smoke. He shifted in his saddle and returned his eyes to the approaching dwarves.

"Those are Confederate banners and colors, Sir," one of his bodyguards said as he squinted at the dwarven infantry. Dragomir nodded as he studied his enemy. So this was what he would defeat today. Could be a challenge, depending on what the army consisted of. Since he had technically attacked to start the day, he would attack to finish it. Once he believed the swordsmen were rested enough, he turned to his hornblower.

"Sound the advance," he ordered. The hornblower put his horn to his lips and blew the order to advance. A moment after the horn blowing stopped, the legion advanced together. The dwarves had halted at the top of the miniature hill for a moment and as the legion drew closer, they began to march down the hill towards them with the sound of loud, deep booming drums.

The front line of the dwarves were medium sword infantry, only wearing mail hauberks and open face helmets with gambeson coats underneath and over the mail that covered their torsos. Their shields were octagonal in shape and covered their torso's and their upper legs. Not peasants, nor levies, but not upper class.

In the center of the front line were what seemed to be dwarven foot-knights, heavy dwarven infantry. They had steel breastplates, vambraces, rerebraces, cuisses, greaves and gauntlets with great helmets. Most of the armor sets were different in appearance.

Some helms had thinner eye slits as others had no armor where the eyes were. Some had feather and horse hair plumes of different colors and designs as others either had some form of metal design or no ornamentation at all. Most all had different sur-coats and coats of arms worn on their breastplates.

The arrayment of weapons wielded by the confederate dwarven foot-knights were scattered, some wielded mace and shield whilst others brandished long shafted hammers that were flat on one side with a long, claw-like protrusion on the opposite side of the head. Some had halberds and many others had great double bladed axes. Many others had short hafted great-hammers that had abnormally large and broad heads. Though the shaft was short, the weapon was still nearly as tall as the dwarf who carried it.

Behind the front line were crossbow infantry. There were nearly as many crossbow dwarves as there were melee infantry dwarves. The crossbow and medium sword infantry had the same colors of fabric that made up the gambeson coats they wore, black and yellow.

The crossbow-dwarves stopped near the very top of the hill and the melee dwarves kept marching down to near the bottom of the small hill, not quite on the flatter ground. The legion advanced closer.

"Shoot!" Came the command from dwarven officers of the crossbow infantry. Crossbow arrows flew through the air to strike upon Emporian shields. A few of the hundreds of arrows slipped past shields and hit the necks, upper arms and heads of the men who were struck.

Arrows shot directly through some necks and others went most of the way through, snapping through the bones and shattering them. Arrows pierced the rerebraces of soldiers and would either pierce into the other side or strike the bone, snapping it. Men who were struck in the arm grunted contained screams of pain. The heads of soldiers that were struck by the incoming arrows were snapped back and the necks were broken. The dead fell to the ground.

Tribunes noticed and called out, "Shields up! Shield wall!" The call was taken up and the cohorts took to the formation that was ordered. The Great-swordsmen had thrown their capes around their shoulders so that it would cover their bodies.

Dragomir wanted to end this quickly. The dwarves pounded their war drums and shouted out their battle cries. Something caught Dragomir's eye. The tenth and eleventh cohorts were flanking the dwarven army. He took this as his chance and turned to his hornblower and said, "Sound the charge."

The horn blew loud and clear in one blast, but the note was broken up. Not like the pivot order where there were two notes, but where the note started, went dead for a split second, then continued as if it never stopped.

A moment after the horn sounded, the melee infantry of the Seventeenth Legion picked up their pace to a jog. The Swordsmen and Spearmen that made up the front line lifted their shields and charged. Crossbow arrows flew through the air and struck shields and bounced off. The impacts jolted through the arms of the men holding them, but other than that and the few arrows that found their marks in arms and legs, the front four cohorts charged. The dwarves held their ground and braced for the charge. The Swordsmen were in the perfect position to wield their maximum efficiency.

The swordsmen spotted the dwarven foot-knights and shouted out to their fellow soldiers, "Armor!" As they shouted out the warning, they sheathed their swords and unhooked their maces. The men carried this shout throughout the rest of the cohorts.

As the Swordsmen came near the tribunes gave out orders, "Slow! Shield wall!"

The men next to them carried the order out through the cohorts and they slowed and formed up tightly. The Spearmen didn't slow though and charged with their spears leveled at the dwarves, up near their heads and pointed downwards to hit the dwarves. They clashed and the dwarves in the center that were lined up to fight the Swordsmen cohorts charged the Emporians and soon there was one bold line of bodies holding the center of the field.

"Hail arrows!" Dragomir ordered.

"NOTCH! DRAW!" Shouted the tribunes of the Longbowmen cohorts. Longbowmen shot arrows into the ranks of crossbow-dwarves, felling many of them. Crossbow arrows shot from crossbows and, at times, found their marks and ended the lives of some humans and seriously injured others. Many arrows still snapped, broke, splintered, bounced off and shattered on Emporian shields.

A spearman thrust his spear at a dwarf and the dwarf deflected it and it ended up striking into the exposed face of a dwarf behind and jerked the head back violently and the dwarf fell to the ground, grabbing at his face, screaming.

An Imperial swordsman blocked the attack of a dwarf's sword with his shield and brought his mace around to strike it upon the dwarf's shoulder and the dwarf's shoulder was broken and he crumbled to the earth, dropping his weapon and grabbing at his shoulder.

The hooves of the tenth and eleventh cohorts alerted the crossbow-dwarves and they turned to see balled lances striking them down to the earth and into their comrades. Some were killed by the lances, but many more were killed by the iron shod hooves of the large war horses as the horses trampled the dwarves as if they were nothing but grass beneath the horses hooves.

Seeing this, the Longbowmen ceased their shooting and began to shoot arrows into the ranks of dwarven knights that were pushing the Emporian Swordsmen back.

A dwarven knight with a great-hammer swung his weapon and landed the hit on the shield of an Emporian Swordsman, knocking him back and into a fellow Emporian. The dwarf quickly recovered and swung his hammer back around and an Emporian jerked away, out of range of the hammer. A flight of arrows came streaking down and struck the dwarven knight in the head, shoulder and neck. The arrows snapped and one penetrated deep into the neck. The dwarf staggered back and fell to the ground.

Another took his place and swung, missed and an Emporian landed a blow with his mace to the side of the helmet. The dwarf dropped his weapon and fell to the ground. And yet another dwarven knight stepped up and hit the Emporian with his long hafted hammer and the man was sent flying back to the ground.

"Get the Great-swordsmen in there!" Legate Dragomir ordered his hornblower and he blew his horn in two regular notes, paused, then blew a long blow to order the advance and the second cohort of the Seventeenth Legion advanced past the Legate and towards the center of the combat line. The Spearmen were holding their ground against the Confederates, but the Swordsmen were bowing, pushing the medium dwarven infantry back and bending to the heavy dwarven foot-knights.

They were pushing more than they were bending, much more. The crossbow-dwarves were wavering, dropping their weapons with buckling knees and shaking legs, and the two cavalry cohorts pulled away from the combat one at a time and charged again and again, never staying in the midst of combat for too long.

As the Great-swordsmen neared the battle line, behind where the battle line was a form that fell from the sky and crashed to the ground. The Great-swordsmen, Longbowmen, cavalry and, well, anyone who wasn't in direct combat paused and were confused as to what it was.

It was too large to be a bird, far too large for that, and there were no siege engines in the area. None that anyone knew of. The cavalry were in the perfect position to see what it was and everyone else could figure out what it most likely was.

A wind dragon.

Every Emporian that was not in direct combat looked up to the best of their ability and saw dragons diving upon them. The Great-Swordsmen needed to lift their face guards to see clearly.

The Longbowmen took immediate action. They drew arrows and shot them up at the nearest dragons. Most every arrow found its mark and either lodged into scales or broke them and sometimes both. Other arrows pierced the wings, tearing holes in them.

Some dragons were thrown off course and the cavalrymen pulled out of the combat area, each cohort took different courses away from the combat line. The soldiers in the combat line didn't notice anything as they fought, or if any saw, they were of very little amount.

The Great-swordsmen cohort's tribune shouted out orders to split into forty-eight groups of ten and sent some into the combat line and sent the others out around the Longbowmen. The third Spearmen cohort advanced quickly to help protect the Longbowmen and the legate and bodyguards cohort. Another few dragons came close to the ground and were paid off with flights of arrows from the Longbowmen that tracked every dragon that came within range.

A group of Great-swordsmen reached the battle line and the Swordsmen parted for their path towards the dwarven knights. The group reached the front of the line and waited for the Swordsmen to be ready to part and let them through.

Legate Dragomir turned to some of his bodyguards and said, "Get to the camp and get messengers to the nearest two forts of what's happening!"

"At once, Sir!" They responded and reeled their steeds off and galloped off.

He turned to the rest of his cohort and said, "The rest of ye, with me!" He drew his sword as did all his bodyguards that hadn't already. He then said, "Centurion Alvin! Take thy century to the right flank!"

"Sir!" He nodded and turned to his century and said, "To the fight!" He rode off in front of his men and they charged for the right flank.

"Centurions Nestoras and Luther! Take thy centuries to aid the tenth and eleventh cohorts!"

"As thou commands, Sir!" The two centurions replied and turned to their men.

"Onwards!" Nestaros shouted.

"To glory!" Luther gave his shout. "GLORY!" Shouted back his century.

"The rest of ye, with me!" Dragomir shouted and raised his sword. His men followed.

The Swordsmen parted and the Great-swordsmen burst through. The dwarves were startled to see them charging, one hand near the larger hand guard and one near the pommel and the hilt near their helmet.

A greatsword swung down and collided with the helmet of a dwarven knight. The dwarf fell down.

Another Great-swordsman brought his weapon and slammed the broad-side against the side of another dwarf and the dwarf staggered away from the blade and down to the ground.

Both were most likely dazed, though the second dwarf could have fallen unconscious.

The dwarves began to recover as the ten Great-swordsmen cut and beat their way through them.

Behind the Great-swordsmen charge, the Swordsmen charged behind and finished off any who had fallen to the ground.

Whether they were already dead when the Swordsmen got to them or not, they were still attacked just in case they were trying to fake it.

The dwarven knights were now pulling back and the swords-dwarves were pulling back even quicker.

A dragon landed in a stumble after being pelted with many arrows and a group of Great-swordsmen attacked before she knew it. They targeted the already cracked and splintered scales. They rarely missed unless the dragon had flinched as they were swinging. With each swing, scales either broke off or cracked some more and shattered or broke into more pieces.

A Great-swordsman striked the dragon's leg and used the rebound and cut at the wing, placing a long cut in the leather of the wing. The dragon whined in pain as she reeled away from the strike.

The Longbowmen were shooting at any dragon that was within range and wasn't being attacked by either Great-swordsmen, Spearmen or the bodyguards of the legate.

The tenth cohort charged into the rear of the dwarven knights and, with their lances, they ran dwarves into the ground and threw them into one another. The great war horses they rode stomped upon the dwarves and cut their lives short. The eleventh cohort was back and looking towards the sky.

The dwarves broke, but they were partially surrounded by Emporian infantry and cavalry. This made them more afraid and they began to panic. The Great-swordsmen that had reached the battle line and were in contact with the confederates were now killing them like pigs to slaughter.

Once the swords-dwarves in combat with the Emporian Spearmen had broken and were running, the Spearmen turned around and looked at the sky at the dragons that were now targeting the swordsmen.

A Swordsman alerted his fellow swordsmen and they lifted their shields above their heads and an at least partially fire dragon strafed the line with a long breath of fire as the dragon flew past.

The fire had little effect on the Swordsmen that had lifted their shields, but the swordsmen that were still exposed were caught in the fire and burned to a quick death.

Longbowmen targeted the dragon with a flight of arrows into his side. Most arrows pierced through the scarlet and white scales and the dragon's wing flinched in as he flinched away from the arrows and fell to the ground where he rolled back onto his talons.

He flinched away from putting weight onto his left side. Cavalry of the tenth cohort placed their balled lances in hook-like straps on the right side of their horses and grabbed a small, hand held crossbow from the left side of their horses. They held the crossbows in one hand and aimed at the dragon. They shot at the dragon once they got within range.

The cavalry of the tenth cohort also ran down fleeing dwarves. Dragons came to the rescue of the dwarves and they raked their talons at the Emporian cavalry.

A dragon with brown scales grabbed a man from his horse with a front talon as she passed over the Emporians. Her tail crushed another man and horse to the ground during the passover.

An Emporian cavalryman completely dropped his lance and quickly grabbed his crossbow as another dragon, that had slightly darker brown than the last dragon had, came near. The man, along with a few of his companions, aimed their crossbows and held them at the ready.

Though, they didn't hold them for very long as they shot at the attacking dragon. Two of the cavalrymen aimed their arrows at the left wing. The others penetrated the scales and sank into the dragon. The other two arrows went into the wing, passing straight through.

The dragon landed amongst them, landing directly on one man, and swiped at another man with one talon and another man was hit with his tail. The dragon clamped his jaws down upon another man. The rest drew their swords and crossbows and attacked the head of the dragon.

Legate Dragomir had led his bodyguards against fleeing dwarves and they had slaughtered many with their swords and horsepower. Fortunately, not many dragons had tried to attack him. The ones that had were either shot at by the Longbowmen or did land a successful strafe.

No fire, simply trying to grab at men and pick them up off the ground or at least knock them off their horses. He had lost nearly thirty men to dragons already. He made sure to stay within range of the Longbowmen and within sight too.

Dragomir surveyed the battlefield to see a cohort of cavalry get attacked by a dragon and several men died. A dragon flew another strafing of fire upon Spearmen and Swordsmen cohorts. Fire reigned about the battlefield.

Great-swordsmen battered and stabbed at a dragon and the dragon fell, dead or dying. Longbowmen shot flight after flight of arrows into the air and struck their targets with almost every arrow, but they were low on ammunition and it would not last much longer.

"We cannot win this. This legion was not prepared to fight dragons!" Dragomir said, obviously and his irritation grew. He turned to his bodyguards in their moment of respite and continued, "Get to the legion and order the retreat! Fall back out of the region and to some form of cover. A fort or a tree line. A town or anything. Fall back steadily. Go! Spread the word! This day is lost."

"Yea, My Legate!" They said together and over each other and split into their groups to warn the rest of the legion that was still battling for their lives. Many of the men still stayed with their legate and he would wait until he was sure that the legion knew of his command.

Back at the camp, three riders rode up to the edge as the rest of the camp were on their feet and looking into the distance and high. The smoke rose from the village they supposed, but now there was more smoke and what looked like figures in the air far off. The riders pulled up and one opened his face guards and said, "Confederate troops have arrived at the battlefield. Get word to as many forts as we hath messengers."

The men turned around to see the two remaining wind dragons of the Seventeenth Legion, the second had landed a bit ago and the other didn't take off because the third had taken off to scout for Legate Dragomir, take off and into the air with great speed after some air had gotten under their wings. Men were blown off balance by the power of their take off.

The rest of the camp burst into action. They armed themselves for a fight and the bodyguard detachment sped back for Legate Dragomir.

The Emporian cavalry reserves already had their horses armored and were armoring themselves and mounting. Longbowmen came together and were then half surrounded by Spearmen and a group of Great-swordsmen. Officers shouted out orders to their reserve men, "Get in line! Get in formation!; Over there! Go!; Mount up!"

The dragons had camouflaged in with the sky so as to not be seen departing. The ground troops were to make sure that they were not followed in some way.

The Seventeenth Legion had received the order to retreat and were doing their best to retreat with order and not chaos.

The Confederate soldiers were taking their advantage and harrying them all the way. The Longbowmen had only one or two arrows each and were saving them for emergencies, like a dragon got too close for their liking.

The dragons knew of this by how they were not being shot at when they came near the ground or other Emporian troops and so they became bolder in their attacks. Instead of strafing with their claws, they would land and wreak devastation on the cohort they attacked. Grabbing men with talons and squashing them into the ground. Grabbing them with their tails and lifting them into the air to land somewhere else, knocking men to the ground with their tail.

Swordsmen pulled out their maces and would land blows to the dragons when they could. The tenth and eleventh cohorts were low on numbers and about fifteen dead dragons to show for it. Though they had many wounded dragons to show for it. Dragons fought off attacking cavalrymen from wounded allies and helped their fellow dragons get away from the fight.

The Great-swordsmen were especially targeted. Though they may be difficult to kill, they were also highly expensive for Emporia to recruit. Only a certain number of men could actually qualify for becoming a Great-swordsman and though that amount wasn't rare, it was certainly not as common as the Swordsmen qualifications.

So it wasn't so much as expenses, but for lower amounts of men who could fill the positions. So as the dragons attacked the Great-swordsmen, they would get injured but would also tire the Great-swordsmen further and, with luck, would kill or seriously injure a Great-swordsman.

Near the southern end of the battlefield is where the wains filled with supplies were. A score of Great-swordsmen guarded the wains and wagons and they prepared to get the supplies away from the battlefield. A few dragons attacked and were warded away or killed by the Great-swordsmen. Another two dragons conspired to attack together.

"I'll go high," one said to the other. The one that spoke had bright yellow scales with orange-red accents near the wings, both under and on his back. His wings were amber and his eyes were as well.

The other had steel gray scales that covered all but her underbelly that was white. Her eyes were icy blue and her wings were a lighter shade of steel gray. She nodded and they split off to attack.

The Great-swordsmen were watching the skies, and any dragons that were nearer than others. A few watched the two that had stopped high for a moment, near each other. "They're planning something. Be ready for another assault!" A Great-swordsman of the rank of centurion ordered in a Praetorian accent.

They couldn't see what scales the dragons had, but they were enemy dragons nonetheless and they were near directly above them. One dragon came in fast, a metal dragon and from where the Emporians could see over the reflection and smoke, they were certain that it was iron scales. They all knew they couldn't fight an iron scaled dragon. Or, they could, but it would be much more difficult.

The dragon came closer, beat her wings hard once and gained some altitude, which made the Emporians think that she may strafe them with her talons. This is when they saw that she had white scales, but at the last second, she furled her wings and dropped on top of a Great-swordsman and crushed him.

The dragon then grabbed a horse of a wain with her jaws and threw it, whinnying, at another Great-swordsman. It hit him dead on and he was thrown to the ground underneath the horse. The horse hit and bounced to roll on, but the Emporian lay on the ground, unable to recover his breath quickly enough and many of his bones were broken.

Great-swordsmen scrambled to attack her. Then the centurion remembered that there were two and he opened his face guard and looked up. He couldn't see the other one, not yet anyway.

The iron dragon took a hit on the snout by a Greatsword flinched away, recovered and fainted another attack to bite the man, who swung again, in which she backed away and he missed. She then sprung forward, got hit in the snout again, which was annoying to her, but she swiped at the man and hit him up into the air and away from the wagons. Other Great-swordsmen attacked her, on many sides, but no attacks really hurt. Only enough to annoy her greatly.

A moment later of the centurion watching the sky, he saw another dragon wheeling around and making a final approach to strike. He had yellow and orange scales, the centurion saw, and his eyes opened wide in shock.

One of the wagons had oil barrels stored within it. He didn't think that they knew that though, but that didn't matter. What mattered was that there was and a fire dragon was on his way to wreak devastation on the wagons.

"Fire dragon!" He shouted at the top of his lungs, which was barely audible because of the magnitude of the sound.

Great-swordsmen turned around to see him coming in too late. The dragon opened his mouth and orange and yellow fire shot out at the centurion, who had tried to evade the attack the moment he saw it coming, and the wagons behind him. The other dragon continued to attack, getting close to the wagons.

The fire killed the centurion and hit the wagons. The wood caught the fire and carried it to the others until every wagon was on fire. The wagon with the oil, which was near the back, was lit on fire and not much later and it erupted into white hot flames as the fire burned to and through the wooden barrels. The oil began to spread rapidly towards the iron dragon.

The iron dragon yelped and jumped away. The fire dragon was less affected, even though he was closer, but still half flinched away from the fire, mainly out of shock. The iron dragon scrambled away and the fire dragon got in between her and the flames to try to shield her from them.

The remaining Great-swordsmen who were not in range of the fire got up and saw their moment to strike. One's cape was on fire, but he charged the dragons nonetheless.

The fire dragon didn't turn around to look until the man was right next to him and laid a long cut, that cut straight through, along one of his wings. He cried out in pain and jumped away.

The heat of the oil fire had lessened and was bearable enough for both the men and the iron dragon to be able to function without feeling like they were melting. The iron dragon clamped her jaws around the man's body and tightened her jaw. Her teeth pierced the steel armor and into the man's body. He screamed in pain and she threw him into the fire.

The fire from his cape had singed her upper lip on the left side of her face. She had reacted by throwing him into the fire and tried to scrape the pain away.

This left her open and a Great-swordsman attacked her underbelly. He got underneath, broke a scale and made an opening for his weapon to pass through and thrust.

It didn't do any lasting damage to the dragon, but did cause her pain and she flapped her wings to get away.

Other Great-swordsmen attacked the fire dragon with ferocity. A few hits landed on his thorax and he ended up burning one, but the other got his weapon into his thorax.

The iron dragon saw and charged to the fire dragon's aid. She killed the man, but the last Great-swordsman found his prime opening as she ripped the head off his fellow man, he got his weapon deep into her eye, through the socket and into the brain. The dragon reeled away and collapsed. The Emporian turned to the fire dragon, who opened his mouth and scorched the man to ashes.

A Great-swordsman elsewhere cut at the eye of a dragon and landed his hit. The dragon half yelped with pain and jerked away. The dragon was missing scales on her thorax, so another Great-swordsman ran up as the dragon was recovering and thrust his greatsword into the opening and through the bones to hit either a lung or the heart. She gave another half yelp, half roar of pain and backed away.

The Great-swordsmen let it go and rested for a brief moment as they continued their retreat and covering of the third cohort. They were exhausting and would not last much longer fighting dragons and lo and behold, there were plenty more of those around.

A dragon saw her opportunity and attacked them. One Great-swordsman was too exhausted to fight her and simply planted his feet and raised his greatsword and said to himself, "This is utter hell."

He stood his ground and half allowed the dragon to beat him around. One blow sent him flying through the air to land on the ground twenty feet from his original position and rolled a little bit before stopping and convincing himself to get back up and to end his life rather than be taken prisoner.

The dragon pursued him and he found that his weapon was no longer with him. His whole body hurt, but he charged for his weapon anyway.

He side-stepped an attack by the dragon, reached his weapon and turned around in time to see the dragon grab him with her jaws and fling him scores of feet away to land in a smoldering building in Korontsy.

The other Great-swordsmen of the dwindling group of ten were feeling the same way their friend did, but some of the remaining four still had some power enough to fight back. None were going to be taken alive today, not very easily at least.

A dragon crashed into the fourth cohort and several men flew through the air to land either on the ground or on fellow soldiers. Some got caught underneath the dragon's talons and claws and their bones were crushed.

Many Emporian Swordsmen either dropped their swords or sheathed them and pulled out their maces and attacked the dragon, targeting individual scales. The multi shade scales of brown were cracked and broken as the dragon swiped at the Emporians with his claws and tail.

A few scales on the thorax were broken off and the skin underneath was exposed and a few men noticed this and dove beneath the dragon's guard to thirst their swords into the cracks in its scales. The dragon flinched back with a stifled yelp and backed away.

A few Great-swordsmen saw their chance and attacked the dragon's flanks and one got before the thorax section and had help aiming his greatsword and thrusting it into the dragon to pierce the heart or at least come close to it. The dragon then bounced away from the conflict and another dragon came to his rescue.

Legate Dragomir waited until he was absolutely sure that the legion had received his order. Several of his bodyguards were attacked and killed in the process and the rest were urging him to retreat himself, but he was adamant that he make sure the legion was retreating together before he left himself. He watched as he and his bodyguards turned to flee from the battlefield, the seventeenth legion split into two.

One was backing away towards the burnt and slowly burning village remains and the other was being pushed to the south east. Dragons attacked him and his bodyguards, but he was able to get away from the conflict as his bodyguards distracted the dragon.

Few banners still hung high above their cohorts, others lay upon the ground near where its holder died. Some were picked up by passing soldiers from the cohort to which it belonged and they carried with them.

The Emporian soldiers that had been pushed into the ruined village were surrounded and being attacked on as many sides as could be at one time. The cohorts dwindled underneath the attacking dragons. The numbers of the cohorts drew low and the morale began to break. All that it took was for the standards of the third, fourth and fifth cohorts to fall to the ground and the men broke and surrendered, but by then, not many soldiers still lived. Most of the living were wounded and dying.

The second, sixth, seventh, and eighth cohorts retreated away from the battlefield and further into Emporian territory. The Confederate dragons did not follow them much farther than the smoking ruins of Korontsy. Legate Dragomir and the tenth and eleventh cohorts slipped away with heavy losses and the Seventeenth Legion was broken and running. Running with order anyway.

Recruit Lebuin saw the fort come into view and checked his surroundings before dropping his camouflage as he decreased his altitude. He neared the fort and circled above for a minute, looking down at the fort and waiting for his signal, as was the protocol for approaches.

Upon an open-roof tower, on a barracks, a man stepped out and the slow wind blew his carmine cape about and he looked up, waved a small silver and carmine flag and waited as Lebuin decreased his altitude.

Lebuin made his final approach and reined up and landed with a heavy thud. A centurion stood near where he had landed and was waiting for him.

"Code," the centurion demanded once Lebuin had secured his footing. The centurion had a Corinosian accent. Lebuin blinked for a moment. He had forgotten it, or at least forgotten how to say it.

Lebuin's nerves got further on edge until he finally remembered and said with a Hugroevanian accent, "Imperialis Robur."

The man nodded and asked, "Superior officer?"

191

"Legate Dragomir of the Seventeenth Legion," said Lebuin. "Rank and name along with what thy purpose is hither?" "Recruit Lebuin with orders to report to, His Highness, High Prince Andronicus."

The centurion looked at him for a moment and mulled over the words before asking, "What is the report?"

"Confederate soldiers reinforced the rebels at Korontsy."

The centurion blinked at him for a moment and others had stopped in their tracks to pay attention to the conversation. He blinked a little more and asked, "What?"

"Confederate soldiers near Korontsy."

The man scoffed and asked, "And how exactly does that happen? Did they come with some winter snow as well?"

"Perhaps. I'm only reporting what I was bid to report. I didn't see anything. I was at the camp."

The man sighed and said, "Sure thing that is," he turned around and looked back and added, "Wait here. I'll report to the High Prince."

"Surely, Sir," replied Lebuin, resting on his haunches and curling his tail about him. The centurion jogged for the legate's tower and conversed with the guards there before being admitted in.

Centurion Vulmar took the steps two at a time as he ascended the tower to the High Prince's room. "Confederate soldiers near Korontsy," he scoffed to himself in a whisper and continued, "What a tale."

He arrived before a door guarded by four bodyguards who stopped him and the centurion of the guards asked with a Rabian accent, "Business here, Centurion?"

"Report from Legate Dragomir for His Highness."

The centurion nodded as he accepted the response and turned around and said, "Let His Highness know."

"At once, Sir," said the guard and he opened the door to inform the High Prince of Centurion Vulmar's presence.

"What's the report?" The centurion guard asked quietly. The other guards sidled up closer to hear.

"Apparently there are Confederate soldiers near Korontsy." The man scoffed and asked, "What? How?"

"That's what I thought... and said."

"Did they sprout from the ground like little flowers from the past winter's snow?"

"That's almost exactly what I said, too."

High Prince Andronicus stepped out of the room and all five soldiers snapped to attention and saluted, bowing to royalty.

High Prince Andronicus pushed past them and down the stairs. Vulmar followed him and the guards shared the news with their fellow guards.

The door to the legate's tower burst open and High Prince Andronicus came out, followed by the landing centurion. Everyone outside saluted and bowed to his presence. Recruit Lebuin folded one front leg beneath him and used the other to support his weight as he bowed to the fast approaching royalty.

"What is the report?" Andronicus inquired. "Confederate sold... soldiers at Koronty... Koronsy..." "Korontsy?"

Lebuin nodded. Andronicus eyed him for a second before looking at the sky as he thought. This was the first time Lebuin saw any type of royalty and he had expected to never see any royalty. What a fool of himself to make in front of such. "Name and rank?"

"Recruit Lebuin, Thy Highness," Lieutenant Vulmar responded before Lebuin could become more of a fool. Lebuin silently thanked him.

"Very well. Recruit, rest for now," he said, turned to a tribune and continued, "Tribune, get the dragons in the air and send them to the nearest forts and cities. Leave one hither. They are to spread the word as quickly as possible. I want them back as soon as possible as well."

Andronicus ordered and a tribune saluted and said, "It shall be done, Thy Highness," and quickened off to the dragon barracks.

Andronicus turned back to Lebuin and Lebuin tensed. "Well done, recruit."

Lebuin bowed and Andronicus turned back to the command tower and closed the door behind him. Vulmar turned from looking at the door and looked at Lebuin and said, "First time seeing royalty?" Lebuin nodded and Vulmar chuckled and laughed.

Dragomir arrived back at the camp and pulled up in front of a line of twenty Spearmen and a centurion appeared and they saluted him.

"I hath sounded the retreat. Now make way back for friendly fortifications," said Dragomir.

"Immediately, Legate," said the centurion.

"Spread this word throughout the camp quickly. There may not be much time left to retreat."

"At once, Sir."

The Spearmen reserves burst into action and went back into the camp proper and spread his order. Soon after the whole of the reserves were filing up to retreat in an orderly fashion. The Great-swordsmen removed their torso armor and helmet and put their capes back on. They left the tents where they were and began to march for the nearest fort with the safest path to, which was Fort Virgiliu. Dragomir did the same, only at his own pace on horseback.

Chapter Twelve

After Math

Day 11, Manylight, Year 2142

"There's another," said Fortis Legate Arnulf with a Britonic accent as the air was stirred by a dragon as he landed in the main courtyard below. Andronicus walked side-by-side with Fortis Legate Arnulf on the walls of Fort Virgiliu as they discussed with one another.

The scouts Andronicus had sent out were returning in full. Some surviving Emporians from the battle of Korontsy had come around Fort Virgiliu, but not many and Legate Dragomir had not arrived yet, which Andronicus found as odd since the survivors that had come up said that he had left the battlefield and back south-west for Fort Virgiliu.

So Andronicus waited for him to arrive, but his patience was thinner than frost now and he wanted to do something soon. The sky was overcast with light gray clouds that made the entire world almost look bland and dull. The sun wasn't shining and even though it was near midday, it still seemed like mid morning.

If the Draken Confederation thought that they could come into Emporian territory, attack Emporian soldiers, then run away and then just get away with it all. Then they were wrong and Andronicus wanted to prove it. His men wanted to prove it.

Andronicus didn't respond to Arnulf. He looked out over the Second Legion, his legion, that was camped just outside of the fort and mostly to the northeast fields of the fort.

The legion was so large that it sprawled out for the entire northeastern quadrant and spread out away from the fort for a distance. It was almost like a large town, larger even.

The land outside the fort was mostly flat, but rose up into a noticeable hill. On the other side of the hill, it rolled back down just as shallow as it rose. Shallow enough to almost seem like it was flat. The grass of the fields was also short, ankle deep at the most. There was grass everywhere besides most of the grounds within the borders of the encampment.

"Is that the last one?" Andronicus asked.

"Nay, Thy Highness," said Arnulf and Andronicus nodded in approval, mostly to himself to make a mental note. They passed a patrol of two Longbowmen as they walked. The Longbowmen snapped to attention and saluted, side-stepping out of their path. Their bows were strung as they patrolled, as was the protocol: Ready thy weapons when on patrol, thou art the first responders of the legions.

"How much longer are they scheduled for then? When doeth the last one return?"

"Tribune Semtimus expects the last of the dragons to not return for another day, Thy Highness."

Andronicus nodded. The encampment of the Second Legion had stables for the horses and medical tents for the sickly and the wounded. All other tents were for the twenty thousand Emporian soldiers and ten thousand auxiliaries.

Banners were posted all over the camp, the banners of cohorts stood near the tent with the commanding officer of the cohort. The banners of auxiliary units bore the Emporian flag at the top and was larger than the banner beneath, which was the flag of the client state from which they came from.

"Thy Highness," Arnulf began and took a deep breath before continuing, "What of the rest of the Seventeenth Legion? Shall they be sent home until they are called upon to finish their service?"

Andronicus thought about that for a moment and said, "Perhaps, but not yet. I want to wait a time longer for Legate Dragomir to arrive. Though at this point I believe he may be no more."

The Drakenmor Confederation had sent supplies here and there, to Ludy Kamnya and Ludy Dvukh Chelovek. Not to any of the others though, he didn't find this odd. The Confederation had been fighting heavily on the Britone front and Emporia and Brandland had not seen a battle in Drakenmor with one another for nearly eight years. Cladaigh an Iarthair and Mirkwood were on the other side of the continent and Libertadia was a sea away from Emporian conquest.

"I agree, that he is no more that is, and what of the spare recruit? Young one he is. He has been volunteering for missions, or anything really."

"He is young. We were all young once. Glory. I want him for the Second Legion. I want such minds in my legion. Attach him to the Second Legion's scout force."

"It shall be done, Thy Highness."

The two of them walked for the nearest tower to descend from the walls. There were no guards near the door into the tower, so Arnulf opened the door into the tower and they entered. The tower was filled with voices and all of the voices within ceased and they shot up from their positions of ease and saluted and bowed.

Andronicus saluted them back and nodded his head to them and they stood at ease as they passed. A soldier closed the door they had opened as they walked past them all and down the stairs that wound clockwise from the bottom to the top, so they descended the stairs counter-clockwise.

Their footsteps were heavy with the weight of their armor. The feathers of his carmine and silver plume bounced slightly as he descended the steps to the courtyard.

Sconces were placed upon the inside of the winding stairwell, to Andronicus' left. It wasn't long until they reached the bottom of the tower and the soldiers at the bottom shot up like the ones above and saluted and bowed. Andronicus saluted in return and almost reached the door when a soldier opened it for him. He and Arnulf exited into the courtyard.

It wasn't the main courtyard, but close to it. They turned to their left and continued to walk to the main courtyard. By this time, soldiers were practicing in the main courtyard.

This happened everyday as multiple cohorts took turns in their practicing throughout the hours and days they spent in the fort.

Andronicus and Arnulf looked on at them as they practiced in rotations. Two dragons relaxed near the dragon barracks and they chatted and watched as well. Longbowmen stood on the walls, looking outwards towards the landscape near the fort and out far away.

"How well are they doing, Fortis Legate?" Andronicus asked as they walked and watched the men go through their rotations.

"Very well. The new Legionnaires are taking it on well. One can not easily tell that there are as many young legionnaires within that cohort as there are," replied Arnulf.

"How many are in that cohort?"

"About two hundred and thirty fresh soldiers. Young men, barely out of advanced education."

"That many? Impressive. Ah, I remember now. They hath been hither for about one month, correct?"

"Correct, Thy Highness," said Arnulf. There was a strong scent of pride in his voice and a growing pride within Andronicus' heart at the sight and notions. Confederates could talk all they wanted about how they would die for freedom with their dying breaths, and Andronicus was compliant with that. He knew that he would be the one that saw the air escape their lungs for the last time.

"Thou and thy Tribunes hath done well. I congratulate thee and thy Tribunes."

"I give thee my thanks, Thy Highness."

They walked around the practicing Emporians and to the legate's tower. The guards there saluted and bowed to Andronicus and he saluted in return. One opened the door and Andronicus went through.

"Shall that be all for now, Thy Highness?" Asked Arnulf. "Verily. Thou art dismissed."

"At once, Thy Highness," said Arnulf as he saluted, bowed and Andronicus saluted in return and went farther into the tower and up the stairs. The guards shut the door and Arnulf went to go do other things. Andronicus climbed the stairs up to his office.

His office was not the Fortis Legate's office, but near it. So he did not effectively remove the Fortis Legate with his stay, but he was in command while he was still there. The two offices were not on the same floor, Andronicus' office was on the top floor and the Fortis Legate's office was on the floor below. He reached the top floor and four guards made their last movements to get in an attentive stance for his presence. They saluted and bowed as he came into view and he saluted in return as he approached. One opened the door and they all stood out of the way for him to pass.

"Thy Highness," they said as he passed into his office.

Just after he entered, the door closed behind him and he walked to the wall with the map of the Drakenmor front. The room was illuminated by an oil lantern that was kept and maintained by his guards and any supply-men that were let past to maintain his office under watch.

He studied the map and looked from it to the world map that was to his left, behind his desk, thinking.

He still had more soldiers coming to embolden the Second Legion. Another fifteen thousand were well on the way to him as he looked at the maps and found the spots of where they should be at that very moment.

There were one thousand dragons from Hugroevania that hadn't left their homeland yet, but would within the next month or so and would arrive not much later after that.

Somewhere on the Great Ocean, near the coast of Luminarch, were four thousand more Emporian soldiers: two thousand Emporian Swordsmen, five hundred Emporian Greatswords-men and fifteen hundred Emporian Crossbowmen.

Somewhere near the point of the Corrue Peninsula were two thousand dwarven auxiliaries from the client state Kingdom of Kende. Along with these auxiliaries were three thousand Emporian Longbowmen and three thousand more Emporian Crossbowmen.

Somewhere in the heart of Emporia were two thousand men that manned five hundred portable scorpions. It would still take at least a month or more for these soldiers to arrive at their meeting point.

That made up the rest of the soldiers he wanted to have under his command. Once they arrived at the coast of Drakenmor, or near it, he would set out to join his son, Flavius, Legate of the Fifth Legion, who was in command of the current siege of the Ludy Kamnya Mountains.

Flavius was on the other side of the small mountain range, or smaller when in comparison to the other mountain ranges in the north, so he wouldn't actually be joining him, but would be there to help during the fighting and ensure that no flanking force could get out.

He then studied the map of the Drakenmor front, specifically around the northern and western areas around the Ludy Kamnya Mountains. He searched for every possible way that those dwarves could attain reinforcements from any of their allies.

Initially, he had thought that only armies from, or of, Ludy Dvukh Chelovek would approach from the border they and Emporia shared, so he hadn't put much thought into Confederate armies coming from that way. Now that it had just happened, or so he was told by many accounts, he felt outsmarted. It was such a plain idea, so simple that he was ashamed that he hadn't seen it.

At first, he had supposed that idea as a possibility, but after a few thoughts and facts, he disposed of it. He knew, or at least thought he knew, that Ludy Dvukh Chelovek disliked the Draken Confederation. Enough so that they wouldn't allow large forces, anything more than perhaps a couple thousand troops at a time, to enter into their land. And those couple thousand troops would be escorts or guards for however many nobility from the Confederation would visit, and if the amount of nobility was too great and warranted more than two thousand, then some of the nobility would be refused for the time being.

But now, he scrutinized their lands, the border between lands, and Imperial lands next to the border. He saw multiple spots where armies could enter into the land and begin raiding, but that would, in the end, trap the army within Imperial land to be hunted down by any Imperial Legion that was sent after them. Though, as stupid as trapping an entire army behind enemy lines was, he didn't put the action past the Confederation's range of actions. He knew that Ludy Dvukh Chelovek wouldn't do such a thing, but if they did, it would only happen just as he and the rest of the legions in Drakenmor were occupied.

Even then, they wouldn't linger for long, nor would they venture as deep as the Confederate army did. As of his current knowledge, the Confederate army had not escaped from Imperial land yet and he believed them to be heading back the way they had entered into the land, most likely directly between forts Adi and Burgwine.

As he studied the map, he made a plan to position his legions in the most advantageous locations to spot and intercept any invading forces from the north and west. He knew by then that he would have to pull soldiers from the garrison at Kamennoye Serdtse to help, and perhaps some from Fort Virgiliu as well. Not much, only a few cohorts each.

He nodded to himself as the plan came together in his mind for the coming offensive to conquer the last of Ludy Kamnya and put an end to the existing royal line and all thoughts of rebellion for good. Securing the last remaining piece of the Empire's foothold on Drakenmor and finally being able to focus more soldiers outside Imperial lands and towards the remaining enemies of Emporia, especially the Drakenmor Confederation.

As much as he hated them and wanted them destroyed for all of eternity, he had to conquer both Ludy Dvukh Chelovek and Brandland first. Perhaps even Bergsee.

He knew that Ludy Dvukh Chelovek would be rather easy, compared to Brandland and Bergsee at least, but once he began to put pressure on the two dragonic factions near the Drache Strait, Magister Hermann would be able to easily win over the waters between Britone and Drakenmor and their fall would be quick as they would get squeezed from two sides at once. Perhaps even a pincer maneuver would be able to work quick enough.

After the long moment of thinking, he stopped himself from getting too carried away in the glory to come. He needed to keep his mind in the moment and on the current front.

The wind picked up and swirled around the fort as a dragon landed. Andronicus turned around and walked to the window and looked out over the landscape and fort beneath.

Below, he saw the soldiers begin to clear the main courtyard and some Emporians were near a wind dragon. One was untying a silver and carmine tassel on both horns and another was talking to the stray recruit.

The wind dragon was nodding and the man that stood before him gesturing with his hands and after another quick exchange of words, the men and the dragon laughed for a short bout. The dragon shook himself off and trotted over to the dragon barracks where he and the other dragons commuted with one another.

The main courtyard was then refilled with the practicing cohorts and they continued their drills. The cohorts that were practicing were Crossbowmen cohorts and they had set up targets on one side of the courtyard and they stood at the other side, winding up their crossbows and shooting the targets.

Each man had a crossbow that he shot and reloaded himself. Each Crossbowman had a quiver as well. Each quiver had about ten arrows. The arrows weren't like regular arrows. They were thicker and shorter than regular arrows.

A man pulled a loaded crossbow to his shoulder and aimed. The line of crossbowmen waited for the command to shoot. "Shoot!" Ordered the tribune of the cohort and a loud thrum filled the air as the crossbow arrows flew through the air in dark blurs towards the targets. The bolts went most of the way through the targets.

One sound rang out from the courtyard as a crossbow arrow missed the target and hit the stone behind the target, nicking and cracking the stone. The arrow snapped and bounced off. Everyone heard it and looked up at the sound.

"Thou missed by nearly three feet!" An Emporian called out and started laughing. Andronicus looked down at the voice to see a few men shaking with laughter. One man just stood there and looked at the wall, target and then the crossbow in his hands, dumbfounded.

"Get back in order!" The tribune called out and the men stopped laughing, still chuckling to themselves, and got back into formation. The tribune then looked at the soldier who had missed and said, "Thou holdst possibly the easiest weapon to use, and thou can not at the least make it look easy to use. Get in formation and thou shalt attempt again when thou get the chance. This should give thee a long enough time to think about how in a battle, thou wouldst most likely be dead and be the cause of many of these soldiers' deaths as well."

"Understood, Sir," said the soldier. He saluted and the practicing continued.

A knock came to his door and Andronicus looked to the door saying, "Enter."

The door opened and he turned around to see who it was. The centurion outside his door and the man saluted and bowed.

"Thy Highness, there is a message for thee," said the guard. "Bring it to me."

The centurion turned around for a second before he walked into the room with an envelope in his right hand. He walked up to Andronicus, bowed at the waist and held up the envelope.

Andronicus took it and the centurion left. He looked at the front of the envelope that had the lettering that addressed it to him and he recognized the handwriting easily enough.

He turned it over and broke the carmine seal and removed the letter within. Holding the letter in one hand and the envelope in the other, he walked over to his desk and tossed the envelope into a tin can for garbage.

He went to sit down at his desk and remembered that he still had his armor on, so he remained standing as he unfolded the letter, which was folded into thirds. He began to read it:

> *Andronicus, My Brother, I hath written this and hath had it sent to thee to inform thee that Validus shall be marching to Drakenmor with a legion of his own. I shall inform him to report to thee the moment he arrives. He'll be there with fifteen thousand Emporian soldiers of various cohorts.*
>
> *I ask that thou wilt guide him well and teach him what he needs to learn. He knows much from his histories, but there is still much to be learned from hand-on experience.*
>
> *Sincerely, Thy Brother, Emperor Servius.*
>
> *Post Note – Remember that.*

Andronicus finished and started shaking his head as his amusement grew, as did his smile at the words.

He set it onto his desk and looked up at the map of the Drakenmor front, thinking of where Validus could be sent to start his time on this front. That mainly depended on when he would show up, so Andronicus grabbed a blank piece of paper from a drawer; it was extremely hard to do with his armor on; that he had opened to get and closed after he had gotten the paper, and a pen that was laying on his desk surface, then wrote:

> *His Excellency, Emperor Servius, I hath responded to thy notice in earnest to discover when thy son, Validus, is expected to arrive and that I shall do what thou hast asked of me. Also to saith that I had almost forgotten about that. I thank thee for the memory.*
>
> *Sincerely, Thy Brother, HIGH Prince Andronicus.*

He ended and folded the paper into thirds, the exact way he had been taught when he was young and still living within the Imperial Palace.

After it was folded, crudely as it was, he opened a drawer and gathered an envelope. He placed the letter within, struggling to get it in for a few seconds before succeeding and closing the envelope. He then wrote:

> *Addressed to His Excellency, Emperor Servius Rubicon.*

With his armor on, he didn't want to try to seal it, so he walked over to the door and said just before he reached it, "Centurion."

He said it loud enough to be heard through the door and the centurion opened it just as quickly. After he had the door open, he said, "Thy Highness."

Andronicus handed him the envelope and said, "Taketh this to Tribune Semtimus and bid him to seal it with my seal. Then he is to send it off."

He took the envelope, bowed to him and said, "It shall be done, Thy Highness."

Andronicus then shut the door and stood there for a moment, thinking, before he chuckled to himself quietly and walked back over to the window.

The sound of crossbows thrumming and arrows finding their marks had filled the air the entire time. The tribunes shouting out their orders to their cohorts.

A few moments later, a dragon bounded out in front of his companions and stood in an open spot of the courtyard.

"Clear the courtyard! Dragon lifting off!" Shouted an Emporian at the rank of tribune. This was Tribune Semtimus. He held an envelope in his hands.

Not much longer, the courtyard was cleared, mostly, as the Crossbowmen were still there, but near the edges.

Tassels were tied onto the dragon's horns and Tribune Semtimus briefed the dragon on his mission. The dragon nodded from time to time until Tribune Semtimus handed the envelope to a subordinate, who then fastened the envelope into a pouch that was with a secured part of the tassels.

The man then held a thumb up to Semtimus and he nodded, looked at the dragon and the two nodded. The Emporians cleared away from the dragon and the wind picked up as the dragon took off.

The Crossbowmen then retook the courtyard and continued practicing. Andronicus stood there in the window for a while as the day wore on.

GLOSSARY

Velum Island

Geography

The Great Ocean - (the)(great)(ocean)
Memorije Forest - (meh-mor-ih-jee)(forest)
Oks River - (awks)(river)
Reke River - (rehk-eh)(river)
The Senka Ocean - (the)(sehn-kah)(ocean)
Velum Mountains - (vehl-uhm)(mountains)

Fortifications

Fort Alban - (fort)(Al-ban)
Fort Rowen - (fort)(rOh-wen)
Fort Tavian - (fort)(tay-vee-in)

Cities and Major Cities

Izubio - (I-zoo-bee-O)
Krvna Voda - (kuhrv-nuh)(vO-dah)
Memorije - (meh-mor-ih-jee)
Planina - (plahn-ee-nuh)
Zaboravio - (zah-bor-ahv-ee-O)
Zemlja-grad - (zehm-yuh-grad)

Senka Island

Geography

Dlinnyy River - (dlihn-nee)(river)
Senka Forest - (sehn-kah)(forest)
The Senka Ocean - (the)(sehn-kah)(ocean)
Senka River - (sehn-kah)(river)
Teniste Gory Mountains - (tehn-ihst-uh)(gor-ee)(mountains)

Fortifications

Fort Branimir - (fort)(brahn-eh-mihr)
Fort Corey - (fort)(kor-ee)
Fort Norbert - (fort)(nor-berht)

Cities and Major Cities

Dlinnorechnoy - (dlin-nor-ech-nee)
Mesto Voina - (mest-O)(vO-ee-nuh)
Portovy Pristav - (por-tOv-ee)(prih-stav)
Vidnorovsk - (vid-nor-ovsk)

Marsh Island

Geography

Arney River - (aR-nay)(river)
Agivey River - (ah-gIv-ay)(river)
Bann River - (bahn)(river)
Edentry River - (eh-dehn-tree)(river)
Granford River - (grahn-ford)(river)
The Ice-Plane Ocean - (the)(ice-plane)(ocean)
Schootport River - (skoot-port)(river)
The Western Sea - (the)(western)(sea)

Fortifications

- None –

Cities and Major Cities

Edentry - (eh-dehn-tree)
Granford - (grahn-ford)
Landbeek - (land-beek)
Schootport - (skoot-port)

Drakenmor; Map 01

Geography

Beag River - (behk)(river)
Conartha Beag Isle - (con-aR-thuh)(behk)(isle)
Conartha Beag Isle Forest - (con-aR-thuh)(behk)(isle)(forest)
Conartha Forest - (con-aR-thuh)(forest)
Conartha Isle - (con-aR-thuh)(isle)
The Conartha Mountains - (con-aR-thuh)(mountains)
Conartha Plains - (con-aR-thuh)(plains)
The Ice-Plane Ocean - (the)(ice-plane)(ocean)
Mirkwood Forest - (murk-wood)(forest)
Mirkwood Island - (murk-wood)(island)
Mirkwood Mountains - (murk-wood)(mountains)
Satt Fjall Mountain - (sat)(fyall)(mountain)
Two Isle Bay - (two)(isle)(bay)
The Western Sea - (the)(western)(sea)

Fortifications
- None -

Cities and Major Cities

Baile - (bI-luh)
Baile Corr - (bI-luh)(kor)
Beag - (behk)
Ceann Baile - (keh-uhn)(bI-luh)
Fiail Ard - (faw-eel)(aRd)

Glen Iar - (glehn)(I-aR)
Halsten - (hahl-stehn)
Jern hule - (yern)(huel)
Kolafjall - (kol-uh-fyall)
Linn Fola - (lihnn)(fuhl-uh)
Oddhvassa Vatn - (awd-hvahs-suh)(vahtn)
Satt Fjall - (sat)(fyall)
Sigur - (sig-ur)
Skilagjald - (skihl-ahg-yald)
Skuggi Fjallsins - (skuhg-ee)(fyall-sihns)
Sprunga - (spruhn-guh)
Tindaborg - (tihn-duh-borg)
Torden Cave - (tor-dehn)(cave)
Vermundr - (ver-mun-dur)
Voldugur Dalur - (vol-duhg-ur)(dahl-ur)

Drakenmor; Map 02

Geography

Bare Island - (bar-uh)(island)
Bare River - (bar-uh)(river)
Dragebyen River - (draw-guh-bee-in)(river)
The Holr Mountains - (the)(hol-ur)(mountains)
The Ice-Plane Ocean - (the)(ice-plane)(ocean)
Mirkwood Forest - (murk-wood)(forest)
Mirkwood Mountains - (murk-wood)(mountains)
The Swirling Mountains - (the)(swirling)(mountains)
The Western Sea - (the)(western)(sea)

Fortifications

Eirik's Hold - (I-rik-ss)(hold)

Cities and Major Cities

Agnar's Grave - (un-gar-z)(grave)
Baren Syn - (bar-en)(sin)
Dal-toppen - (dahl-tOp-en)
Dragebyen - (draw-guh-bee-in)
The Drage-styre Palace - (the)(draw-guh-steer-uh)(palace)
Dyp by - (deep)(bee)
Fjellgap - (fyell-gawp)
Hult Punkt - (hoolt)(punkt)
Kysten Byen - (shist-in)(bee-in)
Lysfjord - (lees-fyood)
Metall - (met-all)
Mostrud - (moost-rUd)
Skrent - (skrent)
Skygge - (shee-guh)
Stor Gruve - (stor)(groo-vuh)
Vegar's Hill - (vay-gars)(hill)

Drakenmor; Map 03

Geography

The Holr Hills - (the)(hol-ur)(hills)
The Ice-Plane Ocean - (the)(ice-plane)(ocean)
Separat Mountain - (sep-aR-awt)(mountain)
Separat River - (sep-aR-awt)(river)
Sky Mountain - (shee)(mountian)
The Swirling Mountains - (the)(swirling)(mountains)
The Swirling Forest - (the)(swirling)(forest)
The Western Sea - (the)(western)(sea)

Fortifications

- None -

Cities and Major Cities

Det Store Fjellet - (deh)(stoor-uh)(fyell-uh)
De Virvlande Skogarna - (dO)(veerv-land-uh)(skO-gah-nah)
Ensomme By - (en-som-eh)(bee)
Flatt Fjell - (flawt)(fyell)
Granittgruve - (brahn-iht-groo-vuh)
Klippekant - (klip-uh-kahnt)
Nytt Hem - (niht)(hahm)
Robust Landsby - (roo-buhst)(lahnds-bee)
Separert Topp - (sep-ar-eirt)(top)
Skog-utseende - (skoog-oot-see-ahn-duh)
Skyen Topp Palace - (shee-in)(top)(palace)
Sommerfrost - (som-er-frost)
Toppen av Kullen - (topp-en)(awv)(kool-en)
Vanngrotte - (van-grot-uh)

Drakenmor; Map 04

Geography

Bergsee River - (berg-see)(river)
The Ice-Plane Ocean - (the)(ice-plane)(ocean)
Kontinental Forest - (kon-tee-nehn-tehl)(forest)
Kultainen River - (kool-tI-nen)(river)
The Nordlanden Hills - (the)(nor-leht-en)(hills)
Nurkassa River - (nor-kahs-ah)(river)
The Swirling Forest - (the)(swirling)(forest)
The Swirling Mountains - (the)(swirling)(mountains)
The Western Sea - (the)(western)(sea)

Fortifications

- None –

Cities and Major Cities

Ende des Flusses - (end-eh)(des)(floos-ess)
Kadonnut Huippu - (kad-O-nut)(hoo-ee-poo)
Kulman Kaupunki - (kool-man)(kau-poon-kee)
Kultainen - (kool-tI-nen)
Lumen Peitossa - (loo-men)(pA-tO-suh)
Meren Ilme - (meer-en)(eel-mA)
Merenranta - (meer-en-rahn-tuh)
Piikkikivet - (pee-kee-kee-vet)
Puun - (poon)
Silvertoppen - (seel-ver-top-en)
Suuri Luola - (sooh-ree)(loo-O-lah)
Tasainen Vuorenhuippu - (tah-sI-nen)(voor-en-hooh-ee-pooh)
Vármvatten - (varm-vaht-en)
Virvlande Bergskant - (veerv-land-uh)(berg-skant)
Vuoren Pohja - (voor-en)(pO-hee-uh)
Vuorenrinne - (voor-en-reen-eh)

Drakenmor; Map 05

Geography

Bergsee River - (berg-see)(river)
Drage River - (drow)(river)
Fjord Mountains - (fyood)(mountains)
The Ice-Plane Ocean - (the)(ice-plane)(ocean)
Kontinental Forest - (kon-tee-nehn-tehl)(forest)
Kreuz-Berge River - (koitz-berg-uh)(river)
The Nordlanden Hills - (the)(nor-leht-en)(hills)

Fortifications

- None –

Cities and Major Cities

Agnetes Bakke - (ahg-nuh-tuh)(bah-geh)
Dragebyen - (drow-bih-in)
Flussbiegung - (fluss-bee-guhng)
Heltebyen - (heehl-teh-bih-in)
Ispass - (eess-pess)
Kontinental - (kon-tee-nehn-tehl)
Kuu Paistaa - (koo)(pah-eest-too)
Nordlanden - (nor-leht-en)
Stjerne Syn - (steer-neh)(soon)
Vacker - (vah-gah)

Drakenmor; Map 06

Geography

The Bergsee Mountains - (the)(berg-see)(mountains)
Bergsee Lake - (berg-see)(lake)
Bergsee River - (berg-see)(river)
Drache Strait - (drah-kuh)(strait)
The Feuer und Wasser Gulf - (the)(foi-er)(und)(vahs-er)(gulf)
Kreuz-Berge River - (koitz-berg-uh)(river)
The Senka Ocean - (the)(sehn-kah)(O-shen)

Fortifications

- None –

Cities and Major Cities

Berggabel - (berg-gah-bel)
Bergkante - (berg-kahn-tuh)
Bergpass - (berg-pass)
Blick auf die Berge - (blick)(auf)(dee)(berg-uh)
Felsiges Land - (fel-sig-ehs)(land)
Grenzstadt - (Grenz-schtadt)

Metallfeld - (meh-tahl-feld)
Mondsee - (mond-see)
Spitze des Sees - (schpitz)(des)(seez)
Ufer des Sees - (oof-er)(des)(seez)
Uferfeld - (oof-er-feld)
Unbedeckt - (oon-beh-dekt)

Drakenmor; Map 07

Geography

Dark Husk Mountains - (dark)(husk)(mountains)
Drage River - (drow)(river)
The Feuer und Wasser Gulf - (the)(foi-er)(und)(vahs-er)(gulf)
The Great Draken-Wood - (the)(great)(drAk-en-wood)
The Ice-Plane Ocean - (the)(ice-plane)(ocean)
Kontinental Forest - (kon-tee-nehn-tehl)(forest)
Kreuz-Berge River - (koitz-berg-uh)(river)
Tributaries of the Dark Husk - (tributaries)(of)(the)(dark)(husk)
Windig River - (vin-dich)(river)
Windig Cirque - (vin-dich)(sur-kuh)

Fortifications

Burg - (burg)

Cities and Major Cities

Altes Dorf - (ahl-tes)(dorf)
Asche-Stadt - (auch-es-schtadt)
Aschgrauer Wald - (auch-grou-er)(valdt)
Cirque Mund - (seerk)(munt)
Donker Hout - (doonk-er)(howt)
Firetop - (fire-top)
Gabel - (gah-bel)
Grabstein - (grahb-stI-n)
Juwelenstadt - (U-vAl-en-schtadt)

Langer Fluss - (lAn-ger)(fluss)
Mond-Splitter - (moond-schpit-ter)
Rivier - (ree-veer)
Waldstadt - (valdt-schtadt)
Windtop - (vind-top)
Zuflucht - (zoo-flucht)

Drakenmor; Map 08

Geography

Dark Husk Mountains - (dark)(husk)(mountains)
Fire Line Mountains - (fire)(line)(mountains)
The Great Draken-Wood - (the)(great)(drAk-en-wood)
The Grenze Mountains - (the)(gren-zeh)(mountains)
Grenze River - (gren-zeh)(river)
The Ice-Plane Ocean - (the)(ice-plane)(ocean)
Kaputt Mountain - (kah-poot)(mountain)
The Senka Ocean - (the)(sehn-kah)(ocean)
Svecheniye River - (svech-en-yuh)(river)
Tributaries of the Dark Husk - (tributaries)(of)(the)(dark)(husk)
Windig River - (vin-dich)(river)

Fortifications

Pantser Gate - (pan-ser)(gate)

Cities and Major Cities

Altstadt - (ahlt-schtadt)
Bos - (boss)
Entfernt - (ent-feh-ernt)
Feuerdorf - (foi-er-dorf)
Feuerstadt - (foi-er-schtadt)
Flussdorf - (fluss-dorf)
Heimat des Terrors - (hI-maht)(des)(ter-ros)
IJsvliegtuig - (els-vlif-tach)

Panster Mine - (pan-ser)(mine)
Schattenstadt - (schahtt-en-schtadt)
Seltsamer Berg - (zelt-sahm-er)(berg)
Sturmfelsen - (schtorm-fel-zen)
Svecheniye - (svech-en-yuh)
Tiefer Ritzen - (tee-fer)(rit-zen)
Vredig - (vrA-duhg)
Vuur Berg - (fUr)(berg)

Drakenmor; Map 09

Geography

The Grenze Mountains - (the)(gren-zeh)(mountains)
The Ice-Plane Ocean - (the)(ice-plane)(ocean)
The Senka Ocean - (the)(sehn-kah)(O-shehn)
The Spire - (the)(spire)
Svecheniye Forest - (svech-en-yuh)(forest)
Svecheniye River - (svech-en-yuh)(river)
Zamok Delta - (zem-Ohk)
The Zamok Mountains - (the)(zem-Ohk)(mountains)

Fortifications

Fort Andrey - (fort)(ahn-dray)
Fort Emil - (fort)(eh-m-eel)
Fort Florin - (fort)(flA-O-rihn)
Fort Marcellus - (fort)(mar-sehl-lous)
Fort Proklos - (fort)(prO-klOz)
Severny Zamok - (seh-vern-ee)(zem-Ohk)
Tsentralny Zamok - (sin-trahl-nee)(zem-Ohk)
Yuzhny Zamok - (yUz-nee)(zem-Ohk)

Cities and Major Cities

Bereg Reckie - (ber-reg)(rek-ea)
Bolshoy Spil - (bal-shoy)(spiel)
Hushtovka - (hoosh-tOv-kah)
Kray Gory - (krA)(gor-ray)
Medvezhyi Peshchery - (med-vyez-ay)(pee-shar-yea)
Morozna Poroda - (mar-rOz-nah)(par-rO-dah)
New Dubovsky - (new)(dU-boov-skee)
Nordvaskin - (nord-vah-skin)
Otkrytoye Mesto - (aht-krit-ah)(mehst-O)
Rasschelina Strelkova - (rush-el-een-ah)(strel-kOv-ah)
Ryadom se Goroy - (rI-ee-dom)(zeh)(gor-ree)
Sosnovy Pritzel - (sos-nOv-ee)(prit-zel)
Svetlograd - (svet-lO-grad)
Vide na Vodopad - (vee-dah)(nah)(vO-dO-pi-dao)

Drakenmor; Map 10

Geography

The Great Ocean - (the)(great)(ocean)
The Ice-Plane Ocean - (the)(ice-plane)(ocean)
The Ludy Kamnya Mountains - (the)(lU-dee)(kahm-nyah)(mountains)
Nevysokie Gory Mountains - (nehv-ee-sO-kee)(gor-ay)(mountains)
Oblachny Sensor - (Obl-ahk-nee)(dach-ek)
Poluostrovnoy Forest - (pool-O-strOv-nee)(forest)
The Senka Ocean - (the)(sehn-kah)(O-shehn)
Vostochny Greben Forest - (vos-tOsh-nee)(greh-beon)(forest)
The Vostochny Greben Mountains - (the)(vos-tOsh-nee)(greh-beon)(mountains)
Vostoke River - (vos-tOk)(river)

Fortifications

Fort Adi - (fort)(au-dee)
Fort Audomar - (fort)(au-dO-maR)

Fort Burgwine - (fort)(berg-vIn)
Cheshuichaty Zamok - (choo-shu-ee-shIt-yuh)(zem-Ohk)
Fort Miller - (fort)(mil-lur)
Fort Titus - (fort)(tI-tous)
Fort Virgiliu - (fort)(veer-jee-lee-oo)
Zheleznye Vorota - (shil-iz-nee)(vor-O-tuh)

Cities and Major Cities

Bolshoy Risk - (bal-shoy)(reesk)
Derevyanny - (dih-rih-vyahn-nee)
Gorny Bereg - (gor-nee)(beer-reg)
Gorod Ivana - (yor-rod)(I-vahn-uh)
Kamennoye Serdtse - (kam-en-oy)(serd-ts-eh)
Mesto Pobieda - (mehst-O)(pob-ee-duh)
Ploshchad - (plOsh-shed)
Poluostrovnoy - (pool-O-strOv-nee)
Postroen na Stali - (post-rOn)(nah)(stah-lea)
Pozdneye Utro - (pooz-nee)(U-trah)
Selo Vlad - (seh-lO)(vlad)
Severny Bereg - (seev-ern-ee)(beer-reg)
Velikiy Kamien - (vee-lee-kee)(kah-men)
Velikiy Sever - (vee-lee-kee)(see-ver)
Vorota - (vor-rO-tah)
Vostochny Bereg - (vos-tOsh-nee)(beer-reg)
Vostoke - (vos-tOk)
Ubezisce - (oo-bees-yes-cah)

Luminarch; Map 01

Geography

Alzeir's Bay - (Al-zair-z)(bay)
Bois de la Baie - (boi)(deh)(lah)(bay)
The Britonarch Channel - (the)(brih-tOn-aRch)(channel)
The High-Lands of Haxier - (the)(high)(lands)(of)(Hahx-eer)
The Low River - (the)(low)(river)

Kleine Bossen Forest - (klI-neh)(boss-en)
The Sea of the Anvil - (the)(sea)(of)(the)(an-vil)
Schaduwrijke Bomen Forest - (shad-doo-hIk-eh)(bO-men)

Fortifications

Fort Boris - (fort)(boh-ris)
Fort Huub - (fort)(hUb)
Fort Louis - (fort)(loo-ee)

Cities and Major Cities

Col entre les bois - (kohl)(awn-trA)(leh)(boi)
De Vinger van het Land - (dee)(feen-ger)(fawn)(et)(landt)
Haxier - (Hahx-eer)
Mountain Back - (mountain)(back)
Port de la Baie - (por)(deh)(lah)(bay)
Schaduwrijk Boomdorp - (shad-doo-hIk)(bOm-dorp)
Verwoeste Vesting - (fer-vOs-teh)(fest-eeng)

Luminarch; Map 02

Geography

Alzeir's Bay - (Al-zair-z)(bay)
Bois de la Baie - (boi)(deh)(lah)(bay)
Border Forest - (bor-der)(for-est)
The Britonarch Channel - (the)(brih-tOn-aRch)(chan-nel)
Golemate Shuma Forest - (goal-A-maht)(shoo-muh)(forest)
The Senka Ocean - (the)(sehn-kah)(ocean)

Fortifications

Fort Alekso - (fort)(ahl-lek-sO)
Fort Kole - (fort)(koal-A)
Fort Vaggelis - (fort)(vag-el-ees)

Cities and Major Cities

Arbres d'armure - (aR-breh)(daw-mi-or)
Au Nord des Bois - (oo)(nor)(dee)(boi)
Foreseus - (for-see-us)
Gradot nha Golemiot - (grad-ot)(nyuh)(goal-ay-mee-yet)
Mochurishna Zemja - (mO-choo-reesh-nuh)(zem-yah)
Treva za Odmor - (tre-vuh)(z)(Od-mar)
Tvrdina nha Drvjata - (tvr-dee-nuh)(nyuh)(driv-yah-tuh)
Voden Front - (vO-den)(front)
Wolvenpool - (wool-vehn-pool)
Zamos - (zam-Os)

Luminarch; Map 03

Geography

The Chechian Crater - (cheh-chee-uhn)(crater)
Plaxident River - (plax-eh-dehnt)(River)
Plaxident Lake - (plax-eh-dehnt)(Lake)
Plaxident Valley - (plax-eh-dehnt)(Valley)
Primus Mons - (prI-muhs)(monz)
Secundus Mons - (sehc-uhnd-uhs)(monz)
The Senka Ocean - (the)(sehn-kah)(O-shehn)
Tertius Mons - (tair-tEE-uhs)(monz)

Fortifications

Fort Vopiscus - (fort)(vO-pees-kous)

Cities and Major Cities

Aeternus - (A-tern-ous)
Aqua Grisea - (ahk-wuh)(griz-ee-uh)
Avena Flava - (ah-ven-uh)(flav-ah)
Collis Basis - (kol-ees)(bah-sees)
Emporenna - (ehm-por-ehn-uh)

Plaxident - (plax-eh-dehnt)
Reaver - (ree-vur)
Tria Emina - (tree-uh)(ehm-ihn-uh)

Luminarch; Map 04

Geography

Baumgestein Forest - (baum-gest-ehn)(forest)
The Mountains of Zulkbar - (the)(mountains)(of)(zulk-baR)
Plaxident River - (plax-eh-dehnt)(river)
Rabe Forest - (rah-buh)(forest)
The Screaming Peaks - (the)(screaming)(peaks)
The Senka Ocean - (the)(sehn-kah)(O-shehn)

Fortifications

Fort Arruns - (fort)(ar-roons)
Fort Bledar - (fort)(bleh-dar)
Fort Dominic - (fort)(dom-in-ik)
Fort Hugo - (oo-gO)

Cities and Major Cities

Alter Berg - (ahl-ter)(berg)
Baumgestein - (baum-gest-ehn)
Dunkles Wasser - (dunk-les)(vass-er)
Tal des Windes - (tahl)(des)(vin-des)
Tiefes Schloss - (tee-fes)(schloss)
Raben-Burg - (rah-ben-burg)
Wassergrenze - (vass-er-gren-zeh)
Windstrom - (vind-strohm)

Luminarch; Map 05

Geography

Bagien River - (bag-en)(river)
The Northern Valley High-Mountains - (the)(northern)(valley)
(high-mountains)
Rabe Forest - (rah-buh)(forest)
Rzeka River - (rz-ek-uh)(river)
The Senka Ocean - (the)(sehn-kah)(O-shehn)

Fortifications

Fort Delcie - (fort)(del-chyah)
Cities and Major Cities
Alps Poli - (alps)(pool-ee)
Bagien - (bag-en)
Burg Zulkbar - (burg)(zulk-baR)
Delcie - (del-chyah)
Nasionami - (nash-O-nahm-ee)
Rabenwald - (rah-ben-vahlt)
Rzeka - (rz-ek-uh)
Rzeka-Kruka - (rz-ek-uh)(kroo-kah)

Luminarch; Map 06

Geography

Bagien River - (bag-en)(river)
The Great Ocean - (the)(great)(ocean)
Koniec Lake - (kOn-yetz)(lake)
The Northern Valley High-Mountains - (the)(northern)(valley)
(high-mountains)
Rozwidlenia Lake - (roz-vilt-lin-yah)(lake)
The Senka Ocean - (the)(sehn-kah)(O-shehn)
Starry Las Forest - (stair-ee)(las)(forest)
Starry Las River - (stair-ee)(las)(river)

Fortifications

Fort Coleman - (fort)(kol-mun)
Fort Ulrich - (fort)(ohl-rikh)
Fort Marcin - (fort)(march-in)

Cities and Major Cities

Bariera Sztormowa - (bar-eer-uh)(shtorm-Ov-uh)
Koniec Wapienia - (kOn-yetz)(wap-EEn-yah)
Rozwidlenia - (roz-vilt-lin-yah)
Start Rzeki - (start)(rz-kee)
Starry Las - (stair-ee)(las)

Luminarch; Map 07

Geography

Alzeir's Bay - (Al-zair-z)(bay)
Alzeir's River Forest - (Al-zair-z)(river)(forest)
Praeterton Valley Mountains - (prA-ter-ton)(valley)(mountains)
Praetregon River - (prA-treh-gon)(river)
Praetregon Lake - (prA-treh-gon)(lake)
Quiescens Forest - (quees-shens)(forest)
Samnite River - (sam-nite)(river)

Fortifications

Fort Spurius - (fort)(spur-ee-ous)

Cities and Major Cities

Cromona - (crO-mO-nah)
Curva in Litore - (cor-vah)(een)(lee-tor-ray)
Exerci - (ex-er-chee)
Praeterton - (prA-ter-ton)
Praetregon - (prA-treh-gon)

Quiescens - (quees-shens)
Samnite - (sam-nite)
Spatium Inter Arbores - (spat-ee-um)(een-ter)(ar-bor-ays)

Luminarch; Map 08

Geography

Alzeir's River - (Al-zair-z)(river)
Alzeir's River Forest - (Al-zair-z)(river)(forest)
The Forest of the Defenders - (the)(forest)(of)(the)(defenders)

Fortifications

Fort Egyed - (fort)(egg-yed)
Fort Liviu - (fort)(lee-vyoo)

Cities and Major Cities

Agri Ligni - (ag-ree)(lee-nyee)
Besiegten-Stadt - (bee-seeg-ten-schtadt)
Courous - (kor-ous)
Defensor Terrae - (deh-fen-sor)(tair-ay)
Holzland - (holz-land)
Schutt - (shut)
Sieg - (seeg)
Siegte-Stadt - (seeg-teh-schtadt)
Statua Gloriosa - (stah-too-ah)(glor-ee-O-suh)
Von Fluss und Wald - (von)(fluss)(und)(vIlt)

Luminarch; Map 09

Geography

Agapi River - (O-gA-pee)(river)
Alzeir's River - (Al-zair-z)(river)
Alzeir's River Forest - (Al-zair-z)(river)(forest)

Blut River - (bloot)(river)
Dunkel River - (duhnk-ehl)(river)
The Forest of the Defenders - (the)(forest)(of)(the)(defenders)
Orino Perasma River - (or-ee-nO)(per-as-mah)(river)
The Screaming Peaks - (the)(screaming)(peaks)
The Swayed Forest - (the)(swayed)(forest)
Tief River - (teef)(river)
The Western Valley High-Mountains - (the)(western)(valley)(high-mountains)

Fortifications

Fort Kolpos Psarion - (fort)(kol-pOs)(sar-ee-on)
Fort Psarolimano - (fort)(sar-O-li-man-O)

Cities and Major Cities

Corinthius - (Cor-in-thE-ous)
Elie-Poli - (A-lee-pol-ee)
Fischer-Stadt - (fish-er-schtadt)
Flussburg - (fluss-burg)
Kolpos Psarion - (kol-pOs)(sar-ee-on)
Maulwurfstadt - (mall-vurf-schtadt)
Neue Amyna - (noi-ee)(am-I-nuh)
Ourliazontas-Poli - (our-laz-On-tas-pol-ee)
Potami-Poli - (pO-tO-mee-pol-ee)
Psarolimano - (sar-O-li-man-O)

Luminarch; Map 10

Geography

Eastern Valley High-Mountains - (eastern)(valley)(high-mountains)
High Valley Forest - (high)(valley)(forest)
Kyzikos River - (kI-zee-kOs)(river)
Naxos River - (nax-Os)(river)
Orino Perasma River - (or-ee-nO)(per-as-mah)(river)

Pur Forest - (pour)(forest)
The Western Valley High-Mountains - (the)(western)(valley)(high-mountains)

Fortifications

Fort Timon - (fort)(tee-mon)

Cities and Major Cities

Akragas - (O-kra-gas)
Benin - (ben-een)
Cosa - (kO-sah)
Kyzikos - (kI-zee-kOs)
Naxos - (nax-Os)
Praga - (prah-gah)
Valea Trandafirilor - (val-ah)(tran-daf-ee-ree-lor)

Luminarch; Map 11

Geography

The Great Ocean - (the)(great)(ocean)
Nisipari Island - (nee-see-par-ee)(island)
Pur Forest - (pour)(forest)
Verde Island - (ver-day)(island)
Zorile Island - (zor-ee-lay)(island)

Fortifications

Fort Amulius - (fort)(am-oo-lee-ous)
Fort Lydus - (fort)(lee-dous)
Fort Patrice - (fort)(pat-rees)
Fort Yannick - (fort)(yan-ik)

Cities and Major Cities

Cerdacul Luminii - (cher-dah-kuhl)(loo-mee-nee)
Codrul Verde - (cO-drool)(vair-day)
Havnflaten - (han-flat-en)
Jagodnia - (yah-gOd-nyuh)
Nowy Sokolnik - (nO-vee)(sO-kol-neek)
Oborlescu - (O-bor-les-coo)
Valea Bujorului - (val-ah)(boo-jor-ool-loo-yee)
Valea Fagului - (val-ah)(fag-ool-loo-yee)

Luminarch; Map 12

Geography

Fleuris Mountain - (flu-ree)(mountain)
Honors Waters - (honors)(waters)
The Southern Sea - (the)(southern)(sea)
Loire River - (loo-ah)(river)
Fleuris Forest - (flu-ree)(forest)
Loire Mountains - (loo-ah)(mountains)
Ode River - (ode)(river)
Montblancette Forest - (moon-blOn-set)(forest)
Great Lake Mountains - (great)(lake)(mountains)
Vaugeois Island - (voo-joo-ah)(island)
Vaugeois Strait - (voo-joo-ah)(strait)

Fortifications

Castel Nouvelle - (cast-el)(noo-vel-eh)
Fort Philip - (fort)(fee-leep)

Cities and Major Cities

Aranykert - (ar-ahn-kert)
Arany Viorica - (ar-ahn)(vee-or-ee-suh)
Belleville - (beel-eh-veel-eh)
Briseval - (breez-eh-val-eh)
Csernoborosk - (cher-nO-bor-Osk)
Ficsorul Mare - (fik-sor-ool)(mar-eh)
Fleuris Port - (flu-ree)
Hargitafalu - (har-gee-tuh-fal-oo)
Loire - (loo-ah)
Montclairon - (moon-cleer-oon)
Verdeszegi - (ver-des-zeh-gee)
Vigne Fleur - (vee-nee)(flur)

Luminarch; Map 13

Geography

Alzeir's River Forest - (al-zair-z)(river)(forest)
Felsig Hills - (fel-sich)(hills)
Flach Berg - (flak)(berg)
La Mort Forest - (la)(mor)(forest)

Fortifications

Fort Aleksandrov - (fort)(al-ek-zand-rOv)
Fort Ludger - (fort)(loot-ger)
Fort Grimwald - (fort)(grim-vIlt)

Cities and Major Cities

Lisztpatak - (leest-pat-ahk)
Montclairia - (moon-clar-ee-uh)
Neuhafenburg - (noi-hawf-en-burg)
Riempuszta - (ree-em-poos-tah)
Silberbachtal - (sil-ber-bache-tal)

Silberweiler - (sil-ber-vI-ler)
Transilvaniendorf - (trans-il-van-een-dorf)
Villerouge - (veel-leh-roo-jeh)

Luminarch; Map 14

Geography

Alzeir's River Forest - (al-zair-z)(river)(forest)
Dunkel River - (duhnk-ehl)(river)
Gedenken Lake - (ged-enk-in)(lake)
La Mort Forest - (la)(mor)(forest)
Orino Perasma River - (or-ee-nO)(per-as-mah)(river)

Fortifactions

Fort Alcesimarchus - (fort)(al-ses-ee-mark-as)
Fort Manius - (fort)(man-ee-ous)

Cities and Major Cities

Argeopolis - (or-gee-O-pol-ees)
Bellevigne - (beel-leh-vee-neh)
Bergenikos - (ber-gen-ih-kOs)
Kalinovia - (kay-lee-nOv-ee-uh)
Nordheimar - (nord-hI-mahr)
Skynthos - (skeen-thOs)
Stelidora - (stAl-ih-dor-ah)
Vintergion - (vin-ter-jen)

Luminarch; Map 15

Geography

Gedenken Lake - (ged-enk-in)(lake)
Lake Kennedy - (lake)(kee-neh-dee)
Oamenii Nordului River - (wah-mee-nee)(nor-dool-loo-ee)(river)

Oamenii de Sud River - (wah-mee-nee)(dee)(sood)(river)
Pur Forest - (pour)(forest)

Fortifications

Fort Cardei - (fort)(kar-day)
Fort Isidor - (fort)(ee-see-dor)
Fort Lascar - (fort)(las-car)
Fort Oppius - (fort)(Op-pee-ous)
Fort Seaghdh - (fort)[Scottish(Gaelic)]
Fort Troy - (fort)(troy)

Cities and Major Cities

Bergtira - (berkt-tI-rah)
Floreni - (flor-en-ee)
Heliodora - (hee-lee-O-dor-ah)
Muntele Argelia - (moon-tel-eh)(ar-gel-ee-ah)
Stelnica - (stel-nee-kah)
Thalassia - (thal-ah-sah)
Valea Lunii - (val-ah)(loo-nee)
Veranopolis - (var-en-O-pol-ees)
Verde - (ver-day)

Luminarch; Map 16

Geography

Brathas - (brah-thas)
Fenthia - (fen-thee-ah)
The Great Ocean - (the)(great)(ocean)
La Mort Forest - (la)(mor)(forest)
Oamenii Nordului River - (wah-mee-nee)(nor-dool-loo-ee)(river)
Oamenii de Sud River - (wah-mee-nee)(dee)(sood)(river)
Procul River - (prO-kuhl)(river)
The Varenian Mountains - (the)(vair-en-ee-ahn)(mountains)

Fortifications

Castle Hake - (hayk)
Fort Tane - (fort)(tah-neh)

Cities and Major Cities

Aquincum - (ah-keen-koom)
Brivas - (bree-vas)
Burrium - (boo-ree-oom)
Byblus - (bI-bloos)
Dunarcani - (doo-nar-can-ee)
Floritoru - (flor-ee-tor-oo)
Fulginiae - (fool-jee-nee-I-ay)
Hadria - (had-ree-ah)
Melta - (mel-tah)
Noreia - (nor-ay-ah)
Piatra Verdea - (pee-ah-trah)(ver-dah)
Puteoli - (poo-tay-O-lee)

Luminarch; Map 17

Geography

Arany River - (ar-ahn)(river)
Fosszel River - (foos-el)(river)
The Great Lake - (the)(great)(lake)
Great Lake Mountains - (great)(lake)(mountains)
Meztelen River - (mes-tel-en)(river)
La Mort Forest - (la)(mor)(forest)
The Southern Sea - (the)(southern)(sea)

Fortifications

Fort Budai - (fort)(boo-dah-ee)

Cities and Major Cities

Csillagpatak - (cheel-lag-pat-ahk)
Fecskefalva - (fech-keh-fal-vah)
Feketehegy - (fek-et-eh-heg)
Fenyvesalja - (fen-vesh-al-yah)
Fenyveshalom - (fen-vesh-al-om)
Kisfalva - (keesh-fal-vah)
Nyugatfalva - (nyoo-gut-fal-vah)
Procul Emporia - (prO-Kuhl)(ehm-poor-ee-uh)
Szaplon - (sap-lon)
Sziklafalva - (seek-lah-fal-vah)

Luminarch; Map 18

Geography

The Great Lake - (the)(great)(lake)
Great Lake Mountains - (great)(lake)(mountains)
La Mort Forest - (la)(mor)(forest)
The Southern Sea - (the)(southern)(sea)
Thanatos Bay - (than-uh-tOs)(bay)

Fortifications

Fort Achille - (fort)(ak-eel)
Fort Decimus - (fort)(deh-sih-mous)
Fort Eclectus - (fort)(ee-lekt-ous

Cities and Major Cities

Baktanya - (bawk-tan-yah)
Borosfalva - (bor-Osh-fal-vah)
Black-Slate Mine - (black-slate)(mine)
Cseresznyealja - (cher-es-nyahl-yah)
Cserfalu - (cher-sal-oo)
Ganev's Mine - (gahn-ehv-z)(mine)

Lushnari - (loosh-nar-ee)
Manev's Mine - (mahn-ehv-z)(mine)
Meridiem Emporia - (mair-ee-dyem)(ehm-poor-ee-uh)
Pirosdomb - (pee-rOsh-dOmbd)
Tiszalke - (tees-al-keh)
Vaudrieux - (vud-ree-yu)

Luminarch; Map 19

Geography

La Mort Forest - (la)(mor)(forest)
Oamenii de Sud River - (wah-mee-nee)(dee)(sood)(river)
Thanatos Bay - (than-uh-tOs)(bay)

Fortifications

Fort Ferdinand - (fort)(fer-dih-nand)
Fort Tyndarus - (fort)(tIn-dar-ous)

Cities and Major Cities

Gjirokastraq - (jee-rO-kast-ratch)
Gurzaj - (gur-zI)
Lushnjeva - (loosh-nyev-uh)
Shkallaj - (shkal-lI)
Sinus Australis - (see-nus)(awst-ral-ees)
Valmonta - (val-mon-tah)
Velezara - (vel-eh-zar-ah)
Vjollca - (vee-ols-ah)

Luminarch; Map 20

Geography

Adıyabakir - (ahd-ee-ah-bak-eer)
Asma Forest - (ahs-muh)(forest)

Denlis - (dehn-lihs)
Erzutep - (eir-zU-tehp)
The Great Ocean -(the)(great)(ocean)
Istanfra - (ihs-tahn-fruh)
Kastabakir - (kahs-tuh-bahk-eer)
La Mort Forest - (la)(mor)(forest)
Procul River - (prO-Kuhl)(river)
Salistan - (Sahl-ihs-tahn)
Tekirhya - (tehk-eer-yee-uh)
The Varenian Mountains - (the)(vair-en-ee-ahn)(mountains)
Yaparta - (yahp-aR-tuh)

Fortifications

Fort Aurel - (fort)(aR-ehl)
Fort Sjef - (fort)(shef)

Cities and Major Cities

Cerdacul Verde - (cher-dah-kuhl)(ver-day)
Ceresani - (cher-es-ahn-ee)
Luminaia - (loo-mee-I-ah)
Lunca Verde - (loon-kah)(ver-day)
Serpentinea - (ser-pen-tee-nah)
Tufanesti - (too-fahn-ehst-ee)
Turanu Mare - (too-rah-noo)(mar-ay)
Valea - (val-ee-uh)
Valea Zambilei - (val-ee-uh)(Zahm-bihl-ee)
Vardela - (var-del-ah)
Zimbria - (zihm-bree-uh)

Luminarch; Map 21

Geography

Dragon Steel Bay - (drah-guhn)(steel)(bay)
The Marteau Mountains - (the)(mar-too)(mountains)

Nord River - (nord)(river)
Praeterton Valley Mountains - (prA-ter-ton)(valley)(mountains)
Quiescens Forest - (quees-shens)(forest)
The Sea of the Anvil - (the)(sea)(of)(the)(an-vil)

Fortifications

Fort Sergi - (fort)(sur-jee)

Cities and Major Cities

Bellemont-sur-Mer - (beel-leh-moon-syur-mair)
Belvigne - (beel-veen-eh)
Montserrat de la Sierra - (mon-ser-at)(dey)(lah)(seer-rah)
Valladela - (val-yah-dey-ah)
Valverde del Mar - (val-vair-ay)(deyl)(mar)

Luminarch; Map 22

Geography

Dragon Steel Bay - (drah-guhn)(steel)(bay)
Honor's Water - (honors)(water)
The Marteau Mountains - (the)(mar-too)(mountains)
Montblancette Forest - (moon-blOn-set)(forest)
Marteau River - (mar-too)(river)
Queue River - (qur)(river)
Rubicon River - (roo-bih-con)(river)
The Sea of the Anvil - (the)(sea)(of)(the)(anvil)
Soltero Island - (suhl-tair-O)(island)
Soltero Mountain - (suhl-tair-O)(mountain)

Fortifications

Fort Auxilium - (fort)(awx-ihl-ee-uhm)
Fort Rubicon - (fort)(roo-bih-con)
Fort Vespasianus - (fort)(vehs-pahs-ee-ahn-ous)

Cities and Major Cities

Bellafleur - (bee-lah-flur)
Cernaville - (sern-uh-vee-luh)
Crespigny - (kris-pee-nee)
Laciosa - (leh-syu-sah)
Montverin - (moon-veer-ahn)
Riosalado - (ree-O-sal-ah-dO)
San Mirador - (san)(meer-ah-dor)
Torrezuelas - (tor-rays-sway-las)
Valverdeja - (val-ver-dey-hah)
Verthier - (verth-eer)
Villeroux - (veel-leh-roo)

Luminarch; Map 23

Geography

Camil - (kam-eel-uh)
Isollier - (eez-O-leer)
Levent - (loo-vOn)
The Marteau Mountains - (the)(mar-too)(mountains)
The Southern Sea - (the)(southern)(sea)

Fortifications

- None -

Cities and Major Cities

Cielmont - (klee-mahnt)
Valperrin - (vahl-puhr-ihn)

Britone; Map 01

Geography

The Britonarch Channel - (the)(brih-tO-nihc)(channel)
The Britone Forest - (the)(brih-tO-nn)(forest)
The Dividing Mountains - (the)(dividing)(mountains)
Nation-Long River - (nation)(long)(river)
Pennince Hills - (pehn-ihn-s)(hills)
Pennince Mountains - (pehn-ihn-s)(mountains)
Topridge Mountains - (top-ridge)(mountains)
The Western Sea - (the)(western)(sea)

Fortifications

Fort Holden - (fort)(huhl-dehn)
Fort Oscar - (fort)(aws-car)
Fort Waldon - (fort)(wall-duhn)

Cities and Major Cities

Boreas Emporia - (boor-ee-ahs)(ehm-poor-ee-uh)
Eli - (ee-lI)
Erinda - (eir-ihn-duh)
Fields - (fields)
Fjellhaven - (fyehl-hAv-ehn)
Irewood - (I-er-wood)
Long Pass - (long)(pass)
Norrskog - (nor-skog)
Pennsville - (penz-vihl)

Britone; Map 02

Geography

The Britonarch Channel - (the)(brih-tO-nihc)(channel)
The Britone Forest - (the)(brih-tO-nn)(forest)
The Dividing Mountains - (the)(dividing)(mountains)
Nation-Long River - (nation)(long)(river)
North Spear Mountains - (north)(spear)(mountains)
The Salt-Flat Peaks - (the)(salt)(flat)(peaks)

Salt Lake - (salt)(lake)
Salt River - (salt)(river)
Salt Spike - (salt)(spike)

Fortifications

Erobra Castle - (ee-rO-bruh)(cahs-ehl)
Fort Alvin - (fort)(ahl-vihn)
Fort Arthon - (fort)(aR-thon)
Fort Gratham - (fort)(grah-thahm)

Cities and Major Cities

Calm Sea - (calm)(sea)
Delorin - (deh-loor-ihn)
Ljusby - (yUs-bee)
Mutina - (mU-tee-nuh)
Salt Lake - (salt)(lake)
Vinterdal - (Vihn-tur-dahl)
White Spear - (white)(spear)

Britone; Map 03

Geography

The Britonarch Channel - (the)(brih-tO-nihc)(channel)
Britonic Plains - (brih-tO-nihc)(plains)
Cane Mountains - (kAnn)(mountains)
Cane River - (kAnn)(river)
Drache Strait - (draw-kuh)(strait)
Halberen Bay - (hahl-bur-ehn)(bay)

Fortifications

Castle Lavvann - (castle)(law-vawn)
Fort Habstrast - (fort)(hahb-strahst)
Fort Mullen - (fort)(mool-ehn)

Cities and Major Cities

Cane - (kAnn)
Halberen - (hahl-bur-ehn)
Long-Grass - (long)(grass)
Marendine - (meir-ehn-dIn)
Fjordlauk - (fyood-luk)

Island Wall; Map 01: City Names

Fortifications

Castillo de Nagoza - (cast-ee-lO)(dey)(nah-gO-sah)
Castillo de Vinedera - (cast-ee-lO)(dey)(veen-eh-day-rah)

Cities and Major Cities

Anzuelo de Colina - (ahn-sway-lO)(dey)(kol-ee-nah)
Calasierra - (kal-ah-seer-rah)
Cieloalto - (seel-O-ahl-tO)
Ciudad Cuervo - (see-oo-dad)(kway-r-vO)
Ciudad Esperanza - (see-oo-dad)(ay-sper-ahn-zuh)
Ciudad Perla - (see-oo-dad)(pair-lah)
Ciudad Sarcia - (see-oo-dad)(sar-see-ah)
Luminosa - (loo-meen-O-suh)
Luzmarina - (looz-mar-een-ah)
Marisierra - (mar-ee-seer-rah)
Monteluz - (mon-tey-loos)
Nagoza - (nah-gO-sah)
Punto Ciudad - (poon-tO)(see-oo-dad)
Riova - (ree-O-vah)
Rocanueva - (rO-kan-wey-vah)
San del Mar - (san)(deyl)(mar)
Solmar - (suhl-mar)
Solmarina - (suhl-mar-ee-nah)
Solmaris - (suhl-mar-ees)
Valldelrosa - (val-dey-rO-sah)

Vinedera - (veen-eh-day-rah)
Verdeanu - (ver-day-ahn-oo)

Island Wall; Map 01: Island Names

Geography

Cieloalto Forest - (seel-O-ahl-tO)(forest)
The Eternal Sea - (the)(eternal)(sea)
Flecha Forest - (flay-chah)(forest)
Riova Forest - (ree-O-vah)(forest)
The Sea of the Anvil - (the)(sea)(of)(the)(anvil)

Island Names

Cangrejo Isla - (kan-grey-hO)(ees-lah)
Cristal Orilla - (krist-al)(or-ee-lah)
Dorado Ensenada - (dor-ah-dO)(en-sen-ah-dah)
Dorado Puerto - (dor-ah-dO)(poo-air-tO)
Elysiano Puerto - (el-ee-syah-nO)(poo-air-tO)
Encantado Islote - (en-can-tad-O)(ees-lO-tay)
Eterno Oasis - (ey-ter-nO)(O-ah-sees)
Gemelo Norte - (geh-mel-O)(nor-tey)
Gemelo Sur - (geh-mel-O)(soo-r)
Goldire Isla - (gold-fI-er)(ees-lah)
Hormiga de Fuego Isla - (or-mee-gah)(dey)(fway-gO)(ees-lah)
Isla Adornada - (ees-lah)(ah-dor-nah-dah)
Isla Ancla - (ees-lah)(ahn-klah)
Isla Astillada - (ees-lah)(ast-eel-yah-dah)
Isla Castigada - (ees-lah)(kas-tee-gah-dah)
Isla Crow - (ees-lah)(crow)
Isla Cuervo - (ees-lah)(kway-r-vO)
Isla de Aislamiento - (ees-lah)(dey)(ay-slah-mee-en-tO)
Isla del Dedo Perdido - (ees-lah)(del)(deh-dO)(pair-dee-dO)
Isla de los Perdidos - (ees-lah)(dey)(lOs)(pair-dee-dOs)
Isla de los Sin Nombre - (ees-lah)(dey)(lOs)(seen)(nom-bray)
Isla Elegida - (ees-lah)(el-ay-hee-dah)

Isla Enferma - (ees-lah)(en-fer-mah)
Isla Esperanza - (ees-lah)(ay-sper-ahn-zuh)
Isla Espinosa - (ees-lah)(es-peen-O-sah)
Isla Granite - (ees-lah)(gran-I-t)
Isla Marisierra - (ees-lah)(mar-ee-seer-rah)
Isla Molusco - (ees-lah)(mol-oos-kO)
Isla Nagoza - (ees-lah)(nah-gO-sah)
Isla Oscuro - (ees-lah)(aws-koo-rO)
Isla Ostra - (ees-lah)(aws-trah)
Isla Plateada - (ees-lah)(plah-tay-ah-dah)
Isla Port - (ees-lah)(poort)
Isla Rana - (ees-lah)(ran-ah)
Isla Rest - (ees-lah)(rest)
Isla Riova - (ees-lah)(ree-O-vah)
Isla Solmar - (ees-lah)(suhl-mar)
Isla Torcida - (ees-lah)(tor-see-dah)
Isla Verde - (ees-lah)(ver-day)
Isla Vil - (ees-lah)(veel)
Isla Vinedera - (ees-lah)(veen-eh-day-rah)
Larga Playa Isla - (lar-gah)(play-yah)(ees-lah)
Luzmarina Isla - (looz-mar-een-ah)(ees-lah)
Perla Isla - (pair-lah)(ees-lah)
Punto Isla - (poon-tO)(ees-lah)
Sarcia - (sar-see-ah)
Solmaria Isla - (suhl-mar-ee-ah)(ees-lah)
Solmarina - (suhl-mar-ee-nah)
Solmaris - (suhl-mar-ees)
Tierra Desnuda - (tee-air-rah)(des-noo-dah)
Tierra Nieve - (tee-air-rah)(nee-vay)
Zafiro Isla - (sah-feer-O)(ees-lah)

Island Wall; Map 02: City Names

Fortifications

Aviador Castillo - (ah-vee-ah-dor)(cast-ee-lO)

Castillo Madre - (cast-ee-lO)(mah-drey)
Castillo Refugio Sereno - (cast-ee-lO)(reh-foo-hee-O)(ser-ey-nO)
Castillo Tranquilo - (cast-ee-lO)(tran-kee-lO)

Cities and Major Cities

Ciudad Cristal - (see-oo-dad)(krist-al)
Ciudad Madre - (see-oo-dad)(mah-drey)
Ciudad Radiante - (see-oo-dad)(rah-dee-ahn-tay)
Ciudad Serena - (see-oo-dad)(ser-ey-nah)
Ciudad Superficial - (see-oo-dad)(soo-per-fis-ee-ahl)
Ciudad Toro - (see-oo-dad)(tor-O)
Ciudad Zafiro - (see-oo-dad)(sah-feer-O)
Costa Naranja - (cOst-ah)(nar-ahn-hah)
Cristal Oasis - (krist-al)(O-ah-sees)
Cueva Hooked - (koo-ey-vah)(hookt)
Escala de Fuego - (es-kal-ah)(dey)(fway-gO)
Eterno Refugio - (ey-ter-nO)(reh-foo-hee-O)
Irene - (ee-rey-nay)
Lugar Honrado - (loo-gar)(on-drah-dO)
Luminoso Puerto - (loo-mee-nO-sO)(poo-air-tO)
Monteluna Verde - (mon-rey-loo-nah)(vair-dey)
Playa Fresca - (play-ah)(freys-kah)
Pobre Ciudad Portuaria - (pob-rey)(see-oo-dad)(por-twar-ee-ah)
Punta de Hielo - (poon-yah)(dey)(yay-lO)
Punto Susurrante - (poon-tO)(soo-sur-ahn-tay)
Sereno Puerto - (ser-ey-nO)(poo-air-tO)
Sereno Refugio - (ser-ey-nO)(reh-foo-hee-O)
Sombra de Luna - (som-brah)(dey)(loo-nah)

Island Wall; Map 02: Island Names

Geography

Escala de Fuego Mountains - (es-kal-ah)(dey)(fway-gO)(mountains)
The Eternal Sea - (the)(eternal)(sea)
Irene River - (ee-rey-nay)(river)

Luna Mountain - (loo-nah)(mountain)
Occidental Mountain - (awk-see-den-tal)(mountain)
Oriente Mountain - (or-ee-en-tay)(mountain)
The Sea of the Anvil - (the)(sea)(of)(the)(anvil)

Island Names

Cristal Oasis - (krist-al)(O-ah-sees)
Cristal Refugio - (krist-al)(reh-foo-hee-O)
Dorado Orilla - (dor-ah-dO)(or-ee-lah)
Encantado Ensenada - (en-can-tad-O)(en-sen-ah-dah)
Esmeralda Isla - (es-mer-ahl-dah)(ees-lah)
Eterno Arrecife - (ey-ter-nO)(ar-reh-see-fey)
Eterno Refugio - (ey-ter-nO)(reh-foo-hee-O)
Isla Airman - (ees-lah)(air-man)
Isla con Forma de Cuerno - (ees-lah)(con)(for-mah)(dey)(kway-nO)
Isla Coral - (ees-lah)(kor-ahl)
Isla Costa Naranja - (ees-lah)(cOst-ah)(nar-ahn-hah)
Isla Costa Roja - (ees-lah)(cOst-ah)(rO-hah)
Isla de Agua Caliente - (ees-lah)(dey)(ah-gwaw)(kal-ee-en-tey)
Isla Deshonrada - (ees-lah)(des-on-rah-dah)
Isla en Forma de Gancho - (ees-lah)(en)(for-mah)(dey)(gahn-chO)
Isla Escala de Fuego - (ees-lah)(es-kal-ah)(dey)(fway-gO)
Isla Larga Desnuda - (ees-lah)(lar-gah)(des-noo-dah)
Isla Mediana - (ees-lah)(med-ee-ahn-ah)
Isla Paralela - (ees-lah)(par-ah-lel-ah)
Isla Viper - (ees-lah)(vI-per)
Luminoso Puerto - (loo-mee-nO-sO)(poo-air-tO)
Pobre Puerto - (pob-rey)(poo-air-tO)
Radiante Puerto - (rah-dee-ahn-tay)(poo-air-tO)
Sereno Ensenada - (ser-ey-nO)(en-sen-ah-dah)
Sereno Isla - (ser-ey-nO)(ees-lah)
Sereno Puerto - (ser-ey-nO)(poo-air-tO)
Sereno Refugio - (ser-ey-nO)(reh-foo-hee-O)
Sombra de Luna - (som-brah)(dey)(loo-nah)
Susurrante Puerto - (soo-sur-ahn-tay)(poo-air-tO)

Tranquilo Laguna - (tran-kee-lO)(lah-goo-nah)
Tranquilo Santuario - (tran-kee-lO)(san-twar-ee-O)
Zafiro Laguna - (sah-feer-O)(lah-goo-nah)
Zafiro Orilla - (sah-feer-O)(or-ee-lah)
Zafiro Santuario - (sah-feer-O)(san-twar-ee-O)

Island Wall; Map 03: City Names

Fortifications

- None -

Cities and Major Cities

A Cidade Dourada - (ah)(see-dad)(doo-rah-dah)
Cerdanita - (sur-dahn-ee-tuh)
Cezaria del Sol - (say-sar-ee-ah)(dey)(sol)
Cidade Armadilha - (see-dad)(air-mah-dee-lah)
Cidadela Mare - (see-dah-del-ah)(mah-ruh)
Ciudad Tridot - (see-oo-dad)(tree-dawt)
Florindela - (floo-reen-del-ah)
Lages de Serra - (lah-ges)(d)(sair-uh)
La Piedra Sagrada - (lah)(pee-ay-dah)(sag-rah-dah)
Marisol da Rocha - (mah-ree-sol)(dah)(rOsh-ah)
Mirandela do Sul - (mee-run-del-ah)(doo)(sool)
Montalva - (mon-tal-vah)
Playa Sagrada del Norte - (play-ah)(sag-rah-dah)(nor-tey)
Serralheira - (ser-rahl-yay-ruh)
Valerosa - (val-ay-rO-sah)
Valverde de Ardeal - (val-ver-dey)(dey)(ar-dee-al)
Vila Verdeira - (vee-lah)(ver-dey-rah)
Vila Verdejo - (vee-lah)(ver-dey-hO)

Island Wall; Map 03: Island Names

Geography

The Eternal Sea - (the)(eternal)(sea)
Grande Floresta - (grahn-deh)(flor-ehst-uh)
Juramento River - (hoo-rah-men-tO)(river)
La Piedra Sagrada Mountain. - (lah)(pee-ay-dah)(sag-rah-dah)(mountain)
Piedra Sagrada Forest - (pee-ay-dah)(sag-rah-dah)(forest)
The Sea of the Anvil - (the)(sea)(of)(the)(anvil)

Island Names

Detenedor de Tormentas - (dee-tehn-eh-door)(dee)(tor-mehnt-ahs)
Grande Ilha Floresta - (grahn-deh)(ee-lah)(flor-ehst-uh)
Ilha Anviled - (ee-lah)(an-vey-vloo)
Ilha Armored - (ee-lah)(ar-moo-rd)
Ilha Batida - (ee-lah)(buh-tee-duh)
Ilha das Baleias - (ee-lah)(dush)(bah-lay-ish)
Ilha Malcriada - (ee-lah)(mal-kree-ah-dah)
Ilha Prateada - (ee-lah)(pray-tee-ah-dah)
Ilha Sangue Osso - (ee-lah)(sayn-goo)(oos-oo)
Ilha Torcida - (ee-lah)(tor-see-dah)
Ilha Torturada - (ee-lah)(tor-tuhr-ah-dah)
Isla Bloodvein - (ees-lah)(blud-vayn)
Isla Desperdiciada - (ees-lah)(des-per-dee-see-ah-dah)
Isla Gem Shore - (ees-lah)(gem)(shor)
Isla Maldita - (ees-lah)(mal-dee-tah)
Isla Obsidiana - (ees-lah)(ob-sid-ee-ahn-ah)
Isla Piedra Sagrada - (ees-lah)(pee-ay-dah)(sag-rah-dah)
Isla Tridot - (ees-lah)(tree-dawt)
La Isla de Ironmane - (lah)(ees-lah)(dey)(I-ron-mayn)
Maleficio de Roca - (mal-eh-fee-see-oo)(deh)(rok-uh)
Pequena Ilha - (peh-kay-nuh)(ee-lah)
Praias Douradas - (prI-ahs)(doo-rah-dah)

Island Wall; Map 04: City Names

Fortifications

Castelo do Sol - (cash-tel)(doo)(sol)
Castelo Serrilhado - (cash-tel)(ser-reel-ah-doo)

Cities and Major Cities

Cidade da Espada - (see-dad)(deh)(shpad-uh)
Cidade de Jade - (see-dad)(d)(jah-deh)
Pequena Cidade - (peh-kay-nuh)(see-dad)
Pescador do Litoral - (pish-keh-dor)(doo)(lee-too-rahl)
Praia do Solzinho - (prI-ah)(doo)(sol-zee-noo)
Rio dos Sonhos - (ree-oo)(doosh)(son-oosh)
Vale Verde do Norte - (val)(vair-deh)(doo)(nor-teh)
Vila Verdeira - (vee-lah)(ver-dI-rah)

Island Wall; Map 04: Island Names

Geography

Espada Forest - (shpad-uh)(river)
Espada Mountain - (shpad-uh)(river)
Espada River - (shpad-uh)(river)
The Eternal Sea - (the)(eternal)(sea)
The Southern Sea - (the)(southern)(sea)

Island Names

Ilha Amarrada - (ee-lah)(am-er-rah-dah)
Ilha Central - (ee-lah)(sen-tral)
Ilha da Aldina - (ee-lah)(deh)(al-dee-nah)
Ilha da Espada - (ee-lah)(deh)(shpad-uh)
Ilha da Luiza - (ee-lah)(deh)(loo-ee-zah)
Ilha da Pedra de Frutos - (ee-lah)(deh)(peh-drah)(d)(froo-toosh)
Ilha da Pequena Espada - (ee-lah)(deh)(peh-kay-nuh)(shpad-uh)

Ilha de Jade em Desvanecimento - (ee-lah)(d)(jah-deh)(em) (deesh-van-see-men-too)
Ilha Devastada - (ee-lah)(deh-vush-tah-dah)
Ilha Dinis - (ee-lah)(dee-nees)
Ilha do Recife - (ee-lah)(doo)(reh-see-feh)
Ilha do Sol - (ee-lah)(doo)(sol)
Ilha do Solzinho - (ee-lah)(doo)(sol-zee-noo)
Ilha do Zeferino - (ee-lah)(doo)(zif-er-ee-noo)
Ilha Serrilhada - (ee-lah)(ser-reel-ah-dah)
Praia do Sal - (prI-ah)(doo)(sal)